TO THE POWER OF
JOURNEY OF A LOST SOUL

Mitch Malin

To Grandma & Grandpa
I love you guys! Thank you
for supporting me and my book!

Editing and Book Development Provided By
The Awakened Press
www.theawakenedpress.com

Cover and Illustrations by Mitch Malin

First edition.

ISBN-13: 978-1-7337734-0-9

CHARACTERS

Name: Vanilla
Species: Crescent Horned Punisher

Name: Xypher "Zero"
Species: Grenzel Blind Demon

Name: Lisa
Species: Mandian

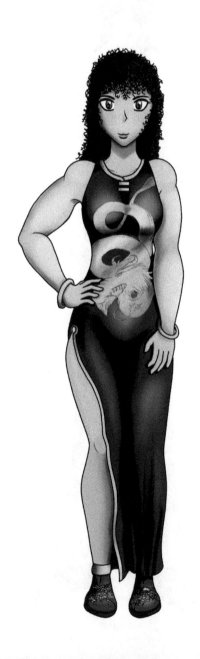

Name: Wake
Species: Mandian

Name: Zallin
Species: Arrow-Top Madite

Name: Raech
Species: Arrow-Top Madite

Name: Soul
Species: Origin Spiritan

Name: Malachi
Species: Unknown

CONTENTS

CHAPTER 1

-Rebellion-

The restless crowd cheered and screamed with excitement as the lights dimmed and flames playfully licked the bottom of the old curtain. Fanboys toward the front lunged at the stage, attempting to break past the barriers that kept them from the band. A smooth, gray fog came billowing down from above to meet them.

"We are *To the Power of 10*! Are you guys ready to rock?" the amplified voice of a young woman shouted. The audience responded by pumping their fists in the air and chanting. From behind the wall of flames, the source of the voice appeared. She was a teenager with a perfect hourglass figure, her smile exuding pride and confidence. Her long white hair cascaded to the ground and swept the floor as she stepped out from behind the now severely charred curtain. Long, pointed horns protruded from the sides of her head and curved upward. She wore a tank top with a low neckline and a gothic style skirt with torn black leggings underneath. Her dress swayed from side to side seductively as she walked atop black stiletto heels. In her hands she held a jagged dark purple bass guitar with the name "Vanilla" etched into its finish. A small microphone was fitted close to her mouth by a wire that ran from her cheek to a wireless transmitter by her hip.

By now the curtain had been completely reduced to falling ashes, revealing three additional musicians: a short, redheaded drummer with dark eyes set beneath thick brows; an athletic keyboardist with curly brown hair and a red dress; and a tall, blue-haired guitarist.

The drummer tapped his sticks together four times and began playing. A heavily distorted guitar solo followed. Each note hit with perfect accuracy and extraordinary speed. The horned woman closed her

1

eyes and started headbanging, wildly tossing her hair in all directions. Then, everything stopped. Spotlights converged on the horned rock star, and the keyboardist played a beautiful, complex riff. As if under a spell, the crowd screamed enthusiastically the moment the teenage vocalist opened her mouth. They were completely taken by her voice.

> *"A life lost with nothing gained,*
> *Now turn and face the pouring rain!*
>
> *Fade to dust with hollow eyes,*
> *This is death; your demise."*

Then the guitar and drums kicked back in along with the bass. The windows and light fixtures in the building shook from the intense volume, threatening to shatter at any moment. Fans jumped around wildly, knocking into one another and flailing with unrestrained energy. To an outsider it would have looked like a full-blown riot. At one point an airborne beer bottle broke one of the theater's windows, causing a cold draft of night air to fill the room, but no one seemed to notice. They were all too entranced by the music.

> *"Die! Die! You won't escape these lies!*
> *You'll never know the truth inside!"*

Suddenly, the thick double doors to the theater swung open and four men dressed in shiny, silver plate mail and padded black armor stepped inside. They were equipped with stun guns and held swords with the crest of the Royal Spiritan Crown, symbolizing that they were part of the Royal Guard. One of them was clinging onto a megaphone, which he promptly held up and shouted into.

"Vanilla Lamberschvak, you're under arrest for cause of excessive and harmful noise in a public place without consent of local authorities. By Spiritan Civil Law section 108-50, I command you to stop at once!"

The young rock star glanced at the knights, but continued singing. "Amp it up! Amp it up!" the crowd chanted, completely ignoring the Royal Guard's announcement. In response to the crowd, the vocalist motioned to the guitarist to turn the volume up on their amplifiers. He nodded and, after taking a drink from an unmarked beer bottle, cranked the knobs on a wall of amplifiers behind him to 10.

The knights of the Royal Guard tried yelling into the megaphone again, but the sound of the music and crowd drowned out their voices. Out of frustration, one of the Royal Guardsmen tried to make his way into the crowd, desperately pushing toward the stage. Before he reached the middle of the crowd, however, he was already bruised and smelled strongly of beer. A group of muscular fans dressed in black leather jackets grabbed ahold of his body armor, the crushing grip of their hands like vises. With barbaric force, they hoisted him above their heads, carried him back to the edge, and tossed him out.

He landed by the entrance with a loud thud. One of the protective metallic plates that covered his thighs had been bent from the impact so that it no longer sat symmetrically against the rest of his outfit. Flustered and looking as though he had been attacked by a lion, the Royal Guardsman scampered to his feet and brushed himself off. He drew his stun gun from its holster and aimed it at the singer, but didn't fire. One of his comrades shook his head and signed something to him with his hands. The first Royal Guardsman looked surprised, but nodded. Then, after giving a long, hateful glare at the singer, he reluctantly followed his allies outside.

The performance continued without further interruptions. The fans cheered until their voices became raspy and dry, and the musicians played until they had no energy left. Somewhere toward the end of the performance, a few of the people in the front row finally broke the barriers that held them from reaching the stage; but by the time they had climbed up onto the elevated wooden floor, the band finished their final song and was thanking their audience for coming.

"Thank you everyone! We are *To the Power of 10!*" the singer said, sounding frighteningly dehydrated. The guitarist tossed her a water bottle, which she quickly chugged, purposefully spilling a bit on her shirt.

Noticing that three of her fans were onstage, the vocalist turned to them and smiled. She bent forward and winked, flaunting her well-endowed figure. The fan boys whooped and whistled at her until the guitarist walked up to them and said, "Hands off, kids. This one's mine." Then he quickly pulled the singer aside.

"Vanilla, I told you not to do that."

"Why not? It could get us some cash, you know."

"Or waste our time on a few idiots. Besides, these jerks aren't worthy of you."

Vanilla, the singer, stood up straight and put her hands on her hips. "Alright boys, I'll have to pay you a visit once I'm done dealing with my boyfriend here." The guitarist was about to speak up when someone stomped their foot loudly backstage and began yelling.

"Hey, you guys better shut up or I'll break your faces! Zero, I'm sick and tired of your hooker of a girlfriend tryin' to seduce our fans."

A short, young man was glaring at the guitarist. His frizzy red hair was up in a spiked ponytail. He was holding drumsticks threateningly like knives. He flexed his chest and stood up to his full height, which was no more than 5 feet tall.

The blue-haired guitarist frowned and stepped forward. "Oh yeah? Well I'm tired of your constant whining, Wake Harshfur! Leave my girlfriend outta this. You're just jealous because I *have* a girlfriend!"

"I'm warnin' you, Zero! I'm about ready to break your face!"

"Really? I'd like to see you even try and *reach* my face with that child-size body of yours!"

"Shut the hell up! I'm not a freakin' child. I may not be as tall as *you*, but that doesn't mean I can't pound your face in!"

"Actually it means you're too *short* to reach my face…even if you had stilts!"

"That's it. I'm not takin' any more of this crap from you!"

The drummer threw his drumsticks behind him and stuck out his chest. Before he could take a step toward the guitarist though, the slender keyboardist stepped out in his path. Her expression was firm and threatening, like a lioness protecting her cubs. Wake stopped in his tracks and struggled to make eye contact with the beautiful teenager. The stunning gold dragon patterns on her dress glistened in the overhead lights like the warning stripes of a wasp. She pointed her finger at the drummer and shook her head. Wake shifted nervously in place and glanced around. His face was red with anger, but he was too afraid to make a move.

After a moment of silence, he mustered up his courage. Looking her in the eyes briefly he said, "Lisa, get out of my way, or I'll…" His voice trailed off along with his dwindling confidence. The woman did not budge, but the fire in her eyes intensified.

Eventually the red-faced drummer turned around and ran for the exit with his equipment, his head hanging in embarrassment. After a few moments, the back door of the theater slammed. Lisa relaxed and went over to her keyboard to pack up.

A fan who was still loitering onstage said, "Wow, I've always liked a girl that could kick some ass. Will you go out with me?"

Holding her keyboard in one hand as if she were going to throw it, the curly-haired Mandian shot a terrifying glare in the young man's direction. His smirk faded and he backed away until he fell off the stage with a feminine shriek.

Ignoring the dull thump of the youth as he hit the floor, Lisa flipped her hair back and made her way out the back door of the theater. It slammed behind her with a mighty bang.

After the dense population of fans had thinned to only a handful of teenagers, Vanilla walked over to the guitarist and held his arm, pulling it between her large breasts. "Hey," she said, "let's see if we can sneak into the bar downtown. I need a drink."

The guitarist looked at her and said, "I know where this is going. Not tonight, Vanilla. I've got to go to Meltdown Music early in the morning to get some new strings for my guitar. I busted one on our last song, so I can't do anything with you tonight."

She pressed her hands on her boyfriend's chest and stood on her tiptoes to kiss him. "That's just an excuse. I know you want to," she whispered into his ear.

He gently pushed her away with one hand and shook his head. Then he held up his guitar to show her the broken string and said, "See? It's not an excuse. We've got another show coming up in two weeks, so I've got to get this fixed as early as possible so I can practice."

The Crescent Horned Punisher gave him a look that seemed to scream, "Liar!"

Zero shrugged and moved to the exit. He stopped at the door and called back, "I'll call you tonight."

Vanilla glanced at the handful of fans that lingered by the front doors of the theater and then back at her boyfriend. "Men!" she scoffed and picked up her microphone. She clumsily adjusted the thin straps of her tank top, which had slipped low enough to expose her pink brassiere. With a wave and a wink to the fans, she followed the guitarist out of the building.

"Hey, if we don't have another show booked for two weeks, why do you have to get guitar strings tomorrow morning? You're just making excuses! Besides, I saw a packet of them in your guitar case when we were setting up," the Crescent Horned Punisher quipped as she hurried to catch up to him. He glanced back at her without responding. As soon as she had reached him, she grabbed his arm. "Hey, what's wrong?"

"Nothing. Let go."

"No, seriously. What's wrong? You love me, don't you?"

"Yes I do! Now shut up."

"*You* shut up! I bet those guys back there wouldn't snap at me like you just did."

"But do they play in a band? Vanilla, without our band, we'd both be eating garbage off the streets. Things are already bad enough as it is right now. I don't need you to make me feel like shit."

"What?"

"Never mind! I don't wanna talk right now."

"Yeah, whatever. You don't give me enough love, though!"

"Don't even start with that!"

Vanilla pressed her chest against Zero's back and wrapped her arms around his waist. "Let's settle this a different way," she whispered softly in his ear.

The Grenzel Blind Demon shoved her away. "We're in public, damn it!"

"If you really loved me, you wouldn't say no."

"Alright already! I'll come over to your apartment later tonight."

The promiscuous Crescent Horned Punisher smiled triumphantly and turned around to walk in the opposite direction. The guitarist watched her out of the corner of his eyes, which were covered by his long blue locks of hair. He sighed and looked down at his feet. "What am I doing...?" he mumbled to himself. Again, he directed his attention at his girlfriend, who was almost out of sight. "I swear she'll be the death of me..."

When Vanilla had reached her apartment, she noticed that the teenager that fell off the stage earlier was hanging around the entrance to the building. Thinking nothing of it, she walked up to the front doors of the apartment building and walked inside. The young man in a dark hooded sweatshirt and baggy jeans watched her closely from beneath a pair of heavily tinted shades.

Once inside, the young rock star hauled her equipment up a narrow staircase until she reached a dimly lit hallway. Her arms were completely exhausted now from lugging around her amplifier and bass. As she heaved it up to the door marked "Room 170" it nicked the wall, leaving a huge gash and exposing the drywall. "Oops," she said nonchalantly. Then, after making sure no one was watching, the Crescent Horned Punisher retrieved a small silver key from within her brassiere and inserted it in the door. It stuck when she turned it and the door did not budge. Cursing to herself, Vanilla set her equipment down and gave it a good kick. The door burst open, but it now had a dent and a black mark from her high heels. As it swung in, she stumbled forward and almost fell face-first into her room, but managed to grab ahold of the doorframe and steady herself. With a furious growl, she picked up her things and carried them inside.

The walls of her room were off-white, or at least appeared to be from dirty handprints and lack of cleaning. Clothes lay strewn on the floor and a mess of gossip and glamour magazines were everywhere, stacked high on the carpet or bursting out of an open drawer. Crumbs of old food littered the room like sand on a beach. Stains from various alcoholic drinks dotted the furniture and carpet like a splatter painting by some long forgotten artist. Worse still, the foul odor of smoke lingered heavily in the air.

The teen set down her musical equipment amidst the chaos and rolled her shoulders. Then, like a ninja, she skillfully navigated her way through the piles of junk on the floor until she reached a raggedy old mattress. With as much grace as an albatross landing, she flopped herself down on the bed and kicked her shoes off. "What a day," she sighed. By the time she closed her eyes, she was already starting to dream.

Through her sleepiness, she heard a soft knock sounding from outside her room. Propping herself up on her elbow, she squinted at the door through half-lidded eyes. "Who is it?" she called out grumpily.

After waiting a few seconds with no response, Vanilla gave an exasperated groan and slowly climbed out of bed. Begrudgingly, she made her way to the door, albeit less skillfully than before.

Without taking the time to peer through the eyehole, she flung it open and was confronted by the young man who was standing outside a few minutes ago. He jumped, obviously startled by the sudden answer.

Vanilla leaned on the doorpost and put one hand on her hip. With her other hand, she began toying with the straps of her tank top, sliding them off and on her shoulder provocatively. A mischievous and seductive smile crept across her face like a succubus. "Hey there, big boy."

"Um...hi. I'm just here to apologize to you about the things I said to you and Lisa at the concert. So...uh, I'm sorry."

"What's there to be sorry about? You have a right to like girls, don't you?"

"Well, yeah, I just—"

"Come on, let's have some fun!"

"No! That's not what I wanted!"

The young man turned around and quickly ran down the hallway. "Damn. He must not like girls," Vanilla scoffed. With a small shrug, she closed the door and walked back to her bed, dragging her feet.

Flopping down again, she took out her cell phone and pressed the Power button. It was an old pink flip phone with two touch screens, both of which were severely scratched and dirty. She gazed half-consciously at the time, which read 9:30pm. "I wonder if Zero has his phone on. I should have taken a picture of me with that guy so I could send it to him. That'd teach him to snap at me," she thought with a frown, mindlessly curling her long, flowing hair around her index finger.

Eventually tiredness overtook her, and she fell back into a deep sleep. Visions of a dark and violent childhood flooded her dreams as she lay there. These moments long passed or created in her head grew darker and scarier as she continued to dream.

Within her nightmares, she saw herself as a young child dressed in faded brown rags. An overweight man with short horns and dark, beady eyes stood in the room with her. His smile was menacing and his eyes were black with his evil intentions.

The young child threw a rock at the portly man and said, *"Go away, Daddy! I hate you!"* The man laughed and slowly walked toward her. The child ran to the far corner of the room, for there was no exit. The scene went black, and the dream faded, but not before the sound of a child screaming could be heard.

Vanilla awoke with a start and jolted into a seated position, holding her hand over her heart. "That was..." she panted. Then she shook her head in an attempt to clear her mind. The room felt silent, but a war raged inside her. She shut her eyes tightly and held the sides of her head. Her body was cold and sweaty, and she felt sick to her stomach.

"Damn it! I don't want to think about you! I hate you!" she yelled at the darkness. "I hate you, Billud! You fat bastard!" In her rage, she hurled nearby objects at the wall, causing more damage.

There was a loud bang as the door to her apartment burst open and Zero rushed inside. His expression showed a bit of shock, but mostly his concern. He hurried over to her and put his hands on her shoulders. "Hey, Babe, are you OK? I came to check on you, and then I heard you yelling so I kinda barged in."

"I'm fine."

"Vanilla, tell me what's going on. You were just yelling something about 'you-know-who' and that really worried me."

There was a pause, and then Vanilla sighed and slumped over. Her gaze was fixated on her dark purple sheets. Zero sat on the edge of the bed and looked at his girlfriend apprehensively. There was a long, drawn-out silence before either of them spoke.

"Did you have a bad dream?"

"I dunno."

"Well, is there anything I can do?"

"Yeah."

"What can I do for you?"

"Help me get my mind off that bastard..."

"So it *was* a bad dream?"

"Maybe."

"Well, I suppose we could go down to the bar and see if we can sneak in. Would that help?"

"No. I just want to die..."

"What!? You can't do that! If you did, I don't know what I'd do!"

"Watch me."

The depressed teen dug through a pile of old magazines until she found a pocket knife. Before she could flip the blade open, Zero grabbed her hands and yelled, "Even if you don't give a damn about your own life, I do!"

He flipped it open and bent the tiny blade sideways with his bare hands, rendering it useless. After a frustrated sigh, he tossed it behind him and said, "I won't let you kill yourself, Vanilla. We both know pain. I've had a shitload of pain in my life and I know that you have, too. That's why we scream about it in our lyrics! And if we run out of breath, we use our instruments! That's the way of a true musician…as long as you and I work with each other and play music, we're freaking unstoppable! Not even one of the Seven Chosen could stop us!"

The young singer said nothing and avoided eye contact. Zero looked at her for a while, hoping that she would see the light. Deep down though, he knew she was too depressed to reason with, so he gently put his arms around her and held her close. Like a ragdoll, she went limp and rested her head against his strong shoulders. Before she knew it, she was asleep.

The shrill, beeping cry of an alarm clock filled the morning air as the Crescent Horned Punisher sat up in bed. She groaned and blindly batted her hand in the direction of the noise. There was a thud as the device crashed to the floor, and then there was silence. Slowly, she pulled herself into a sitting position and rubbed her eyes. After a quick look around, she realized that her boyfriend was gone.

Breakfast consisted of a day old bagel, a half-eaten chocolate chip cookie, and two energy drinks. As she was finishing her meal, she glanced at a wall clock that hung above the doorway and counted backwards an hour to calculate the time. "Wow it's lunchtime…I almost slept in again. I better call him and see if he's at the studio," she mumbled to herself.

Still chewing a chunk of bagel, the Crescent Horned Punisher flipped her cell phone open and dialed her boyfriend's number. The phone rang six times before going to his voicemail. "Hey, it's Zero. Uh, leave a message and shit. If this is a prank call, you can just go to hell. I don't give a shit," the recording said. A quiet beep sounded.

"Hey, it's me. I'm just calling to see if you're at the studio already. I'm headed over there in a bit, so if you're not there I'm going to be pissed off. Bye." She hung up and gave a frustrated sigh.

After getting dressed, the young rock star gathered up her microphone, bass, and amplifier and headed out the door and into the rainy streets of 1st City Realm.

The rain gently tapped on the ground as she hurried into a small, cylindrical building at the corner of an intersection. A large neon sign hanging overhead read, "Transport House," and glowed bright green through the dreary afternoon.

Inside, the building bore a striking resemblance to a public restroom. The walls were tiled with a dull yellow. The air was somewhat stale with just a hint of cigarette smoke and body odor. There were stalls lining the perimeter and a chained down garbage can with graffiti on it by the exit.

Vanilla stepped into a compact, metal-walled stall and waited. An automated voice said, "Please state your destination."

"Meltdown Music Studio, West City, 5th City Realm," the Crescent Horned Punisher recited in an irritated tone. The walls of the room glowed with a sickening shade of yellow, and then the automated voice said, "Destination is valid. Please proceed to the exit once stall number three is unlocked. Thank you."

She rolled her eyes and tapped her foot impatiently. *Why does it have to take so long for this stupid thing to work? Maybe I should just buy a teleportation watch. Besides, only homeless people use these places,* she thought angrily. *Jeez, my arms are going to freaking fall off carrying this amp before this thing is done.*

Eventually there was a loud pop followed by the automated voice, "Transportation complete." The singer kicked the door to the stall open and stumbled outside.

City Realm 5 was enormous. West City here seemed much larger and more densely populated than in the other City Realms. Most of the buildings in the area were brand new, or at least very well kept. There were glossy, towering skyscrapers everywhere and a sea of people in the streets and sidewalks. Businessmen dressed in crisp, gray suits weaved skillfully through the crowds as they made their way to appointments. Street vendors shouted about their products, attempting to be heard above all the noise and not be trampled in the process. Spoiled children cried or complained loudly to their mothers about meaningless things, screaming when they didn't get their way.

Vanilla navigated clumsily through the mass of people and sound, ignoring the occasional flash of cameras from the paparazzi or the whistle of a male fan. Unfortunately for her, the closest she could get to Meltdown Music Studio by way of the Transportation House was still a few blocks away, and she still had to fight through the unending flood of pedestrians.

Soon Meltdown Music Studio was in sight. It was a small brick building that sat nestled between an abandoned warehouse and a multi-story office building. There was a vast parking lot in front, which was usually vacant. Once in a while an old hovercar was parked in the far right corner closest to the offices, but today it was nowhere in sight.

As she came up to the glass double doors of the recording studio, Vanilla heaved her amplifier into the metal handle bars, flinging both the doors open simultaneously with a loud bang.

At first sight, the interior resembled a casual coffee shop. Soft, sagging couches as old as the building itself were situated around a low rectangular table. A coffee machine sat on a shelf in the far corner of the room with a little paper slip that read, "Donations" in permanent marker. An arrow was drawn pointing to the left, where there was a broken coffee cup.

On the other end of the building was a mess of various recording equipment and multiple rooms with soundproof walls—much like cubicles, only providing more privacy. It was obvious that the studio was well-loved and well-worn by all kinds of musicians. Posters of various bands lined every vertical surface in the building, including some windows.

Vanilla set her amp and microphone down with a loud thump and gingerly massaged her wrists. "Hey Zero! Are you here?" she called out. A few seconds later she was answered by the sound of someone playing a distorted guitar in one of the less-soundproof rooms. Without much thought, she walked up to the room and knocked loudly on the door.

The guitar playing stopped and the door opened. Zero stood in the doorway with a red V-shaped guitar. After brushing back a few strands of his long blue hair, he gave her a hug and said, "Hey. I'm sorry I didn't pick up when you called. I'm meeting with someone who wants to join our band."

"Wait, there's someone else here? Are they hot!?" she asked. She quickly combed through her hair with her fingers and adjusted the straps on her tank top.

Zero raised one eyebrow and leaned against the doorframe, shooting an amused smirk at her. "Unless you're interested in women, I'd say this person's not for you." Vanilla scowled at him and elbowed her way past.

A blonde-haired woman was standing next to a large amplifier and holding on to a bass guitar. Her sweatshirt had a black heart on it with a line drawn diagonally through it. A series of tangled, blackened vines with the words "Die Heartless" written in fancy cursive was tattooed on the side of her neck.

Vanilla looked her over from head to toe with obvious disapproval. "You look like you're afraid to show your skin, girl," she said, pointing to the woman's modest clothing. Zero quickly walked in between the two.

"Please excuse her, Angie. She's had a rough upbringing, but I'm sure you'll warm up to each other soon. Angie, this is my girlfriend, Vanilla. Vanilla, this is Angie. She'll be our new bassist."

Vanilla's eyes widened. She faked a cough and said, "You want *her* to be in our band? Zero, this chick doesn't even look like the kind of person that could play dirge metal! She looks more like a…country singer."

In response, the woman angrily slammed her bass down on a nearby chair and glared at the singer with the ferocity of an enraged lion.

"What makes you think I can't play gothic metal, bitch?"

"Everything! And it's D-I-R-G-E M-E-T-A-L, not gothic metal. Get it straight, moron."

"They're the same damn thing! I took four years of music school and I know that you haven't even attended grade school. So don't you dare call me a moron!"

"I can call you whatever I want, you whore!"

"Well! I thought this was a serious band, not a group for spoiled little babies to run rampant and have temper tantrums. Zero, the deal's off. You can find your own way into the 5th City Band Battle."

Angie flipped her hair back and picked up her equipment. With one last glare and rude hand gesture at Vanilla, she marched out of the room and straight to the exit.

As soon as the front door to the studio slammed, Zero whirled around to glare at his girlfriend. His face was beet red with anger. "Why the hell did you mouth off to her!? We need her to get us into the 5th City Band Battle. She's one of the judge's daughters, so she could have completely covered the entrance fees! You just ruined a once in a lifetime chance for us!" he exclaimed. His teeth clenched so tightly that his jaw was trembling.

Vanilla shrugged casually and rolled her eyes. "I thought she looked like a rich girl and I don't like snotty people like that. Besides, I can play bass, so we don't need her."

"Vanilla, she *is* rich, but that means we'd pretty much have our lives made with her on our side! She could take care of all our band's expenses since you keep using our money for drugs and alcohol!"

"So now you want to sneak her in as a manager? Is that it?! Oh, and in case you've forgotten, I'm not the only one who buys the goods. You do, too, so you can't put all the blame on me."

"Fine, you win that one, but I'll always be the front man of *To the Power of 10*! I'd never let anyone replace me. She was just gonna be our roadie and help us out financially and you just *had* to ruin it!"

"Well, I'm sorry *you* didn't tell me that earlier, jerk! I just didn't like her."

"Whatever. I don't wanna argue anymore. Our next show is on the twenty-fifth, so just be ready."

"What? Are you leaving now or something?"

"You know what? Just shut up."

With that, Zero grabbed his guitar and stormed out of the building.

Vanilla flinched as the door slammed behind him. "Jeez, he's such a baby," she muttered defiantly as she headed toward the entrance to get her equipment.

The rain was pouring heavily outdoors, the sky was dark, and the argument with her boyfriend had set Vanilla in a very foul mood. She sighed loudly with frustration and gazed out the glass doors at the large raindrops splashing on the pavement. It seemed as if each drop symbolized some part of her that was becoming detached and cast away, never to return.

A strange feeling came over her as she flopped down on one of the old couches in the studio. Though it was warm, a chill ran down her spine. Then the rebellious teenager reclined her feet, closed her eyes, and drifted off to sleep.

In her dreams, she once again envisioned herself as a young girl dressed in rags. This time, however, she was in a primitive stone hut, dimly lit by a crude fireplace. Something about the house gave her an uneasy feeling, like unseen dangers lurked around every corner. There was no door to escape; only a small hole in one of the walls. She went up to it and peered through.

Outside there were piles of jagged gray rocks, Stone Age houses similar to the one she was in, and very little plant life. It occurred to her that she was inside a massive cavern—presumably thousands of feet below the surface—for the ceiling of the cave was incredibly high. Her eyes immediately fell upon a tall, muscular teenager with black hair who was walking down a gravelly path. There was something intriguing about the young man. Vanilla felt as though she had once known him long ago in some forgotten time and place.

As she continued to watch, she saw Crescent Horned Punishers, much like herself and the man, come out of their stone houses and throw rocks and sharp bones at him. Some even ran up and hit him on the head or kicked violently at his legs. Though he was obviously in pain, the man refused to fight back.

"*Hey you, do something! They're hurting you!*" Vanilla shouted out the window. The young man stopped and turned around. His gentle eyes met hers and a sheepish smile appeared on his kindly face, which was now wet with blood.

"*These hands weren't meant to destroy, only to build and protect,*" he replied calmly.

Vanilla pressed her face harder against the opening in the wall. "*Then protect yourself, you idiot!*" she exclaimed. To her surprise, the black-haired teen only shook his head and kept on walking.

The dream faded and the beautiful Crescent Horned Punisher awoke to find herself still lying on the couch in the studio. "Who was he? I keep seeing him in my dreams, but I can't think of who he could be…" Then her next concert came to mind. "Shit. I'd better practice." Reluctantly she pulled herself together and began to warm up her voice.

The hours passed by, only disrupted once by another musician entering the building. She took no time to see who it was, but stopped to listen and see if it was a man. To her dismay, it was a woman, so she carried on with her practice.

When she was finished, she packed up her equipment and began the long trek back to the nearest Transportation House. It was rather late by the time she reached the main streets, but there were still crowds of people swarming around like mosquitoes on a warm summer evening after a rainstorm. It was also much hotter out than when she had arrived. Her arms ached from hauling her heavy amplifier, but she was resilient and kept on going, telling herself that she would sneak into a bar later and drink to numb the pain.

As she arrived at the old Transportation House, a red sign on the exterior caught her eye. Setting down her amp, she leaned over to read it.

IMPORTANT NOTICE: On October 25, 3046 (5th City Realm time), all Transportation House in City Realms 1, 3, and 5 will be removed in accordance with the City Councils' requests. For security reasons, all incoming traffic will be redirected to the nearest warp plateau.

"Shit! I guess I'll *have* to get a watch now," Vanilla groaned. Picking up her amplifier again, she headed inside the building to teleport, but not before giving the sign a good, hard kick.

Once she was finally in the safety of her own apartment, she set her things down one last time and flopped back onto her bed to take a nap. Her arms were now exhausted and throbbing so hard that she could barely move them—nor did she want to. Her stomach growled, but she ignored it and closed her eyes. Sleep was upon her within seconds.

The night before the concert, Vanilla and the band were sitting in a restaurant in 1st City Realm, waiting for their waitress to return with Zero's debit card. The Crescent Horned Punisher was sitting next to the blue-haired guitarist, with Wake and Lisa seated across from them.

"So," Zero said, looking at Vanilla, "I was thinking we could stay in a hotel tonight."

Dumbfounded, the Crescent Horned Punisher raised her

eyebrows and replied, "A hotel? You mean those run-down places people who can't afford houses or apartments stay at? What the hell are you on?"

"It's what bands used to do before teleportation watches were invented."

"This isn't the early 2000s, Zero. We're *not* staying at a hotel, right guys?" Vanilla turned to Wake and Lisa. The drummer said nothing and moved his head to the side to avoid eye contact. Lisa looked like she wanted to tell the singer something, but gave a small shrug and smiled sheepishly.

"No. Just no. I'm not going to do this. It's a load of shit, that's what it is!"

At that moment the waitress walked up to their table. She had heard what Vanilla said—as did everybody around them. Cautiously, she handed Zero's card back to him and forced a smile. "Is there something the matter?" she asked nervously.

"No, everything's fine. Sorry about my girlfriend's outburst. She does that sometimes," Zero replied, shooting a nasty glare at Vanilla.

The Crescent Horned Punisher was irate. She stood up abruptly and pointed at her boyfriend. "It's all your fault, asshole! If you think I'm going to stay one night in a freaking ghetto boarding house, you can go to hell!"

"Hey, calm down! It'll be no different than your apartment."

"Yeah right! At least I don't live in a trailer like you!"

"So? My trailer is cleaner than your apartment!"

The waitress looked frightened. She took a step back, her body tense with uncertainty and anticipation. Some of the customers around the band got up and left as quickly as they could. The manager appeared out of the back room and hurried over. His expression was that of surprise and a hint of anger. "What's going on?" he asked.

"This sorry excuse for a man wants me to stay in a run-down hotel!" Vanilla shouted.

Confused, the manager frowned and eyed the band skeptically. "Ma'am, I'm sorry, but I'm going to have to ask you and your friends to leave. This restaurant is supposed to be a safe and family-friendly place for people to—"

"Then fuck you! Nobody cares about me!"

The Crescent Horned Punisher stormed to the exit and kicked the door open, cracking the glass pane on the lower half. The manager looked bewildered. He began talking to the other band members, who were about to leave as well, though Vanilla couldn't hear exactly what he was saying—nor did she care.

As she marched down the sidewalk, ignoring the looks pedestrians were giving her, she realized something. *Damn it! We all used Zero's watch to get here and I don't know where the nearest Transportation House is!* She glanced back at the restaurant. Zero and the other members had just exited and were walking toward her. Like a rebellious child, Vanilla briskly turned back around and kept walking to snub them. "I'll find a way back," she told herself defiantly, "I don't need those idiots!"

She went on for a few blocks without looking back, but then another thought came to her. *I wonder if there are any guys staying at that hotel? I could get back at Zero and show him that it was a terrible idea to make me go!* Turning around, she began making her way back toward the band, a wicked smile curling her lips.

"Dude, what the hell were you thinking back there?" Zero said as she neared.

"Oh, sorry. I thought it over and I'm willing to go," Vanilla replied innocently.

The guitarist was taken aback. "Y-you are?" he stammered.

"OK then. Uh, let's...let's go." His eyes scanned the Crescent Horned Punisher's face carefully. She smiled sweetly and held out her hand. He typed an address in on a hologram keyboard on his watch and took his girlfriend's hand in his. Wake and Lisa put theirs on top of the other two's and, with a bright blue flash, everyone teleported.

The hotel Zero chose was situated out in the barren flats of a wasteland known as the DeGalful Plains in the far south of Crandenbow. There was little to no vegetation in sight. The only things that acted as landmarks were a few vacant shops scattered alongside an old highway. Each of these run-down buildings stood out like a sore thumb against the plain landscape, and they were all a long walk away from each other. A fine grit hung in the air like a light fog, creating the illusion that objects in the distance simply faded away into the bleak horizon, swallowed up in the abyss like the hopes and dreams of all who lived there.

The feeling of despair and poverty was present even within the small village of stores. Homeless people with dirt-smudged faces and faded clothes roamed around aimlessly, sometimes fighting with each other or collapsing from exhaustion on the dusty ground. The deserted parking lots were piled with litter, making them appear more like a dump.

As the band walked into the hotel, a bearded man sitting behind a counter glanced up at them as though they were illusions. His eyes looked glazed over and his overalls were as dusty as the ground outside. A bent cigarette hung loosely in his mouth, threatening to fall and singe his red plaid shirt.

"We'd like to stay one night and check out tomorrow at six in the morning...so I'll take three rooms," Zero said laconically.

Startled, the bearded man jumped up and said, "Holy—! I was sure my mind was playing tricks on me! Are you really gonna stay the night? It'll run you 30 Gold Crests, if you please, sir."

He was almost drooling with anticipation as Zero dug out his wallet and handed him three gold-colored coins with a clear centerpiece. Each bore the words, "10 Gold Spiritan Crests" on them.

"Here, take it. If we're pleased with your service, I might just top that off with twenty more," Zero added slyly.

"Thank you kindly, sir! Your support is much appreciated. Not many people use these hotels anymore. In fact, I'm one of the only hotel owners in these parts. I can assure that this will be a most enjoyable experience. If there's anything I can do for you, please let me know," the man replied, his smile widening. Zero shook the man's hand after the keys were handed out, and then he and the band headed toward their rooms.

"Zero…you've hardly spoken to me this past week. The only time you've said anything to me was at that restaurant. Are you avoiding me or something?" Vanilla asked, unable to fathom why her boyfriend was being so quiet and cold to her. The guitarist avoided eye contact as he unlocked the hotel room and stepped inside.

"Zero…seriously, what's going on? I hope you're gonna talk to me before the concert tomorrow."

He stopped and stood stock-still for a moment. His expression was solemn and filled with emotional pain. He was taking controlled breaths though his nostrils.

"Zero…come on. What did I do to deserve this?" she asked innocently, walking over to one of the two small mattresses in the room and laying down. The Crescent Horned Punisher could feel tears of her own rising within her, so she buried her face in the pillow to cry.

He walked over to the other mattress and let himself fall backwards onto it. After taking off his T-shirt, he pulled the covers over himself and closed his eyes. "Vanilla…I'm sorry in advance," he whispered distantly.

The singer propped herself up on her elbows and looked up at him. The soft, white skin around her eyes was pink from weeping. "What do you mean?" she said, climbing out of her bed and coming over to him. The guitarist made no reply. She leaned in to kiss him, but he quickly turned onto his side, facing the wall. Upset and feeling rejected, the Crescent Horned Punisher sulked back to her bed to try and sleep, hoping that a new day would resolve the mysterious conflict.

The golden light of morning shone through the white shades of the hotel room and cast long shadows on the floor. Somewhere outside a bird was tweeting happily with its friends as they searched for food. Vanilla opened her eyes and blinked in the bright daylight. "I hate mornings…" she grumbled, stretching her arms and legs.

Then she remembered the concert. Without a second thought she sprung out of bed and grabbed her suitcase. "Hey Zero, wake up! We have to—" her voice trailed off as she looked over at the bed on the other side of the room.

Clean sheets had already been put on, along with a new fluffy pillow. Further still, Zero's luggage was gone from the floor. Vanilla frowned. "He must be getting breakfast," she thought, walking to the door. A small slip of paper was tucked halfway in the doorframe, but she thought nothing of it and let it fall as she opened the door.

"Hey Lisa! We should get going," she called into the keyboardist's room. The Crescent Horned Punisher listened for movement, but no sound came from the room.

The Crescent Horned Punisher's heart started to beat faster. "What's going on?" Frantically, she tried turning the doorknob to the room. It was locked. "Come on, sleepy head! I'm not joking!"

The room Wake was in was locked and silent, as well. "Guys? Are you here? Anybody!?" she called out.

"Oh, I was wondering who was yelling. Your band left this morning." A voice said from behind her. Vanilla whirled around and, to her dismay, found that it was only the scraggy, bearded owner of the hotel.

"Where did they go?"

"Wait, you mean you don't know where your own band was headed? Well, there's no point in asking me. I sure don't know."

"When did they leave?"

"Well, about six o'clock this morning. That blue-haired guy told me not to wake you up…I feel kinda bad, but I guess I don't really have authority in that area. He paid me, after all."

"H-he said that? He told you not to wake me up?"

"Yep. If you need to get back home, I can call for one of my buddies to escort you with his transportation watch. It's a long walk to the nearest town if you don't have one and the bus doesn't run anymore. Ever since hovercars became a rich person's toy it's been pretty lonely out here."

"No way… He couldn't have done that…"

"Miss? Are you OK? I don't want you doing anything you might regret. I'm more than happy to get someone to help you."

Ignoring the bearded man, Vanilla stumbled out the front doors of the hotel like a panicking drunkard. Her legs shook violently, threatening to make her fall. As if on the verge of psychosis, she twitched and mumbled gibberish, unable to accept the reality that was before her. Her eyes were open so wide that it gave her an unnatural and disturbing appearance—almost like that of a nocturnal monster. She could feel her sanity quickly slipping away like sand in an overturned hourglass. "Lisa…

Wake… ZERO!!" the Crescent Horned Punisher screamed, lifting her head toward the morning sky. Then she fell to her knees on the dusty ground and thrashed about, beating her head with her fists. She was alone.

"ZERO!!" she called out again, though deep down she knew he could not hear her painful cries. Tears streamed down her face and her voice became dry from screaming. Desperation overtook her. With dwindling energy, she sat up and pulled out a small knife from her pocket and held it to her neck.

"I hate myself," she whispered and began to press, but before the knife could pierce her snow-white flesh, it was forcefully knocked from her grasp by another metal object. She looked up to find that a string of short, sharp, metallic squares had flung the knife to the ground. A thick silver cord attached each one together, forming some sort of segmented sword.

A man with messy white hair and a pale face stood before her. His eyes were strikingly different from a Mandian's; they resembled more of a monster's than anything. His sclerae were black as the night sky and his irises were pure yellow and had slit pupils like a cat. Two dark lines ran down his cheeks, making it appear as if he had cried with black eye makeup on. He was holding the handle of the extended weapon, which he quickly pulled back, causing it to retract into what looked like a normal one-handed sword. The sinister man smirked, revealing his sharp teeth, and then hung the weapon on a loop on his belt.

"What did you think you were gonna do with that knife, huh? I couldn't let a pretty young lady like you hurt herself, now could I? I'm Dan. What's your name, beautiful?" he said slyly and moved closer. Vanilla noticed that he was not making eye contact with her. Following his gaze, she realized he was staring lustfully at her chest. "Come on, girl,

I couldn't let *anyone* waste a nice rack like that…I saved your ass, so at least tell me your name."

"I-I'm Vanilla…"

"Vanilla? Boy did I hit the jackpot! Aren't you in some band? Well, it doesn't matter. Come with me, I'll get you out of here."

With trembling legs, she started to get up. Dan quickly reached out and grabbed her arm, pulling her to her feet with more force than necessary. She tried to break free of his grasp, but he was too strong.

"Alright, you're with me now. You got that?" he said, leaning in so close that she could smell his foul breath. Vanilla's heart beat wildly in her chest. She swallowed hard and looked away.

"W-where are you taking me?" she asked weakly as Dan prepared to transport.

He gave her a mean smile and shook his head at her. "Didn't I answer that before? I'm taking you away from here."

"But where?"

"Shut it. Speak again and I'll knock you out cold."

Vanilla firmly pursed her lips as the evil man's grip on her tightened. "We're outta here!" he said and they were both warped away from the barren wasteland.

CHAPTER 2

-A Life Worth Leaving-

"Here we are!" Dan said gruffly as he and Vanilla arrived in front of an abandoned apartment building.

It was in the middle of a vacant complex that was equally run-down. All she had time to see was the building in front of her, however, and the gleam of the man's silver teleportation watch. *Where are we!?* she thought frantically, her eyes darting around for a clue. Most of the small, dusty windows on the multistory apartment were broken or cracked and the paint was chipping from the siding, which was covered in graffiti. Still clutching his hostage's arm, the evil Origin Spiritan led her inside and slammed the door behind them.

It was humid inside and smelled of chemicals and cigarette smoke. The warped, gray floorboards were stained and filthy, and the walls had deep gouges in them, presumably from a sword or a knife. In one corner of the room there was a large, empty cage with a few strands of blonde hair caught on the door.

With a jolt, Dan shoved the rock star into a nearby chair. It nearly toppled over as she hit the backrest. Mounds of yellowing fabric stuffing protruded from long gashes and its poorly stitched seams. The arms were stained maroon in places and it smelled horrendous. Unable to block out the odor, Vanilla was left to gag and suffer until olfactory fatigue set in.

"Now stay put or I'll hunt you down like a dog," he said, coldly staring into her eyes. She nodded nervously. Her muscles were rigid as a statue, but her whole body was shaking violently. She could hardly breathe.

It was only then that she realized that her kidnapper was of a species she had never seen before—or could not recall seeing in the chaos of the moment. His cat-like eyes looked somewhat like Zero's, but they were scary and full of hate. His teeth were sharp and pointy like a shark's and yellow with plaque. The dark vertical lines under the man's eyes stood out against his snow-white face and messy white hair.

"What do those markings under your eyes mean?" the curious Crescent Horned Punisher asked out of impulse. Her heart stopped as she heard the words come out of her own mouth. *Shit! Why did I say that? I'm dead!* she thought, shrinking back into the rancid armchair.

Dan whirled around, his face scrunched up in a menacing scowl. His hand darted toward her and slapped her hard across the face, leaving a red mark on her left cheek. She let out a cry and recoiled.

"You don't know what they mean?"

"N-no..."

"They mean I'm an Origin Spiritan—and a member of the Destruction Dynasty!"

"I'm sorry!"

The Origin Spiritan hit Vanilla again and spat on her. "We were the first Spiritans to be created. The whole dimension of Spiritia and everything in it is rightfully ours! Now shut up and keep still, woman. I'm trying to think!"

The Crescent Horned Punisher did her best to hold back the oncoming tears. The muscles in her face strained and she pursed her lips together as tightly as she could. She was beyond petrified.

After a long, threatening glare at her, her captor walked into the next room and began frantically digging through some cupboards. Each time she heard something hit the floor or bang against another object, she flinched and shuddered.

I've got to get out of here somehow! she thought as Dan reentered the room holding up a plastic bag to inspect the contents. He was smirking triumphantly at the pills inside.

"Hey girl, eat these. It'll make you feel better," he said, extending his hand toward her. His false sincerity was blatantly obvious, but refusing his offer seemed out of the question. Not wanting to get hit again, she cautiously took them from Dan's hand. As soon as her skin touched his, a cold shiver ran down her spine. The Origin Spiritan seemed pleased with the reaction and cackled.

The pills were square with blue writing on them. They didn't seem like something that was made with machinery, as each one was a slightly different size. Powder was also coming off them as she turned them over in her hand. After hesitating for a fearful moment, she swallowed them and braced herself. Immediately she felt strange; it was as if her body was floating in the waves of an ocean. Her thoughts became unclear and bright, haunting colors filled the room. The only thing that she could truly interpret was the sound Dan made as he snickered sinisterly.

She wanted to speak, but her vocal cords felt dry and painful. She panicked and stood up with great difficulty. The room was spinning and every object within the small apartment was engulfed in the odd, ever-changing colors. She felt Dan push her back into the chair and yell something, but the words did not register in her mind. They sounded foreign and deadened, like some primitive utterances being spoken underwater.

Soon the hallucinations that danced around her grew into a blinding light that swallowed everything. Time seemed to slow and the sounds became low and even more distorted. She felt her body still, and then her world faded into white silence.

In what seemed like moments later, she awoke. The sound of a muffled voice could be faintly heard nearby. She could not see anything and her body felt heavy and limp. *It's so dark...am I blind?* she thought.

31

Groping around in the dark, her hands came across something damp and spongy. It squished between her fingers and released strange, lukewarm liquid. Startled and afraid, she let out a scream.

Suddenly, light was shed on her as a door opened to reveal Dan. He stood still with his hands in his pockets. Vanilla squinted and held her dry hand up to shield her eyes.

"Are you awake, bitch?" he asked.

With much effort, she sat up and looked around. Her world was still wheeling. She was sitting on a pile of black garbage bags in a small closet. A few decaying cardboard boxes were stacked on shelves behind her. Each box had strange words scribbled on the side with red ink. It occurred to her that what she had put her hand into *was* a sponge, but as for the liquid, she couldn't recognize what it was. It was a dark, grayish green and had a musty odor.

Dan reached out and pulled her to her feet. "I'm surprised that you fainted so fast. Most girls stay awake for at least an hour after taking that drug. I have to lock them in a cage so they don't cause me trouble."

Vanilla opened her mouth to say something, but quickly thought better of it. Her whole body trembled from fear. Being in the same room with Dan made her feel sick to her stomach. He was repulsive; from his lustful eyes to his arrogant demeanor.

"Well, it doesn't matter what happens to you now," the Origin Spiritan scoffed. With a firm grasp on his victim, he led her out of the closet and into a small room. The door slammed behind them with a loud bang, making her jump.

Inside, it was humid and smelled strange. The walls were tinted yellow with mold and were peeling. There were no windows, only a hole in one of the walls with old bloodstains around it. An old, moldy mattress lay on the floor with crumpled sheets over it. Vanilla caught a glimpse of a ripped pair of pink panties pinned beneath the edge of the mattress and the wall. Dan shoved her onto the bed and ordered her to undress.

Out of fear, the poor Crescent Horned Punisher obeyed. Dan's stare pierced her like needles in a voodoo doll. Her mind had gone completely numb, possibly from the drug she had taken earlier. Right before she had taken her underwear off, she had a vision—or so it seemed.

She stood in a temple very much like a cathedral. Heavenly rays of light streamed through the stained-glass windows, forming colorful patterns on the floor. Gorgeous images of mystical beings and places were painted on the walls to form what appeared to be a story. The ceiling towered high above with magnificent stone arches. The entire space was engulfed in complete silence.

In the front of the room, five wide marble steps led up to a raised platform. Sitting in the center of it was a massive pipe organ. It was constructed of pure white rock and its long, tubular brass pipes shone pure gold.

A man with long golden hair and a priest's robe was standing at the instrument with his back turned. He had flowing golden hair that cascaded down his back like a waterfall. Though his body and limbs were slender, he exuded a noble presence, powerful and wise, but also a bit frightening. Strangely though, his body was motionless, completely frozen in time.

Mustering up her courage, Vanilla walked cautiously toward him, not knowing if she was dreaming or had been transported somewhere. *Maybe I died and this is the afterlife,* she thought fearfully.

It was so quiet in the building that to her, each step she took sounded like canons going off. She could even hear her own heartbeat. With each pulse of adrenaline she grew weaker. As she reached the end of the last isle of wooden seats, she stopped. If she climbed the short flight of stairs, she would be only a few feet from the strange man. Something deep inside told her to keep going and ignore her fear. Hesitantly, she lifted her right foot onto the first of the marble steps.

Instantly, sound returned to the room like a raging flood. The faint chirping of birds from outside, the ambient noises of people going about their business on the streets, and the low rumble of air circulating though the vaulted ceiling filled her ears. It was so sudden and drastic that she had to cover her horns for a moment as she adjusted.

The man in front of her turned around. His skin was made from light and he wore a mask that covered all but his left eye, which glowed blue like a sapphire. His stare was piercing, as though he could see into her soul and knew everything about her. At the same time, his gaze was also kind and mysterious. His presence was even more overwhelming now, like a mighty king upon his throne. The Crescent Horned Punisher could feel immense power radiating from him. She was petrified as the divine being reached out and gently placed his hands over her eyes. When he spoke, his words were foreign, yet somehow understandable. His voice was like thousands of people talking all at once, each in a different language. With every second of his speech, she felt that he was reciting millenniums worth of knowledge. It was far too much for her brain to handle or retain.

Finally, she was able to distinguish a single word out of all that was being said. "Know," said one of the many voices. It repeated itself again and again, growing in volume until her head started to hurt. Just when she could bear it no longer, they stopped and she was face-to-face with the man of light, his intense blue eyes only inches from hers.

The vision ended as quickly as it began. She was still sitting on the mattress and before she knew what she was doing, a scream painfully tore from her throat. Surprised at the sudden outburst from his hostage, Dan stepped back, allowing his captive just enough time to bolt out of the room.

When she had reached the front door to the apartment, she flung it open and raced outside. There she fell to her knees, almost completely naked, and yelled at the top of her lungs. "I repent! I REPENT!"

Somehow the strange man of light's words had brought her to a revelation. Something had changed. She knew that her eyes had been opened and she had been given wisdom. She could see what her life had become from years of making bad choices. Her legs trembled from guilt and her eyes filled with tears. In the cold night air, the young rock star's cry echoed far beyond the run-down apartment complex and into the cloudy sky. Exhausted, she fell face-first in the dirt and blacked out.

Through the bitter darkness, she felt twig-like fingers slowly wrap around her motionless body. They were frigid and lifeless, like icicles. Whatever it was, it gently tightened its grip and hoisted her up.

Am I flying? Is this *death?* she thought. It was impossible to see, but she could just barely make out the sound of wind howling past her. Soon her body became numb and the constant battering of emotional agony left. Her mind was at peace as she fell into an unusually serene sleep.

When she awoke, Vanilla expected to find herself naked and tied up in the old apartment that Dan had taken her to. To her surprise, however, she was lying in a cool room on a very soft featherbed with purple sheets pulled gently over her.

The room was very quiet and plain. The walls were bare wooden boards that looked like they had just barely survived a thousand-year deep freeze, for they had turned gray from age. The many nails that held them together were rusted, but surprisingly, there was no draft from outside.

The floorboards were dented and gray as well. A faded square maroon rug lay under the bed. Its edges were frayed and tattered as if it had been chewed on by different animals over time. There was a small, flickering candle on an antique dresser that sat next to the bed. A foot away from the candle was the few clothes she was wearing when she had fainted. They were torn and muddy.

Feeling unusually embarrassed, she quickly reached for them. It was then that she realized that she was already fully clothed with a long purple sweatshirt and black sweatpants. *How did that happen…? Did someone rescue me? Well whoever did this knows my cup size,* she mused, feeling her mysterious new brassiere. *Where am I?*

Suddenly, she heard the loud clack of high-heeled boots on the wooden floorboards in the next room. They were headed toward her. Thinking quickly, the Crescent Horned Punisher lay back down and pulled the covers over her just as the door slowly creaked open. Someone had entered the room.

Out of the corner of her eyes, she saw a very skinny and tall woman. She wore a long, purple patched-up skirt and a dull gray shirt that hung on her fragile frame like a rag draped over a stick. Her twig-like fingers were gray and lifeless, and her legs were as skinny as the handle of a broom. A pair of black leather thigh-high boots covered them.

What stuck out most of all about the woman to Vanilla was the purple conical hat atop her head. It had a pair of yellow eyes and a zigzagged mouth that was sewn shut. The eyes on the hat, though barely visible from how sunken they were, looked around the room while the eyes on the woman's face stayed closed.

What is she? She looks like a half-dead witch or something. She's almost like a Madite, but no Madite is that skinny, she wondered. *It's like something out of a horror movie,* she thought, and shuddered. The odd

36

woman did not appear threatening, however.

The skeletal being hesitated, and then walked over to the far corner of the room where a large mirror hung. Heart racing, Vanilla squinted just enough so that she appeared to be asleep, but could still see the woman.

There was a long silence, which was finally broken by the woman beginning to cry, although there were no tears. "My body is thousands of years past its limits…I can't keep this up for much longer."

Though she did not know why, the Crescent Horned Punisher felt the urge to climb out of bed and comfort the woman. The sight of the woman's anguish tore at her heart with a seemingly unnatural magnitude. It was almost as if she could feel her pain. However, before she could make up her mind, the woman left the room and shut the door quietly behind her. The room fell silent once more.

After waiting for a moment, she climbed out of bed and walked toward the door. She stopped for a moment, her hands trembling with anxiety. *What could be beyond this door? Is this all Dan's doing? I need to know,* she thought, and opened the door.

Coming into the next room, she realized that she was in a bare kitchen. The only furnishing that the room had was an old gas stove, an open cupboard with metal pots and pans, and a small dining table beneath a window.

"I wonder if I can find my way home from here…?" Vanilla said to herself as she headed over to look out the window.

She gasped as she gazed outside and saw a desolate landscape, covered in purple slime. There was no vegetation. Only a few large, slime-covered rocks scattered here and there could be seen for miles. There were no animals or insects, either. The whole realm was bleak and barren. Up above, the sky was shrouded in dark gray rain clouds. She could hear the faint howl of wind, though it seemed out of place because nothing in the landscape was moving. It was like a vast, slimy desert.

Startled at this strange and foreign world, she whirled around and ran back toward the bedroom. Before she had reached the doorway, her foot caught on something under a rug and she fell face-first onto the floor with a thud.

As she pulled herself up, she realized that there was something unusual about where she landed. The floorboards beneath her had sounded hollow when she hit them. Feeling curious and completely forgetting her fear, she removed the rug and searched for a loose edge to grab onto. To her delight, she found a suspiciously wobbly plank. Getting a firm grasp, the young rock star pulled hard until it lifted up.

A long, dark staircase was revealed as the floorboard clattered aside. The Crescent Horned Punisher stood for a moment, gazing down the stairwell. The low rumble of air coming up from the passage brought with it a sense of foreboding. It took her several seconds before she could muster the courage to enter. Finally, she took a step.

The farther she descended, the mustier the air became. Gradually, the damp basement smell grew so potent that it was making her dizzy. She remembered hearing a story about a robber who had just looted a shop and went into the sewer to escape pursuit. A week later, he was found dead a few yards from where he had entered it. The authorities claimed that he suffocated from the toxic stench. The thought of dying from hazardous odors or suffocation made her feel even queasier. She held her hand over her mouth and slowed her breathing as much as she could.

Just then, she reached the last step. There was a dark hallway ahead of her, but the air had become surprisingly less thick. Soon an ominous presence flooded the passage. She trembled from fatigue and squinted to see if there was any light farther down.

A faint glow emitted from something on the left side of the hallway. It flickered and danced against the shadows like candlelight. Drawing closer to it, the young rock star saw that it was the light from a room.

Maybe that woman from the house is in there, she thought to herself. With curiosity giving her courage, Vanilla inched her way toward the open doorway. Each step she took drained more energy than the last. And finally, when she felt like she had no strength left, she realized that she had already reached the opening.

She was standing in a doorway that led into a large room. A stone table sat on the floor surrounded by 10 strange looking people. As she looked around, she noticed a man who was dressed in a black cloak. One hand rested upon a golden hilt of a sword and the other was clutching his wide rice hat. The man's face was covered by a blank white mask. He seemed to have noticed her before she had even peeked around the corner. "Hm. Excuse me," he said quietly to someone who was just out of view, "but it appears your guest is eavesdropping."

Heart still beating wildly, Vanilla turned around to run away. Her knees buckled, causing her to fall face-first onto the hard floor in the corridor. Scrambling to her feet in desperation, she saw a tall, skeletal woman in front of her.

She was the same person Vanilla had seen in the house. Something was obviously different about her, though. Gray, cadaverous wings stuck out from the woman's back, creating a blockade behind her. They resembled decaying hands with long, pointy fingers. Before she had a chance to do anything, they reached out and engulfed her in darkness.

When she came to, she was lying on a bench in a quiet park. A slight breeze was blowing, creating waves on the endless fields of grass. Somewhere in a distant tree, a lone bird was singing. Vanilla slowly sat up and looked around in bewilderment. *Was I drunk? How the hell did I get here?* Then she looked at her clothes.

These are the clothes I got from that creepy woman... So I guess I wasn't drunk. I suppose I'd feel pretty hungover if I was drunk. Something really weird is going on here. First I have a vision about some priest guy with a mask, and then I get taken to some old house in some sort of slimy place. The last time I did drugs was a few days ago, so it's not like I would still be hallucinating from that. I suppose it could have been caused by that pill that Dan made me take. And if this is one of the City Realms, I must have been out for hours because it's already evening.

As she was pondering, she started to feel something that she had not felt in many years. It was an uncomfortable, heavy feeling in her stomach. Part of her wanted to suppress it, but she couldn't. It was guilt. The vivid memory of how she had escaped from Dan's apartment and repented—something she had never done before—kept replaying in her head.

What am I doing? Something just isn't right. I feel bad. Maybe I just need to get some food. I don't think I've even had breakfast yet and it's already past lunchtime... No, that's not it. Is this guilt? Why?

The Crescent Horned Punisher stood up. As she did, a letter fell from the bench. Instinctively, she bent down and picked it up. The handwriting on it was gorgeous. The swooping curves and steadiness of each line looked like something that had been done by a computer, but at the same time it seemed too organic to be artificial. Curious, she began reading.

Dearest Vanilla Lamberschvak,

By the time you will receive this letter my already prolonged life has ended. But you need not worry, for your future will be bright as long as you follow my instructions.

As soon as you are able, escape to the planetoid ream of Glunke. On your 18th birthday you will find my father from the past. He is a young adult named Zallin. To you and this world, I have not been born yet. But that story is for another time and place—a story you will help write.

You may have already guessed what I am implying…I am your future daughter, Raech. My appearance will not be like it was at our first and last meeting. I will be born young and healthy, if you choose to fulfill this prophecy as instructed.

On a closing note, do not feel turmoil in your heart from my death, as long as you and Zallin are together, there is no doubt I will be reborn to you as a child.

Yours truly,
Raech Lamberschvak

Vanilla's slight disbelief vanished as she pulled another object out of the envelope. It was a very old, faded picture of her, along with two other people.

The photograph showed a family outside a wooden cabin. There was a man with a pointy blue hat that had strange yellow eyes and a

41

zigzagged mouth, and also a young girl with a purple hat, like that of the mysterious woman's. Holding hands with the child was Vanilla. She was smiling at both the man and the young girl.

The Crescent Horned Punisher felt the urge to cry. Something inside her told her that her life was going to change if she followed the instructions that this woman wrote. *This is all so surreal. It feels right though,* she thought. *I've got to go to…what was it called? Glunke? Yeah, that was it. I wonder if there are any Teleportation Houses around here. I must be in 3rd City Realm. Damn—er, darn. It looks like I'll have a ways to walk before I can get into the city. I'm so hungry…*

She carefully folded up the letter and tucked it into her pants pocket. Then, with a reluctant sigh, she trudged onward, following the winding sidewalk and trying not to think about food.

As she was nearing the street, she noticed a young Mandian couple with two children having a picnic. She was reminded of Zero and frowned. *They can be happy. Why can't I?* she thought bitterly. As she walked closer, she could smell apple pie. *Oh man, I've got to eat… Come to think of it, I don't even have my purse! It wasn't with me when I woke up back there and I don't think it was with me when I got kidnapped. Crap. That means that it's still at that dingy hotel in the DeGalful Plains. It's a lost cause… At least my cell phone is still with me. Hm. Maybe I should ask those people for food. Ugh! But why does it have to be* them?

"Excuse me," Vanilla said, coming up to the couple, "I hate to ask this, but would you be willing to let me have something to eat? Anything will do—even a cracker. I haven't eaten all day and I have to walk really far. I can autograph something for you in return."

The couple looked at each other and then back at her. "Wait, *who* are you?" the husband asked, eyeing her suspiciously.

"I'm Vanilla Lamberschvak."

"I've never heard that name before. Have you, Sweetie?"

"No," the man's wife responded, shaking her head.

"Well, we don't need your autograph, but here, you can take this apple and a cheese stick. I'd offer you some pie, but it would be difficult to eat while you're walking," the man said.

"James, she can sit with us if she wants to. Would you like to join us, Vanilla?"

"That's OK. I don't want to butt in or anything. Oh, is this 3rd City Realm?"

"Um, yes. Why?" James said, looking quite puzzled.

"It's kind of a long story. Some weird stuff just happened to me."

"Oh, is everything OK?"

"James, she's hungry! Give her the food."

"Oh right! I'm sorry! Here you go."

Vanilla took the food with trembling hands and wolfed it down while the couple watched her empathetically.

As she was finishing the apple, one of the children came running over with a dandelion. "Daddy! Look! A flower!" he said, holding up the weed with both hands. He was about five years old and had very curly brown hair and bright blue eyes.

"Oh, cool! Do you know what that one's called, Joshua?" James said, smiling at the child.

"Uh, yellow flower?"

"It's a dandelion."

"Dandelion?"

"Yup. Where's your brother?"

"Over there. Who's that?" the child said, pointing a short, stubby finger at Vanilla.

"Her name's Vanilla. Can you say 'hi?'"

"Where's her nose?"

Vanilla blushed and almost coughed up a chunk of apple that she was in the process of swallowing. The couple looked equally shocked—if not more.

"Joshua! That was mean. Not every species is the same. Your friend Jimmy is a Grenzel Blind Demon and you know not to tease him about his chin and eyes. I want you to apologize to her," the child's mother said sternly.

"I'm sorry!" Joshua said, rather angrily.

"T-that's OK," Vanilla replied, trying hard to quell her temper.

"I'm so sorry, Vanilla. He's usually well-behaved around strangers," James said.

"Uh-huh. Well, I better get going. Thanks for the food."

"OK, hang in there. I hope things brighten up for you. Do you want to take another apple with you for the road?"

"Thanks, but I think I'll be OK."

Vanilla turned around and quickly walked away from the family, firmly locking her gaze on the street. *Stupid kid,* she thought. *Not everybody is a Mandian. You have it pretty damn good and you don't even realize it.*

It was just starting to get dark as she reached the street. The tall streetlights flickered on in pairs, row by row. Moments later, small swarms of gnats and moths were already circling around them, seemingly oozing out of the woodwork just to frantically dance the night away. The air was surprisingly still, and very few people were around. To the Crescent Horned Punisher, it felt unnatural and eerie. *I don't think I've ever been in this part of 3rd City Realm. It seems like there should be more people here, but there isn't. I wonder if it's a holiday… I hope I can still find a teleportation watch somewhere. I don't recognize this part of 3rd City Realm at all.*

Where she now stood, there were towering buildings in front of her, like hulking giants of glass and metal whose very figures etched the sharply undulant horizon. They rose into the darkening sky, disappearing as they pierced the heavens. It was a common sight in all the City Realms, but also did nothing to alleviate her feeling of disorientation. It was like trying to piece together a puzzle that only had one color; everything blended together and looked the same.

Behind her was the park she had woken up in—a moderately sized plot of land with grassy fields and a few trees that were hardy enough to survive the abuse of city life. Like the concrete jungle before her, it was generic—a repeated image that she had seen in other parts of the realm thousands of times.

As she wandered through the vacant streets, gazing distantly at the illuminated shops, she noticed a neon sign for a bar. Instinctively, she headed toward it but stopped herself midway. *No, I shouldn't. That won't help me out of this. Besides, I really shouldn't be drinking,* she thought. Then her stomach began to growl. *I guess it'd be OK if I snuck in for a bit. Maybe I can snag some cashews or pretzels from one of the tables.*

The closer she drew to the entrance, the stranger she felt. Again, she stopped herself, this time right outside the doorway. She could hear the muffled throbbing of a steady bass line coming from inside. Someone was shouting, too, although it was impossible to understand what they were saying. The colorful glow from the signs in the window reflected in Vanilla's eyes as she struggled with her conscience. It was almost hypnotizing.

Suddenly, someone burst out of the front doors and stumbled onto the sidewalk. It was an Origin Spiritan. He was dressed in plain gray and black clothing that was stained with beer. His white hair was unkempt and wet. Like a sailor walking on a rocking ship, he staggered around, singing gibberish and occasionally letting loose a thunderous belch. When he noticed her, he stopped his drunken carol and stared at her. His vertically slit pupils widened like a cat preparing to pounce.

"Heh, yer a purty thang! A…a purty…purty THANG! Hahaha," he blurted, teetering from side to side.

Frightened and completely disgusted by the drunkard—and his smell—she turned around and ran. The man called something after her, but she couldn't understand it, nor did she care what it was. Her mind was racing now.

That was horrifying! I can't believe that I used to think drunken people were funny! I hope he doesn't try to follow me—not that he really could. I should get inside one of these shops. It'll be a lot safer than the streets. Maybe I can find someone who can help me, too. Choosing the nearest and most brightly lit store, she darted inside.

Exhausted, she bent over and put her hands on her knees, panting for breath. Her heart was still beating wildly in her chest like a drumroll. Running had made her feel even more hungry and weak, but she knew that she was safe.

Once she had caught her breath, she straightened up and looked around. As irony would have it, she was in an electronics store. The floor was tiled and so clean that she could almost see herself in it. The walls were light gray and illuminated with all sorts of interesting gadgets. There were numerous hologram computers on display in the center of the room, their projected screens creating little walls of pictures and text. In the far corner of the building there was a big glowing sign that read, "Multi-Rings." A variety of brand names were listed underneath it in smaller text.

Jeez, it looks like they have everything, Vanilla thought as she made her way into the showcase of modern technology.

Before she could find an employee to ask, however, she spotted someone a few feet away from her that she recognized. He was looking at noise-canceling headphones in the clearance isle.

The young man was a short, red-haired Mandian with a ponytail and was wearing a blue and gray sleeveless shirt that had seen better days. His cargo shorts were also well worn, having smudges of permanent marker on the waistband where someone had once sloppily scribbled "Wake Break" as an invasive prank.

"Wake..." she said automatically.

Surprised, Wake looked up. As soon as their eyes met, the vertically challenged drummer cast his gaze at his feet. "All I'm gonna say is that it wasn't my choice. We—me and Lisa, that is, voted against kicking you out, but that blue-haired bastard wouldn't listen to us. Why would he, anyway? He's just a stubborn son-of-a-bitch!"

Vanilla wanted to say something, but couldn't. The brew of strong emotions within left her speechless. Eyes stinging with oncoming tears, she did her best to fight back the urge to cry. Wake could see her struggle, but didn't know how to comfort her.

"I...well, good luck, Vanilla. Sorry, but I need to go."

"Wake, wait!"

"Hm?"

"I need help buying something."

"No, I won't help you buy drugs. You've got...too much talent to waste your life on that shit."

"It's not that! I need a teleportation watch. It's a long story, but there's somewhere I need to get to. It's very important."

"A teleportation watch? Uh, alright, sure. Go pick one out."

"Thank you so much! I really appreciate it."

"Y-yeah, whatever. Hey, are you OK?"

"As OK as I can be at a time like this I guess. Why?"

"You just seem…I dunno. Never mind."

"What?"

"Nothin'. Just go find a watch."

"OK."

Vanilla quickly found a teleportation watch she liked on a nearby display stand. It was bright silver and as smooth as a river washed stone. There were a number of small buttons on both sides and one large one right under the screen with the word "Send" printed in bold, green letters. She found a box with a matching model number and brought it to her friend.

"I found one."

"Good. Let's go check out."

"Thanks again for doing this for me. I promise I'll repay you when I can."

"Sure, whatever. You know, somethin's different about you. You're not…I dunno."

"Mean?"

"I guess."

"A lot has changed."

"I'll say," Wake mumbled.

"Huh?"

"Nothin'. There, there's nobody in line on register four."

"OK."

The clerk smiled when he saw them. "Say," he said in a hushed tone, "aren't you guys from *To the Power of 10*?"

Wake looked around to see if anybody else was listening. "Why? You want an autograph or somethin'?" he asked, a hint of impatience in his voice.

"Sure! I was at your concert a few days ago. You guys rocked! You were way better than the band that opened for you. Say, where were *you?*" he replied, pointing at Vanilla.

"She was sick," Wake interjected. Vanilla bit her lip. She wanted to explain how Zero abandoned her and how she was kidnaped and almost raped because of it. She wanted to shout it out so everybody in the store would know and her ex-boyfriend's reputation would be ruined, but she hesitated and her opportunity was lost. Wake had just finished signing a photograph for the clerk and was walking away from the counter with the watch in a plastic bag. There were people waiting in line behind her, so she collected herself and went after him.

"Here," the drummer said, holding out the item as she approached.

"Thanks. Hey."

"Hey what?"

"You could have told him what happened."

"I thought you'd get mad at me."

"Why would I?"

"Girls get mad at everything."

"Excuse me? What about *you*? *You're* the one always getting mad at everything."

"Hey, I just bought you somethin'. I usually don't do that for people, so be grateful!"

"Well I…I'm sorry. I guess I'm still really upset about what happened."

"And why wouldn't you be? Hell, even I'm pissed off about it. You're a way better singer than that boneheaded Grenzel Blind Demon. He can burn in hell for all I care!"

"Why don't you quit the band?"

He broke eye contact for a moment and fidgeted with one of

49

the zipper pockets on his shorts. "Um… It's kinda hard to explain." His cheeks had taken on a slightly rosy hue.

"Tell me," she said, leaning forward.

"I-I can't! It's personal. You'd laugh at me."

"No I won't."

"That's what they all say."

"Oh, come on! Hey, maybe we could form our own band!"

"I dunno… Don't you have some place you need to be?"

"Yeah, but…"

"Maybe that's where you should go then. Ugh, I really hate long goodbyes."

"But—"

"Look, whatever future awaits you, I'll always…be your friend, Vanilla. You're smart and talented and—gah! I don't know!"

"Wake…"

"What?"

"Thank you."

"Hm?"

"I said thanks. It's weird getting compliments from you—not that I'm complaining or anything."

"Yeah, well don't get the wrong idea. There's a girl that I like already, so—"

"Really? Who? Is it Lisa?" Her eyes lit up with an insatiable curiosity.

"I won't say."

"It's Lisa, isn't it? It has to be."

"Shut up! I said I won't say!"

"Alright, alright… Well, I guess this is goodbye then."

"Yeah. Good luck… Vanilla."

"You too, Wake."

The two musicians stood in silence for a moment, staring at one another. Wake gave a small smile and nodded. Vanilla answered with the same. A crystal clear tear escaped from her eyes as he teleported, leaving her alone in the warm summer night. She took a look behind her just in time to see lights in the store dim, signaling that it was closing time.

"Alright," she said to herself, unboxing the teleportation watch. "Let's see if I can figure this thing out. I hope it doesn't need to be charged."

As she turned it on, a small hologram appeared above the screen. A lady in a gray business suit bowed and began talking.

"Hello! Thank you for purchasing a Zeth-brand teleportation watch. Please listen carefully as I explain the End-User License Agreement and Privacy Policy. If you are unable to hear this message clearly, press the Plus button located on the side of this watch. If not, I will proceed in five seconds."

"Ugh, I don't want to hear this. Maybe it will skip over it if it knows I can't hear it," Vanilla said and pressed the Plus button. To her dismay, the message began to play again from the beginning, this time a little louder.

"No! Stupid thing! How do I skip this?" she said, hastily digging through the papers in the box for an instruction manual.

"If there's something you missed, you can always play this message again. You can access it from your Settings under 'Terms and Conditions.' A printed copy of this is also included with the product's instruction manual. Now, let's begin. By using this product, you agree to be bound to the following Terms and Conditions. If you do not agree, do not use this product."

"Argh!" she growled. "Just let me use the freaking watch!" Out of frustration, she pressed all of the buttons at once, hoping that it would somehow stop. There was a flash and the hologram disappeared. A string of cryptic messages scrolled across the screen too quickly to read, and then the device turned off.

"Shit! This better not be broken!" Vanilla said, frantically mashing the Power button with a trembling finger.

To her delight, the device powered on without showing the hologram. Instead, the word "Welcome" was displayed on the screen, followed by a menu with nine icons. The first said "Enter Destination," and had a picture of a planetoid realm with "ABC" printed in the middle.

Vanilla tapped it, and then a floating blue, translucent keyboard was displayed above the screen. Her fingers hovered over it for a few seconds, hesitating. "Uh…what was the realm called again?"

Reaching into her pockets, she withdrew the handwritten letter from her future daughter and skimmed it over. Eventually, her eyes fell on the name of the slimy purple planetoid. "'Glunke…?' OK, with an 'E' at the end like that?" Stowing the letter again, she quickly typed it in and hit the Send button. Before she knew what had happened, she was standing outside in the darkness of another realm. The air was chilly and silent like a winter in the countryside. The purple ground beneath her was soft and mushy like putty, and sunk as she stood on it.

"Wow, it's so cold! I'm lucky I have this sweater," she said, folding her arms and hunching over. *I wonder where that house is. I'd better find it quick. I hope it's unlocked…*

No sooner had she turned around and taken a step forward that her face hit something hard. "Ouch!" she said as she fell onto her rear and dropped the box. The instruction manual slid out and plopped into the purple slime. Panicking, she grabbed it and the box. There was goo all over both items, but luckily the watch itself was still safe in her grasp.

Oh, great! My pants are all gooey! Ew! What is this stuff anyway? Well, I know I'm in the right place...

As she lifted her gaze from the strange substance, she realized what she had run into: it was the cabin. It stood in the middle of the eerie purple landscape like a lone signpost in a desert. Aside from what she assumed was a dead tree off in the distance, there was nothing else in sight.

"Wow, I guess I'll be safe from the paparazzi here," she stated. *I wonder if I'm the only one in this entire realm? I suppose I'll have to go into City Realm 1 or 3 for groceries...not to mention a social life. Crap! I almost forgot. I don't have any money. I shouldn't have agreed to let Zero manage our income... Shoot! I'll have to figure something out...*

Slowly, she got up and wiped off as much slime from her pants as she could. Fortunately, it was less sticky than she thought, but it had still soaked in and was making her even colder.

Vanilla tried the door and—to her relief—found that it was open. As she pushed it ajar and stepped inside, she realized that it was the same temperature in the cabin as outside. Feeling slightly irritated, she set the teleportation watch's packaging on a nearby table and set off in search of dry clothes.

The house was so quiet that it felt a little unnerving. Vanilla half-expected to hear the scurrying of a mouse or the sound of wind blowing against the windows, but there was none. Everything was lifeless and still, like something in a nightmare, but somehow it didn't seem all that threatening. Still, it was a little bit unsettling.

The cabin was obviously very old. The wooden walls were gray and warped with age. The carpet—where there was any—was tattered and faded. All of the furniture was antique and covered in a thick layer of dust, making it look like the morning after a snowstorm. There was a grandfather clock in the main hallway, but it, like the rest of the house, lay frozen in time.

In the bedroom, she found an old dresser. Its finish was cracking and chipped, and it was missing a few of its knobs. She knelt down beside it, shivering as her wet pants pressed against her bottom, and opened the top drawer.

Inside were rows of folded purple and gray shirts. The Crescent Horned Punisher pulled one of them out to take a look at it. "Hm. That's modest," she said out loud to herself, a bit disappointed. *Come to think of it, the Raech of the future was much skinner than me. This looks like it's my size. They look brand new, too. I wonder if she got these for me.*

She clumsily pulled off her shirt and tried the new one on. It fit perfectly, not an inch too tight or too loose. *Well, I suppose I could go back to my old apartment sometime and get the rest of my stuff later. Though the thought of going back there makes me feel anxious. It's a life I'm trying to leave behind.*

Next, she slid the shirt drawer shut and opened the one below it. It contained an assortment of long pants. *For someone who's supposed to be from my future, she sure doesn't know how I like to dress,* she mused, picking out a pair of plain gray pants and setting them on top of the dresser.

The last drawer had undergarments. *Tch. Granny panties. I should have guessed.* "Well, it'll do for now," Vanilla said, selecting the least modest undergarments from the drawer and turning them over in her hand.

After she had dressed, she went into the kitchen to find food. It had been hours since she had eaten last and she was feeling dizzy with hunger. The sparseness of the kitchen worried her, but as she opened the cupboards, her doubt was quickly shattered. They were full of various kinds of food. "Oh, thank you Raech!" she said out loud, grabbing the first sugary thing she saw.

"Well, this *looks* like a strawberry-filled doughnut. As long as it's not cherry!" she said, sitting down at the table to unwrap the treat. The lettering on the package was foreign, but a clear plastic window on the front showed red jelly oozing out of a frosting-coated pastry. Sure enough, she tasted strawberry when she took her first bit. *It doesn't matter what realm it's from; it's good as long as it's sugar,* she thought, wiping her mouth with the back of her hand. *I suppose I should have something more substantial though.*

When she had finished off the treat, she got up and reluctantly rummaged through the cupboards for something both healthy and tasty. "I wish I could just eat doughnuts and not get fat," she said to herself, eyeing a can of beans with distaste. "I wonder if there's like a pill or something that could just negate the bad effects of sugar. There's a multimillion-Crest idea. Oh, well."

Eventually she found a box of cereal that looked fairly healthy and poured some into a bowl. "I don't know how those health nuts do it. They're missing out on all the good stuff."

Off in the distance, there was a low rumble. She stopped and listened. *Is that thunder? I guess it would make sense. It's pretty cloudy outside.*

Suddenly there were loud bangs on the roof of the house. Panicking, the Crescent Horned Punisher ran for cover, leaving her cereal on the table. *What's going on? Am I under attack?* she thought, frantically stuffing herself in a closet and throwing a large coat over herself.

The strange sound continued, never slowing or speeding up. *Maybe it's hail. I didn't think it was cold enough for that though. It sounds too loud to be rain, unless there are just really big drops. I guess I would know by now if something was attacking the house.*

Cautiously, she slid the closet door open and peered out. From what she could see of the house, everything was fine. She could just barely see one of the windows from where she stood. It looked as though rain was falling, but something was different. Instead of tiny clear droplets, blobs of purple were coming down.

Wait, that looks like the stuff on the ground, she thought, stepping out of the closet and going over to the window. "It is! Ew!" she shrieked. "I'm glad I wasn't outside when it started."

She stood watching the slimy rain fall for a few minutes. It was mesmerizing and somehow a little soothing, like staring into a bonfire. Each drop created a small pit on the soft ground, only to be replaced by another one moments later.

"It's kind of like life... We have our fleeting time here, but we all die someday, and then someone else comes along. Jeez, I sounded like a philosopher there for a second! Maybe I *am* drunk," she said to herself with a sarcastic smile.

Then she had a thought. *Wait, I wonder if that trapdoor is still open. I don't want anybody or anything coming into the house from down there. I should put something heavy over it just in case.*

A quick walk across the house brought her back to the kitchen. She pulled back the purple rug and tapped around with her foot, expecting to find the secret entrance. Surprisingly, each board sounded the same as the next. *Maybe the rug got moved,* she thought, getting down on her hands and knees and trying to pry up random planks. Still, nothing seemed out of the ordinary.

Could it have been filled in? No, that can't be. I'm sure it was right around here... Finally, she gave up and slid the rug back where it was. *I guess I'll probably stumble across it while I'm walking around sometime. I really wish I could find it though.*

Just as she was about to leave the room, something caught her eye. A small slip of paper was sticking out from under the refrigerator. Curious, she walked over to it and bent down to pick it up.

Much to her disappointment, it tore slightly as she tried to retrieve it. The paper itself was very old and yellowed. There were wrinkles and creases all over it, and it was covered in a thin layer of dust. It looked like something important was written on it, but it was in a language that she had never seen before. Each character was square-like and connected to each other, like some sort of Stone Age cursive.

Huh. I wonder what this says. Maybe I should save it. She was about to tuck it in her shirt, but remembered that she wasn't wearing a tank top. *Dang it! Stupid old lady clothes… Well, I guess it's not as bad as a turtleneck or something.*

A wave of dizziness hit her as she stood up, reminding her that she had yet to eat something substantial. The bowl of dry cereal was still on the table behind her, but a quick glance in the fridge revealed that there was only rice milk. Vanilla stared at it hesitantly, debating on whether she should find something else to eat. A rumbling from her stomach decided for her. Reluctantly, she opened the container and poured some on her cereal.

Why rice milk? Will Raech be lactose intolerant? Rice milk is a sorry excuse for milk! It's pretty much grody flavored water. Oh, well… I'll have to pick up some real stuff when I have the chance.

When she had finished, the Crescent Horned Punisher got up and walked into the living room, leaving the empty bowl on the table. She was still feeling a bit off balance, so she decided to sit down next to one of the old dressers and rummage through it.

In the first drawer she pulled, there were stacks of blank paper and pencils. The paper was either new or had rarely been disturbed. The topmost sheet was covered in a film of fine dust. At first it felt soft to the touch, like velvet. Vanilla drew lines in the powdery substance with her index finger, but soon realized that there wasn't enough light to see her picture.

The sky outside was much darker than when she had first arrived. Quickly checking her cell phone, she saw that it was only 8pm. *That's weird. This place must be a few hours behind the City Realms. I am kind of tired. Maybe tomorrow I can use some of this paper to write sheet music. Oh dang, I don't have my bass...* "Well, I can still write songs," she sighed. "This is going to take some getting used to."

CHAPTER 3

-Prophecy-

The morning was cold and quiet. There was no sound of busy streets, no low rumble of underground traffic, and not a single bird chirping or even an insect tapping desperately against a window. As Vanilla slowly opened her eyes, she was expecting to see the smoke-tainted walls of her apartment and smell the odor of unwashed laundry piles on her floor. It took her a few seconds to realize where she was.

Oh, that's right, she thought. *I moved. It's been a few days, but I'm still waking up thinking that I'm at my apartment. This is so weird. At least it's quiet here.* With all the speed and dexterity of a lethargic sloth, she propped herself up on one elbow and brushed her long white hair away from her face. *I need food, but I don't want to get up yet. It's too early...* Then another thought came to her that woke her up instantly. *Today's the day I'm going to meet Zallin! Oh my gosh! I have to get ready!*

Filled with newfound energy, the Crescent Horned Punisher sprung out of bed and ran into the kitchen to find breakfast. As she rounded the corner, she stubbed her big toe on the doorframe and keeled over, grasping her now throbbing foot. "Damn it! That hurts like a... *Ugh!*"

When the worst of the pain had passed, she gingerly stood up and limped to the refrigerator. *I'm so glad I was able to get real groceries yesterday. Still...I feel like a bit of a jerk for taking all those coins from that fountain in 3rd City Realm. It was for a good cause, though. I had to get money somehow.*

As she retrieved the carton of skim milk from the fridge, she couldn't help but wonder what the day had in store for her. *I wonder what kind of man Zallin is. I mean, I know he's a Madite. That or he was just wearing a weird hat and blinking when that picture was taken. Although, Raech had a hat, too. As long as he isn't into hip hop or country music, I'll be fine. I don't understand how anyone can tolerate that load of crap. It doesn't take any talent at all to talk into a pitch-corrected and quantized microphone. Hm...maybe he's a musician, too. I can't wait!*

After wolfing down a bowl of cereal, she brushed her teeth and got in the shower. The water was chilly when she turned it on and took several minutes to heat up. *Come to think of it, how does this house get water and electricity? There's no water tower around from what I've seen and anytime it rains, it's always that purple slime. There has to be something taking it from somewhere,* she mused, clumsily undoing the back strap of her black brassiere and throwing it vaguely toward a basket filled with clothes.

Once she had undressed, Vanilla stepped into the old tiled shower, hoping that it was warm enough. "Oh! That burns! Ow!" As she turned the knob back down, she glanced at her left thigh. It had a tattoo of a generic red heart with an arrow through it. The name "Xypher" was written diagonally across it in fancy black letters. *I never thought I'd regret getting this. I hope Zallin isn't the kind of person who would get mad at me for having this. I suppose I could get it removed someday... Besides, I'm not with that blue-haired idiot anymore.*

The bathroom felt icy cold as Vanilla stepped out of the shower and reached for a towel. To her dismay, she had forgotten to hang one up. A quick search through the closet reminded her that she had yet to take the laundry out of the dryer. Chilled and disgruntled, she reached for the hand towel by the sink to cover herself. *I suppose I don't have to do this since nobody lives here except me. Darn, why didn't I think of getting a towel before I got in? I guess it's still kind of early for me. I hope Zallin doesn't wake me up early every morning.*

Out in the hallway, she hastily made her way to the laundry room, casting a careful glance at the windows before she passed them to make sure no one was looking in. Her bare feet felt good against the soft carpeting. *This isn't so bad,* she mused, a lewd smile creeping across her face. The Crescent Horned Punisher's imagination was starting to get the better of her, but she forced herself to think about other things. *I can't let myself fall back into my old ways,* she thought, shifting the hand towel higher over her chest.

In the laundry room, she bent down and pulled the dryer door open. "At least I was able to by some tasteful clothing with the remainder of my grocery money," she mumbled to herself, pulling out a black tank top and a pair of acid washed jeans. "I sure hope Zallin has money. I can't just live on coins from a fountain."

When she had dressed and hung a dry towel in the bathroom, Vanilla set about picking up the house the best she could. In the few days she had lived there, it had become very messy. Dirty clothes lay strewn all over the bedroom, bowls of half-eaten cereal were stacked by the sink and on the kitchen table, papers with ideas for lyrics were piled on the cabinet in the living room, the bathroom mirror was covered in watermarks, and a splotch of mint toothpaste was dried on the edge of the sink.

Ugh. I hate having to clean. Maybe I can get Zallin to do this. "Listen to me! I'm already acting like we're married and I haven't even seen him in person! I wonder where we'll meet. I wish Raech would have told me in her letter. I guess I could walk around outside. If it's really destiny, then I'm sure I'll see him."

Suddenly, there was a bright flash in the sky. It was so strong that it left Vanilla dazed for a moment. Struggling to compose herself, she stumbled outside as quickly as her trembling legs could carry her. From the little that she could see through her slowly recovering vision, something was falling through the clouds in a burning ball of orange flames. "What is that!?" the Crescent Horned Punisher exclaimed in panic.

Moments later, there was a loud, sickening splat. A horrendous image of a corpse hitting the ground went through her mind, but then she remembered that the ground itself was covered in goo. *Anything that falls on this slime would make a noise like that. It's alright, Vanilla. Calm yourself. Maybe it was... Oh, I don't know!* she thought to herself and ran in the direction of the sound.

As she neared the site where the object had landed, she felt a wave of energy pulsing through the air. "What is this? Is it magic? Maybe it's a piece of top-secret military equipment!"

A few steps forward gave her the answer. A man was stuck in one of the sinking pits of goo. It was apparent that he was trying to use magic to escape, but was unable to. The slime was absorbing the colorful bursts of energy like a sponge.

Is that *Zallin? It must be! This is destiny, after all,* she thought rather skeptically. *I've got to help him! But what can I use to pull him out? If I get stuck too, it'll all be over!* Whether by fate or luck, she noticed a blackened tree branch a few feet from the pit. It was rotting and covered in goo, but it was her only option.

Wrenching the stick from the ground's gooey grasp, she swung it over the pit and anchored herself as best she could. "Zallin, grab onto this! I'll try to pull you out!"

Surprised, the man looked up. He was not a Mandian, but looked very much like one except for his strange, cone-shaped hat. It was pure blue and had yellow eyes on it that moved. It also had a mouth with jagged teeth made out of the same blue material.

The eyes on the man's face remained closed, although he was

obviously able to see. From his appearance, Vanilla knew right away that he was a Madite. "How do you know my name?" he asked hesitantly.

"Just grab the damn thing! I'll tell you when you're out."

"Alright."

Zallin wrapped his hands tightly around the branch and braced himself as she began to pull. She strained her whole body, desperately trying to free him. Though he was skinny and lightweight, the slime was relentless in his grip. The stick felt as if it was about to break. She could sense the rotted fibers giving way, but refused to give up. Just when she thought she could tug no more, there was movement. With one last heave, he was free. The two of them toppled over, the Madite falling awkwardly on top of her.

"Oh, I-I'm so sorry, ma'am! I assure you, that wasn't intentional," he said, jumping to his feet and extending his hand to help her up. He was red in the face with embarrassment—and Vanilla with exhaustion.

"That's OK. I don't mind."

"Well, thank you for saving me. That slime must nullify levitation magic somehow... More importantly, how did you know who I was?"

"It's kind of a long story. Where do I even start? There was this prophecy and—no wait. Let me back up. Uh... Can we just go to the house? I need to sit down on something besides this gunk."

"Is that your house over there?"

"Yeah... I guess it is."

"Uh, 'you guess?'"

"It is. I promise! It was given to me."

"I see. Just who are you?"

"My name's Vanilla. Vanilla Lamberschvak. I'm supposed to marry you." Vanilla cringed as she heard the words leave her mouth. *Shit! What am I saying? He probably thinks I'm crazy now!* she thought, sick to her stomach with anxiety.

"Uh, w-what?"

"Th-the prophecy. I mean, there was a prophecy. This woman gave it to me in a letter. That's how I knew your name. I have it inside. I'm sorry. I'm just so amazed right now that it's hard to talk."

Zallin eyed her suspiciously. "I see," he said carefully. "Do you know for sure if it was really a prophecy? And who is this woman you speak of?"

"I know this will sound ridiculous, but she's my future daughter—or was. She...she passed away after she wrote the letter."

"Hm. And you believe her words?"

"Please, just come inside with me. You can see the letter for yourself."

He glanced behind him, as if looking for an excuse to leave. "Alright. But please, let's make this quick. I was in the middle of something."

"Yeah, a pit of goo."

"That's not what I...never mind. Lead the way."

He cautiously followed the white-haired maiden back to the house, his eyes darting to and fro, as if expecting there to be a trap. Vanilla could sense his tension. She too felt tense, but for a different reason. *I have to figure out a way to make him believe me,* she thought. *Why does he have to be so skeptical?*

Once inside, she hastily dug through a dresser in the living room to find the letter Raech had given her. Zallin stood by the doorway with his arms crossed, doing his best to be patient. Just as he opened his mouth to speak, she found the letter.

"Here it is!" she exclaimed, holding it up triumphantly. He stepped closer and glanced over it. Much to the Crescent Horned

Punisher's dismay, his expression was unchanged as he finished reading.

"Well?" she asked nervously.

"I'm sorry, but I'm still having a hard time believing this."

"Why? You're Zallin, aren't you?"

"Yes."

"And this is my eighteenth birthday. It *has* to be real!"

"Happy birthday. Unfortunately, I'm in no position to be blindly stepping into marriage with someone I just met. This woman who gave you the letter has no credibility as it stands. Anyone could make something like this up with enough psychic power. She probably read your mind to get your name and maybe she knew that I would be in this realm today."

"Zallin!"

"I'm sorry, Vanilla. Perhaps if I had been able to meet this woman, I would be a bit more willing to believe this whole ordeal. Please try and understand it from my perspective."

"I... Wait! There's a picture too! I almost forgot! Here, take a look at *this*."

"Hm."

"See?"

"I'm very sorry, but this could have been easily made with any photo manipulation software."

"It *isn't*!"

"How do you know?"

"I-I have a feeling!"

"Feelings are meant to enrich our life, not guide it. I do apologize, but I must be going now."

"But... Um, can I at least get you some food? I'm sure you're hungry from whatever you were doing before."

"No, I really must go now. Thank you for your hospitality, though."

"How about something to drink then? I have coffee, water, juice, milk, tea, and beer."

Zallin hesitated. His right hand was already on the doorknob. Vanilla crossed her fingers behind her back and prayed. Slowly, he relinquished his grip. "Er, I suppose tea would be fine, thank you."

"OK. How do you like it? Your tea, I mean."

Zallin frowned. "Um, plain? I didn't know there are multiple ways of having tea."

"Oh, yeah. I guess not. I'll be right back!"

The Crescent Horned Punisher bustled off to the kitchen, blushing from embarrassment. *Why do I keep saying awkward things? This isn't like me. I can't believe I asked him "how he likes it." Now he probably thinks I'm a prostitute or something!*

The electric burner flicked on and she set the pot over it. The coils on the old stove hissed and hummed as they heated up, radiating a faint orange glow. Tapping her foot nervously, the Crescent Horned Punisher glanced back at the living room.

The Madite was slowly pacing with his arms still crossed. He seemed to be inspecting the house's ancient wooden interior, or at least pretending to do so. The Crescent Horned Punisher crossed her fingers and hoped that he wasn't going to lose his patience. He was obviously not enjoying the wait. Every second felt like an hour, chock-full with anxiety. She drummed her fingers against the counter, trying her hardest to calm down. *If this doesn't work, I'll have failed. All of this will have been for nothing,* she thought. The knots in her stomach were almost too much to bear.

Finally, the water came to a boil. She turned the burner off and poured the hot water into cups. Fumbling a bit with the bags of tea leaves, she somehow managed to drop them into the water. The tremor in her hands was making it hard to hold onto anything and she feared she would spill the tea and have to start over—if Zallin gave her the chance.

Without realizing it at first, she began to sing. Her voice was shaky at first, but gradually grew steadier and more confident.

"Bleeding Heart, why are you sad?
Hold to the courage you always had.

Bear with your pain,
In the midnight rain,

Hold my hand and let's be glad.
Through weary smiles,

And daybreak's sorrow.
You and I will see tomorrow.

O Bleeding Heart, you will heal.
For only I know how you feel."

"Miss Vanilla, that's quite an interesting song that you just sung… Where's it from? You have a beautiful voice, by the way."

His voice made her jump. He was standing at the doorway to the kitchen. All signs of impatience were gone from his body. She had not expected him to listen to her sing, much less have an interest in her song.

"It's from a song someone wrote for me when I was with my band," she said. Then tears filled her eyes as she remembered Zero and the others. Head hung in shame, Vanilla quietly lifted the bags of tea leaves from the water and weakly tossed them into a nearby garbage can.

Taken aback by the young woman's sudden mood swing, the Madite glanced briefly at his feet and said, "Oh, I'm sorry. Did I upset you? I didn't mean to."

"No, it wasn't you. I just…well, never mind. I don't want to make you depressed, so I'll keep my mouth shut."

"Miss Vanilla, I can't just take a woman's hospitality and food without taking her emotions into consideration. You're obviously depressed and I wouldn't feel right just leaving you like this, lest you harm yourself. If it's something that I can help with in a morally appropriate way, I will."

"Let's just sit down and have our tea. I…I'll try to explain." Vanilla handed a cup of warm tea to him and sat down across from him at the kitchen table. The steam from the hot beverage she held felt cleansing to her teary eyes. She took a deep, slow breath.

He waited patiently.

Fidgeting with the ratty tablecloth, she opened her mouth, but no words came out. Swallowing hard, she tried again. "I…" Her heart felt as though it were about to burst from her chest.

Zallin shifted noiselessly in his seat. Though her eyes were on her cup of tea, she sensed it. Closing her eyes tightly, she said one last, desperate prayer in her mind and tried once more.

"…Wh-when I was a little girl, I lived in a place called, um, the Underworld—the one in Keduel. M-my f…parents were…" she paused for a moment and drew a sharp breath. Her voice died down to less than a whisper as she struggled to finish her sentence, "…terrible. They hated me…and I hate them because of what they did to me.

"One day my sister and me found a way out and we escaped to

the surface. Somehow we managed to tag along with some scientists who were about to transport back to 3rd City Realm. We left them and wandered together for a while. I grew sick of my sister whining and crying, so I abandoned her in a park while she was sleeping. I feel terrible about it though…

"Eventually I met a boy named Xypher a day or two later outside a music store. He insisted that I called him 'Zero.' Anyway, Zero was thirteen then and I was ten. He was staying with some musicians that were in a heavy metal band called *Death by Love* and he asked them if I could stay with them for a while. Seeing as I didn't have any food or shelter, they agreed.

"Zero and I started learning music together since we were always around instruments and had nothing better to do. He loved playing the guitar so much that he would even skip meals sometimes so that he could practice. Sometimes his fingers would get so worn out from playing that they would bleed, so he had to spend a day or two resting."

Zallin's eyes were still fixed intently on hers. He sat completely still with his hands around the cup of tea.

Her body wasn't shaking as much as before. She took a deep breath and continued. "As for me, I learned to sing by listening to *Death by Love*'s albums and whatever other music they had at the house. The band leader, Monty Scythen, also helped me by giving me short lessons here and there. 'Scythe,' as he liked to be called, taught me some simple bass lines, too, but I was more interested singing than playing the bass. The other band members taught Zero and me how to read and write since neither of us ever had any schooling. They were always very busy though, so we were on our own a lot. I guess that wasn't always a good thing…

"Years later, we decided to make our own band under the name, *To the Power of 10*. We had no clue how to find members for our band, so we just wandered around the city until we came across willing and able musicians."

She paused briefly to swallow. Her mouth was getting dry from talking. Zallin nodded and shifted in his chair, but didn't take his yellow eyes off her face.

After taking a quick sip of tea, she went on. "Eventually Zero picked up a girl who could play keyboard, so she became our keyboardist. Her name was Lisa Connerway. She's mute because of an accident that happened a few months before we met her.

"I met a short drummer with a red ponytail whose name was Wake Harshfur. He and Zero would always fight over everything.

"I'm sure you've heard of our band if you've spent a lot of time in the City Realms. That's where we were the most popular. Zero was even featured in Meltdown Music's monthly magazine a few times.

"But…he dumped me some time ago. He just left me at a hotel in the middle of nowhere. I don't know if I'm more angry at him or sad that he's gone. He's most likely found another singer by now and she's probably way better than me—prettier too. I guess that's my story. I'm surprised that you're still listening. Are you still awake?"

Zallin nodded and leaned forward in his chair. He gently clasped her hands in his and looked into her eyes. She blushed and held her breath, hoping with all of her heart—which was now racing faster than ever—that he had decided to stay.

"I understand. There is one more thing that I'd like to know, though. Do you truly believe that the story about your future daughter is true?"

"Yes, it has to be. I mean, who else could have predicted our meeting like this?"

"Hm. I…I'm sorry. I still find it hard to believe that a prophecy would be used to predict the relationship of a heavy metal singer and a healer from an independent military organization."

"You're not going to leave, are you?"

"To be honest, I'm still contemplating it. Please let me have some time to think this through. This isn't something that I can just decide on the drop of a hat."

"Zallin!"

Vanilla stood up abruptly and desperately flung her arms around the strange man. He took a step back and hit his head on a shelf above him. With a grunt, he fell to the floor and blacked out.

The next morning, Zallin awoke to the feeling of someone's arms around him. He panicked and sat up quickly. "Who are you?" he shouted out of reflex. Then he realized that the Crescent Horned Punisher was lying in bed next to him and that his clothes were draped over an armchair just out of reach. "Oh no... This is bad," he said, shaking his head to try and clear his mind. Gingerly, he pulled the sheets over his body and got up to retrieve his clothes.

"Oh, good morning..." Vanilla said, rolling over and yawning.

He glanced at her, but quickly turned away, realizing she was naked, as well. Face burning red with embarrassment, the modest Madite bit his lip for a few seconds and then spoke in a quivering voice, "I don't know what just happened and I don't want to, but could you please put some clothes on?"

She rolled her eyes. "I think you *know* what happened and I'm thinking we should get married...just in case."

The Madite's face turned pale and his hands trembled. He began sweating profusely as he searched desperately for an excuse. After a tense pause, he spoke slowly and carefully.

"I take that as blackmail, Vanilla. I am a man of morals and virtues, but now I've lost my virginity to a woman I barely know. I...I can't believe this."

"That was your first time? Well, you were unconscious for the whole thing, if that helps. Please though, we need to get married."

"...Alright," Zallin replied after a long pause, realizing that he could not worm his way out of the situation.

She threw her arms up and exclaimed, "Yes! Finally!"

CHAPTER 4

-Fire and Ice Part I-

Vanilla looked up at her 14-year-old daughter and said, "And that's my story. About a year after that, the 'Rebirth of Raech' happened. I think you can probably remember the rest."

Raech blushed and instinctively brushed through her long black hair. "Thank you for sharing more about where you've come from. I'm thankful that you were able to pull through so many hardships."

"Oh, well I'm glad I didn't make you bored."

"Of course not! Your life story sounded very exciting. It would make a great book!"

"Oh I don't know about that. It would probably make a boring book to most people. Well, it is what it is I guess. Anyway, here I am at thirty-two years old with a wonderful fourteen-year-old daughter and a husband that's supposed to be getting me a cake. Raech, will you call your father and see what's holding him up?"

"Yes, Mother."

She touched her conical purple hat as if to adjust it, and then began to dial a number on her cell phone. Vanilla gazed out the living room's wide window as she did so. The familiar view showed gentle valleys of purple slime, gray skies, and little else as it had been for more than 14 years.

The quaint room that had been barren nearly a decade and a half before was now fully furnished with two couches and a brand new blue armchair situated around a low coffee table, an antique cabinet set at an angle in the corner, a secondhand stereo system, and family photos hung on the wall by the front door. There was also a potted plant next to the adjacent closet. Beneath the windows there was a table upon which

73

various odds and ends had been set in hopes of someday finding their rightful place in the old house.

A few moments of silence passed before the teenage Madite set the phone on a nearby table with a quiet thump. "I think he must be on his way because he didn't answer."

Ironically, the front door opened right after she had spoken and Zallin walked in. He was carrying a fancy cake box with the words, "Happy Birthday" on it. With dramatic movements and a bow, he handed the cake to his wife. She laughed cheerfully and gave him a hug. "Aw, thank you!"

Zallin sat down at the dining room table and said, "Well, we usually don't have cake for lunch, but since it's your birthday we can make an exception." Sensing his attempt at humor, Vanilla rolled her eyes and opened the box of cake.

Each slice was frosted with sparkly white icing that would have given a health nut nightmares and a sugar addict wet dreams. Large slices of brilliant red strawberries were arranged in the shape of a smile on the top of the dessert. Using the plastic fork and knife from inside the box, Vanilla scooped generous pieces onto plates and handed them to her family.

"It's too bad your parents couldn't make it, Zallin. All these years and I've never met them. Have you talked to them at all recently?"

Zallin's mouth twitched, but he forced himself to continue smiling. "No. So, what should we all do today? I hear that the 150th Annual Glass Chime Festival starts in 1st City Realm today."

"Oh that sounds fun! I'm sure Raech would enjoy it," Vanilla replied, oblivious to her husband's avoidance. Raech noticed, however, but kept quiet.

The family sat down at the round dinner table and ate in an eerie silence. Vanilla felt a sense of foreboding looming in the atmosphere. *Something's not right. Maybe it's just the weather,* she told herself.

"So, how is your day going so far?" Zallin asked, scooting his chair closer to the table.

"It's been good. I just finished telling Raech my story. Fortunately it didn't put her to sleep or anything."

"Oh Mother, sleep would have never crossed my mind! It was very interesting and exciting. I'm glad that you were willing to share it with me," Raech interjected.

Vanilla smiled. "Well, I figure it's good for a child to hear their parents' life stories at least once, right Zallin?"

"Oh, of course," Zallin said quietly, his eyes quickly darting to his half-eaten sliver of cake.

"Come to think of it, we've been married for fifteen years and you still haven't told me that much about your childhood. I don't even know what realm you grew up in."

Zallin told a bite of cake and started coughing. He hastily held a napkin up to his mouth and stood up.

"Are you alright?" Vanilla asked worriedly.

The Madite nodded and cleared his throat. "Yes, I just swallowed wrong. I think I'll go get a glass of water."

"I can get it for you."

"No, that's alright. It's your birthday. Enjoy the cake."

"OK. Let me know if there's anything I can do, though."

Zallin simply nodded again and hustled off to the kitchen. Raech eyed him curiously as he went, but said nothing. Vanilla set her fork on the edge of her plate and leaned back in her chair.

"I don't know if I can eat any more of this right now. It's so rich…"

"Mother?"

"Yes, Sweetie?"

"Um…well, never mind."

"Hm?"

"No, it's nothing."

"Alright."

"Oh, what would you like to do today?"

"You know, I heard that there's a music festival going on in 1st City Realm this week. I'd kind of like to check it out."

"That sounds like fun! What kind of music?"

"All kinds, I think. It's being held at a park in West City. I'll just need to put on some dark glasses and a scarf or something."

"Why?"

"The paparazzi. Yesterday someone was taking pictures of me while I was at the grocery store. Surprisingly I haven't had to deal with it much for the past ten years or so. Maybe my old band has become a lot more popular recently."

"I thought they were already really popular."

"Yeah, around the City Realms, but not much more than that. Or at least that's how it was when I was with them last. Even then, I didn't have to deal with the paparazzi *that* much. Once in a while I'd have people come to my apartment, but I usually just ignored them or…well, never mind."

"Ah. Do you still talk to your former band members?"

"No. I…we had a falling out, as I said during my story."

"I see."

"Maybe we can just go for a walk as a family or something instead…I kind of don't want to be reminded of *him*."

"You mean your ex-boyfriend?"

"Yeah."

"Where shall we walk, then?"

"Hm. That's a good question. There are a lot of good trails in Rembren, but a while back I heard that there was a big monster outbreak in some parts of the realm."

"What about Dreamic?"

"I've never heard of that. Is it a realm?"

"Yes. It's one of the ten safest realms in our dimension. I'm surprised you've never heard of it before."

"Well, there's like three billion realms or something in Spiritia."

"I know, but Dreamic is quite famous. I read that it exports the largest amount of produce of any realm."

"Where did you read that?"

"It was in an agricultural science book I rented from the library a month ago."

"Then maybe that's where we should go. Hang on. I need to see where your father is. Zallin, where are you?"

"I'm upstairs!" the reclusive Madite's voice called back faintly.

"We're going on a walk. Do you want to come?"

"Hold on, I can't hear what you're saying."

Vanilla sighed. "I said we're going on a walk! Do you want to come with?"

There was a pause. Just as she was about to shout again, her husband appeared in the doorway leading to the stairs. He was wearing a light jacket and jeans.

"Where are we going?"

"On a walk. I've been trying to tell you that."

"Oh, I said 'sure.' You must not have heard me."

"I guess not."

"So, where to then?"

"Dreamic, right Raech?"

"Yes."

"Dreamic? Are any more non-residents being allowed in there right now?" Zallin asked, looking quite surprised.

"I don't know," Raech replied.

"I guess we'll find out when we try teleporting there," Vanilla said with a shrug.

"I suppose so. Raech, did you check what season it is there? I wouldn't want to get there and be freezing or anything."

"No, I just thought of it, so I haven't had time to check."

"Vanilla, do you have your phone handy?" Zallin said.

"Yeah, I'm on it… OK, so it looks like it's January and the temperature is…minus forty degrees!? Oh wait, that's for one of the mountains. Hm, this place actually looks really neat. Alright, here we go. Oak Village has the highest temperature right now at seventeen degrees."

"We'd all better bring something warm to wear then. I'll go get our coats," Zallin said.

"Oh, Hon?"

"Yeah?"

"Can you grab my black one? The other day I accidentally poked a hole in the purple and white one when I was checking the pockets for one of my rings."

"Sure."

"Thanks."

As Zallin hurried off to collect warmer clothes, Vanilla went to the front room to put her shoes on, followed by Raech.

"Mother?"

"Yes Sweetie?"

"I love you and I'm glad that you've held on all these years."

"Aw, thanks. I'm glad too. I love you more than you could know."

"Thanks Mom." Raech smiled and gave her a hug.

Moments later Zallin reappeared with two winter coats in his hands. He was wearing a dark blue parka with yellow trim and silver buttons. Extending his arms, he handed one to Vanilla and the other—a purple one—to Raech.

"Thanks Hon. You know it's not like it's not below zero. If we're going to be walking, I wonder if a thick sweater would be better," Vanilla said as she clumsily wrestled her coat past her horns and pulled it down over her tank top.

"Oh, well I can always unzip it if I get too warm."

"I suppose."

"Alright, are we ready?"

"I think so."

Together, the family stepped outside and, after Zallin had locked the front door, he teleported away with them using a spell.

The instant they arrived on Dreamic, they were met with a world of sparkling white and breathtaking snowcapped mountains in the distance. The air was crisp and clean, the sky was overcast, and the branches on the deciduous trees were crystalized in a thin layer of ice. For a moment Vanilla forgot that they were in the middle of a village. It was only when she heard the sound of some passersby's feet crunching through the powdered ivory ground that she remembered. Somewhere deep inside, she felt like she had come home. Though she had never been to Dreamic before, it now seemed like the only place she truly belonged. "It's beautiful…" she whispered to herself in awe.

"So, where would you like to walk?" Zallin asked, stepping closer to her.

Vanilla blinked. "Wait, what? Oh, yeah. Uh…anywhere! This place is just so gorgeous."

"Fair enough. Why don't we just go through the town? Perhaps we can ask someone if there are any trails nearby…Vanilla?"

"Yeah, sorry! I'm still taking in the scenery. It's so different than the City Realms or Glunke. There are just so many plants. I mean, I know it's winter, but still."

"Well, during the warmer months this *is* the greenest inhabited realm in Spiritia—inhabited by people, that is."

"I'll bet. So this is Oak Village then?"

"Yes."

"I'd love to live here. Everyone looks so happy."

"You'd probably have to work."

"Why? Is it that expensive?"

"It's not just the expense. There's a law here that requires the residents to farm with a percentage of their land."

"That's dumb. What about old people or little kids?"

"I'm sure there's an exception for them."

"Why farming though?"

"I think it's because they want Dreamic to continue exporting large amounts of produce. It's good for the local economy. Also, I heard that there are some crops that can only be grown here," Raech cut in.

"I'd think that'd be hard on the land though. All those crops would deplete the nutrients in the soil. Then again, I'm sure farmers have found a way to work around that. Crop rotation, was it? I really haven't been around any farms or read about the process, so I can't say I fully understand all the details," Zallin said.

Vanilla sighed. "I'd be fine with some gardening if it meant we could live here."

"It would be a bit more than a little gardening, Vanilla."

"You're making it sound impossible…"

"Hm. That wasn't my intention."

The family continued to stroll through the small village, taking their time to enjoy the scenery. Like a child at a theme park, the Crescent Horned Punisher gazed dreamily at everything from the log cabin-like buildings to the mirror-like icy ponds. Her husband watched her worriedly through the corner of his eyes.

"Say, Vanilla, is everything alright?"

"Hm? Oh, yeah! Everything is awesome! Why do you ask?"

"No reason. I was just curious."

"Why?"

"Oh, nothing."

"Zallin, there has to be a reason. Are you worried about me?"

"Well…"

"Oh, come on! Can't I be happy without you thinking something's wrong with me? It's not like you haven't seen me happy before."

"I'm sorry. I just wasn't sure if…"

"If what? If I was going crazy?"

"No, not that."

"Then what?"

"Please, let's just enjoy our time here."

"It's going to be hard now that I know you think I'm going crazy or something."

Zallin bit his lip and said nothing. Raech glanced anxiously at him, and then at her mother, who had a scowl on her face. Her eyes were focused on her husband like the crosshairs on a sniper. He was looking at the ground, but could feel his wife's piercing glare.

Miraculously, the tension in the Crescent Horned Punisher's

body faded and she apologized. "I'm sorry. It was childish of me to get all wound up like that. I know you were just being protective of me."

Both Madites were taken aback. The speed of her resolution seemed almost as uncanny as her newfound obsession with Dreamic.

"Th-that's alright. I forgive you," Zallin said with a nod, his eyes quickly scanning the moody Crescent Horned Punisher's face.

"You know, I'd kind of like to go into the forest. I don't know if I've ever actually been in a real forest like that before," Vanilla said after a pause.

"It won't be very green, you know. Aside from any pine trees, that is."

"I know. I'd still like to."

"Hm. It looks like there's some 'No Trespassing' signs and barbwire fencing though. I suppose they don't want anybody causing mischief or harming endangered species. I've heard that there are some wild plants that only grow on Dreamic," Zallin replied, motioning to the wall of dark green pines a short distance away.

"So it's not only crops? I wonder if there are any animals that can only be found here," Raech said, squinting at the trees, hoping to see some exotic creatures half-hidden by the crest of a snowbank.

"Well…we could sneak in, couldn't we? One of you could use magic to teleport us in or something," Vanilla said quietly, glancing around to see if anyone was listening.

"I'd prefer not to do anything against the rules. I've heard that there have been Dreamic residents who were fined 1,000 Crests for cutting down a sapling growing at the edge of their lot. I get the idea that the laws here are pretty strict. I suppose they have to be to keep things as green as they are in the growing seasons," Zallin said.

"That's terrible! I'd fight that in court if I were them! There's no way a judge would let that fly. Well, a good judge, I mean. I've been in front of plenty of bad ones in my day…"

"I'm sure those people tried to fight it in court. That being said, I think we should just stick to the town unless we know for sure that it's OK to go into the forest."

"Oh, OK…"

As they walked through the pleasant little village, Vanilla noticed that there was much diversity. She had already counted five different species of Mandianoids and was still seeing more. Most of them she recognized, such as Madites, Mandians, and a few Grenzel Blind Demons, but there were some she had never seen before. *It's like a melting pot of different species,* she thought, trying not to stare at anyone too long.

Zallin noticed his wife's curiosity and smiled. "Dreamic draws people from all over. There are many potential tourist attractions here, but much like in Rembren, the local government doesn't like all the extra attention so they actually limit the amount of tourists that are allowed in."

Vanilla looked perplexed. "Why? I would think tourism would be good for the economy in a place like this."

Zallin shook his head. "Me, too. I think it has something to do with protecting the environment. The more people who they allow in, the higher the chance of something bad happening is. Since the environment *is* the economy here, it's only natural that keeping it safe is their top priority."

"I guess. But that's kind of a risk you have to take if you want to make money off a location."

"In some cases, yes. Really though, I think the economy is as good as it is here because of the mandatory farming."

"Oh. I really don't like the idea of being forced to farm."

"I don't think most people do, but it's a small price to pay for getting to live in such a beautiful place."

"I don't know if I'd call it 'small'… Say, aren't farms usually smelly? I haven't noticed any bad smells the whole time we've been here. I mean, I know I don't have a strong sense of smell, but…"

"Be careful how you word that. Some people could find that to be very offensive. As far as odors go, that would primarily come from livestock, but I haven't seen any so far. Perhaps the residents of Oak Village concentrate more on growing produce. I'm sure there are places here that raise animals though."

"Hm. People take offense to everything."

"Some people. I personally wouldn't like it if somebody associated my living with foul odors."

"Well, I know, but that's not what I meant by that. I mean—oh I don't know! You know what I meant, right?"

"Yes, I know what you were trying to say. I'm just pointing that out."

"Alright, sorry."

"No need to apologize."

"Dad, look! There's a sign for a hiking trail over there," Raech cut in.

The couple stopped and looked in the direction that their daughter was pointing. Sure enough, atop a small hill several yards away was a little white sign showing a stick figure walking with a backpack. Next to it were two great pine trees forming a sort of gateway. They were dark and lush—a stark contrast to the numerous brown, skeletal deciduous trees. From where they stood, the family could see that the trail ran adjacent to the reservation, but was separated from it by a single barbwire fence. "Good observation, Raech!" Vanilla said, patting the young Madite on the shoulder.

As the family neared the trailhead, Zallin pointed at a second sign that had been obscured by a thick, tangled, leafless bush. "That looks like a warning of some sort," he said, uncovering it and glancing over the text.

"What does it say, Hon?"

"It says not to touch glowing blue lichen if you see any. There's also some information here regarding the laws… Hm. I was right. You can't cut anything down or take anything from the forest. That makes sense. The penalties are pretty severe, too."

"How will they know when someone does something like that? It's not like they have Royal Guardsmen posted on the trail or something, right?"

"I'm not too sure, but I'd rather not find out."

"Well, duh! I'm not going to do anything bad, you know."

"I didn't think you were."

"Hmph. Usually when you say something like that it means that you're worried that I might do something."

"Not necessarily. Anyway, shall we take this trail?"

"Sure."

The moment the family passed the gate of trees, it felt as if they had just walked into a different world. Vanilla had to look back just to be sure they hadn't. The trees on either side of her stood tall and proud like kings despite their lack of leaves. Their branches were like hands reaching to the sky in prayer. Tiny snowflakes had begun to fall, glistening like diamonds in the midday light as they drifted slowly to the ground.

"Whoa," Vanilla said in wonder. "It's like something out of a movie. Even without their leaves, the trees are really beautiful."

"I agree. Hm. This is unusually warm for this time of year," Zallin replied.

"What's the temperature like normally?"

"I can't remember exactly, but I think it's typically about five degrees this late in the fall. The summers can get up to ninety, but they rarely pass eighty-five."

"Where did you learn that from?"

"A fellow Council member, but it was many years ago. Why?"

"I was just curious. That's all."

"Oh. It will be interesting to see where this path leads."

"I agree! Let's walk!"

The trail was narrow and crooked because of a small mound and the ground beneath them became damp and sludgy, but it was not enough to deter the three adventurers.

As they pressed on, the family couldn't help but feel a deep peace. Even Zallin seemed to be caught up in the beauty of it all. There was a rare look of nostalgia in his eyes. They passed crystal clear streams, snowy groves of unique and gnarled oak trees, and the occasional grassy glade, which was no more than a field of white where the horizon line was lost in the ivory backdrop of hills. Each pocket of the realm had such magnificence and character that it looked like something that would only be found in a dream.

"This reminds me of Glennoc…" Zallin thought out loud. The instant the words left his mouth, he cleared his throat and quickly added, "Don't mind me. I was just thinking out loud."

"What's Glennoc?" Vanilla asked.

"It's a realm that's kind of like Dreamic, only with less strict laws regarding the environment. I read about it in a book a while ago. It has the largest public library in the entire Spiritan dimension," Raech replied before her father could stop her.

"That sounds interesting. Maybe that'd be a better place to move to if it's anywhere as beautiful as it is here, that is."

"It's really not, unfortunately," Zallin said hastily.

"Really? That's too bad."

"But I thought—" Raech began, but Zallin gave her a quick look that stopped her mid-sentence. "Well, never mind. I was probably mistaken," she said, casting a curious glance at her father.

"Is everything alright?" Vanilla asked, eyeing her husband suspiciously.

"Yes, I just had a bad experience in Glennoc once, that's all. I'd prefer not to bring it up."

"Alright, whatever. Hey! Did that tree just move?"

"Where?"

Vanilla pointed to a young aspen in a clearing to their right. Zallin and Raech watched it closely in anticipation, but nothing happened.

"Are you sure it wasn't the wind? There's a slight breeze right now. Or maybe it could have been an animal," Zallin asked.

"I'm almost positive I saw it moving just now."

"Well, there *are* legends of tree-like people in ancient records that have been found here. I think they're called Elganvi. I haven't really looked into it through. Maybe it's one of them."

"Are they friendly?"

"I really don't know. I'd assume so, considering Dreamic is such a safe realm. We'd best be wary of our surroundings from now though, just in case."

That kind of ruins it for me, Vanilla thought with a sigh of frustration. Her husband was quick to notice the sudden change in her mood.

"Maybe I'm being too cautious. I'm sure it's safe here, otherwise there wouldn't be a trail for people to walk on."

"Are you sure?"

"Well, this *is* Dreamic, after all. The City Realms are considered safe, but nowhere near as safe as Dreamic."

"They're not *that* safe, Zallin. I lived in 1st City Realm for a few years and have spent a lot of time in 3rd and 5th. There are a lot of creeps and weirdoes there."

"They're still safer than most of the other realms, though. A lot of other realms have monsters in them."

"I guess."

"Really, I think we should be safe here."

"OK, if you say so."

The family pressed on for another hour without further interruption, going even deeper into the woods until they reached a strange stone pillar. It was beyond the fence, just out of reach. Vanilla stopped and stared at it curiously. It was as wide as the thick trunks of the old oaks around it, but only twice the height of an average person. It was leaning quite badly to the left and had cracks and chips all over it, but had a proud look about it as if still boasting of the Golden Age it was made in. The vines that grew around its sides were thick and heavy, and only added to its mysterious allure.

"I wonder what this is from," Vanilla said as her husband and daughter came up behind her to have a look as well.

"It looks like part of a temple, perhaps. The forests here are very sacred according to folklore. I wouldn't be surprised if they had built some sort of place to worship woodland deities at some point in time," Zallin replied, eyeing the pillar.

"Where's the rest of it then?"

"Buried underground, I'd assume. Or maybe it's all worn away with time."

"That's so sad. I bet it was really beautiful when it was still intact."

"I'm sure it was. Are you getting tired at all?"

"A little."

"Shall we head back?"

"I guess. I want to take a picture of this thing first."

"Go ahead."

Vanilla took out her phone and snapped a few pictures. While she was taking the last photo, something in the background caught her eye. It was the aspen tree from before. She recognized it instantly, as it looked very out of place amongst all the oaks. Grasping her phone tightly, she carefully swung one leg over the barbwire fence, steadying herself with her other hand on a wooden post.

"Vanilla, wait! We aren't allowed to go beyond the fence," Zallin called out, jogging up to her.

"It's that tree from before! Look over there!"

Zallin stopped and looked, but the mobile aspen was gone without a trace. There were no spots of dirt or holes that could have had roots stuck into them. Even the snow on the ground appeared to be in the same place as before.

"Where? I don't see anything."

"I swear it was just over there! It must have moved."

"If it was, there would probably be a trail. If it could move, I'm sure it would leave tracks of some sort and I don't see anything like that."

"Are you calling me a liar?"

"No, that's not what I'm saying. Who knows? It may have been there and moved. I just don't have enough evidence to support that."

"So you're calling me a liar."

"Vanilla, that's *not* what I'm saying. Besides, even if it *is* real, we can't go chasing it through the forest. It's illegal to stray from the trail."

"Here, look at this picture I took."

Vanilla held out her phone for Zallin to see. He squinted at it for a second, and then shook his head.

"It's not there."

"Yeah, now look at this one."

Zallin's raised his eyebrows in surprise. Sure enough, the mysterious tree was in the photograph.

"I-I see. That's proves it, I guess. I'm sorry I doubted you."

"So you *did* think I was lying."

"Vanilla, please don't start this. I was only using logic and the available evidence to reach a conclusion. I would assume that you would do the same when faced with a similar situation."

"Well, I was right."

"Yes you were. Now let's start heading back. It's getting a bit too chilly."

"Let me just take a peek behind those trees. It might still be in the area."

"Vanilla, we don't know if it's safe—whatever 'it' is. Besides, I don't want you to get in trouble with the law."

"Who's going to find out? There's no one around."

"That doesn't mean no one will find out. There could be some sort of hidden monitoring equipment set up."

"Come on, Zallin. It's my birthday."

Zallin hesitated for a moment, and then sighed. "Fine, but just for a minute, but *please* don't go where I can't see you. I'm going to stay here with Raech."

"OK. Now help me over this fence. I don't want to rip my pants."

Using magic, the reluctant Madite carefully levitated his wife over the fence and gently set her on her feet on the other side. Her feet sunk into the cold sludge, but it didn't faze her. Curiosity overpowered the desire for comfort.

Zallin stood watching her like an overprotective parent, occasionally casting a nervous glance at the trail to check if anybody was coming. Raech was at his side, watching out for people as well. She was obviously worried, casting nervous glances around and fidgeting with her sleeves.

Vanilla had reached the edge of the glade and was standing between two great oaks. Their many branches were curled like the legs of a dead spider. Straining her ears, she took a cautious step forward.

"Vanilla, you're too far!" Zallin called out. His voice made her jump, but she was quick to regain her composure and acted like she had not heard.

"Vanilla, come back!"

As she wandered farther in, ignoring his calls, an ominous, foreboding feeling came over her. She began to shiver, though she couldn't tell if it was because of the weather or fear. A few yards away there was another fence. Unlike the one running alongside the trail, this one was made entirely from dark, rotting wood. It looked as if it would crumple at the slightest touch. Then she realized something else—the chickadees had stopped singing. In fact, there was no movement in any of the trees around her. Nervously, her eyes darted back and forth, scanning her surroundings for danger, but there was nothing in sight. Finally, she could bear it no longer and sprinted back to safety. Her husband was waiting for her at the fence, predictably with a scowl on his face.

"Vanilla, you agreed—"

"I know, I know. I just wanted to make sure it wasn't hiding a bit farther in."

"What if something had attacked you?"

"Then you would come rescue me."

"Well, yes, but I'm not Chosen or anything. There are many things that even I couldn't defeat. I'd never forgive myself if I let something happen to you."

"You just worry too much. There was nothing over there except another fence."

"I'm glad to hear that. Let's head back now."

The mood was as cold as the evening air as the family exited the forest. Vanilla refused to look at Zallin and both of them remained silent. Raech kept quiet as well, fearing that she would upset them further if she talked.

It was dark when they arrived at the house. The air was humid and thick with the smell of slime. The roof was covered in a layer of purple ooze, which slowly dripped large wet globs onto the ground. Zallin unlocked the front door, turning the key with more force than necessary, and held it open for the girls, but said nothing. Raech thanked him, but Vanilla stepped inside without even a glance in his direction.

A while later, as the Crescent Horned Punisher was brushing her teeth to prepare for bed, the blue-hatted Madite came up and apologized. "I'm sorry, Vanilla. It was wrong of me to act so cold toward you after what happened today. I guess I was raised as a strict rule follower. It was never an option to do something that might get me in trouble, so I have a hard time making exceptions to that. I really didn't want you to get in trouble with the law, especially in Dreamic."

The Crescent Horned Punisher spit her toothpaste into the sink and sighed. "I know. I guess I wasn't a good example for Raech back there."

"I wasn't, either."

"I was really curious about what that thing was. I felt like it wanted to talk to me—if moving trees can talk. Maybe I was just too caught up in the beauty of that place."

"That's alright. I understand. Perhaps we can go back there sometime soon for a walk or something."

"Sure. I bet they have good sledding hills. I think the last time I went sledding was when Raech was five."

"It certainly has been a few years."

"Do we still have those sleds in the attic?"

"I would assume so. I don't recall throwing them out. We may need to purchase one for Raech, though."

"That's true. Zallin?"

"Yes?"

"I love you."

"I love you too, Vanilla."

CHAPTER 5

-Fire and Ice Part II-

The next morning Vanilla awoke with a start. In her tiredness, she heard shouts from outside. Using the little energy that she had, she stumbled out into the living room to look out the window.

To her surprise, Zallin was standing outside with his staff raised in a fighting stance. His right leg was wounded badly and blood was slowly trickling over his left eye. "Give me my daughter, Echo!" he yelled, his head toward the sky.

Vanilla gasped and rushed to the front door. To her dismay and bewilderment, it wouldn't budge. "Zallin, what's going on? Why won't the door open?" she cried.

"Stay in the house, Vanilla! I don't want you to get hurt!" he called back, his voice cracked with emotion. He twirled his wooden staff around and brought it down on the mushy ground with a loud smack.

The Crescent Horned Punisher dashed back to the window and watched in terror as a masked man stepped into view. He was wearing a black high collared cloak that was torn toward the bottom. A wide brimmed rice hat sat atop his head to shade his face, which was partially concealed by locks of silvery-blue hair and half of a blank white mask. He drew a blade of fire from beneath his cloak and began to speak, his voice sounding like that of someone on the verge of psychosis.

"You can't save everybody, Zallin. As proof, you have already failed at protecting your only child… And to think Crescent took you in as a lieutenant for the 55th Council. You're just a pathetic weakling who got lucky a few times!"

"I'll tear you to shreds for that! Give Raech back! She has nothing to do with this!"

"Ha! I think you know my answer to that question. You're just wasting your breath!"

"Then I'll take her back by force—and avenge my family!"

Zallin aimed his glowing staff at the masked menace, who then rose into the air and began floating above the brave Madite, as if continuing to mock him.

"Almost thirty years have passed since that day and now I—" Zallin started, but a woman stepped out from behind Echo. She looked very much like Vanilla, except her horns were more jagged and she was considerably taller. Her white, sheet-like dress flowed gracefully even though there was no wind. She could see from the window that the woman was holding onto Raech's arm. The young girl was hanging limply by the Northern Punisher's side.

"Be still," she said with her hand outstretched toward Zallin. Large roots shot up from the ground and wound around his limbs, causing him to drop his staff.

"Damn it!" he cursed as he struggled to move. Then the masked man flew toward him like a hurricane, brandishing his fiery weapon. With a quick movement, he chopped at the roots holding Zallin's right arm. The tough plants were incinerated instantly, leaving the helpless Madite's arm smoldering on the ground.

He yelled in pain and fell to his knees. The eyes on his hat rolled back, and his whole body quivered. With a violent jolt, he vomited and collapsed onto the purple slime.

In sheer horror, Vanilla instinctively screamed, *"Please! Let them live!"* in Lambervan from the window, bashing at the thin wire screen with her fists.

The woman who held Raech hostage cringed slightly upon hearing this. She looked at her with a gaze that seemed to show suppressed sympathy. Though the desperate Crescent Horned Punisher was unable to see it, a tear escaped the woman's eyes. She said something to Vanilla in a language that sounded much like Lambervan, but it was too hard for her to hear over the chaos of everything.

Echo whirled around to face his companion. "Just what the hell did you say? I don't recognize that sort of talk," he asked fiercely, grabbing the woman's chin and wrenching her head to face his. He quickly doused his plasma blade and stowed it beneath his cloak.

"It was nothing."

"What? Are you trying to play me for a fool!?"

"No, Captain. I was just—"

Echo thrust his hand out and slapped her across the face. The impact of the blow almost knocked her out of the air. Blood began trickling slowly down her forehead.

"Don't you dare try and hide anything from me. Remember that! Hmph! I'll leave the blue-hatted Madite to die in agony. His wife will just have to watch—just like he did so many years ago. Now, let us leave this place," the cloaked man sneered.

After another harsh glare at his subordinate, he clapped his hands together. Two large fancy doors with the number 57 on them appeared in midair. "You're weak, Zallin!" Echo snickered as he opened the door and stepped inside. The woman holding onto Raech followed him. The door shut with a soft click, and then quickly shattered into tiny fragments.

"Zallin!" Vanilla cried desperately. She rattled the door handle in an attempt to break the mysterious outdoor lock. After a few seconds that felt like hours, she was finally able to force it open with her heightened adrenaline. The solid brass knob snapped off and clattered to the ground.

Like a marathon runner in the last stretch of a race, she ran to where her husband lay. Her vision was blurred with tears and her palms were terribly bruised from her attempts to move the doorknob. Physical pain had no meaning to her now. She flung herself over him and began sobbing. "Zallin, you can't die here! This can't be real! It just can't!" she wept.

The brave Madite was on his back, clutching the stub of his severed limb. A crimson puddle was widening beneath him, mixing with the purple ooze of Glunke. From the faint color of his skin and the distant look in his eyes, she knew that her husband was near death.

He winced and slowly lifted his remaining arm up. She couldn't move. His nearly lifeless hand gently stroked her beautiful white hair, leaving it stained red with blood. "Wait for me... Love..." he whispered. Taking one last labored breath and gazing into her heartbroken eyes, he let his arm fall limply back onto his chest. He was dead.

The Crescent Horned Punisher's eyes widened and she let out a painful scream that resonated throughout the realm. Shaking violently with anger and sadness, she beat the ground with her fists and pulled at her hair. Then she buried her face in Zallin's yellow scarf and wept bitterly. She was beyond suicide; the weight of anger and depression in her was strong enough to sink the heavens into the darkest depths of the Underworld.

Every movement felt taxing, as if her bones were made from lead. The Crescent Horned Punisher threw her head back and screamed at the sky until her voice went dry. With her mind and heart now completely hollow, she laid her head on her husband's cold chest and blacked out.

Seemingly moments later, she came to. Dim light from a cloudy dawn shone upon the dreary, purple landscape. The ground was covered in a thin, cool fog. Vanilla slowly lifted her head, only to receive a horrid reminder of what had happened before she lost consciousness. She cried out in agony and put her head back upon her deceased husband to weep again. Her eyes were sore and her body felt weak from hunger and depression, but she had no desire to leave the courageous Madite's side.

The entire day went by in what felt like minutes. Soon dusk had arrived, and then night, plunging the lonely planetoid into darkness. Still the Crescent Horned Punisher refused to move. It was only until she opened her eyes to gaze distantly at the clouds that she noticed a towering figure in a white flowing dress standing over her.

At first she thought it was an angel, but soon she realized that it was the woman who had accompanied Echo. Her hair was colored black with charcoal—a sign of remorse in the Underworlds. She stared silently and sympathetically at Vanilla, who felt her stomach churn with rage.

"Vanilla… I just wanted to—" the tall woman began.

"You evil *bitch*! You killed him! You killed my husband!"

With a fierce screech, Vanilla leapt up and tackled the woman. Together they fell onto the slimy, purple ground with a loud splat. The widow screamed insults and, holding her by the horns, viciously beat the woman's head against the goo. In all of this the woman did nothing, but simply let herself get pummeled until Vanilla was too exhausted to move and collapsed on top of her like a rag doll.

The woman slowly sat up and wiped some of the slime off her face. "As I was about to say, I feel terrible for what I did to your husband. I'm here by my own will to atone for my sins—though I know nothing I could possibly do would ever make up for what was done. Please allow me to help you, Vanilla."

The woman paused to see what her response would be, but there was none. The young widow lay motionless, still draped across her lap.

"My name is Ceilia. I'm a Northern Punisher from the Underworld beneath the Snowcrest Mountains in Ghedzar. I am a member of the 57th Council and a mage who specializes in nature-based magic." Again she paused to see if Vanilla would reply. Like before, she was met only by the sound of the widow panting.

Ceilia carefully picked her up and set her on her back on the ground in front of her. Vanilla's teary, white eyes were wide open and burned with hatred and sadness.

"Vanilla, Zallin *isn't* dead. I suppose I should have told you that first…I'm so sorry."

The Crescent Horned Punisher slowly turned her head and glared at Ceilia, as if she had just been mocked in the midst of her depression. The Northern Punisher cast her eyes down for a moment.

"I'm not joking with you. That would be a horrible thing to do at a time like this…though I guess my credibility *is* a bit lacking now. Let me explain."

Vanilla scowled, but had no strength to rebel again.

"I happened to notice that when Echo struck him down, your husband had a small dagger in his hands." Vanilla's eyes widened and began to water again, so Ceilia hastily continued. "No, no. It's not like that. He *saved* himself with it. Well, sort of. I mean he used a technique called 'Faith Suicide.' His body is currently in a state similar to a coma, but he's slowly healing himself. The Divine Point—the dagger he used—temporarily overwrites and alters his Soul Code to give him a limited amount of regeneration. It's something that his soul can only withstand once. He may appear dead now, and he isn't conscious of the world around him, but he *will* be back."

Vanilla kept on crying as if she hadn't heard.

Ceilia opened her mouth to speak again, but reconsidered. After a moment she reached out her hand to put it on Vanilla's shoulder, but changed her mind once again.

She gave a hesitant glance at the lifeless Madite. As she got up and took a step toward his corpse, Vanilla lunged forward and grabbed ahold of her right leg. "I'll freaking kill you!" she said in a dry, painful scream and fainted.

When she came to again, she found herself lying in her bed with the covers tucked over her. For a brief moment she had a spark of hope that it was all a dream, but this was instantly shattered as she realized that Ceilia was sitting on the floor at the foot of the bed, resting her head in her hands.

Vanilla recalled that her pocketknife was in the top drawer of her dresser, but she had no way of reaching it without making noise, much less the strength to even move.

Even though she had barely made a sound, Ceilia seemed to notice that she was awake. As the tall Northern Punisher rose to her feet, the widow quickly closed her eyes and pretended to be asleep. Her heart raced as she heard the woman walk to the side of the bed and stood there for a moment before hustling out of the room.

Slowly, she reopened her eyes. The house was almost completely silent. Only the sound of the ancient grandfather clock could be heard ticking in the hallway. It was terribly lonely and she felt the urge to cry welling up inside her, though she had no tears left. Exhausted, broken and extremely hungry, she closed her eyes again and sank down beneath the covers.

There were footsteps in the hall, but she neither cared nor had the energy to look. Ceilia reentered holding a warm bowl of soup with both hands. She knelt on the floor next to the bed and gently put her hand on her shoulder.

"I brought you some food."

Vanilla lay stone-still.

"You need to eat, Vanilla. It's been a few days."

The widow gave no reply.

Ceilia set the bowl of soup on her nightstand and stood up. Then, to Vanilla's surprise, the tall woman gently lifted her into a sitting position. Though Ceilia was skinny, she was incredibly strong.

The Northern Punisher picked up the soup bowl again and held it under Vanilla's chapped lips. Then, like a mother feeding a helpless infant in a highchair, she dipped the spoon into the warm broth and put it in her mouth. She shuddered as she swallowed—not because of the taste, but because of the thought of her being dependent on an enemy. She was too hungry to spit it out, though. Ceilia continued spoon-feeding her until all of the soup was gone. Finally, she got up and took the empty bowl away.

The widow stared blankly at the ceiling, thoughts of Zallin still burning in her mind like a reopened wound. Suddenly, there was a loud *dong* noise out in the hallway. The grandfather clock signaled three.

Ceilia reappeared in the doorway with a book in her hands. She gave a weak smile at Vanilla, who continued to gaze emotionlessly into the distance. The Northern Punisher's smile faded, but not the kind look in her eyes. "Would you like to be alone?" she asked softly.

To this she made no reply.

"I see. I'll leave you alone then. Just so you know, I put Zallin in your daughter's room for now. He'll be OK."

Once the Northern Punisher had left, Vanilla silently climbed out of bed using the little strength she had regained from eating the soup. Her legs were terribly shaky, but her sheer determination kept her from falling. Like a master ninja, she noiselessly retrieved her pocketknife from the top drawer of her dresser and tiptoed out of the room. Her head was swimming and she felt sick to her stomach, but the desperate Crescent Horned Punisher told herself that no pain was greater than losing her family and pressed on.

Soon she found Ceilia sitting in the living room reading a book in Zallin's blue armchair. It was all Vanilla could do to contain her rage. The Northern Punisher was so engrossed in the tome that she did not notice her—or so it appeared.

Quietly, and taking even more care than before, the Crescent Horned Punisher snuck up behind the tall woman and thrust the blade of the tiny pocketknife into the back of her neck. There was a painful sensation of recoil in Vanilla's hands, as if she had just punched a brick wall. Startled, Ceilia dropped the book and jumped to her feet. She was completely unharmed, but the blade was unusable now. In fear, Vanilla dropped it and stepped back, but lost her footing and fell.

"Oh, you startled me! Are you OK?" Ceilia said, placing one hand over her heart and taking a deep breath.

The widow was too afraid to move, much less say anything. Ceilia then noticed the small pocketknife lying on the floor. Its blade was bent and twisted, as if it had hit a rock instead of flesh. The tall Northern Punisher's eyes filled with sadness as she stooped over and picked up the weapon.

"Oh, I see… Well I'm glad you didn't use this on yourself," she said quietly as she straightened the blade out with her bare hands and set it on a nearby end table. "Vanilla, I understand that you don't trust me and I suppose you have every reason not to. Please though, I want to help you. I want to do everything I can to atone for my sins, though I know that no amount of good deeds could truly pay for what has been done."

Still petrified with fright, Vanilla sat on the floor, staring at the Northern Punisher with wide eyes. Sweat dripped from her forehead and her whole body was trembling.

"Vanilla, I'm not going to hurt you. I couldn't live with myself if

I took another innocent life… Though I already find it hard to live with myself after what I did."

Vanilla swallowed hard, still anticipating being hit by the powerful Northern Punisher. It was only after a long, tension-filled pause that she started to relax a bit. Ceilia's eyes were downcast and her body language told her that she was sad, not preparing to attack.

"You're so young, Vanilla," the Northern Punisher said at length. "If only I could take back what I did. He and I—Zallin and I, that is, were friends."

The widow felt sick to her stomach. Whether it was rage or hunger, she could not tell. Even so, Ceilia continued.

"Back in the old days when the Councils used to meet together, I met your husband. We quickly became friends. Both of us were in a similar predicament: we both had undergone many hardships and we were forced into the Councils." She paused for a moment and closed her eyes. "There was never any love interest between us. We were just friends… The Councils stopped their mutual meetings after Echo succeeded my captain."

Vanilla stared in wonder at the woman, desperately trying to silence her conscience. Deep inside, she was beginning to feel sorry for her. Try as she might, she could not harden her heart anymore. The more she told herself that the 57th Council lieutenant's story was a lie, the more convicted she felt. Eventually, a small tear escaped from her right eye. Quickly, the widow turned away in fear that Ceilia might notice.

To her surprise, Ceilia suddenly jumped to her feet and closed her eyes, as if thinking very hard. *I knew it! She was just waiting until I relaxed,* Vanilla thought in panic.

"Your daughter is safe. One of my fellow Council members has just informed me via Mind Messaging."

Vanilla was dumbfounded. The sudden change of events left her speechless and confused.

"W-what? She is?" she stammered.

"Yes."

"Why did you and that Time Wizard take her anyway?"

Ceilia looked at her feet for a moment before answering. "Echo thought that she might be the key to defeating Marissa."

"Why? Who's Marissa?"

"She's one of the Seven Chosen and she dislikes the Councils."

"What are they doing to her?"

"To be honest, I don't really know. All I know is that she's not in any danger at the moment…"

"'At the moment?' Then what about later?"

"I don't know."

"Tell me! I need to know!" Vanilla's temper was flaring up again. She had quickly forgotten about the nagging of her conscience and was about to cry again.

"I'm sorry, but I really *don't* know."

Big tears began to well up in Vanilla's eyes. Instinctively, Ceilia reached out and placed her arm on her shoulder. The widow jerked her shoulder away and covered her eyes to cry. The Northern Punisher continued to stare sympathetically at her, trying to think of how to provide comfort.

"You *will* get her back, Vanilla."

"That's easy for *you* to say! This is just too much for me! I can't take it anymore!"

Struggling to make eye contact, Ceilia looked down. The weight of shame lay heavy on her. Vanilla's eyes widened and she took a step back.

"They're going to kill her aren't they…?"

Ceilia glanced up for briefly and bit her lip. "I-I don't know," she stammered.

"No! They can't! She's my daughter!! Th-they can't do that! NO!!"

Not knowing what to say or do, Ceilia embraced Vanilla and prayed that it would somehow calm her. She was irate and tried to push her away at first, but soon gave up, realizing that she was far too weak. As she cried into the tall woman's shoulder, she miraculously began to feel peace. Though she was still in tears, her muscles relaxed and her heart rate slowed.

"How am I feeling this way at a time like this?" she thought. "Is this magic of some kind?"

Even Ceilia was a bit surprised, but did her best to hide it. "There, there," she said tenderly, taking advantage of the moment. "Your daughter *will* return, Vanilla. I won't let anything more happen to you."

Suddenly, the widow slipped from Ceilia's arms and lay unconscious on the floor. The Northern Punisher was quick to check her vitals and scan her body for evidence of magic. "What just happened?" she thought out loud. "Why did she…? Oh. That soup probably wasn't enough for her. Poor dear, she must have fainted from hunger and stress again."

When Vanilla finally came to a third time, she was back in her bed. Ceilia was already at her side, ready with another bowl of soup. "Here," she said gently, holding a spoonful of the warm food in front of her face. She had forgotten how hungry she was, but instantly remembered as the smell of the broth filled her mouth. Hastily, she wolfed it down with the grace of an albatross landing. Ceilia watched her patiently.

"If there's any food you want me to make for you, feel free to tell me. I may not be a five-star chef, but I know my way around the kitchen," she said when the hungry Crescent Horned Punisher had finished.

Vanilla looked her in the eyes and gave a small smile. "Thanks. It's a bit hard to think right now though."

Ceilia nodded. "That's understandable."

"I...I'm sorry I keep lashing out on you."

"That's OK, Dear. Things are very difficult for you right now. You have a good reason for being upset. Just know that I'm here for you."

"Th-thanks."

Again, a silence came over them. It was so quiet that they could hear the ticking of the grandfather clock in the hallway, but it was somehow calming.

"Could I have a glass of water please? I'm really thirsty," Vanilla said after a while.

"Sure. I'll be right back."

As Ceilia got up and walked from the room, Vanilla noticed that she was not wearing any shoes or socks. From the glimpse that she caught of the bottoms of her caretaker's feet, it seemed that they were rough and heavily scarred. She frowned and tried to think of why.

"Ceilia, what happened to your feet?" she asked when the Northern Punisher returned.

"Oh, that. I don't like wearing things on my feet. I feel like it distances me from nature. I hope you don't mind. I made sure they were clean before entering the house."

"It's fine. Why would going barefoot help you get in touch with nature?"

"I'm not sure how to describe it. I've always felt very close to the plants and animals, and when I wear shoes or something like that it just feels like I've thrown a bag over my head. Maybe it's because I specialize in nature-based magic."

"Wait, so what *is* 'nature-based magic?' I've heard Zallin mention it a few times."

"It refers to water, wind, plant, and ground magic as a whole. I can actually manipulate some natural elements as well as create artificial ones with magic."

"That's cool. I wish—" Vanilla began, but remembered the gruesome image of Zallin being trapped by the big roots and having his arm cut off by Echo. She tried to fight back the tears, but was unable to.

Ceilia set the glass of water on Vanilla's nightstand and put her arm right around her. "I'm sorry. That was triggering, wasn't it? I should have known."

"N-no, I was the one who asked."

"Well, anyway… Here, why don't you take a sip of water?"

"Thanks."

Vanilla's hands were so shaky that she spilled most of the water onto herself as she took it from Ceilia. The Northern Punisher quickly gathered up the ends of her dress and dabbed her shirt. Taken aback, Vanilla blushed and pushed her away, wide-eyed with surprise.

"Oh, I'm so sorry! I was just acting out of instinct. I…I'm sorry," Ceilia said, going red in the face as well.

"T-that's OK," Vanilla stammered, a bit flustered. "I know you didn't mean any harm. It just surprised me a little."

"I'm really sorry. That wasn't appropriate of me. I should have thought that through before acting."

"Really, it's fine. It was just an accident."

"Um, let me get you a towel and some more water."

Vanilla crossed her arms over her chest and shivered. The ice water had made her very cold and even thirstier. Fortunately, the motherly woman was quick to return and handed her freezing friend a nice warm towel and a second glass of water, this time making sure that she had a firm grip on it before letting go. Curiously, the Northern Punisher was still blushing.

"You don't need to worry, Ceilia. I know you didn't mean to touch my chest like a pervert or anything. You were just trying to dry me off," Vanilla said, noticing the lingering redness in her face.

Ceilia smiled shyly and said, "I know, I just... Well, never mind."

Vanilla raised one eyebrow. Before she could reply, the Northern Punisher sighed and said, "That was really awkward."

"I said it's fine. There's no reason to perpetuate about it."

"Y-yes, sorry. Can I get you something more to eat? I think we're out of canned broth, so I'll have to make some from scratch if you want soup. Not that that's a problem or anything."

"I'm not really hungry right now," Vanilla said quietly, but was answered by her stomach growling.

"Your stomach seems to say otherwise. Really, I don't mind cooking for you. It's the least I can do."

"OK, I guess."

"Is there something specific you'd like me to make?"

"I'll let you choose. I'm tired of thinking right now."

"Alright. I'll do my best."

While Ceilia set about cooking a meal, Vanilla wandered around, trying to keep her mind off the absence of her husband and daughter. Every room she entered had pictures or some sort of memento of them, however. She finally concluded that there was no way of escaping without leaving the house. So, after finding her purse and hastily brushing through her hair, she stepped outside to transport.

As she was typing in an address in her transportation watch, Ceilia called out to her from the kitchen window.

"Wait a minute, Dear! You haven't even eaten yet!"

"Oh, well how much longer will it be? I'd like to get out of the house for a while."

"About five more minutes. Please don't go anywhere until then, alright?"

"OK."

"In the meantime why don't you come inside? It's awfully chilly out there."

"I'm used to it."

"Alright. I'll call you in when lunch is ready then."

Vanilla stood in place a few yards from the house. A slight breeze caressed her pure white hair, folding it over her face and playfully tangling it around her horns. Try as she might, the young widow could not suppress the memories of her brave husband and daughter. She sighed heavily and bit her lip to hold back oncoming tears.

Eventually Ceilia came outside to retrieve her. The two went back into the house and sat at the table together. After a hearty serving of the Northern Punisher's unique cooking and assuring her that it was delicious, Vanilla went outside again to transport. Once again the tall woman told her to wait.

"Dear, just hang on a second!"

"Why?"

"Um...I don't know how to say this, but you really shouldn't leave."

"What do you mean? I have the right to go somewhere if I want to. I'm not a baby or anything."

"I know. It will just be better if you stay here. At least until Zallin is revived."

"You can't keep me cooped up here any longer! I'll go crazy!"

"But—"

"No. Just no. I'm going *now*. I'll be back later."

The instant before Vanilla's finger could touch the Send button on her watch, Ceilia appeared beside her and grabbed her hand, preventing her from transporting. Fearfully, she looked up at her towering guardian, expecting to be attacked, but the tall woman just stared back calmly into her wide eyes.

"We need to stick together and stay with Zallin until he comes back to life, Vanilla."

"Let go of me! Help!"

"I think you should know by now that I mean you no harm. If I meant to hurt you, I would have by now. I'd be far too strong for you to resist anyway. Let's go inside now."

"You can't do this to me! This is evil!"

"Evil's intention is to cause pain and sorrow. My intention is to protect."

"You're causing me pain right now! My wrist hurts!"

Ceilia fell for her trick and loosened her grip just enough for her to escape. The desperate Crescent Horned Punisher jammed her hand down on the transportation watch and vanished. Ceilia put one hand to her head and gave a frustrated grumble. "I'm just trying to help! …Oh, I guess you can't hear me."

With a quick, systematic movement of her hands, the Northern Punisher made a set of fancy navy blue doors appear in front of her. 57 was written in gold across the top of both of them. She grasped the curved brass handle of the left door firmly in both hands and flung it open. A blast of dark energy shot out as if it had been under intense pressure. Ceilia leapt into the blackness, slamming the door behind her. There was a crackling noise like ice breaking, and then the door shattered into millions of tiny fragments.

Meanwhile, Vanilla was sitting at the base of a shady pine tree in the middle of a large park. In the distance a group of small children were playing in a sandbox while their mothers sat together on a bench, talking and laughing loudly. In the opposite direction, a young teen and his friends were flying a colorful kite, skillfully weaving around the trees and tall light poles.

Just as she was drifting off to sleep, the blue double doors appeared in front of her. Startled, she let out a scream and jumped to her feet. The people nearby looked at her for a moment, and then continued about their business as if they had not even seen the ornate freestanding doors.

Vanilla started to run, but Ceilia was already upon her. Before she knew what happened, she was back on Glunke, being escorted through the front door of her own house.

"I really don't like being this rough with you, Dear, but I need you to stay put. If someone from my Council were to attack you while you were in another realm, I would have to abandon my post here to go and save you, leaving Zallin's body unguarded. I'd much rather keep both of you safe at the same time. I hope you'll forgive me," Ceilia said as she released her hold on her captive and put her hands on her hips.

Ignoring her words, Vanilla ran to her bedroom and locked herself in. Her heart pounded wildly against her chest as she struggled to keep from crying again. When Ceilia had grabbed her arm a second time, it had triggered the terrible memories of her abusive father. The Crescent Horned Punisher backed up against her closet door and sank to the floor, petrified with the vivid imagery of her childhood.

She was eight years old, hiding behind a group of jagged gray spires in the Underworld. The stained rags she wore hung loosely on her body and felt itchy as they brushed against her skin. The unforgiving ground beneath her was made up of hard clumps of decaying tissue, dust, sharp rocks, and broken bones. Her feet ached and hurt to stand on, but she was too afraid to stay in one place for too long. Her little hands trembled with fatigue as she began to crawl toward another hiding spot.

Out of the corner of her eyes she saw a crowd of male Crescent Horned Punishers dressed in brown loincloths creeping toward her. Upon realizing she had seen them, they began moving faster. Soon they had surrounded her, laughing and sneering and spitting on her face. An obese Crescent Horned Punisher with beady black eyes and dark hair came through the crowd and grabbed her.

"You worthless piece of shit! How dare you run from your own father!" he snarled, brutally cuffing her on the head. Vanilla screamed in agony and squirmed in her father's grasp, but could not break free. He threw her on the ground and kicked her hard in the ribs, cursing loudly in Lambervan as she continued to cry out in pain.

Then, as sudden as it had come, the nightmarish flashback faded, leaving Vanilla gasping and crying on her side. It took a moment before she knew that her relived nightmare was over. Slowly, she uncovered her eyes and sat up. Ceilia was standing at the door with a box of tissues in her hands, a bit startled at what she had witnessed.

"I-I'm sorry," she said quietly. "I heard you yelling and I had to make sure you hadn't injured yourself. Are you alright?" Vanilla shook her head and gazed distantly at the floor.

"Is it something you'd like to talk about?"

"M-maybe," she replied in a tiny, tear-choked voice. The motherly Northern Punisher sat down next to her and handed her a handkerchief.

"Well, go at your own pace and don't feel pressured. You don't have to tell me if you don't want to."

After a long pause the young widow began her tale, starting with her abusive childhood, her fateful encounter with Zero, how he abandoned her at the hotel, and how she met Zallin. Ceilia listened patiently, occasionally nodding her head solemnly or wiping a small tear from her own eyes.

When Vanilla had finished, the tall Northern Punisher gently hugged her and whispered, "It's OK. My story is very similar. Know that it isn't your fault for the way that he treated you, and that you're strong for having come this far. You did the right thing by running away."

The dissociative Crescent Horned Punisher just stared ahead blankly, her sad, glazed over eyes giving her the look of someone who was dying. As she sat there, a small flash of blue light from outside caught her attention. At the same time, Ceilia jumped to her feet and signaled to be quiet.

The ensuing silence lay thick and tense upon the household. Both of them strained to listen for the slightest noise, but there was nothing but the monotonous ticking of the grandfather clock in the living room. Finally, Ceilia rose and motioned for Vanilla to stay put. She nodded and watched as the Northern Punisher crept out of the room and made her way to the front door.

Suddenly, a surprised shout rang out, sounding like the blast from a canon and shattering the stillness. Instinctively, Vanilla rushed to the front of the house to see what had happened. At first, nothing appeared out of the ordinary, but upon further inspection she noticed that the front door was slightly ajar and Ceilia was nowhere to be found. Starting to panic, the Crescent Horned Punisher dashed outside.

To her astonishment, the tall Northern Punisher had engaged in combat with someone. When Vanilla realized who it was, she froze in fear.

Echo had returned.

CHAPTER 6

-Savior-

"I should have known you'd be moved into helping that bitch by your pathetic 'motherly instincts.' You're a disgrace to my Council! Egdabin was a fool to have taken you in!" Echo snarled.

"He was more of a leader than you could ever dream of being, Echo! The Councils are supposed to protect Spiritia, not cause chaos!" Ceilia retorted, spreading her arms wide and standing tall.

"Enough! You shall die!"

A dark aura burst forth from Echo's body, blowing the Northern Punisher's hair and dress back with a force like a massive hurricane. The windows on the house rattled and the walls groaned and creaked under the strain. Vanilla was blown back into the house. The door slammed shut behind her with a mighty bang. Everything around her was being shaken so violently that she was sure the whole house would suddenly collapse and bury her at any moment. Even so, she pulled herself together and looked out the window in horror.

Outside, Echo's cold eyes now burned with hatred and bloodlust as he whipped his sword out from his belt. Fire instantly erupted from the fancy golden hilt and formed a blade. The air around it was distorted from the heat and quivered as if it, too, feared the powerful weapon.

Ceilia put her hands out and exclaimed, "Nature, be my fortress!" The ground shook with the might of a full-blown earthquake as jagged, rocky spires shot up from the purple slime and completely enveloped the house, cutting off Vanilla from the two combatants and plunging her into complete darkness.

Panicking, she stumbled away from the window and groped around wildly for the light switch. The sound of muffled blasts and shouts rang out from outside. "Shit! Where the hell is it!?" Vanilla cried, frantically sliding her hands around the wall. Finally she felt the hard nub of the light switch at the tips of her fingers. Ferociously, she smacked it and the lights flickered on.

The house seemed undamaged, but the only thing Vanilla could see from the windows was a wall of solid gray rock. Completely disoriented by everything that had just happened, she fearfully paced around in circles as she listened anxiously to the battle. Her mind was racing. She couldn't decide if she should seek better shelter or stay and wait for an opportunity to run. There was no escaping from the rocky tomb. Then she remembered she had her teleportation watch in her purse.

Like a marathon runner she sprinted down the dark hall, using the light from the front room as her guide. As she neared her bedroom, she thrust her hand into the open doorway and hit the light switch. Before her eyes had even adjusted, she had her purse in hand and was rummaging in it like a desperate thief.

At last she found the little device. The screen had gone black and the keyboard hologram did not display when she touched it. Thinking that it had been turned off somehow inside her purse, Vanilla pushed the Power button and waited anxiously. To her dismay, nothing happened.

She tried again, this time holding the button down somewhat vigorously. Still, the device refused to start.

"What the hell!? Is the battery dead? Now, of all times?" she exclaimed, wanting more than anything to hurl the inexpensive watch at the wall. Then a thought came to her. *Zallin didn't run when Echo attacked the first time. He risked his life to protect me and Raech. Even now he hasn't technically left my side. He could have run, but he chose to stay and fight...I can't fight, but I'm not going to leave his side. If Glunke is destroyed with me in it, at least we will have died together.*

Time stood still as Vanilla slowly walked out of her room and into the hallway again. The sounds from the battle that raged outside gradually became less frequent and quieter. As if she were in a tragic movie or a bad dream, the Crescent Horned Punisher solemnly made her way to the front of the house. With each step she felt heavier with the weight of fear, but she remained focused on her goal.

Just as she reentered the front room, there was a ground shaking roar followed by earsplitting crashes and splats. The glass on the windows shattered and flew inside, narrowly missing her. Vanilla screamed and crouched down, instinctively covering the back of her head with her hands. Light and cold air rushed into the room, followed by the unmistakable smell of the outdoors. Then, all was still.

Cautiously, the Crescent Horned Punisher raised her head and looked around. The furniture was covered in purple slime, gray rocks, and shards of broken glass. The rock barrier that Ceilia had erected had crumbled and caused a tidal wave of slime to hit the house. Strangely, nothing had come through the ceiling even though the barrier had gone over the top of the house. It was quiet outside, except for the whistle of wind through the open windows.

"I-is it over?" Vanilla thought out loud.

As she approached one of the broken windows, she saw a body lying on the ground in a pool of red liquid. It was Ceilia.

Without hesitation, Vanilla rushed to her guardian's side and knelt down. "Ceilia, are you OK!?" she asked, trying to keep calm and ignoring the widening puddles of blood. The Northern Punisher coughed up clear liquid and painfully raised her head to look her frightened friend in the eyes.

"I'll be fine, Dear...my time is close now."

"No! You can't die! You're a Council member!"

"That I am, Vanilla, but nothing lasts forever."

"Well then who's going to protect me and Zallin?"

"I did what I could, Dear...I let him beat me so our fight wouldn't end up destroying this realm with you and Zallin in it."

"But... Then it was my—"

"It's OK, Dear. It's not your fault... It was my choice."

"No, it can't end like this! I-I can't let you die because of me!"

Gingerly, Vanilla helped the tall woman to her feet and wrapped her arm around her for support. Ceilia shook her head slowly as if to say, "It's no use," and together the two women walked to the house. Each step felt like an eternity, heavy and slow. Vanilla's legs were shaking so hard she could barely keep upright.

When they reached the front door, she kicked it open and helped her wounded friend inside. Gently, she set her down so that she was sitting with her back against the door. The tall woman winced and gave a small gasp, but forced a smile.

Vanilla looked around frantically, caught in indecision. "What would Zallin do?" she asked herself in a desperate attempt to calm herself. She knelt down by her friend and brushed her bloodstained hair away from her eyes. Their gaze met, and the Crescent Horned Punisher felt her heart race even faster.

"Ceilia? Can you hear me!?"

The woman whispered something.

"C-Ceilia!? N-no! You're not going to die! You can't! I won't let you! Please...please live!" She embraced her carefully and cried.

The white dress that the Northern Punisher had on was now almost completely crimson, as were the floorboards beneath her.

Vanilla stood up abruptly and cursed through the stream of tears, quickly turning in circles and flailing her hands. "What do I do? What do I do!?" Then she remembered there were bandages in the bathroom cabinet.

"I'll be right back! Hang in there!" she said and made a mad dash down the hall.

When she reached the bathroom, she grabbed the doorframe with one hand and swung herself inside, sliding on the tiled floor as she entered. Hands shaking violently, she wrenched open the medicine cabinet double-doored as a mirror and reached for a package of gauze tape and sterile cotton pads. The box of the former was old and had never been opened. By the time she had it in her grasp, the entire contents of the little storage space were scattered over the sink and on the floor.

On her way back to the front room, she tore the cardboard lid clear off, almost emptying the roll of gauze tape onto the hallway floor in the process. She fumbled with it for a moment, cursing her clumsiness.

Ceilia had not moved at all, but the pool of blood had not been so cooperative. It was much wider than it had been only seconds ago, like a timer counting down the seconds she had to live.

Back by her dying friend's side, Vanilla did her best to dress her numerous wounds, but the bleeding still wouldn't stop. Her skin was starting to feel cold. Vanilla forced herself to smile and tried to say, "You're going to be OK," but her mouth refused to utter the words. She herself was starting to feel faint.

Suddenly, she heard footsteps coming from behind her. Whipping her head around, she saw a familiar man enter the front room from the hallway. His tattered and burnt blue robe with the right sleeve singed off, his torn black pants, and his conical hat that was the color of the ocean was unmistakable. There was a light scar on the base of his right arm where his shoulder connected to his torso. Her eyes widened.

119

"Z-Zallin, *you're alive!*" she cried, standing up and throwing herself on him.

He caught her in his arms and she kissed him repeatedly.

"Vanilla, you're safe! Thank goodness!" Then he turned his attention to Ceilia, who had slumped over.

Zallin hurried over to her and knelt down, quickly inspecting her wounds. His eyes widened as he recognized her. "Ceilia!? Is that you? So that was—"

"I'm sorry… Zallin." Her voice was barely audible.

"I… I forgive you. I know it wasn't your choice. Here, let me heal you."

"No, I want to go… There is no pain on the other side."

The two Council member's eyes met, and a look of understanding came over Zallin. After a moment's hesitation, he nodded solemnly and put his hands on her shoulders. "Thank you, Ceilia. You may go…and may peace be with you on the other side. You're more of a hero than I was," he said quietly, trying not to cry.

Completely astonished, Vanilla watched in tears as her courageous caretaker slowly closed her eyes and fell sideways onto the floor with a light thump. Zallin hung his head and wept.

"Zallin, why didn't you heal her?!"

"Vanilla, it's not like that! She was my friend, too…"

"Then why didn't you do something?!"

"I-I don't really know how to explain it… She and I have known each other for a long time. To her, her own death was better than continuing to live with the things she has witnessed and gone through."

"But—"

"Vanilla, just trust me. It hurts me to see her go more than you realize, but she's free now and happier than she was in this life."

"How can you be sure though?"

"I can't, but I have faith. I'm going to bury her outside. She deserves a proper funeral."

With one last gaze at his fallen comrade's face, Zallin picked up the deceased Northern Punisher's body and carried her outside, followed by his wife.

A steady breeze was blowing through barren purple land, creating small wavelike marks over the numerous sinkholes. The sky was much darker and cloudier than before, and the air smelled of oncoming rain. Vanilla stuck close to her husband, still feeling torn between sadness for Ceilia and joy for Zallin's revival.

When they had come to a flat spot atop a gentle hill, Zallin carefully set the Northern Punisher's body down and teleported his staff into his hands. Then he closed his eyes and whispered something. The ground parted, forming a small pit the perfect size for a grave. The Madite and his wife lifted Ceilia's body up again and lowered it in. Once she was in place, he used magic to seal the hole again. Taking a large stone from the ground, he carved an epitaph in it with his staff and placed it on top. The couple stood together at the grave in silence until nightfall.

Minutes after they returned to the house, a heavy downpour started. Gooey purple drops the size of golf balls pelted the roof with a sound like gunfire, and then slid reluctantly off and to the ground. Bright flashes of yellow lightening tore across the sky, accompanied by low rumbles of thunder in the distance.

The couple headed for the basement immediately. They sat together on an old dusty couch beneath the stairwell. Vanilla had brought a thick purple blanket with her that she used to cover their legs for warmth. She was resting her head against her husband's shoulder while he fidgeted with a loose string on the edge of the blanket.

"Zallin…?"

"Yes?"

"What are we going to do?"

Zallin closed his eyes and sighed. "I'm thinking."

"It's just so sad… Why do things like this happen all at once? First our daughter is kidnapped, then you're killed, Ceilia gets killed, the house is almost destroyed… What next?"

"…Pain is a part of life, even when it may seem unfair. I will choose to hold fast to hope, though."

"It *is* unfair! We didn't do anything to deserve this! Raech has always been such a kind soul. Why'd they have to take her? She wouldn't hurt anybody!"

"I agree. It hurts to think that I couldn't even save my own daughter… What kind of father am I? If I had only been stronger…"

"*Our* own daughter. You gave your life for her. What did *I* do though? I'm completely useless…"

"No, you're not. There wasn't much that either of us could do… Hm. The only person who I know that would be strong enough to help us would be Crescent. There's no guarantee he will though and I'm a bit nervous about meeting with him again after so many years. He may be our best option as things stand."

"Who? I think I've heard that evil Time Wizard mention that name."

"Crescent is my captain. He's one of the Seven Chosen."

"I didn't think 'Crescent' was a man's name. It doesn't sound very manly."

"Well, maybe not, but don't say that to him. He'd…well, it'd be bad. Trust me."

"He wouldn't hit a girl, would he?"

"He's done it before, so I strongly advise against upsetting him."

"But you'd protect me if I did, right?"

"Yes."

"Hmph. To think, we've been married for nearly fifteen years and this is the first time you've told me what your captain's name is. I really wish you'd talk about these things more."

"I'm sorry. It's not easy, as I've said before."

"Well maybe if you keep trying it will get easier."

"Perhaps."

"What do you mean 'perhaps?'"

"Oh, nothing. It sounds like the weather is starting to calm down now. I think we should go upstairs and clean."

"Wait a minute. You're avoiding my question."

"No, I'm just prioritizing."

"Oh, so my questions aren't as important as cleaning? Is that what you're saying?"

"No, Vanilla. Please, I don't want to start an argument."

"You're right...I'm sorry. I just...I don't even know anymore. I can't stop thinking about Raech. We *need* to get her back, whatever it costs. I don't think I'll be able to sleep until I know she's home."

"Me, neither. We'll get her back, Vanilla." He hugged her from the side. She rested her head against him and wiped her tears with the back of her hand.

"Why her? Why our only daughter...? She didn't do anything wrong!"

He stroked her hair. "I know."

"When are you going to connect with your captain?"

He hesitated, his body going rigid for a moment. "I...I suppose I can do that now." Closing his eyes, he focused his mind and began to relay a message via telepathy. Vanilla had seen it a few times before in the years they had been together, but had always wondered about its authenticity. There were no visible traces of magic, and no noticeable burst or fluctuations of energy as far as she could tell.

After a few minutes, he opened the yellow eyes on his hat again and looked at her.

She leaned forward. "Did you ask him?"

He nodded.

"What did he say?"

"He says he'll do it tomorrow."

"T-tomorrow? But, what if something happens to her by then? I don't even know if she's been hurt!"

"I'm sorry. I can't argue with him. We're lucky enough that he's agreed to help us at all."

"But—"

"There's nothing more we can do, Vanilla."

She felt the tears returning. "Why…?"

"I'm sorry…I think we should fix things up in the meantime. It'll be freezing tonight if the windows aren't covered. I think I may be able to repair the glass with magic."

"Y-yeah…I'll clean the carpet and the furniture. This is going to be a long night…"

The next morning Vanilla awoke to the smell of coffee brewing. She rubbed her eyes sleepily and yawned. As she rolled out of bed, she glanced at the alarm clock and saw, to her dismay, that it was still very early. "Zallin," she called, feeling a bit annoyed. Then she remembered what had happened and felt tears returning to her eyes.

A few moments later Zallin appeared at the door dressed in his Council uniform. After a nervous glance behind him, he cleared his throat and spoke in a low voice, "Vanilla, Crescent is here. He says he wants to meet you. Be warned though, he's...um, a character, if you know what I mean."

The Crescent Horned Punisher stared at her husband's serious face for a moment, trying to understand his inference. Just then, a towering, 7-foot tall man with multi-colored hair barged into the room. He was so large that the ceiling fan nearly hit the top of his head as it spun around lazily. The brute wore a fancy white jacket with a black swirl print, a light green T-shirt, bright orange pants with red fire patterns toward the bottom, three gold rings on his right index finger, and blocky wooden sandals that made a clapping sound as he walked. However, the man's fashion sense wasn't nearly as bad as his manners, as became apparent moments later.

He smiled and gave a hearty laugh. "Now isn't that precious! Zallin, you let the missus sleep in! Boy, you sure married a cute one!"

Vanilla screamed and hid under the covers. Crescent rubbed his perfectly square chin with a big, beefy hand and shrugged. "Hey, at least *I* didn't just wake up. The early bird gets the worm, as they say. Of course, if the hunter is earlier, he'll kill that damn bird before anything. Come to think of it, I'm hungry for chicken now. Where's your kitchen?"

"Um, let's go back to the living room, sir. Then I can cook you something if you'd like. I don't think we have any chicken, though," Zallin hastily interjected. "Let's just let my wife have some time to wake up. Yesterday was a rough day for her."

"Alright, sounds good! Damn, I'll say it again, Zallin, you've really nabbed yourself a beauty!"

Zallin nodded nervously, trying to mask his impatience and

cautiously guided the massive brute into the other room. Vanilla lay motionless underneath her blankets, completely mortified by what had just happened.

That man is the rudest person I've ever met! she thought angrily. *What kind of person just barges into a woman's room like that? He talks like I'm an object, too! No woman in her right mind would ever love* him. As she steamed over the incident, she heard Crescent's booming laugh from the living room. Wincing, she plugged her horns and buried her head beneath the covers again.

Eventually, hunger drove the frustrated Crescent Horned Punisher to get dressed and sneak into the kitchen. It was almost Noon and Zallin had been cooking something for his abrasive captain. The delicious aroma that drifted through the house would have driven anyone who had not eaten in days to the brink of insanity.

The kitchen was still warm from the oven being on. Vanilla noticed that her red oven mitts were hanging on the door to the pantry and a food-encrusted spatula was lying on the counter. *It looks like Zallin was in a hurry to serve that jerk. I can't believe anyone would just ask their host to cook them something.* As she fumbled around in the cupboards, she overheard the Madite mention Raech, so she stopped to listen in.

"Sir, do you think you'll be able to get our daughter back?"

"Do I think I can? What a stupid question! Zallin, you've known me for a long time. You and I have fought battles with Darklords more powerful than any one of the Councils combined—not more powerful than me, of course! Besides that, I'm one of the Seven Chosen! You've got to be a complete idiot to even wonder about something like that. I ought to break your arms for asking me something so trivial. Come on, Zallin. You're a smart guy—not as smart as me, mind you—so use your damn brain. Of course I can!"

"Th-thank you sir. You truly are a lifesaver."

"You bet I am. I've saved more lives than you could ever dream of and I'm not even a healer! Ahahaha! What a riot!"

"May I ask when's the soonest you'd be willing to do this? If it's not too much trouble, Vanilla and I would like to have our daughter back as soon as possible."

"'If it's not too much trouble?' Just listen to you! I could go now if I wanted to, but let me just finish eating. It's no good fighting on an empty stomach—for most people, that is—and I'm not most people, but I do like this meat thing you've cooked. I'll have to come over again sometime and you can make it for me again."

Zallin simply nodded and waited patiently as the tall brute wolfed the food down. As he was chewing the last piece, he wiped his sauce-covered hands on the white sofa. The Madite cringed and bit his lip.

"So how many years have you and that woman been together? It's been so long since I've heard from you. I had just figured that you had died or something. I replaced you already with somebody better, so I don't mind that you got hitched. I may still call you in from time to time now that I know your corpse isn't rotting somewhere out there."

"Fourteen years. It will be fifteen this November—here, that is."

Crescent coughed, sending tiny food particles flying onto the carpet. He gave Zallin a look of distaste and wiped his mouth with one sleeve. "Well," he said after a pause, "that's…a long time. She hasn't done anything bad to you yet?"

"I don't appreciate questions like that, sir. She is my wife and I am her husband. We are a team."

"Alright, alright. No need to get all upset. I was just wondering. Can't a man be curious? Freedom of speech, you know."

A small beeping noise came from one of the large man's pockets.

He stood up abruptly, knocking over the low tea table in front of him. "Well, looks like my Council needs me. If they were strong like me, they wouldn't have to call on others for help. Damn, sometimes I wonder why I took the position of a captain. It's practically just babysitting a bunch of wimps who can't stand on their own! Bah!"

At the front door he stopped and said, "Tell the missus I said goodbye. I still can't get over how beautiful she is. You're a lucky man, Zallin! Or unlucky, perhaps. I've been told that looks are the only thing Crescent Horned Punisher women have."

Before the offended Madite could reply, the tall brute stepped outside and slammed the door shut with so much force that two framed family photos nearby fell off the wall. Zallin flinched as he heard them shatter on the floor, but just as he was turning around, his captain opened the door again and popped his head back in.

"Oh, Zallin. I…hm, never mind. I forgot. I'll think of it later. If forgetfulness was a person, I'd wring their neck and rip their spine out!" The door slammed a second time, bringing another picture crashing to the floor along with a delicate vase of flowers. Zallin took a deep breath and shut his eyes tightly.

"What broke?!" Vanilla called out from the kitchen. The volume and tone of her voice was proportionate to her anger. At first Zallin did not reply, so she came into the living room to see for herself.

"Our pictures—and my vase! That *bastard*, how dare he!"

"I'll clean it up."

"*He* should, not you!"

"I don't have authority over him so it will be my responsibility."

"Well what kind of man wouldn't clean up after his own stupidity? He's got a lot of nerve, that— The sofa! Shit! Just look at what he's done to our house!"

"I know, but he's going to get Raech back for us."

"I hope he treats her better than he treated our furniture. Zallin, that man is despicable! How could you be so loyal to someone like that?"

"I don't have a choice. I've been placed under his authority and I must honor it. I'd much rather deal with some stress and keep my life than disrespect him and be killed. There will always be leaders that we don't agree with, but the wise thing to do is respect those in authority, regardless of how we feel."

"Well Council Captain or not, after he brings our daughter back he's no longer welcome here."

Again, Zallin made no reply. He stooped over and began carefully picking up the numerous sharp fragments of the vase as Vanilla watched, her temples pulsing with rage. "You shouldn't have cooked anything for him! He's nothing but a big, clumsy, ungrateful...swine!" she quipped and stormed out of the room. The Madite hung his head and stared at the stained white carpet.

Back in the kitchen, Vanilla was vigorously digging through the cupboard under the sink in search of cleaning products. Bottles of soap, dishrags, sponges, and various other items were carelessly flung onto the gray tile floor until she was fed up with looking. "Zallin, where's that stuff for removing stains from furniture? It was just here last night," she called out impatiently.

There was no reply. "Zallin!" she tried again, but the result was the same. The upset Crescent Horned Punisher stood up and marched back to the living room, expecting that her husband was ignoring her.

To her surprise, the living room was empty and the stains on the couch and carpet were completely gone. Vanilla slowly brushed her hand over the sofa's fluffy white armrest, staring hard at it as if it might be an illusion. "It's perfect," she said in wonder. Then she glanced at the table where the vase had fallen from. It had been mysteriously fixed, too. Even the pictures were as good as new and were hung neatly back in their rightful places.

"I said I'd handle it, didn't I?" Zallin's voice came from behind her. Vanilla jumped and whirled around.

"Don't scare me like that! How did you do all this so quickly?"

"Magic. I was a bit hesitant to use any type of power for such delicate work, but it turned out quite nicely."

"Have you always been able to do stuff like that?"

"Not always. It's a similar technique to healing broken bones and internal damage. Or at least the use of psychic magic."

"I'm sorry I took my anger out on you. I'm just...really stressed with this whole ordeal."

"Me, too. You have every right to be. I forgive you and I'm sorry that my captain caused you so much stress. I really wish I could have done something to prevent what happened, but there's only so much I can do without evoking his temper."

"Well I love you. I feel like a total jerk. You were just revived yesterday and I've already started an argument with you."

"No. Don't worry about it. Let's just forget this whole thing. I assume Crescent will be returning with Raech shortly."

"Are you sure?"

"For which one?"

"Oh, both I guess."

"Yes, it's fine and no, there's no way to be certain. But I am sure that we will get our daughter back. He's Chosen and even Echo knows not to mess with him."

"Then we'll have to plan a celebration."

"Of course. What would you like to do?"

"I don't know. Give me a while to think. I just need to put my feet up for a few minutes."

Vanilla retreated to a chair on the opposite side of the room and sat down. Zallin took a seat on the floor beside her, leaning against the side of the chair. It was a few minutes before either of them spoke, but both knew that the other was thinking about their missing daughter. Finally, she broke down and cried with her face buried in her hands.

"I can't take it anymore! I can't keep pushing this away! Oh Raech, please come back safely!" she sobbed. Her husband got up and put his strong arms around her. She shifted in place slightly so that her head was resting on his left shoulder and continued to weep.

"It'll be OK. Soon we'll be back together again. I know it. Have faith, Vanilla, and hold fast to hope."

"But so much has happened... When will it all end? When can we live our lives in peace?"

"Someday. This is just a passing moment. You can pull through this, Vanilla. I believe in you."

"How can you be so calm? What if something else happened to her? What if Crescent doesn't come back with Raech?"

"He will. Nobody is more powerful than the Seven Chosen and in all my years of being his subordinate, I've never seen him with more than a few scratches."

"Can we really trust him though?"

"I trust him with this and I think you should too. Though he may not seem like it, when my captain makes a promise he will always see it through—primarily to build his own ego, but he always follows through to the end nonetheless."

"What if something bad has already happened through?"

"Trust me."

"I'm trying…"

A loud knock at the front door interrupted the couple's worried silence. Zallin sprinted to the door to answer it while Vanilla remained seated. The Crescent Horned Punisher closed her eyes and whispered a prayer, hoping with all her might that it was Crescent bringing Raech back safe and sound.

"See? I told you I could do it," a familiar booming voice said the moment the door was open. Vanilla jumped up and ran to meet him.

The tall brute was grinning triumphantly like a spoiled child who had won a footrace. Raech's fragile body was draped limply over his muscular arms. She was unharmed and alive, but seemed to be unconscious. Her mouth was partially open as if she had been drooling.

Crescent set the girl on the couch with surprising gentleness and looked at her face. "She doesn't look anything like either of you," he said bluntly. "Are you sure she's your child? Anyway, the only reason it took me so long was because the 57th Council is a bit hard to track at times. Not too hard for me, mind you, just most people. In fact, I should have killed that bastard Echo while I was there. He's so weak that sometimes I forget he's a Darklord! Actually, he wasn't even with the rest of his Council, the damn coward! He probably knew I was coming and ran for cover like a little crybaby!"

Vanilla had already flung herself upon her daughter and was crying tears of joy. Crescent scratched his head and stared blankly at them for a moment. "Don't smother her. She's unconscious, you know," he blurted. The protective mother glared sharply back at him, but before she could respond Zallin stepped forward.

"Sir, thank you so much for all you've done. I'm sure you must be a bit tired from fighting with the 57th Council."

"Tired? Zallin, what have I told you before? The Chosen don't get tired from fighting weaklings. The only thing I'm tired of is people not listening. You should be thankful that I'm a nice man. Most people probably would have slit your throat or burnt your eyes out for saying that."

"My apologies, Captain."

"Speaking of weaklings, it looks like the 57th Council lost a member recently. There's some new guy on their team now. I don't like it. Maybe I'll kill him next time I see him, the little rat. Why does a Council like theirs get new members so fast? Whenever I lose someone in the 55th, it takes me months before I find someone strong enough to join— except in your case. Did you know that at one time the 57th Council had two members who were Chosen? Why can't I have that? Not that I *need* comrades or anything. It's just nice to have people to order around. Heck, if I was allowed to fight the other Chosen, I'd beat all of them and then force them to join my Council."

"That is a thought, sir."

"Anyway, I can't stand all this mushy reunion shit. I'm out of here! People should start being more careful with their children. I swear being a parent must be the biggest waste of time there is. Where's the fun and fighting? Where's the bloody battles and heads getting torn off?"

Again, Crescent was out the door before his former lieutenant or Vanilla had a chance to reply. As the tall brute slammed it shut behind him, the entire font side of the house shook, rattling the windows and dislodging all the hanging pictures. This time however, Zallin was prepared. He quickly held out his hands and used magic to levitate them, and then hung them back up.

"I need to check if there's anything wrong with Raech. Stand back for a moment," he said, motioning for Vanilla to move. She nodded and stepped back. The Madite gently held his daughter's hand and closed his eyes. The seconds ticked by as the older Madite stood motionless, furrowing his brow in concentration.

Just as Vanilla was about to speak, the eyes on his face opened, a rare sight for the Crescent Horned Punisher. The spell caster's eyes were darker than a midnight sky, and wiser than almost anything she had seen before. Neither of them had a pupil, but were completely black and slightly transparent. Finally he spoke, slowly and in a very calm voice.

"She's OK. It appears that she's an Endekko. The 57th Council must have known that before they kidnapped her. Perhaps that's why they came after her."

"Actually, Ceilia said something about Echo thinking that Raech might be the key to defeating some woman named Marissa. Apparently she's one of the Seven Chosen. But what's an Endekko? I think I've heard that somewhere before."

"It's a word to describe a beneficial mutation of an individual's Soul Code. To put it bluntly, a person who is born an Endekko is capable of becoming far more powerful than normal. I wouldn't have guessed our own daughter was one since it's a fairly rare condition."

"Are you an Endekko? Maybe it was passed on from you."

"Yes, all Council members are, but something like that can't be passed on. The occurrence of that specific flaw in Soul Code is completely random. It can't be forced, either. Otherwise there'd be lots more Endekkos."

"Well Raech has always been so smart. I guess that explains why."

"No, that's something entirely different. I'm concerned though. If the 57th Council's reason for capturing her was because they think she's the key to defeating someone, they may come back for her in the future.

Or another Council may, for that matter."

"What should we do then?"

"I honestly don't know. We'll just have to be on our toes."

"Can't you get Crescent or your Council to help again? Er, maybe not Crescent."

"It's not that easy. They have other duties, one of which is to protect the entire Spiritan dimension. To ask them to come and watch over us for even a day would be asking a lot—too much, really. We were fortunate enough that Crescent had enough free time to help out."

"Zallin, I'm scared. I don't want this to happen again."

"Well now that I know there is a potential danger, I'll start training harder. I should have known that evil would strike the moment I lowered my guard. I have a few friends I could contact if we need help. Unfortunately I wasn't able to get ahold of them when Echo attacked. I was caught off-guard…"

"Do you think we should move to a more populated place? Like City Realm 1 or 3 maybe?"

"I don't think it's necessary since we can just teleport if need be."

"I guess you're right. It just seems like nothing extreme ever happens in the City Realms… Well, I love you and if there's anything I can do to help please tell me."

"Alright. I love you too. I'm going to lay Raech down on her bed. I figure it'd be best if we let her come to naturally."

"OK."

Zallin hoisted their daughter into his arms with little effort and, with Vanilla by his side, went into the young Madite's room. Though she still had not moved the slightest bit, Raech's face looked healthy and bright as if she somehow knew that she was finally home. The couple stayed at her bedside for a long time talking in low whispers.

"Zallin, do you think she'll have any bad memories? I hope she won't need any counseling…"

"No, I think she'll be fine. Strangely, her body doesn't show any signs of emotional trauma and neither does her soul. I was going to ask Crescent if he knew what they did to her, but I didn't get the chance."

"Maybe that's for the better."

"Maybe."

"Did you notice *any* changes at all?"

"No, I really didn't pick up on anything out of the ordinary. I'm starting to wonder if someone in the 57th Council was watching over her…"

"Why would they do that if they wanted to kidnap her?"

"I don't know. Either way, she's home now and that's what matters."

"Yeah. How long do you think it'll be before she comes around?"

"Honestly, I don't know. It could be hours, I suppose."

"You've been saying that a lot lately."

"I know. It's the truth, though. If I did know I would tell you." Vanilla smiled weakly.

"Have you eaten anything yet? It's already past lunchtime. I can make us some sandwiches if you'd like."

"That's fine."

"What would you like on yours?"

"The usual."

"OK, I'll let you know when they're ready."

When Zallin had gone to the kitchen, Vanilla got up from where she was kneeling and sat on the bed beside Raech. "I know you can't hear me now, but I'm proud of you for pulling through. Whatever the 57th Council did, you survived it and now you're finally home. We were so worried…" Just as the Crescent Horned Punisher had finished talking, the eyes on the girl's purple hat opened halfway.

"Oh, Raech! I'm so glad!" Vanilla exclaimed and burst into tears of joy again. She flung her arms around the sleepy teen and held her in a warm embrace. Startled and confused, Raech flinched and then relaxed after realizing where she was.

"Zallin! Zallin, come quick! Raech is awake!" The blue-hatted Madite came hurrying into to the room with a partially unwrapped block of yellow cheese in his hands. He hastily set it on the wooden writing desk by the door as he entered and wiped his forehead with one arm.

"Raech!"

"Mom! Dad! I thought I'd never see you guys again! I was so afraid. Who rescued me?"

"My captain, Crescent, did."

"Where is he? I have to thank him."

"He left a while ago. Tell me, are you feeling alright?"

"Yeah, I think so. Hey, wait a minute. Dad, didn't your arm, um…get cut off?"

"Yes, it did. I healed myself, though."

"Sweetie, are you OK? Are you in any pain?" Vanilla interjected.

She shook her head. "I'm a little tired, but I think I'm OK."

"Are you sure?"

"I'm so glad you're OK! We were so worried! I wouldn't be able to live with myself if something had happened to you."

"Can we get you anything to eat or drink? I'm sure you must be starving," Zallin said.

"Oh, thank you. I'll have water please."

"Just water? Nothing to eat?"

"Well, I guess something small like an apple would be fine."

"I'm surprised you aren't hungrier," Vanilla said, furrowing her brow.

"Would you like a sandwich?" Zallin asked. "I was just in the process of making one for your mother and I."

"OK. If it's not too much trouble could I have a peanut butter and jelly sandwich?"

"Of course! Just one second."

As Zallin bustled off into the kitchen again, Vanilla proceeded to ask the young girl the one question that had been burning in her mind. "What did they do to you?"

"Um...I don't really remember, actually. I recall being handled roughly, but nothing else."

Vanilla frowned slightly. "Oh... Are you sure?"

"Yes. I think this is the first time I've completely forgotten something... Did you get to meet Dad's captain?"

"Yes, I regret to say."

"Why? Did he do something?"

"Many things. He's a rude slob that has no respect for others and their property. He barged into my bedroom before I had even gotten out of bed. On top of that, he made your father bake him something, and then he made a huge mess on our couch! Each time he closed our front door, he used so much force that those framed pictures in the living room fell off the wall. In all my life, I've never met anyone so inconsiderate and idiotic! I told your father that that man is no longer welcome here."

"Oh... I-I see."

"That being said, I *am* grateful that he went and got you from that evil 57th Council."

"As am I," Zallin added from behind them. "Your sandwiches are ready. Let's sit at the table, though. Raech, why don't I carry you? I don't want you to overexert yourself. After all, I'm sure your body is weak with hunger."

"I think I'll be OK. Thanks for the offer, though."

"Are you sure? I don't mind carrying you."

"I'm sure."

"Alright."

The family went into the dining room, both Zallin and Vanilla keeping close to their daughter. The older Madite watched her closely, starting at any sudden movement that could indicate a fall.

When they sat down at the table, Vanilla scooted her chair closer to Raech. As she ate, the motherly Crescent Horned Punisher gave occasional glances at her.

Eventually the teen had finished her meal and got up to take her plate to the sink.

"Here, I'll do it," Zallin said.

She blinked. "Oh, thank you."

"How are you feeling?"

"I'm doing better now that I've eaten."

He eyed her suspiciously. "I see. I'm glad to hear that."

"Raech," Vanilla said, setting the remainder of her sandwich down.

"Yes?"

"Are you really OK? After all that just happened…"

She nodded. "I think I'm alright. I don't actually remember what happened when I was taken."

Zallin closed his eyes and spoke to Vanilla through telepathy. *"Vanilla, she appears to be telling the truth. Perhaps it isn't a good idea to pressure her any further. If she forgot what happened, there may be a good reason for it, though I suppose that may be a cause of concern in itself."*

She looked at him, and then back at her daughter. "Sweetie, maybe you should rest a bit."

The girl glanced at her father. "Um, OK. I guess I am kind of sleepy."

Vanilla got up and hugged her. "I'm so glad you're OK, Raech… You really had us worried."

"I'm sorry."

"You don't have to apologize. It wasn't your fault."

"I love you, Mom and Dad."

"We love you too," Zallin said.

She yawned. "I guess I *am* getting tired."

"I'm sure when you regain consciousness, your adrenaline kicked in, which is why you felt more awake for a while." He offered her his hand. "I'll walk you to your room."

"OK. Thanks Dad."

He nodded.

"Hon," Vanilla said, turning to her husband. "I think I'm going to step outside for a second."

He looked at her curiously. "Is everything OK?"

"Yeah."

He glanced back at their daughter. "Are you going for a walk?"

She hesitated and then shook her head. "I just need a little fresh air."

"OK."

She headed straight for the front door, consciously slowing her pace.

Outside, she made her way to where they had buried Ceilia, taking care to avoid the well-hidden pits of goo that were scattered across the lonely planetoid.

When Vanilla reached the grave, she stopped and took a deep breath, filling her lungs with the cool, damp air. Looking up at the gray, cloudy sky, she let the tears stream down her face. "Thank you, Ceilia..." she sobbed. "Thank you. If you hadn't shown up when you did...I don't know what would have happened to us. Thank you for protecting Raech. If there's a heaven, I'm sure you're there."

As she stood there, consumed by the contradiction of sorrow and joy, something caught her eye. A slip of paper was sticking out of the edge of a sinkhole.

Wiping the tears from her eyes, Vanilla cautiously walked over to it and bent over. A brief flashback of her fateful encounter with her husband went through her mind as she did so.

Grasping the object firmly in one hand and using the other to maintain her balance, she began to pull. From the large amount of resistance, she quickly realized that it was more than just a small piece of paper.

With a sickening squelch, the slime relinquished what appeared to be a leather-bound book. Strangely, the purple goo only stuck to the cover. It was as if the pages repelled it.

Clearing off the residue from the front and back, she turned it over in her hands and squinted at the title. "*Eon's Unbeatable...*" she read aloud. "Huh. I've never heard of this before. I wonder who left it here. Whoever it was, I don't think they're coming back for it. It looks almost as old as some of Zallin's books on magic. I should ask him if he knows anything about this."

When she arrived back at the house, Zallin was sitting in the front room reading a book. He looked up at her with surprise and got up. "Back already?" he asked, looking curiously at the raggedy book in her hands.

"I guess. I saw this stuck at the edge of a sinkhole. I decided to bring it back and ask you what you make of it. The pages didn't tear when I pulled it free, so it must be something special. I haven't looked inside or anything yet."

She handed her husband the book. The intelligent Madite turned it over and gazed intensely at the back cover, but did not open it. "Well?" Vanilla said after a while. There was a hint of impatience in her voice.

"We need to get rid of this right away."

"What? Why?"

"This book is cursed."

"Cursed? How so?"

"It was written in a time known as the Writer's Destruction Era. From what I've been told, some of the books made back then had the ability to suck their reader's soul into the world within the story."

"That sounds pretty cool, actually."

"No, it's not. If someone were to get pulled in, they could never return to reality. At least that's what I've heard."

"And who did you hear that from?"

"Initially, a member of the 50th Council who I trust informed me about it. I did some research on my own, too."

"Have there been any accounts of people getting trapped inside a story world like that?"

"Well, no, but that doesn't mean it hasn't happened. There are certain events in history that have been well hidden from us by the Old Government, like the creation of Dark Runners."

"What if it's just a rumor, then?"

"Vanilla, this is serious. Rumor or not, it's not a risk I'm willing to take."

"You don't have to. I'll read it."

142

"No you won't. Now let me dispose of this accursed object."

"Wait!"

"What?"

"Can I do it?"

"What, dispose of it?"

"Yeah."

"I think it'd be better if you let me take care of it."

"But Zallin, I found it. Shouldn't it be my responsibility?"

Zallin eyed his wife with uncertainty. "Are you really going to get rid of it?" he asked slowly.

She nodded.

"Alright. Here." The Madite reluctantly relinquished the leather-bound book and sat back down. Vanilla cautiously made her way into the kitchen and, with a quick glance behind her, hid the cursed item under a cloth beneath the sink. Then she went out the back door, hoping to make Zallin think that she was going outside to dispose of it.

That night as Vanilla was lying awake in her bed, her mind kept wandering to the book. Excitement and curiosity was burning in her as she waited for Zallin to fall asleep so she could sneak out to the kitchen and retrieve her hidden tome.

Eventually her husband's light snore broke the night silence, signifying that he had fallen asleep. Cautiously, Vanilla slipped her feet out from under the sheets and onto the plush carpeting. *I'm glad we don't have a hardwood floor in our room,* she thought as she imagined her claw-like toes clacking on the floorboards and waking Zallin from his slumber. Then, with one last glance at her sleeping husband, she held her breath and tiptoed out of the room.

Once the stealthy Crescent Horned Punisher had reached the hallway, she exhaled a sigh of relief and continued on into the kitchen.

It was pitch black as she entered and she feared that she would trip over something and make a loud noise. With one hand on the wall, she groped around in the dark until she felt the handles of the cupboard under the sink.

As she carefully opened them and stuck her hands inside, she knocked a plastic bottle over. The ensuing clunk sounded like a cannon firing against the stillness of the night. Vanilla froze and listened, her heart pounding franticly in her chest. She counted to 10 in her head while she strained her ears to listen for movement. Luckily, the sound had not awoken anyone. So, moving even slower, the Crescent Horned Punisher continued rummaging.

Her hands finally came upon the rag which she had used to conceal the book, but the book itself was nowhere to be found. Perplexed, Vanilla withdrew and tried to recall the events of the evening to remember if anyone was in the cupboard. *Zallin was in the kitchen before bed, but I'm sure he would have said something to me if he had found it. Raech never goes through these cupboards, so it couldn't have been her. Besides, she would ask whose it was before doing anything with it. I'm sure that I hid it in here, though.*

Feeling disappointed, she retreated to the living room, which was lit by a single dim lamp, and sat down on the couch. As she raised her feet to place them on the footrest, she noticed a lump underneath one of the blankets that lay across the far left seat. She leaned over and tugged the quilt aside. To her delight, there was the book. *Zallin must have been reading it. I knew the whole cursed thing was just made-up. After all, who would curse a book?*

Without hesitation she opened it up to the first page and read the title in a whisper. "*Eon's Unbeatable.* 'Chapter One: Contract of Man and Machine.' Hm, sounds interesting."

Hours passed before she became weary of reading and set the book down. She was too tired to go back to the bedroom, so she lay down on the couch and closed her eyes. As she was drifting off to sleep, strange black markings silently coiled their way up her arms.

CHAPTER 7

-Welcome to Andalli-

Vanilla felt her body begin to fall through time and space as she slipped into a deep sleep. Panicking at the odd sensation, she tried to wake herself up, but it was too late. Images from the first chapter of *Eon's Unbeatable* swam around in a haze of colors. It was nauseating, so much so that she felt the urge to vomit. Just when she could stand it no longer, she awoke with a start.

"Hey, wake up!" an unfamiliar voice called out to her. She opened her eyes. Through her grogginess, she saw a handsome young man with dark messy hair and a kind face. She instantly knew he was a knight, but not one of the Royal Guard or Spiritan Alliance. The armor that he wore shone metallic green with an almost unnatural glow.

"Are you alright?" he asked, holding his hand out to help her up. Unconsciously ignoring his hand, Vanilla sat up, rubbed her eyes, and looked around. She was on a hill in the middle of a vast, grassy field. There was a pleasant breeze blowing, but not a bird to be seen in the clear bluish-purple sky.

A few clusters of small trees dotted the serene landscape. In the distance was a gigantic metal wall, a stark contrast with the peaceful environment. It went on for miles and towered over everything near and far from it. Though it gave off an almost ominous vibe, it reflected the fading daylight like a mirror, making it appear as if it were made of light. Quickly averting her eyes from the blinding wall, she stood up and brushed herself off.

"So, Mr. Knight, where are we?"

"We're in the outskirts of Andalli, at the Meadow of Silence."

"Oh no! Then Zallin was right. I'm trapped inside the book!"

"Who's Zallin? And what book? This is the real world as far as I know."

"Zallin is my husband and this isn't the real world. There's no such realm as 'Andalli' in any dimension I know of. I was reading this book called *Eon's Unbeatable* and my husband said it was cursed and—"

"Whoa, hang on a minute. Eon is *my* name and I know nothing of such a book. Are you sure you're alright?"

"Yeah, I'm fine! As I was saying, the world in this book I was reading was called Andalli, so I must have ended up in this imaginary world when I fell asleep."

"Are you suggesting that this is a dream?"

"Um, I guess. I mean, it might be considering I fell asleep and woke up in a place that doesn't really exist."

"Hm. I don't mean to be argumentative ma'am, but I can assure you this isn't a dream. I've lived in this world all my life and this is the first time I've met someone like you and heard of different worlds."

"Well, I'm right—argument over."

"Hm... Anyway, we have more important matters at hand. I need to get you to safety. The day is almost done and nighttime is full of danger."

"Well I still think this is a dream because there's no way I could have been sucked into a completely made-up book world. Therefore, any danger is just in this dream."

"Ma'am, I told you that I'm not going to argue this any further. And even if it *was* a dream, would it really be wise to test that?"

"Fine! Lead the way, *Eon*."

The young knight started walking briskly down the hill. Seeing that the Crescent Horned Punisher still hesitated, he motioned for her to follow, but she shook her head. "I changed my mind. I'm going to try and wake myself up," she called back.

With a sigh of frustration, Eon jogged back up the hill, swept her off her feet, and ran with her in his arms.

"Put me down!" she exclaimed, beating her fists against the knight's armor. Each time her hands touched the mysterious green metal, it flashed turquoise. Eventually, though, she grew tired of fighting and put her head back to look at the sky. There were strange lights that dotted the sky—something she had never seen before. They twinkled against the oncoming darkness like tiny crystals in a cave.

"This *is* a beautiful place, even for a dream. What are those lights in the sky?"

"You mean the stars?"

"Stars? No, I mean those little shiny things. Are they Photose—or whatever that's called?"

"If that's what you call 'stars,' then I suppose so."

"Photose is what makes daylight."

"That sounds more like the sun."

"Whose son?"

"No, the *sun*. S-U-N. It's technically a star, too. It gives light to all the land."

"Are you...on drugs or something?"

"No. Why would you think that?"

"Because this 'sun' you speak of sounds like something a total crackhead would come up with. A star is just a shape. How could a shape give off light? Maybe it's just because this is a dream."

"I beg to differ, but you're entitled to your opinions, I suppose. We're almost to the forest, ma'am. There may be trouble before then, so be prepared."

"I wonder when I'll wake up."

"Like I said, I won't argue with you about this anymore."

Soon the dark wall of trees was in view. The dense forest was situated at the bottom of a deep valley. The tall sea of grass had faded into gravel and large rocks, and a small river lay to their right. Vanilla could hear it gurgling and splashing as it made its way into the woods. Eon stopped and set her down.

"Something's coming," he said in a harsh whisper. Before the Crescent Horned Punisher could ask what it was, a massive human-shaped machine was upon them.

Eon drew his sword as Vanilla ran for cover. The robot bellowed a synthetic war cry and began charging its many guns. The Crescent Horned Punisher watched from a ditch as the brave knight skillfully fought with the mechanical foe.

He dashed around the robot, jabbing his broadsword into it whenever the chance arose. It swirled in circles trying to maintain its guard, but the knight was too quick and eventually it succumbed to his technique and toppled over in a heap of sparks and twisted metal.

Eon had just sheathed his sword and was heading over to where Vanilla hid when a loud bang sounded from the machine. It had fired a short black rocket toward the ditch with its last bit of power. The projectile flew through the air with blinding speed, zooming past him before he could counter it.

Vanilla felt her arms go above her head out of instinct as a deafening explosion went off around her. Everything went white for a few seconds, and then she heard Eon's voice desperately calling out to her. It was faint at first, as her ears were ringing. The world was swimming in slow motion and all noise seemed to be distorted as her senses gradually returned. The brave knight was kneeling by her side, gazing steadily into her eyes.

"Thank goodness you're alive! I honestly can't imagine how you survived that without sustaining any injuries. You must have some magical power or something."

"I-I'm alive?"

"Yes, you're alive."

"OK, I admit this isn't a dream. It can't be."

"I'm just glad you seem to be OK, ma'am."

"You can call me Vanilla."

"Well, Vanilla, shall I carry you again? It may be a good idea to get off your feet after a shock like that."

"Uh, sure."

The valiant warrior scooped the fair-skinned maiden back into his arms again and continued on, now at a walking pace. As they continued their slow decent into the valley, Vanilla felt herself nodding off to sleep, trying to forget the alarming encounter with the robot. Just as she had begun to dream, Eon's voice woke her.

"Hey, I've been meaning to ask you… What are those markings on your arms? I first noticed them after that missile blew up. Are they some sort of magic power that you have?"

"What markings?"

The Crescent Horned Punisher sleepily glanced down at her arms. To her surprise, there were black spiral lines that started from her wrists and ended by her shoulders. She gasped and almost fell from the knight's arms. "What is this?!"

"You don't know, either? Well, like I said, maybe it's some sort of power you have. I'm sure it's not a curse because you'd know if it was. Let's see if my queen, Yaying, knows anything about it."

"Yaying? She's the forest's guardian, right?"

"That's correct. How did you know?"

"It was in a book that I read. I'm not going to argue, though. I believe you now, even for how much I'd rather not."

The forest was less than 10 yards away. Tall pine trees formed a barrier against the surrounding field. The underbrush was extraordinarily dense. In fact, it reminded her of a jungle. Sprawling branches tangled with adjacent trees, creating an almost unnaturally complex network of flora. Eon gently set the white-haired maiden down and together they went up to the edge of the woods.

"How will we get in? It's so thick and I just bought these sweatpants. I don't want them to rip or get muddy."

"Don't worry. I'll tell the plants to move."

Vanilla blinked. She knew that he could speak to the wildlife here, but regular plants didn't have intelligence—none that she could think of, at least. *Then again,* she told herself, *this is a fantasy world. The author of* Eon's Unbeatable *could have written anything he or she wanted.*

Facing the trees, Eon held out his hand and closed his eyes. He strained the muscles in his outstretched arm and said, "Open the forest, Temple Guards." To her surprise, the plants began to move. Groups of robust bushes and tall weeds crept aside as if they were crawling with their roots. Even the branches and vines nearby bent out of the way, creating a doorway wide enough to walk through. "After you," the knight said, stepping aside politely. She thanked him and gingerly stepped through the opening.

Inside the forest, it was cool and damp. Bugs hovered casually overhead, zooming in and out from the shelter of branches. A thick layer of spongy moss covered the ground in hills of green and ran up the bases of nearby trees. The trickling of a nearby stream could be heard, along with indescribable bird songs of unmatched beauty.

Vanilla took a deep breath and stood still for a moment to listen to the forest sounds. "This is amazing!"

"Yes, isn't it? This is the Sacred Forest, the last stronghold against the Machines."

"It's so tranquil…it's almost hard to believe that there's conflict at all."

"Well, it is now, but I fear that the Machines will lead a full-on attack sometime within the next few days. If there is a battle, I want you to stay with Yaying. That'd be the safest place."

"But wouldn't she be their main target?"

"No. The Machines can't differentiate her from the other plants and animals."

"That's weird. In the world I'm from technology is so advanced that there are strict laws in place for how smart you can program things to be. I heard that our government also controls resources for learning so it makes hacking or rogue programming more difficult."

"That seems a bit extreme, if you ask me."

"I agree, but everyone says that there's a fine line between civil protection and freedom. I think information should be free, but then again what do I know? I never even went to school."

"You seem well educated for someone who didn't go to school."

"Oh, thanks. I do wish I could have had a former education, though. I guess it's too late now."

"Never say never."

"*Right…*"

As they walked side by side through dense undergrowth, ducking under low branches and picking their way across marshy ditches, Vanilla began to feel strange. Eon's voice grew distant along with the feel of soggy moss underfoot. She was no longer walking now, but lying down. The sweet scent of the breeze was replaced by the aroma of coffee brewing, and the sound of gushing streams and whining cicadas were no longer present.

"Good morning," Zallin's voice came from beside her. She quickly sat up and smiled at him. The stern Madite's face showed a slight annoyance, but more concern. "I see you couldn't keep from reading that cursed book. This is a serious matter, Vanilla. That book could have trapped you forever! It may have only been chance that you woke up in the real world."

The naïve Crescent Horned Punisher's smile faded. "I obviously *did* wake up, so none of that really matters now!"

"Maybe so, but that doesn't change the fact that you need to get rid of it."

"Well, what if I'm immune to its effects or something?"

"I've never heard of anyone being immune to this sort of thing and I know for a fact that there's no cure or even proven preventative measures that exist for someone who gets sucked into a cursed book's world. It's almost like death in that the victim never wakes up. They just lay there 'till they die of hunger or thirst or an outward cause. I'm not willing to risk such a terrible thing happening to my wife."

"How do you know for sure? You said that there weren't any cases on record of it happening?"

"I trust my sources and I'm not going to let there *be* any cases."

Zallin snatched the book off the table and marched outside. Vanilla's heart suddenly began beating wildly and sweat beaded on her forehead. She clenched her fists tightly and gritted her teeth. An unnaturally potent anger was aroused in her as she jumped to her feet and ran after her protective husband.

He was standing a few yards from the house with his staff in one hand and *Eon's Unbeatable* in the other. A tall orange flame and thick black smoke billowed from the pages, but mysteriously no harm was being done to the mysterious book.

"Zallin, wait! Don't do anything to my book!" Vanilla cried, running up and trying to rescue the book from her husband's clutches. He skillfully kept it out of her reach, taking care not to let the enlarging fire touch her.

"Vanilla, stop! I don't want you to get burnt!"

"Then put out that fire! Please, I want my book!"

"I need to get rid of it. It's too dangerous!"

"Give it back!"

"Listen to me, Vanilla. You're acting like a child!"

Vanilla stopped. Tears filled her eyes and her lip started trembling. "Y-you..." she stammered, backing away slowly.

Zallin took a deep breath, his eyes downcast. "That was wrong of me to say. I'm sorry...I was just trying to protect you. Please try to understand."

"You... Jerk! How could you say something like that to me? I-I hate you!"

"Vanilla, why are you attacking me all of the sudden?"

"Oh, as if you didn't know! What kind of husband calls his wife 'childish?' I'm not a kid or something! Aren't men supposed to be the protectors in a family?"

"Hold on. I just said that I—"

With an irritated scream and a spiteful glare, the Crescent Horned Punisher stomped away toward the house. When she reached the front door, she slammed it with so much force that the framed family photo above fell and shattered. Cursing loudly, she stormed into the kitchen, taking care not to step on any of the dangerous fragments.

Making her way to the pantry, she retrieved a broom and

dustpan. Then she went back to the front room. The tools felt unfamiliar and cumbersome in her hands. Her first few attempts to balance them resulted in the broom falling and hitting her in the side of the head. She muttered cusswords under her breath and tightened her grip on it. At one point she almost threw it across the room. Eventually, however, she began to get the hang of it.

Though she failed to notice it, at one point Raech appeared in the hallway and was about to say something. Once the young teen sensed the tension though, she went straight back to her room as quietly as she had come.

As Vanilla stood by the entrance sweeping up the broken glass, the guilt started to build. Try as she might, it was a one-sided battle and her conscience was winning. With each tiny piece of glass that she corralled into the white plastic pan, she was filled with more shame. She glanced at her wedding ring and sighed. *What's wrong with me? It was utterly pointless for me to act like that. If the book's bad, it's bad. I'd better apologize. Zallin just revived recently and I treated him like crap... What am I doing?*

Out of the corner her eye, she saw odd, black spiral markings on her arm, the same as she had seen the night before. Hastily dropping the broom and wiping the tears from her eyes, she blinked a few times and even pinched herself. Regardless of what she did, the markings remained. Rushing into the bathroom, she locked herself inside and stood in front of the mirror.

Quickly turning the faucet on, she held her arm underneath the stream of water and rubbed it hard with her other hand. Like the tattoo on her upper thigh, it didn't come off even when she scratched at it with her fingernails. As expected, soap did nothing to it, as well. *I don't think I'm hallucinating and it's not washing off. That's one-hundred percent proof that the world in Eon's Unbeatable must be real! This is getting really weird.*

A soft knock on the door snapped Vanilla out of her pondering. Turning off the faucet and frantically drying her arms, she went to the door and opened it a crack.

Zallin was standing outside, leaning against the opposite wall. He looked down for a moment when he saw her peeking out from behind the door. "Vanilla, I—" he began, but she interrupted him.

"It's OK, Hon. I don't know what came over me back there...I'm the one who should apologize. I love you and I know you're just trying to protect me."

"W-what? Oh...I forgive you and I love you, too. I wanted to tell you that I wasn't able to get rid of the book. It must have some sort of spell on it to guard it from most forms of magic and physical force. That really troubles me, so I contacted a friend of mine who works at the Spiritan Research and Development Branch. He specialized in enchanted objects years ago and said that he'll take a look at it tomorrow. So until then, I'm going to keep this locked up. I think there may be more to this than meets the eye."

"That's fine."

"I'm glad you understand. By the way, what are those markings on your arms? It's not another tattoo, is it?"

"I've been trying to figure that out myself, actually. It's definitely not a tattoo. Trust me. Getting something this big inked anywhere would take hours and it's only been a few minutes since I came in. I only have one tattoo and you know where *that one* is."

Zallin blushed and cleared his throat. "I see. It looks very much like something I once read about. Over the course of history there have been a number of individuals who have had strange markings appear on their skin, mainly their arms. They said it—well, I don't exactly remember, so never mind. I don't want to assume anything," the wise

Madite's voice trailed off as he reconsidered what he was about to say.

"I see," she said, eyeing him suspiciously. "So, do you think it's something we should look into? I mean, I'm sure you must at least remember if it's bad or good."

"Well," Zallin began cautiously, "in my personal opinion, no. Unless you behave in an unusual way when the mark appears, I don't think it's anything to fret over. If it were a curse of some sort, the appearance of markings on your skin would always be accompanied by strange behavior or some other symptom. I *did* notice that you were unusually upset about the book a while ago, but no markings were on your arms then. The extreme anger thing is a bit more disquieting than the markings."

"I really don't know what came over me. Again, I'm really sorry. I didn't mean anything I said back there. I love you."

"It's alright. Perhaps the book has some sort of unusual psychological influence on people who read it. Either way, I love you too, and that will never change. I'm sorry for calling you 'childish.'"

Vanilla opened the door all the way and stepped into the hallway. Tears had formed in her eyes again and were trickling down her fair cheeks. Zallin took her in his arms and they stood embracing for a long time. Then she had a thought.

"Where's Raech? I haven't seen her yet today."

"She's in her room resting."

"Is she doing OK? Has she been resting a lot since Crescent brought her back?"

He nodded and spoke in a hushed tone. "I think she's alright. Her muscles seem to have been stuck in a fight or flight response for a while, so I think rest is the best thing for her right now and she knows that."

"I'm still worried with what happened to her..."

"I've been keeping a close eye on her. I haven't seen anything out of the ordinary. I really don't think she remembers being taken, which is probably for the better."

"That's true..."

Halfway through a light sigh, he winced. To most it would have been barely noticeable, but Vanilla could have seen it from a mile away. "Hon, are you OK?"

"Yes, I'm fine. Don't worry."

Her eyes searched his face. "It's your right arm, isn't it?"

For a split second, his eyebrows raised a mere millimeter. "There may have been some foreign contaminant on the muscle tissue as it was reconstructing. I just have to let it continue to heal naturally, I guess."

"Can't you use magic?"

"I'm trying to be careful not to. The temporary regeneration that a Faith Suicide gives a Madite is incredibly strenuous on the body. I need to rely on natural healing for a while until I've fully recovered."

"Oh... Are you sure you're alright?"

He smiled. "Yes, thank you."

There was a short pause.

Vanilla glanced around. "Um, what time is it?"

"It's a little after Noon."

"Has Raech eaten anything?"

"Yes. I cooked the rest of the pork that was in the freezer for her."

"Is there any left?"

"Unfortunately, there isn't. Can I make you eggs and toast? I could do pancakes, too, if you'd rather have those. Just name something and I'll gladly make it for you."

"That's OK. I think I'm just going to have a bowl of cereal. Thanks for the offer, though."

"Of course."

She made her way into the kitchen and prepared her meal. While she sat at the table eating, she heard the rumbling of thunder outside, followed by the pitter-patter of slimy rain against the roof. It was soothing, she thought, to hear storms outside. The pale light that shone from the clouded sky cast soft shadows on the dark hardwood floor, flickering every now and then when lightning flashed.

Raech entered the kitchen a few minutes later and gave a cautious glance at her.

"Hey, Sweetie. Did you have a good nap?"

"I think so."

"Are you hungry?"

Raech shook her head. "Um, is everything OK?"

There was a sinking feeling in Vanilla's chest. "Uh, y-yeah. Why do you ask?"

The polite teen shifted in place. "I thought I heard you yelling. I wasn't trying to eavesdrop."

Vanilla set her spoon in the empty bowl of cereal with a clank. "Oh, that was... Well, it's nothing to be concerned about, OK?"

The girl hesitated. "OK."

"Hey, would you like to go to 1st City Realm with me? I need to get out of the house and get some fresh air."

She nodded. "When are you going?"

"Whenever you're ready."

"OK. I'll go get my shoes on."

"I'll meet you by the door."

Leaving her dishes at the table, Vanilla got up and went to her room. Zallin was sitting at his desk engrossed in a heavy book when she entered. He appeared to be deep in thought. She knocked on the doorframe softly. He looked up.

"Hey, Raech and I are going to go to 1ˢᵗ City Realm and walk around for a bit."

He nodded. "Alright. Thank you for letting me know."

Before she was out of the room, he spoke again. "Vanilla?"

"Yeah?"

"I love you."

"I love you, too."

Raech was patiently waiting in the front room. Vanilla smiled at her and stooped over to retrieve her shoes.

"Thank you for letting me come with you, Mother," Raech said.

"Yeah, sure thing," Vanilla replied distractedly, clumsily double-knotting her shoelaces.

"Where will we go?"

"I haven't really decided. I was thinking we could just meander."

"I like that word."

"'Meander?'"

"Yes. It's very laid-back and calm. It reminds me of walking in a park or an art gallery."

"Hm. I guess so. OK, I'm ready."

Once they had stepped outside onto the familiar purple, slimy ground, Vanilla held her daughter's hand and used her watch to teleport to 1ˢᵗ City Realm.

They arrived on a vast, raised concrete platform in the middle of the city. There were stairs on all four sides leading down to the sidewalk. Newly painted railings lined the edges along with benches that looked as though they had never been used.

"Wow, this must be a new warp plateau," Vanilla said, examining her surroundings.

"Was it not here last time you were in this area?" Raech asked.

"I don't think so. I thought they had finished putting all of them in last year. I know they haven't put all the T-directors in yet. Or at least they haven't activated all of them."

"When did they start?"

"Oh, gee. Let me think...it would have probably been around the time you were born. I know the project has been going on for *at least* thirteen years."

"That's a long time."

"I guess. I mean, from the sounds of it their aim is to put these platforms in every mile. I remember the days when you could just teleport right outside where you wanted to go. Er, well kind of. I guess you can still do that in other realms."

"Oh. Where should we go?"

"I'll let you decide."

"OK. Um... How about north?"

"Alright. Let me just get my phone. I think I have a compass app."

"That sign says north is that way."

"Huh?"

Vanilla looked in the direction her daughter was pointing. Sure enough, there was a sign by one of the staircases that read, "North."

"Oh, wow. I didn't even notice that. You're so observant."

Raech smiled.

Together they descended the long flight of stairs and stepped onto the warm sidewalk. They passed a variety of shops as they meandered about. At one point they stopped by a fountain to rest. Vanilla saw a few coins and reached in to grab them. Raech gave a nervous glance around as she did so.

"Um, is it really OK to take coins from there? They belonged to somebody, didn't they?"

Vanilla stopped. "Oh, I guess you have a point. Actually, when I first moved to Glunke, I took some coins out of a fountain like this so I could buy clothes and groceries. My situation was a bit different then than it is now, of course..."

She hesitantly tossed them back in. When the ripples died down, she saw her reflection. *Have I really changed since then?* she thought with a slight frown. As she was pondering, Raech moved closer. Her face was reflected now, as well. *Yes, I have changed—a lot.*

"Mother, what are you thinking about?"

"Just life. Should we keep walking?"

The teen nodded. "If you're not too tired."

Vanilla laughed. "Oh, come on. I'm not *that* old. Thirty-two is still a young adult for my kind."

Raech blushed. "I-I didn't mean it like that!" she said quickly. "You're not old at all!"

"It's alright, Sweetie. I'm just teasing you."

"Oh...I see."

"Come on. Let's explore some more."

They ventured deeper into the city, taking in the sights. As they passed a humble little music store on the corner, something caught the Crescent Horned Punisher's eye. There was a poster in the window of a blue-haired Grenzel Blind Demon holding a V-shaped guitar. "New Signature Items in Stock!" was printed in bold red letters over the top. The Crescent Horned Punisher closed her eyes for a moment and sighed.

"Mother?" Raech said.

"Yes, Sweetie?"

"If it wouldn't be too much trouble, could we go to that music store?"

"Er…well, y-yeah, sure."

"It's OK if you don't want to. Never mind."

"…I guess I'm a little worried someone will recognize me in there."

"That's understandable."

"Hey, I have an idea. Let's go get some ice cream."

"Oh, OK!"

"I think there's a place around here somewhere. Let's see…if I remember correctly, it's like a block or two from here. I've only been to it once and that was years ago."

Soon they had found the little ice cream shop. It was a small building tucked away in one of the less busy parts of the city. Many of the stores around it were empty and had old "For Lease" signs posted in the window. They made their way inside and up to the counter.

"What are you going to get?" asked Raech.

Vanilla thought for a moment. "I'll probably get a scoop of triple chocolate. How about you?"

"I don't know. Does the cookie dough one have raw cookie dough in it?"

"Yeah, but I don't think there's raw egg, or anything. They probably make it without that."

"Are you sure?"

"I think so. Would you like me to ask?"

"No, thanks. I think I'll get cookies and cream instead."

"OK."

Vanilla stepped forward to greet the server. "I'll get a scoop of triple chocolate in a waffle cone and she'll have cookies and cream."

"One scoop, or two?" the server asked, looking at the girl.

"One, please," Raech replied politely.

"Alright. That'll be 3 Gold Diamonds."

Vanilla retrieved three small, gold-colored coins from her pocket and handed them to the employee. He tossed them in the cash register and took two cones from a rack. After scooping one generous serving of each into the cones, he handed them to the girls and smiled. "There you are. Have a nice day."

Raech was first to thank him. Vanilla followed suit.

"So," Vanilla said, grabbing a few napkins, "do you want to sit outside?"

"Oh, sure."

The two of them went outside and sat down at a table that had an umbrella over it. Vanilla handed one of the napkins to her daughter and leaned back. "It sure is hot, isn't it?" she said.

Raech nodded. "I don't mind it."

"I thought you liked the cold."

"Sometimes I like going to warm places."

"I guess I'm the same way. It can get really gloomy on Glunke."

As they were sitting, they saw two teenagers go by on skateboards. One of them was a Crescent Horned Punisher dressed in a tube top and short denim shorts. She had tattoos on her arms and a shiny bellybutton piercing. The other was a Grenzel Blind Demon with red hair. He wore baggy jeans and a black leather jacket that had the sleeves torn off.

Vanilla had a flashback as she watched them. She was 14 years old, wandering the ghetto of 3rd South City. She was sucking on an ice cream treat and twirling a strand of her long white hair.

The air was warm and muggy, a typical summer in the realm. Heat radiated off the pavement like a stovetop. She could feel it all the way up to her waist, which was left uncovered by her loose-fitting crop top. Her shorts—if they were truly long enough to have been considered such—

did little to shield her fair skin, as well.

She was in a back alley behind a vacant machine shop. There were rusted metal scraps piled along with ripped garbage bags and miscellaneous waste. A faded "No Trespassing" sign had been fixed to one of the twisted barbed wire fences that rested up against the corrugated siding of the warehouse. The buildings on both sides were practically murals of graffiti.

Suddenly, a group of neighborhood delinquents jumped out from behind a dumpster. The two boys were dressed like the typical inhabitants of the area: baggy jeans; wrinkled, sleeveless shirts; and shoes with more holes in them than the victim of machinegun fire. There was a girl with them, as well, who dressed similarly; albeit with less covering her upper half.

"Hand it over, dwil," the tallest of the boys said.

Vanilla scowled at them. "Fuck off, shithead. I stole this fair and square."

The boy's face turned red. "Well it belongs to me now, you little bitch!"

"Go back to your dumpster, hobo! It's *my* ice cream!"

"Fuck you!"

"You wish you could. Looks like your girlfriend doesn't have much to offer a man."

"You're gonna pay for that!"

The boy took out a switchblade. Vanilla threw the treat in his face and turned around to run. The shorter of the boys caught up with her and grabbed her hair. She kicked him in the groin violently and he let go, but the other two had reached her and held her down.

"I'm gonna cut you up!" the towering bully bellowed.

Before he had a chance to do so, there was a flash of white

165

and blue. Zero had run up and punched him in the jaw. He staggered backwards, reeling from the Grenzel Blind Demon's powerful blow.

"Get your damn hands off my girlfriend!" the blue-haired hero roared.

The knife-wielding miscreant spouted as many hateful cusswords as he could before rushing at his opponent. Zero quickly picked up a pipe that had been lying on the ground and swung it at him. It connected with his hand and broke his wrist instantly.

Dropping the blade, he held his hand and screamed in pain. Zero gave him no time to recover. He leaped onto the boy and pummeled him with his fists. By now the delinquent's comrades had fled in fear, leaving him to his well-deserved fate.

"Kick his ass!" Vanilla cheered.

Soon the adolescent was beaten to a bloody pulp and thoroughly stripped of his pride—and his pants. Zero finally let up and wiped the blood off his hands with his jeans. "And *never* touch her again, motherfucker!" he shouted as the broken-wristed bully scampered away like a dog with its tail between its legs.

When the boy was at a safe distance, he turned back and yelled, "I'll freaking kill you!" in a tear-choked voice.

Zero flipped him off and replied, "Come over here and say it to my face! I dare you!" Then he looked over at Vanilla. "You OK? Did they hurt you?"

"I'm fine. What an asshole! He made me lose my ice cream."

"Let's go get another one, then."

She shrugged. "I don't feel like it now."

"Alright." He gave her a hug. "I won't let them get you, Babe."

The bittersweet flashback faded, leaving her to stare distantly at the empty street.

"Mother, is everything OK?" Raech asked.

"Huh? Oh…yeah. I'm fine. How is your ice cream?"

"It's delicious!"

"That's good."

"How is yours?"

"Great. Oh, I guess it's almost melted, though…"

"What were you looking at?"

"Oh, nothing. I was just spacing out. You're done already?"

"Yeah."

"Don't you get brain freeze from eating it that fast?"

"Did I eat it fast?"

"Oh, maybe not. I guess I wasn't really paying attention. It just seemed like it. Maybe it's because I was distracted. Should we head home? It's almost suppertime."

"Oh, no!"

"What?"

"I had dessert before supper."

"That's fine. It's not like you're the type of kid who won't eat healthy food or something."

"But Dad says it's bad to have dessert before supper because it can form unhealthy habits."

"Well if he complains I'll tell him I said it was OK."

"Are you sure?"

"Yeah, of course. I'm the one who suggested we get ice cream, remember?"

"Alright. Thanks for spending time with me today, Mom. I had lots of fun."

"I did, too! I'm glad we could hang out. You spend so much time in your room reading. I think it would be good if you spent a little more time outside with friends."

"I guess you're right. I'll try."

"You're a good kid, Raech."

"Thanks, Mom."

"I really mean it." After preparing her watch to teleport, she hesitated for a moment. *Does she really not remember anything about getting kidnapped? I could ask her again, but maybe it's not a good idea to bring that up,* she thought, looking at the girl's pure, innocent smile.

Vanilla held out her hand. Raech took it, and together they warped back to Glunke.

Zallin was in the front room when they entered the house.

"Welcome back. Did you have a good walk?" he asked.

"We did!" Raech replied.

"Where did you go?"

"1st West City—just around the edge of a residential area," Vanilla replied.

"That sounds nice."

"Hey, Hon?"

"Yes?"

"I think I'm going to take a bath and get ready for bed."

"Oh, are you feeling OK?"

"I'm just really tired for some reason."

He looked at her for a second. "I see. Would you still like some supper?"

"Maybe."

"I could bring it to you."

"While I'm in the tub?"

"I suppose. I was thinking after you got out, though; if you're going to bed, you probably won't want to eat right before you lay down."

"Yeah. Just bring me something small that I can snack on while I soak in the tub."

"Alright."

Once she had taken off her shoes, she headed straight for the master bedroom to get a change of clean clothes.

A little over an hour later, Vanilla had finished bathing and climbed into bed. Sleep was more fickle than usual. Her dreams were strange and filled with ominous trees that came to life. She tossed and turned, eventually waking up after her husband had already gone to bed.

An eerie feeling came over her as she lay beneath her covers trying to calm her mind. It was as though something was beckoning her to get up and go into the living room. Fear crept over her as she imagined dark things roaming about the house. Every sound felt odd and unnatural.

She reached out to place her hand on Zallin's shoulder and shake him awake, but something seemed to prevent her from doing so. Finally, she gathered the courage to get out of bed. As silently as she could, she put on her purple robe and fuzzy blue slippers and tiptoed out into the hallway.

The house was still and nearly pitch-black. Gingerly, she felt her way around until she came to the living room. She could almost hear her heart pounding in her chest and groped for the light switch. At last her fingers found it and she hastily flicked it on. The room lit up and she squinted in pain as her eyes adjusted.

At first, it appeared as though things were exactly as they had been only hours before. The furniture was still in the same place, the books on the bookshelf were untouched and Zallin's laptop was still plugged into a wall outlet near the couch. *Well, if there was something or someone here, it wasn't a robber. I guess Zallin would have woken up if someone had come into our house, anyway.* As she turned to leave, however, something caught

169

her eye.

On the far left couch cushion sat an old, leather-bound book with an eye-shaped stamp on it. Eon's Unbeatable! *I thought Zallin locked it up,* she gasped. Nervously glancing around, she sat down on the couch and reached for the cursed book. As her fingers touched its rugged cover, the spiral markings on her arm vanished and a sense of greed came over her. She found herself angry at Zallin again for trying to keep the book from her. "He doesn't understand," she muttered as she opened to the page she had left off and began to read.

The fear of being caught had left her and soon she had finally read the rest of the first chapter and was nodding off to sleep. Before she had shut her eyes, the Crescent Horned Punisher saw a glimpse of the black marks reappearing on her arms, but she hadn't the strength to move anymore. Her will to stave off tiredness was gone and sleep had won.

Again she woke with a start, but this time her surroundings were hard to make out. Odd shapes moved about in front of her, growing brighter and more colorful with each second. It gave the appearance that she was looking through a pair of binoculars while adjusting the clarity. Eventually she could make out the figure of a young knight clad in green and blue armor walking beside her. She was back in the forest of Andalli, right where she had been before Zallin had awoken her.

"...And wherever Yaying is, the forest grows healthy and strong. I'm not boring you, am I, Vanilla?"

"Oh—what? No! Not at all!"

"OK, good. You looked like you were dozing off on your feet there for a moment. Are you sure you're alright?"

"Yeah. Something really weird just happened though."

"What's that?"

"It's going to be hard to explain, but I think I fell asleep in this world, and then woke up in my world. I went through another day there and when I fell asleep again I woke up here. I don't know if that makes any sense to you, but that's the best I can describe it."

"Interesting. Are you sure it wasn't a vision?"

"I'm sure. I think I'd know if it was. It *is* strange that I'm still in my old clothes though."

"Well, I won't argue with you then."

"So, how much farther do we have to walk?"

"We're almost there, actually."

"Oh."

At last they reached a clearing in which the stream had made a large, crystal clear pond. Tall, sturdy reeds stuck out near the shore, providing perches for various birds and insects. Standing in the center of the pond was a dome made from a circle of young trees that had been bent inward and bound with flowering vines. Vanilla caught a waft of an enchantingly sweet fragrance that she assumed came from the flowers.

"Well, here we are! Yaying is quite talented at constructing things like this, if I haven't told you already," Eon said proudly.

As she followed Eon across a narrow bridge of land, Vanilla felt her feet sinking into soggy patches of moss and mud. She anxiously glanced down at her wide skateboarding shoes, which were now wet and covered with grass and mud. "I just bought these last week," she moaned.

Eon was staring straight ahead and seemed not to notice her distress. "Vanilla, I'm going to open the door here, so stay back."

"Alright. It's not like I'm *tired* of standing in this damp, flooding mess or anything!"

"I know it's not what you're used to, but this is the only way to get to the queen. She can hear you as long as you're in the forest, I might add."

"Oops. I'm sorry Yaying, wherever you are."

Eon held his hands in front of him and closed his eyes to focus. The Crescent Horned Punisher waited quietly, watching the trees closely for any sign of movement, but even the birds and insects seemed to have stilled. Sweat was beading on the young knight's forehead and he knit his brow as if he was pushing his mind to its limits.

Eventually she began to feel skeptical and was about to speak when a loud creaking and groaning interrupted her. The dome of trees shook, casting some of their leaves and small twigs to the ground, and then bowed low in the opposite direction to reveal a well with short stone walls and a ladder going down into it.

"OK," he panted, opening his eyes and stretching, "after you, milady."

She hesitated, recalling the time she had descended the dark passage that was once beneath her house. She pictured herself walking down a cold stairway and into the suffocating darkness of an underground hallway.

"I-I think you should go first. After all, you know Yaying."

"Are you sure? I was always taught 'ladies first.'"

"No, no, you first."

"As you wish."

Eon casually strode over to the well and mounted the old wooden ladder. "One thing before I forget—try to be as quiet as possible while you're in this well. The creatures here are sensitive to noise and will appreciate us being extra careful not to disturb them," he called out to her before climbing down with surprising stealth. Once the brave knight was out of view, the Crescent Horned Punisher shuddered and tried not to think of what kind of creatures would live in dark, quiet wells.

Vanilla stood for a moment arguing with herself, struggling to muster up enough courage to follow her guide. Suddenly, the trees began slowly moving back into place, rustling and creaking as if they were talking to one another. Panicking, she dashed between them and lost her balance at the edge of the well's stout, rocky walls. She let out a frightful cry and was instantly plunged into deep darkness.

CHAPTER 8

-Crossover-

"Vanilla, are you awake?" Zallin's stern voice came from beside her. Sitting up with a jolt and opening her eyes, Vanilla was met face-to-face with the yellow eyes on her husband's hat. They blinked and stared firmly back at her. "You were reading the book again, I see."

"Zallin, I—"

"How did you get ahold of it? I locked it up in the safe in the basement."

"It was here on the couch when I got up last night!"

"That's impossible. An inanimate object can't break out of a safe that was sealed with strong spells, open a locked door, and appear in front of you. Did you have someone help you?"

"No! If I had anyone over last night you would have heard me let them in. Why are you always blaming me? It wasn't my fault this time, I promise."

"I assume that you willingly read the book, though. Your soul shows no signs of mind control, so it would be wrong to say that you had no part in it. I'm concerned about you, Vanilla, and Raech too. I don't want her to be at risk, either. As we discussed yesterday, I'm taking the book to my friend today after lunch. I need to put an end to this."

"No, don't!"

"Wait a minute. You gave your consent to this yesterday."

"I didn't mean it!"

"Well you certainly fooled me then. This isn't like you. It's kind of reminding me of your outburst yesterday."

"I don't care! Let me keep the freaking book! I found it and I want to read it. You can have it when I'm done."

Zallin's gaze intensified, making Vanilla cower back into the couch. As she glared back at him to the best of her ability, she noticed the strange markings forming on her arms again. The tension in her muscles eased and her anger quickly changed into guilt.

"Wait, aren't those the markings you showed me yesterday?" Zallin said, taken aback slightly.

Vanilla nodded. "Yeah. Come to think of it, they appeared at a moment like this, too—after I had been so mad about the book."

"Are…you still mad?"

"No, oddly enough. Again, I'm really sorry…"

"That's alright. I think this proves that your anger must be caused by the book. I personally don't know everything about cursed books— only enough to know why to steer clear of them. I'll mention this when I take it to Baine."

"Baine Dalton?"

"Yes."

"But I thought you told me he worked for the weapons division. They don't do anything with magical items unless it's for military use, do they?"

"He works in multiple places."

"Oh, I see."

"I might let him hold onto the book, if he has a place to keep it secured. If the book is here again tonight, it will prove that it has some sort of power to keep itself within reach of its reader. Please wake me up if you end up not being able to sleep or get up in the middle of the night. I want to make sure you're not tempted if it reappears. Can you do that?"

"Sure…"

"Good."

They hugged and Vanilla relinquished the book again. Her eyes followed it as her husband took it and moved to the door. He stopped and glanced back at her.

"Don't worry, I'm sure Baine can figure this out. By the way, I recall what those markings were in the book that I read."

"Really? What were they?"

"They're a form of protection called 'Absolute Purity.' It's incredibly rare and powerful. However, it's not flawless. It will only protect you from some things and can be bypassed by various powers."

"You knew, didn't you?"

"What do you mean?"

"You never really forgot about the marks, did you?"

"Well I… No. I was afraid that you might continue to read the book, thinking that your Absolute Purity would protect you."

"And it did, didn't it?"

"So far yes, but it would be unwise to push your luck with a thing like this. Trust me. I guess knowing or not you still read the book, though."

"You said it protects from some things and so far it's protected me from the book. Isn't that proof enough?"

"No. 'Some things' meaning its power is erratic. You could say that you've gotten lucky two times."

"Three. A robot fired missiles at me and—"

"What!? When? Where?"

"While I was in the book's little world for the first time."

"Vanilla, you could have been killed! I'm taking this to Baine right now."

"Jeez."

"Jeez what? I won't let my wife walk into danger—willing or not! The job of a husband is to protect and support his family. I'm trying to do exactly that. I see the Mark of Purity is fading now and I don't want to get into another fight about this. I'll be home a bit later."

The protective Madite hurriedly slipped his shoes on and left, accidentally slamming the door behind him. Flustered, Vanilla got up and stormed into her bedroom. "He thinks he can just snatch something from a lady like that. What an idiot! I can't believe him!" she vented while gathering a clean change of clothes from her dresser. "'It's for my protection,' he says. Ha! It's just another way for him to control me; not letting me read what I want. I'm still alive, aren't I? Jerk."

As Vanilla was rinsing off in the shower, she heard a strange melody. It sounded like a massive pipe organ being played somewhere far away. She held still and strained her ears to see if she could make out the tune, thinking that it was Raech's portable music player. "That's not 'Alleyway' by *It Granted Life*, is it? No, I don't recognize it. It doesn't sound like something Raech would listen to. It's far too avant-garde for her," she mused.

Suddenly the drops of water in the shower stopped in midair. Startled, Vanilla jumped back, slipped on the wet floor, and fell. When she had recovered from shock, she realized that the splash she had made had frozen, too.

"Oh my gosh! Is the house under attack? Raech! Raech, where are you?" she exclaimed. She stood up and cautiously opened the steam-covered door. To her surprise, the water her body touched flowed normally, but became still when it was no longer making contact. Heart racing, she glanced at the clock. It, too, had stopped. She put her hand on it, and it began to move again. "Something must have stopped time! I didn't think that was possible!"

After hurriedly getting dressed, Vanilla crept through the house, listening for any sign of an intruder. All that she could hear was the distant droning of an organ, now playing a bit slower and clearer.

When she arrived at Raech's bedroom door, she flung it open expecting to find her daughter huddled up in the closet or under the bed. Vanilla let out a little scream as she saw that the young girl was frozen in time, as well. She was sitting upright at her desk in the middle of writing a poem. Before the Crescent Horned Punisher could do anything, the organ music stopped and was replaced by the sound of thousands of voices all talking at once in a foreign language.

"Wait a minute! I've heard this somewhere before," Vanilla whispered to herself. The noise grew louder as she stood and listened. Finally, a single voice stood out among the rest.

"I see you have come a long way since our last encounter," it said. Vanilla whirled around. She was in a cathedral-like building, standing at the foot of a short flight of carpeted stairs. Beautiful rays of colored light streamed in through stained-glass windows, casting mysterious pictures upon the old wooden floorboards. There were empty pews on either side of the room, but it felt as though many people were present. At the front of the room, standing next to a huge pipe organ, was a tall, golden-haired man with a strange mask. The mask had one eyehole that was merely a small slit and three blue lines on the opposing side near the base. He wore a robe of white and gold, much like Sheneephiist priests that Vanilla had read about in one of Raech's history books. He stepped forward and extended his hand, which was completely covered by his long sleeves.

"Greetings, Vanilla Lamberschvak. The last time I spoke to you it was only one word—or perhaps everything. Now we finally have the chance to converse normally. I am Malachi, one of the Seven Chosen."

"So that was you who I saw here so many years ago?"

"Yes, it was I. I apologize for the unusual transition you experienced. At times it is difficult to bring people here from other realms. Do you know why I summoned you?"

"I was just about to ask you that."

"It's about that book, *Eon's Unbeatable*. You were never supposed to come across that, but now that you did your fate has changed once again—or it should have at least, but I intervened on your behalf."

"I don't understand. Have you been watching over me all these years?"

"Your whole life."

"Then why did you let Billud...?"

"My job is not to make the lives of others perfect. It was by my own will that I decided to help you. I could have let you die in the Underworld, but I provided a way for you to escape, did I not?"

At this Vanilla was speechless. Malachi noiselessly sat down on the bench in front of the organ and waited as the Crescent Horned Punisher struggled to think of words to say. Finally, head down in shame, she apologized.

"...I'm sorry. If it's true that you've been guarding me this whole time, then I've been extremely ungrateful. I don't even deserve your kindness."

"You are forgiven. You certainly have grown wise since we last met."

"OK, but... Why me?"

"I have my reasons, but know that I will not prevent everything bad from happening. After all, I am not omnipresent and our struggles in this life are often a good opportunity to grow. Now let us discuss why you are here. Your Mark of Purity is starting to weaken from excessive use. If it fails while you are in Andalli, you will be trapped there for eternity. You need to stop reading the book. Do I make myself clear?"

"But I can't. It just somehow shows up and it's just too tempting.

Can't you just destroy the book?"

"I have my reasons for not doing so. Your husband asked you to let him know at once if the book reappears, did he not?"

"How did you know that?"

"I know many things."

"Obviously. But you can't know everything."

"Perhaps, but I know every step that you have taken and every thought that has passed through your mind."

Upon hearing this, Vanilla's face turned bright pink. She took a step back and inspected her shoes to avoid eye contact. Malachi remained in his place, unmoving.

"You need not be embarrassed, Vanilla. What has passed has passed. I am going to send you back now. Heed my warning about *Eon's Unbeatable*. Your Absolute Purity may break soon if it does not have a chance to recover."

Vanilla looked up and realized that she was back in her daughter's room, standing next to the desk. Time began flowing again and the sound of the organ could no longer be heard.

Startled, Raech dropped her pen and stood up. "Oh, Mother! Please don't scare me like that!"

"I'm sorry, Sweetie. Something really weird just happened."

"What was it?"

"It'd be kind of hard to explain… Never mind. I'll be in the living room if you need me."

"Is everything alright?"

"Y-yeah… Don't worry about it."

She hurried out of the room.

Out in the hallway, she leaned up against the wall and closed her eyes. *That was so creepy!* she thought. *It was like time stopped! And how did he teleport me to that place?*

Slowly, she opened her eyes and stared at her arms. As they were, it would have been impossible to guess the markings had ever appeared. *...And why was I given this power? I can't learn to use magic... It doesn't make sense. "Mark of Purity?" You'd think I'd be the last one to get something like that... Maybe I need to get out again.*

Rushing to the front door, she quickly put her shoes on and transported to 3rd City Realm.

Upon her arrival on one of the many warp plateaus, she was met with the searing heat of midsummer. She squinted in the bright light that shone down from the sky. "It's definitely summer," she said to herself.

Descending one of the four staircases, she made her way to a small park that the warp plateau was overlooking. Deciduous trees dotted the grassy plot of land, becoming denser around a manmade pond. There were tall reeds and cattails lining the perimeter, and frogs could be heard within the water. She sat down on a bench in the shade to think.

What if I can't stop reading the book? What if my soul gets sucked into the story? Wait...if my soul was in the story, why didn't Zallin think I was dead? I guess he knew about the book and he's an experienced healer... This is all so confusing! I just wish my life could be normal!

While she was lost in thought, a family of ducks waddled past her. She only noticed them when one began quacking.

I have a family now. I have to work this out somehow. There was a sinking feeling in her chest and she watched the benign animals preen themselves.

Soon the Photose began to set. The layer of fading light gradually made its way back into the ground. It was like a luminous, ghostly blanket that hung over all the land, descending silently into the depths. Dusk had come. Getting out her watch, she teleported home.

Zallin was in the front room reading when Vanilla entered the house. He looked up at her and frowned. "Where were you? I tried calling you."

"Oh, I'm sorry. I accidentally left my phone here, I think. I was in a park."

"You were gone for hours."

"I just needed some time to think."

"I see."

"Are you going to stay up?"

"Yes. It's only six-thirty."

"Oh, that's right. I forgot about the time difference. I've had a lot on my mind."

"So have I."

"Did you already make supper?"

"I did."

"What did you make?"

"Lasagna. There's some left in a pan on the stovetop."

"OK."

Retreating into the kitchen, she took a plate from the cupboard and proceeded to heap a pile of the cheesy meal onto it. It was still warm enough to not need reheating, so she sat down and began to eat.

When she had finished, she went into her bedroom and sat on the edge of the bed. Tears were forming in her eyes and her body felt heavy. She took a shaky breath and lay down, pulling the covers over herself. Her world began to fade to black.

When she awoke, night had arrived, bringing with it a heavy rain. Vanilla lay in bed with her back to her husband, imagining the consequences of her rare power giving way to the cursed book. Suddenly she felt the familiar urge to leave the room. Panicking, she reached over to wake Zallin, but hesitated. The longing to revisit the forested world of Andalli was taking over her will. She began sweating and shaking as vivid green landscapes with flowing rivers and golden light popped into her mind. It was too much for the Crescent Horned Punisher and soon she gave in and went to the living room and found the book in the same place. She sat down and read until she had fallen asleep.

Seemingly moments later, the Crescent Horned Punisher awoke in Eon's muscular arms. They were at the bottom of the well with pale moonlight streaming in overhead. All around them were damp, moss-covered rocks and large mushrooms that gave off a soft, blue glow. A stream of crystal clear water ran down a long, dimly lit tunnel that stood before the two adventurers.

"Vanilla, are you alright?" Eon whispered, nervously glancing around. The fair maiden opened her mouth to speak, but was interrupted by a sinister hissing from the shadows. Above them, the opening of the well was covered and the light from the fungus disappeared, plunging everything into complete darkness.

The hissing grew steadily louder until it was too much to bear. Out of fear and pain, Vanilla wrapped her hands tightly around her horns and let out a piercing scream. In response, the fungus flickered on and off like a strobe light, giving the two heroes momentary glimpses of the passageway.

For a split second they saw a shadowy, skeletal figure hanging upside-down on the ceiling, looking at them through livid white eyes. The next second it was gone, as well as the hissing.

The fair maiden's cry reverberated in the passage, echoing back and forth as if mocking her for being afraid. As soon as it had faded away, the moonlight reentered, and the mushrooms steadily radiated their eerie light. The tunnel was silent once again.

Eon took a deep breath as quietly as he could, and carried the still petrified Crescent Horned Punisher down the rocky corridor. She dared not make a sound, much less move about. The haunting image of the dark creature was still vividly ingrained into her mind, its boney hands poised to strike and its malicious, threatening gaze watching her from the darkness. She could feel his pulse still frantically running through his strong arms. *Even a brave knight like him,* she thought, *can still be afraid of monsters in the dark.*

Finally, the long hallway opened up into an enormous stone shaft. Holes big enough to walk through dotted the walls, providing what appeared to be individual living quarters. Aquatic plants grew out from a clean lake in the center, providing a makeshift walkway around the perimeter. Reeds and mossy islands were dotted here and there across the water. Vines as big as tree trunks climbed up to the highest point ceiling, housing various small animals. To Vanilla's surprise, the moonlight streamed in from large holes in the roof of foliage. It was so breathtaking that she had already forgotten why she was afraid by the time Eon had set her on her feet.

"What is this place?"

"It's the Heart of the Forest, Yaying's temple."

"It looks like there's an opening up there. Couldn't we have just walked to it above ground and then climbed down one of those vines?"

"No. It's surrounded by a huge castle on an island in the middle of a lake. Even if we were to get there, it would be almost impossible to reach the hole. Also, I've only been on the island outside the castle once, so I wouldn't know my way around very well."

"I see. What in the world was that thing back in the tunnel?"

"Yaying calls them 'Skull Carvers.' She says that they're monsters who've come from a distant land and act as guards for the temple."

"That's still really creepy."

"Yes, I know. I trust that she knows what she's doing, though."

"Speaking of Yaying, where is she? We don't have more walking to do, do we?"

"I am here, child," a soothing voice said from among the reeds. Vanilla turned and saw a woman made from wood wading in the water. Her eyes were as blue as the ocean and her smile as sweet as honey. She wore clothes made from leaves and a crown of white flowers on her head. A dense network of branches grew from her back, tethering her to the lakebed.

"Your Majesty," Eon said, bowing low, "this is Vanilla. She claims to be from a world outside our own, and has been transported here by means of a 'cursed book.' I have brought her here for safety and so that she may seek your wisdom." Vanilla gave a clumsy, delayed bow and began to explain, but the kindly queen held up one hand.

"There is no need for an explanation of what world you come from, young one. All who are of good intentions are welcome in my kingdom. I am curious, however, to know of what species you are."

"I'm a Punisher, Your Majesty. Er, a Crescent Horned Punisher, to be precise."

"A Crescent Horned Punisher? I've never heard of such a being before. Tell me, child, for what do you seek my knowledge?"

"Well, my question was actually answered before I got here. It's kind of complicated, but I ended up going back to my world briefly. When I came back here it was as if I had never left. Time must have paused for me or something. I hope that makes sense. I myself am really baffled by the whole thing, to be honest."

"I see. There seems to be a greater power at work, one outside of Andalli."

185

"I guess. Really though, I don't know much about powers and stuff like that. My husband is a mage, so he knows way more than I do."

"Really? Have you asked him about this then?"

"Yes, but…"

"But?"

"But he doesn't want me to get too involved."

"Perhaps that is wise, then. A lack of understanding can be as dangerous as fighting without a weapon."

The instant Yaying had finished speaking, a group of red-colored birds that were sitting nearby shrieked and started flapping their wings. Other animals responded with their own cries. To Vanilla it was pure chaos. She covered her horns and shut her eyes tightly, trying to endure the sound. A grave look came over Eon and the queen. "The Machines are somewhere in the forest! To arms, to arms!" the brave knight shouted over the ruckus.

Hordes of animals poured into the passage leading to the well. The air was filled with one last roar of excited creatures, stomping feet and flapping wings. Eon, too, joined the stampede, bellowing a vicious war cry. For one horrifying moment, Vanilla thought she was going to be trampled, but the beasts went around her as if she was a large stone or tree. Then it was still, leaving the terrified Crescent Horned Punisher and Yaying alone together.

"I assume you're not used to this sort of thing, Vanilla?"

"Heck no! Oh, pardon my speech. I'm just a bit…shaken, that's all."

"You needn't apologize. I can sense that you've never been in the presence of royalty before. Speak to me how you would a friend. It may be amusing for me to hear how people from your world converse on a daily basis."

"It's not too different, actually. Will Eon be alright out there?"

"I'm sure he will be fine. Never have I seen a more skilled warrior than he. I am thankful to have such a man on my side. After all, he is our only hope…"

Yaying's voice trailed off as she stared down the tunnel. The leaves on her branches wilted slightly, hinting that a great sadness had come over her. Vanilla looked into her eyes and found that the queen was doing her best to look emotionless and strong.

"Your Majesty?"

"Yes, child?"

"Is everything alright?"

"Yes, of course. Why do you ask?"

"It's just, you look so sad all of the sudden. Is it about Eon?"

"You are very perceptive. Yes, but now isn't the time for that. Come, I will show you where you will be staying."

Yaying closed her eyes and placed one hand over her heart. Out from the water shot a group of sturdy-looking vines. They wound around the rocky walls, marking a spiral staircase up to a small opening. Vanilla shuddered at the thought of climbing and considered telling Yaying that she was afraid of heights. *That would be awkward, though. I don't want her to feel offended, or to think I'm needy. I'll just have to tough it out,* the uneasy Crescent Horned Punisher thought nervously.

"There you are. That is the closest available room. It will be yours as long as you're staying in Andalli."

"Thank you. I really appreciate it."

"You're most welcome, Vanilla. Why don't you get some rest now? Nothing good ever came from lack of sleep."

Vanilla nodded, but inside she felt walled in by obligation and fear of climbing. After hesitating as long as she dared, the Crescent

Horned Punisher plucked up enough courage to reluctantly begin her ascent. The steps seemed solid, but this provided little comfort. She knew if she were to fall, it would undoubtedly take her life. Finally, she reached to the top and stooped to enter the cave.

It was small, but cozy. The floor was covered with pale blue grass that felt like silk. A cluster of mushrooms identical to the ones she had seen earlier clung to the top left corner of the room, giving off their cool, blue glow. Underneath them was a bed made from tree branches covered with soft leaves and down feathers from various birds. *I'm guessing that these were molted and not plucked,* she thought, taking off her shoes and laying down. Though it may not have looked like it, the bed was incredibly comfortable and soon she fell into a deep sleep.

Morning arrived all too soon. The shrill cry of exotic birds filled the air, shaking Vanilla from her restful slumber. With a huge effort, she rolled over and reached for something to cover her head. As her hands groped about, she realized that she was not in her own bed. A rush of panic shot through her and she jolted upright, her heart pounding frantically in her chest. Then she remembered where she was and lay back down with a heavy sigh.

It looks like I still haven't returned yet. I miss my family. She held her arms out before her, checking for any sign of the mysterious markings, but to her dismay there were none to be found. She recalled Malachi's warning and bit her lip. *Could it be like he said? Am I really trapped here now?*

Suddenly a soft knock sounded from the mouth of the cave. Eon poked his head in, and squinted in the dim light. "Hey, I hope I didn't wake you. I just wanted to know if you'd like some breakfast before it's all gone," he said, half-whispering.

Vanilla smiled and rubbed her eyes. "I woke up a while ago. What are we having?"

"There is meat, vegetables, fruit, grains, and water. I might be able to get you some milk, but I'm not too sure."

"Isn't that considered like, cannibalism around here?"

"What, meat? There are many carnivorous animals on Yaying's side. There's a difference between good and evil animals, if that's what you were getting at."

"What about the plants? I mean, wouldn't eating a vegetable or a fruit be like eating a baby to Yaying?"

"There's a difference between good and evil plants, as well."

"That's still like a Royal Guardsmen eating the child of a criminal."

"Do you want breakfast or not?"

"OK, OK. I was just trying to see things from their eyes. This world is so different from mine, or at least what I'm used to."

"Haha, it's OK. Come on, I'll walk you down."

Clumsily, Vanilla climbed out of bed and stumbled over to her friend's side. He was clothed in an ornate, green robe that was inlayed with dots of gold and beads of sapphire and emerald. His hair was still unkempt, but his dark brown eyes shone with unsurpassed brilliance. Around his neck he wore an earthy necklace of twine, colored clay beads and a quiver full of arrows on his back.

"That's a really neat outfit, Eon. Where did you get it?"

"I bought this from a store in the city before I fled here. There are some silkworms in the kingdom that are making me more clothes—by Yaying's orders, of course. I can't speak to insects."

"Cool. I always thought bugs were pretty much brainless."

"Shh! That's rude. Many animals here can understand our language and they might pass on something like that. I don't want to be at odds with anyone here, and neither do you."

"Sorry. I feel bad. I didn't mean it! Bugs are awesome! Yay bugs!"

Eon rolled his eyes, but smiled. Vanilla moved closer to her friend, feeling that he would protect her if a sudden swarm of bees or a group of angry spiders appeared. Being closer to the brave knight also made the open floral stairway less intimidating. Before she knew it, they had already set foot on the soggy ground and were headed toward a wide stone table at the far north corner of the lush paradise.

There were still a few creatures at the table. They turned to welcome the late-eaters with a combination of words and primitive noises. Upon hearing them, Vanilla instinctively clung to Eon's arm. "Don't worry," he said reassuringly. "These are the elite members of my division. A friend of mine is a friend of theirs. All of them speak in our tongue, too." Vanilla felt little from this, however, and continued holding her friend's arm until they were seated on the ground by the table.

A heap of something green was suddenly placed in front of them by a moss-covered golem. *That must be the chef or waiter, or whatever they have here,* she thought, forcing a smile. The odd pile that she had been served looked to be made of mashed vegetables and fruit, and gave off a pungent odor. *This looks repulsive!* she thought, but she was now too hungry to argue and shoveled a glob of green mush into her mouth. The taste was better than she had anticipated and soon she had eaten her fill.

As she was standing up, she felt a sudden change in the atmosphere. A shockwave of energy passed her, causing her hair to stick up for a moment with static. The plants started to wilt and the ground trembled at seemingly random intervals. Beside her, Eon had already drawn his sword and was barking orders to his men.

"Vanilla," he said, turning to the astonished Crescent Horned Punisher, "I've got to go make sure Yaying is safe. Follow me and try not to fall behind, OK?" Without waiting for confirmation, the heroic knight dashed back toward the center of the lake, skillfully weaving a path across floating logs and large rocks. Vanilla did her best to keep up, but she was not used to the complex terrain and soon was lost in the commotion. Animals and plant beings went by her in a stampede, obscuring her view. Birds zoomed overhead, shrieking warning cries and carrying stones in their talons.

Completely dumbfounded, the beautiful Crescent Horned Punisher fell to her knees and cried for help. To her dismay, her voice was drowned out by the chaotic screeches, grunts, barks, and yelps around her. None of the creatures would take notice of her, no matter how loud she was. Then, amidst all the insanity, she heard a voice.

"Vanilla, can you hear me? Please wake up! Vanilla!" It was Zallin.

The vivid green of the forest quickly faded away, taking the sounds and smells with it. She was now in her living room, Zallin's strong hands shaking her by her shoulders. It was evident that he was upset, but mostly worried. Raech was beside him, weeping quietly.

"Hey! What are you doing? Raech, why are you crying?" the Crescent Horned Punisher asked.

Zallin stopped and sighed heavily with relief. Raech wiped her eyes with her sleeve and rushed forward to hug both of them. Vanilla sat for a moment, startled by the abrupt awakening. The hour hand on the wall clock caught her eye, and then it dawned on her. "How long was I asleep?"

"Almost two days," answered Zallin, his voice shaking with emotion.

"Mom, I was so worried about you! I thought you might have gotten trapped forever inside that evil book."

"I...I don't know what to say. I feel awful, making you guys worry

191

like this."

"Never will I let that book take you into its accursed world again, Vanilla. Even if I have to stay up for months or years, I *will* stop this," Zallin said, hugging her a second time. She felt tears welling up in her own eyes as she pictured her family waking up to find that her soul had been taken for good by the book, her body lying empty and lifeless on the couch. The image scared her, but what was even more frightening was her inability to stop reading at night. The weight of worry hung heavy on her as she brainstormed for a way to stop it.

"Zallin, maybe you should tie me to the bed tonight."

"W-what? Why?"

"To prevent me from sneaking out here to read. I can't really control it when it happens…"

"I'd only do that as a last resort. Even then, it seems kind of inhumane. I'll stay up with you tonight and sleep for a while tomorrow during the day."

"I'm afraid that this curse—or whatever it is—might cause me to hurt you if you try and stop me, though."

"Vanilla, I'm Lieutenant of the 55th Council. It takes a lot to hurt me."

"I know, but…"

"Just trust me."

"Alright. As for now, I'm really hungry…"

"Oh, uh… W-what can I make for you?"

"Just a bowl of cereal would be fine… Maybe pancakes too."

Before the caring Madite could reply, Raech was already in the kitchen getting a white ceramic bowl from the cupboards. "I guess I'll mix up some pancake batter then," Zallin said. With much effort, the Crescent Horned Punisher got up and went to sit at the table.

Soon the delicious smell of warm pancakes and syrup filled the kitchen. By the time Zallin brought three full plates of food out, Vanilla had already finished two big bowls of cereal and was playing a game of cards with Raech. It was hard for her to resist the aroma of cooked food, though she was feeling rather full, so she ate what she could of her portion.

As Zallin was finishing what was left on his plate, his cell phone began to ring. He glanced at it and stood up abruptly. "Excuse me. I have to take this," he said, briskly walking into the hallway. Vanilla eyed him suspiciously until he had left the room.

After some time Zallin returned, a grave look on his face. He sat beside his wife, his eyes downcast. There was a minute tremor in his hands that caught her attention immediately.

"What's wrong? Your hands are shaking. Who called you?" Vanilla asked, putting her arm around her husband.

"My captain."

"Oh, him. What does he want?"

"We're going to war with a Darklord named Greemil who's been rising in power lately."

"War!? What? Now?"

"Crescent and the other members of the 55th Council will be here shortly."

"Well I'm not letting him in! You can't leave now."

"I don't want to, but I don't really have a choice. I have to obey my captain's orders. If I don't, he'd probably kill me."

"But Zallin, what will I do about the book? Who will protect us while you're gone? When will you be getting back?"

"I don't know, Vanilla, but this I promise: I will return."

At this Vanilla began to cry. Raech hugged her and said, "Dad, I'll miss you. We believe in you and I know you're strong. I love you."

Zallin rose to his feet and forced a painful smile. "Thanks, Raech. Don't worry about me, I'll be fine."

"Zallin, you can't leave!"

"It's OK, Vanilla. I'll be back. Small battles like this usually take about a week. Besides, Crescent is one of the Seven Chosen, so the enemy doesn't stand much of a chance."

The brave Madite stooped over, embraced the emotional Crescent Horned Punisher and kissed her. *He seems like a different person all of the sudden,* she thought. *I can almost sense courage flowing from him…still, I can't let him go. Crescent may be one of the Chosen, but Zallin's not!* As the family held each other for one last heartbreaking moment, a loud knock rang out from the front door.

"Hey Zallin, we've been waiting for almost a minute! Darklords don't sleep, you know. Or maybe they do, just not if they know I'm coming for them. Aw heck who cares? They all die by the sword and that's what matters! Ahahaha!" the booming voice of the insensitive brute came from outside. Zallin jumped, hurried to the door, and vanished with his fellow Council members moments later.

Vanilla still sat at the table, weeping with Raech. *I feel terrible for getting so upset at him over the book,* she thought. *Why do things like this always have to happen?*

The house felt completely lifeless. Like a bad dream, nothing felt real. The Crescent Horned Punisher stood up and gazed distantly out the window. The purple landscape was desolate and cold. She could feel the chill from where she was—the familiar sensation of despair.

Trudging into the front room like a zombie, she collapsed on the couch and closed her eyes. A deep darkness engulfed her. She had felt it many times before, but it now seemed to consume everything; her heart, her mind, and even her memory. It was like a void, devouring all that it touched and always wanting more.

The hours seemed to pass like minutes as she lay motionless, drowning in her depression. The sights and sounds around her had faded from her consciousness, all becoming one stream of noise in the background. Stress pulsed through her body, making her feel weaker by the second.

Raech sat by her quietly for some time, though how long she couldn't be sure. At one point the young Madite brought her some hot soup, but she couldn't bring herself to eat.

It grew dark fast and occasionally a distant rumble of thunder could be heard, but it was not until nightfall that the rain began. By the time they had prepared for bed, a heavy, slimy downpour had started. It sounded harder and more violent than it had ever been before.

Vanilla lay in her bed wide awake, struggling to calm her mind. Zallin's absence and fear of the cursed book weighed heavily on her heart, and the grave warning from Malachi repeatedly reminded her of what may happen if she were to continue her nightly reading.

Suddenly, a clap of thunder shook the house. Instinctively, Vanilla pulled the covers over her head and held her breath. As her muscles slowly eased up, the familiar feeling she had dreaded came, beckoning her out to the living room. Her mouth opened to call for Raech, but no sound came out. Her limbs began to move against her will, forcing her out of bed. Desperately, she tried to resist, but her will was already fading.

In the living room, sitting innocently upon the ottoman, was the book. Burning pain shot down the helpless Crescent Horned Punisher's arms as she drew nearer. Out of the corner of her eyes she caught a glimpse of red spiral marks, winding their way from her wrists. She cringed and tried to push back the feeling with anger. *It's useless to try to stop me. I'm going to read my book! It was mine in the first place. It chose me!* she thought, trembling with uncontrollable greed.

Her hands rushed for the book, her mind yearning to read. Vigorously, she flung it open. Her eyes tirelessly scanned the pages, chapter after chapter until she came upon the last page. The moment she had finished, she dropped the book and fell into a dark and unnatural slumber.

Before long, she was jolted awake by the loud cries of animals stampeding around her. Her eyelids felt stiff, but after some effort she managed to open them and look around. Once again, she had reappeared in Andalli at the exact place and time she had left.

This is it then, she thought. *I'm trapped here for good!* Sick with depression and anger at her cruel fate, the Crescent Horned Punisher lay down on her back and wept.

The hordes of animals eventually cleared, leaving her alone in the middle of the floral cavern. Only a few songbirds and insects were left, chortling cautiously in the safety of the tree branches.

"Oh dear, did they frighten you again, young one?" a soft, feminine voice said from somewhere among the dense foliage. Though she knew it was Yaying, Vanilla ignored her, thinking only of her own sorrow. "I see," the queen continued. "If there's anything that I can do to help, don't hesitate to ask."

After what seemed like hours, the first of the warriors returned with news of their battle against the Machines. From where she lay, the Crescent Horned Punisher overheard one of them—a mighty black bear with a scar on his snout—tell Yaying that they had been victorious, but Eon had disappeared. The queen's response was a terrified shriek, followed by sobbing. At this the animals began whispering amongst themselves in their native tongues.

Propping herself up on her elbows, Vanilla strained her ears to try and make out any more information. To her dismay, the creatures did not revert to speaking Alking. Deep inside, she felt the urge to comfort Yaying. Vanilla's intuition told her that the brave knight was not dead, or in any immediate danger.

By the time she had made up her mind, more creatures of the forest had arrived, bringing in the wounded to be treated. The room rapidly grew crowded and noisy again, though not as it was hours before. Struggling to navigate her way between the soldiers, Vanilla finally reached the queen. To her surprise, however, the elegant tree woman had disappeared.

That's odd, she was just here, she thought, scanning the area closely. There was no visible sign of Yaying; the plants where she had stood moments ago showed no traces of being broken, patted down, or even slightly bent. The Crescent Horned Punisher squinted, trying one last time to spot her friend. The commotion from the animals made her task even harder, as their noises robbed her of concentration. Eventually she gave up and retreated to the staircase leading to her room.

As she trudged up the steps of vines and branches, Vanilla glanced down at the crowds below. The warriors were seated at the stone table, feasting to their hearts' content. A group of large birds provided music as a bear danced along, stepping from side to side and occasionally balancing on one foot. Still, Yaying was nowhere to seen amidst her subjects' merrymaking.

When she had reached the small opening that led to her room, Vanilla stopped to gaze up at the higher rooms. For the first time since her arrival in Andalli, she began to feel at home—sad, but thankful that she was welcomed. "I guess I'll be here forever..." she mumbled, feeling tears returning.

When she awoke, it was still dark. The forest kingdom was ominously still, as if foreboding an imminent disaster. In the back of her mind, she knew that something terrible was about to happen. Clambering out of bed, she went to the open doorway and surveyed the area. Nothing appeared out of the ordinary, but still something seemed amiss. Quietly, the curious Crescent Horned Punisher descended the floral staircase.

Upon reaching the bottom step, she heard movement like the sound of rustling leaves. She quickly darted behind a nearby bush and pressed herself against the ground. As Vanilla lay motionless in her hiding spot, a small orange light shone, creating large dancing shadows on the stone walls around her. Then, to her horror, the smell of smoke reached her. Panicking, she jumped up and ran toward the source shouting, "Fire! Help! Something's burning!"

To her astonishment, she found Yaying lying on the ground, engulfed in flames. Fortunately, the lake was only a few feet from them. Vanilla rushed to the water's edge and splashed the queen with the crystal clear liquid. The fire hissed and died down, but not before its beautiful tree goddess had suffered mortal injuries. Her limbs were charred and crumbling like used firewood.

The animals had now awoken from their sleep, tired and confused by the ruckus. Once their eyes fell upon their queen, however, they were wide awake and stampeded to the scene. Vanilla knelt by Yaying's side and laid her hands on the woman's shoulders. "Yaying, are you alight? Speak to me!" she cried.

As everyone held their breath, Yaying's eyes opened slowly. She stared distantly at Vanilla and gave a small smile. "You tried to save me...? Silly girl, I couldn't even save my own kingdom...let alone myself. I am not worthy of life."

"What do you mean? It's not over yet!"

"No, it was over the moment Eon disappeared… Without him, our hope is lost. Goodbye, friends…"

"Yaying! No!"

Then the queen closed her eyes again for the last time. The green, dreadlock-like vines on her head shriveled and her skin dried and turned grayish-brown like dead wood. At first the crowd's reaction was dumbfounded silence, but moments later howls of agony and remorse filled the air. Bears roared and clawed at the ground. The birds squawked and shrieked with deafening volume. Tigers and jaguars growled and fought with each other. A group of elephants began trumpeting and shaking the ground as they stomped their feet. Once more, Vanilla feared that she might be trampled in the chaos, but her fear was short-lived. Before she knew what had happened, she was lying wide awake on the couch in her living room.

"Oh my gosh, I'm back!" she exclaimed. Instinctively, the Crescent Horned Punisher pinched her arm to make sure she wasn't dreaming and was met by seething pain. The spiral Marks of Purity were still on her skin, but now they appeared more like rashes. "Ow! What happened to my arms?" Then the memory of the night before came back to her. "I wonder if this is what Malachi had warned me about. It still worked though…"

Suddenly there was a sharp rap on the door. Startled, Vanilla jumped to her feet. It was still dark out and visitors were rare on Glunke, especially at night. Suspicion began building inside the vulnerable Crescent Horned Punisher as she stood stock-still, deciding what to do. Then a thought came to her. *What if it's Zallin? He said he wouldn't be gone for very long. Maybe he's back already.* Hoping to romantically meet her hero with a hug and a kiss, she ran to the door, undid the lock, and flung it open.

To her surprise, no one was there. "Somebody's playing a prank!" she exclaimed angrily. Then, two fat white hands came out from the shadows, covering her mouth and dragging her farther outside. Vanilla flailed wildly in her pudgy kidnapper's strong grip, but could not break free. His free hand moved to her bosom and start fumbling with her shirt buttons. Out of desperation, she bit her captor's fingers. He grunted and tightened his grasp in her.

"*My, you're more feisty than last time I saw you, Vanilla,*" said the man in a deep, sinister voice. His words were not in Alking, but rather Lambervan, the native tongue of the Gar Underworld. "*I must say you've grown to be quite the sexy lady. I couldn't resist paying you a little visit. After all, it's been a long time since we've spent some father-daughter time.*"

Vanilla's heart skipped a beat and her body became petrified. She now knew the evil man behind her was her father. "N-no!" she stammered.

"*I see you remember me. How nice of you. Now let's go back to the Underworld, shall we? My friends will be excited to see you as an adult,*" the filthy Billud laughed, shoving his hand deeper into Vanilla's clothing.

"Hold it right there!" a young man yelled. The bulbous Crescent Horned Punisher jerked his blubbery head in the direction of the newcomer. Standing only a few yards away was a black-haired boy dressed in green armor. In his hands he held a beautiful broadsword with ancient symbols engraved upon the blade. It was Eon.

Billud threw Vanilla to the ground and drew his own weapon; a crude, rusty executioner's sword with a small animal skull as the pommel. "*How dare you interfere with me, boy! I'll kill you and feed your bloody corpse to the Dorvek-Shaal!*" With simultaneous battle cries, the brave, noble knight and the portly, barbaric villain charged at each other. There was a loud snap as Eon's powerful sword shattered his opponent's blade, sending a rusty fragment flying past him. It grazed the obese Crescent Horned Punisher's bare shoulders, causing him to flinch. The knight's next strike landed with a sickening squelch, cleaving Billud's head in half.

Vanilla let out a bloodcurdling scream as the gruesome mess of her evil father's remains spilled onto the ground. Eon rushed over to attempt comforting her, but as he ran his body began to disintegrate like burning paper. Vanilla reached for her friend, but the moment they made contact, the knight was reduced to ashes. As a chilly breeze gradually blew away the burnt particles of her savior, the depressed and emotionally scarred Crescent Horned Punisher covered her face and wept.

CHAPTER 9

-Encore-

Summer was progressively fading into autumn in 1st City Realm. Amber-tinted leaves scurried across the pavement with each subtle breath of wind, swirling into small, invisible tornadoes against the buildings. Dragonflies zoomed in and out of sight, chasing down the last of the mosquitos. Night was making its gradual approach as the dim light of evening cast long, spidery shadows on the ground. Vanilla strolled quietly with her 14-year-old daughter on the sidewalk.

The white-haired Crescent Horned Punisher let her mind wander aimlessly while she gazed into the distance. A few weeks previously she had witnessed the death of both a close friend and her violent father, Billud. There was much remorse for her friend, but a great burden had been lifted with the parting of her father. Ethically, she knew it was wrong to view a family member's death as positive, but she had no sympathy for him. She was now free—not only physically, but mentally, too. She continued to muse over the past until her daughter gently tugged at her sleeve.

"What is it, Raech?" Vanilla asked, bringing herself back to reality.

"I hear music," she replied.

They stopped and strained their ears to listen. Through the slight breeze and rustling leaves, Vanilla was able to make out a mellow tone. The sound of an acoustic guitar was carrying quietly through the streets like a siren's song. It was a sad and lonely melody, but somehow vaguely familiar...the soft plucking of each note, the haunting rhythm, and the unmistakable emotion of a musician from Vanilla's past. Daunting flashbacks flooded through her head as she stood frozen in time.

Nostalgia overtook her whole being and tears welled up in her eyes. Nothing could have made her forget that tune—much less the guitarist who wrote it. Her mind told her to leave, but her heart tugged violently in her chest, beckoning her to go forward and find the musician. Without further hesitation, she came to her decision. Abandoned her thoughts and following her heart, she ran in the direction of the music. Her daughter sprinted after her. "Mother! Wait!" she called out.

To Vanilla, the city seemed unusually vacant, as though fate had carefully crafted the moment to remove all distractions, directing her down the path it had chosen. The decorative trees that had been planted in even intervals along the long, straight sidewalk passed by her like mile markers in a race—each was a countdown to her destination.

At the end of it, she quickly reached an intersection. Taking a left would lead her back toward the heart of the city. The illuminated outline of skyscrapers rose above her to form an endless undulant horizon. Their numerous lights were like a sequence-clad dress, sparkling against the fading backdrop of dusk.

To her right, the jungle of concrete, metal, and glass gradually thinned, easing into an unpopulated dog park that stretched for almost a full mile. It was lined with old trees almost acting as a fence, had there not already been one—a simple chain-link wall that encircled the circumference of the plot of land.

She stood for a moment and closed her eyes, focusing on the sound. It was louder when she turned her head to the right, so she quickly ran in the direction, scanning the streets for a guitarist.

After a few blocks, Vanilla came upon the source of the sound. A pale, skinny man was sitting on a bench near the sidewalk. He was hunched over a dark acoustic guitar, calmly picking at the strings. At his feet was an open guitar case with a few paper-form Gold Crests pinned down by a packet of spare strings. There was no tuning fork or guidebook to be found upon its velvet interior—nothing to aide him but his own skill.

Though the man's eyes were hidden by his long blue hair, Vanilla could feel the passion in them as he played. The music was beautiful and filled with sorrow, each note played upon the acoustic's nylon strings equally smooth and haunting. His voice, though not quite as honed as hers, penetrated the night like gentle ripples on the surface of a quiet pond, permeating the area.

> *"Bleeding Heart, why are you sad?*
> *Hold to the courage you always had.*
>
> *Bear with your pain,*
> *In the midnight rain,*
>
> *Hold my hand and let's be glad.*
> *Through weary smiles,*
>
> *And daybreak's sorrow.*
> *You and I will see tomorrow.*
>
> *O Bleeding Heart, you will heal.*
> *For only I know—"*

With her heart pounding more rapidly than ever, Vanilla stood in front of the man and said, "That's 'Little Bleeding Heart.' You composed that for me one night when I was very depressed. I'll never forget it, Zero."

A bit startled, the man looked up. His disheveled hair fell over his eyes, only to be parted by his long nose. There was an unnerving pause as he squinted at her from beneath his veil of blue hair. "Wha—" he began, but then he recognized her. For the Crescent Horned Punisher's curved gray horns, pure white skin, and beautiful figure were unforgettable.

The musician exhaled a drawn-out sigh through his nostrils. "So you came back…"

"I— Well, not like that. I'm married, now…"

"Good for you. Let me guess. Your husband's not a lowlife musician like me, right?"

"Zero, you're not a lowlife."

"Whatever. I'm sure you still hate me, so why don't you just leave me alone and be on your merry little way?"

Vanilla raised her hand and smacked her ex-boyfriend hard across the face. The sound echoed loudly in the empty street. A few teardrops rolled down his cheeks, which he quickly wiped away and then hung his head in shame.

"I'm just a jerk, aren't I? I abandoned you at a hotel when you were only seventeen and I never came back. You disappeared and people started to say that you had died. Hit me all you want, maybe it will make you feel better."

"Zero, shut your mouth and listen to me. I got over my grudge on you ages ago. I'm thirty-two years old, married, and have a fourteen-year-old daughter. I've moved on since then and chosen a different path than the one I was on. I had sincerely hoped that you had done the same."

He stared at her for almost a minute, his mouth hanging open in surprise. "Hmph. You sure *have* changed, haven't you, Vanilla?"

Just then Raech caught up. Panting from exhaustion, she leaned on her mother's arm to catch her breath. Vanilla looked at her, and then at her feet.

"Raech, I'm sorry. I shouldn't have bolted without warning like that. What kind of mother am I, leaving you behind in the city at night...?" she said, hugging her tightly.

"Mom, it's OK. I was worried about you, though. Why *did* you take off so suddenly?"

Then Raech saw Zero. She hastily curtsied and introduced herself. "Oh. Good evening, sir. My name is Raech Lamberschvak. My mother and I heard you playing guitar and—"

Zero waved his hand to dismiss her formal greeting. He set his guitar aside and rose to his feet. Slouched over and with both hands in his pockets, he mustered a faint smile. It wasn't entirely genuine as far as the two girls could tell.

"So, that means you must be my ex-girlfriend's kid. Well isn't that sweet."

"Oh, yes sir. I am. May I ask what your name is?"

"I'm Xypher Endock. Call me Zero, though. I couldn't give a shit for my given name."

Vanilla cleared her throat and put her hands on her hips. "Zero, please don't swear in front of my daughter. I don't want her to start."

The blue-haired man rolled his eyes. "Pfft. Kids ruin everything like always. I can swear if I damn want to," he muttered under his breath. "Sorry, kid. I guess I'm not really a 'good' person, if good people don't swear."

"It's alright, Mr. Endock. You couldn't have known under these circumstances. I'm sure you're a great person."

"Yeah, whatever. Again, it's 'Zero.' I don't give a...care for my real name."

"I'm terribly sorry. I didn't mean to offend you."

Eyebrows raised, the guitarist shook his head and mouthed

another cussword. With a small jerk of his neck, he flipped his long hair back and looked up at the sky for a moment. "Yeah, things sure have changed," he laughed. "Thirty-five years and I still don't get women."

The women watched as the anti-social man quietly packed up his instrument. Vanilla noticed a few gold-colored coins in the cushioned guitar case, leading her to believe that he was playing for money. She instinctively reached for her wallet, but hesitated too long. He had already closed it and was locking it with a silver key he had drawn from his pockets.

"Well, I'm out of here. Take care, Vanilla. Make sure this kid of yours stays out of trouble."

"That's quite a statement coming from you."

"Hey, that was just a friendly joke."

"And I'm just giving you a hard time. You know I could never hold a grudge against you for too long, Zero."

"I'll bet you 10 Gold Crests I can make you hold a grudge against me."

"Oh, hush. Anyway, are you still living in—?"

"Yeah. I still live in a trailer. No need to even ask."

"You should come visit me and Zallin. We live on Glunke."

"You live on what?"

"Glunke. It's a planetoid realm. It would be nice to have you over one of these days. We're actually the only people there…"

"Jeez, maybe I shouldn't have felt so bad about leaving you on your own. 'Glunke' sounds like a noise you'd hear while taking a—"

"Hold it! I don't know if I should slap you again for saying that."

"Heh, you know me."

Vanilla just smiled and put one hand on her hip. "You know, it's hard to believe it's been fourteen years since I saw you last."

"I know, right? So how often do you come to the City Realms?"

"A lot, actually. I like to hang out at coffee shops with friends or go for walks in the parks. I do my grocery shopping in 1st West City. How is the band?"

He sighed and slouched over. "I dunno. We're struggling."

"Struggling? How so?"

"Our last concert had less than fifty people show up. Not sure if you've heard, but we're not signed with a record company anymore, so we're paying for everything again. We really gotta figure out something to keep the band alive."

Her eyes widened. "Really? Yikes…"

He shrugged and shook his head. "Maybe this is what I get for leaving you like I did."

"No…I forgive you."

There was a pause, broken suddenly by a buzzing sound. The Grenzel Blind Demon reached into his pockets and retrieved a cell phone with a cracked screen. Glancing at it briefly, he frowned and put it away.

"Shi…" he muttered under his breath. Then he looked up at Vanilla. "Hey, Lisa just texted me. I need to head out right now. This sucks…"

"What happened?"

"Just…I don't want to get into it. Shit's—I mean, stuff's going on."

She nodded.

He slung his guitar case over his shoulder and turned to walk away. After a few steps, he stopped and looked back. There was a small light of excitement in his eyes as he kicked a small pebble and spoke.

"Hey, um, have you been practicing singing lately?"

"Somewhat. Not as much as I used to, though. Should I know

where this is leading?"

"Maybe. I was just thinking…the band and I are gonna be performing at Felix Park in a week. Would you be up to attending?"

"You just want me to sing for you guys, don't you?"

"Well, yeah. That's…that's pretty much what I meant. Our new bassist just quit, the damn—er, dang freak. I was thinking we could make it a little reunion concert for old time's sake, you know?"

"You bet! You'd better be prepared if I fail epically, though. It's been close to fourteen years since I last sang heavy metal. And a week isn't much time to prepare."

"It's 'dirge metal.'"

"Oh be quiet."

"Ha. I knew you'd say that. So, do you still have the same phone number? I'll need a way to stay in contact with you if you'll be preforming with the band."

"No, I had to change it shortly after I met Zallin. Some of the guys that I use to hang out with kept calling me and sending explicit images. My new one is G7-Q89-32A-767-20A."

"That 'G' reminds me of something you used to wear—or maybe you still do."

"Ahem."

"Oh right, the kid. Sorry. Anyway, I'll call you tomorrow morning and we can arrange a time to practice."

"Sounds good. I really *am* glad to see you again, Zero. A lot has happened in these past fourteen years and it will be good to catch up. You're welcome to visit me anytime, you know."

"I might take you up on that offer. I hope your husband won't mind. I *am* your ex-boyfriend, after all."

"He's actually away on a mission right now, so it don't worry

209

about it. I'll be waiting to hear from you tomorrow!"

The guitarist chuckled and, with one last wave, teleported away with his watch. Vanilla stared happily at the place where he had just been, basking in nostalgia. She found herself grinning wider than she had in years as she thought about her band.

A gentle tap on her shoulder brought her back from her thoughts. "Mom," said Raech, "was that man really your ex-boyfriend?"

"Yes Raech, that was him, alright. I think I've told you quite a bit already about my former life as a musician."

"You've never said too much about him, though. I'm guessing it's a topic that you'd prefer to avoid?"

"Well, we had a very bad break up…it feels kind of weird seeing him again. I'm not mad, though. I think I was more nervous than anything when I saw him there. I wasn't sure how he would react."

"I see. It appears as though you two made up very fast. I was actually surprised at that. Doesn't it take a long time to mend a broken friendship of that sort?"

"You're right, it usually does…but over the years I've come to realize that I'm content with what I have. It wouldn't make sense to keep a grudge about a past relationship like that. After all, if I hadn't broken up with him, I wouldn't have had you. You're the best decision I ever made, Raech."

"Thanks Mom. You're the best mom ever."

"Oh, I don't know about that. Thanks though. I appreciate the compliment."

"Well, I really do think you are. So are you going to get back together with your old band?"

"Just this once. I'll need to practice like crazy for the next few days. A week isn't much time at all and I'm actually feeling nervous about going in front of my old fans again…I've tried to keep everything about my past at a healthy distance after I moved to Glunke. Let's just head home for now. The more time I sit around worrying, the less prepared I'll be."

Raech nodded and held her mother's hand. The ex-rock star was trembling with excitement. With a flash of blue light, they transported home.

The air was chilly on Glunke. The two ladies' footprints stuck into the frigid purple slime that covered the ground as they walked. Vanilla was lost in thought again. *This realm has hardly changed at all, unlike everywhere else…and unlike me. It's almost like time is frozen here. It's always cloudy and cool, and there are practically no trees or other buildings. For all I know the rest of the dimension could have blown up and I'd be completely unaware of it if I was here. But it's peaceful and safe. It just baffles me. … The first ten years of my life I was a victim of sexual abuse. The next seven I spent living a life of rebellion. I got addicted to drugs and alcohol at such a young age and I did so many bad things, but yet I'm still here. On the other side of things, these last fourteen years have been a blessing. I've been able to have a family of my own and live my life away from all the drama of being a rock star, for the most part. It's not perfect and I know it never will be, but I'm thankful for it.* She brushed a few strands of her pure white hair away from her face.

I wonder if things will start to go back to the way they were before— after I do this concert? No, it's just a one-time thing. Still, I miss being in a band. We used to stay up late playing music and doing all sorts of dumb things. We'd get to go places and meet people… Man, it makes me so sad that I can't really do that now. At the same time, I have a family and I know that's my duty. I'm a wife and a mom, and I wouldn't trade that for the world. I guess my family is like my band now in a way, even though I'm the only one out of them who does music.

The Crescent Horned Punisher glanced over at her daughter, who was walking quietly by her side, and smiled. *She sure is a good kid. I'm glad she's not like I was at that age. I remember smashing one of Scythe's guitars because he wanted me to clean my room. Raech cleans her room without ever being told to. If I could go back and do things differently, I certainly would. Then again, would that mean I wouldn't have met Zallin? If it was fate... Well, it doesn't matter. What's passed is the past.*

The house key slid into the lock on the front door. With a little more effort than necessary, Vanilla flung it open. The brass doorknob slammed against the wall with a loud bang. Raech flinched and cupped her hand to her ears. The yellow eyes on her hat blinked and then relaxed.

"Sorry, Sweetie. I guess I did that a little too hard, didn't I?"

"It's OK."

"Well, I should probably see if one of the old band uniforms still fits me."

"OK."

Vanilla went straight to her room without even bothering to take off her shoes. With much vigor, she dug through her closet, opening box after box. Stilettoed high heels, tight fitting corsets, fishnet leggings, and black leather collars with metal spikes were carelessly flung onto the floor along with other items from her old band.

Raech stood at her mother's bedroom door and watched, curious and embarrassed by the things that she saw. The deeper the rock star dug, the smaller and skimpier the clothing was. Now blushing, the modest Madite said, "Mother, I-I didn't know that you owned clothing like that..."

Vanilla stopped. Her white cheeks turned bright pink as she hastily gathered up the things on the floor and stuffed them into the corner of her closet.

"Oh, th-those were just… Those belong to some friends of mine. They must have left them here a long time ago."

"It's OK. I won't tell anyone."

Cheeks still radiant, the ex-rock star clumsily set the lids back on top a couple of the boxes and pushed them into the corner of the closet's topmost shelf with a heavy sigh.

"Raech, I'm sorry I just lied to you."

"It's OK. I'm not upset or anything. I was just a bit surprised that you had such revealing apparel, that's all. I'm not judging you though. I know you're not the same person you once were."

"Well, I know this will make me sound like a hypocrite, but please don't follow my example. Even when you're an adult, don't fall into what I did…"

"Please stop being so hard on yourself, Mom. That stuff is behind you, right? I mean, Dad doesn't appreciate you wearing those sorts of outfits in public but I'm sure that you've gotten past all that by now. The fact that I've never seen you in them is proof of that."

Then silence fell over the room. Vanilla's knees were trembling. Eyes downcast, she took a deep breath.

"…Let's just forget this. What would you like for supper?"

"Oh, um…I can make something for myself. I'll let you concentrate on getting ready for the concert."

"Thank you, Sweetie."

"Of course."

With one last glance at her mother, Raech politely left the room, shutting the door gently behind her. Now completely alone, Vanilla sat down on the edge of her bed and gazed at the ceiling. Tears filled her eyes as guilt began to overwhelm her. *Did she figure it out? No, it was just clothing, nothing else. I don't think anything else got thrown out of those boxes, did it? I can't ask or else she'll suspect something. Not even Zallin knows. Or he thinks I'm over it, at least. He never goes digging through my old stuff. I just have to try not to think about it...but I know I have to stop sometime.*

The harder the Crescent Horned Punisher tried not to think, the more she felt her addictions clawing at her mind. She made fists and held them firmly at her sides, trying to focus on something else. If she closed her eyes, she knew she would be tempted by her imagination, but if she left them open, she would be reminded of it by the boxes.

Swallowing hard and fixing her eyes straight in front of her, she stood up and paced, taking controlled breaths. "It's feels like forever since Zallin's been home. No, I need to think about music. I just need to... Ugh, I can't do this!"

Tension hung so heavily in the room that the air was suffocating. Her old self beckoned her like a siren, singing its false promises. Then a thought hit her. An escape was right in front of her: music. Beautiful, emotional music. Her voice was a sword to cut through the temptation.

Hands shaking and eyes wet with tears, she stood up and closed her eyes. "Yes," she told herself, "this is what I am. A musician. A creator. An artist. This pain is a part of me. That's why we scream about it in our lyrics. And if we run out of breath, we use our instruments. That's the way of a true musician...'"

The rock star pictured herself on stage in her favorite venue. The lights converged, bringing her to the center of attention. Her adoring fans were cheering for her and calling her name. They jumped up and down, pumping their fists in the air and proclaiming their love for her songs with every fiber of their being.

The calming, low rumble of thunder sounded in the distance,

bringing her back to reality. A storm was rolling in. The light gray sheers on the bedroom windows billowed up with a sudden gust of cold wind. Loud splatting sounds echoed from outside as the purple slime of Glunke rained down upon the realm.

Hunching over, Vanilla listened to the droning of the planet's strange goo hitting the roof. Somehow, it created a tempo that was almost consistent enough to put words to. She brushed her disheveled hair back and took a deep breath.

"I weep these tears of blood and sorrow,
The pain of losing a new tomorrow.

Frigid rain beats the skin,
Where ice-cold teardrops dwell within.

Hollow eyes and heart of stone,
I pity those who are alone."

Suddenly, there was a knock on the door. Vanilla jumped and went to open it. Raech was standing in the hallway, a concerned expression on her sleepy face. The angular yellow eyes on her hat were struggling to stay open.

"Mother, I thought I heard you yell. Are you OK?"

"Yes Raech, I'm fine. I'm just practicing my music for that concert. It's in a week, so that doesn't give me much time to get ready. Were you asleep?"

"Not yet. I was just putting away my dishes."

"Oh, alright. Sorry if I startled you."

"That's fine. Goodnight Mom, I love you."

"I love you too, Sweetie. Goodnight."

The door slid shut and Vanilla was left alone to the steady pounding of raindrops again. The depressive, artistic presence slowly seeped into the room again. Vanilla sat in the darkness, letting her emotions build like water behind a dam.

Energy started to rush through the Crescent Horned Punisher's body as she envisioned powerful moments from her past. Again, she pictured herself on stage. Lyrics riddled with emotion flooded into her head like a stream of raw, unaltered creativity. Songs of sorrow began to come to her naturally again for the first time in years. Slowly, she stood up and gracefully brushed her hair over her left eye. Tears trickled down her cheeks, but a small, triumphant smile spread across her face.

She had won.

Then, like a mighty burst of flames, she sung. Her voice erupted and shattered the silence.

"I am the whisper of death,
The prelude of despair,

Hear my hollow call,
You don't feel my pain,
You have no heart at all.

Have you seen through the eyes of the insane?
Has your heart been broken?
Have you watched your loved ones fall?

The hands of the grave reach deep and wide,
They seek this soul that I keep inside.

But I will not fall.
I will stand strong.

I will rise above,
And keep holding on.

My heart has hardened and my hands grown numb.
You will taste my pain until the end has come."

A massive thunderclap boomed outside. It rattled the house so violently that a picture fell in the hallway. The Crescent Horned Punisher flinched and reluctantly made her way over to the door.

Just as she was reaching for the handle, Raech knocked softly. "Mom, do you think we should go in the basement?" The girl's voice was almost drowned out by the noisy splattering of the purple ooze-rain.

Vanilla opened it. The young girl was in her pajamas with fuzzy slippers on her feet. She had wrapped herself in a pink blanket to keep warm.

"Sure. That's probably a good idea, Sweetie. Let me just get my robe." Rolling back the door to her closet, the musical mother retrieved her warm garment and draped it over her shoulders. "Alright, let's go," she said and followed her daughter down the hallway.

The cellar was cool and damp as always. A pungent musty smell lingered in the air, though the concrete floor was clean and as new as the exposed water heater and laundry machine in the northeast corner.

"I feel like we're never down here..." Vanilla mused as she looked around. The walls around them were made from large, square blocks of sealed stone. These were caged in by long wooden planks and pink

217

insulation. Only three small hanging light bulbs provided illumination to the dreary masses of cardboard boxes and miscellaneous pieces of dusty furniture.

The girls seated themselves on a sagging red sofa with a tea table acting as a footrest.

"What should we do?" Raech asked.

Her mother reclined and thought for a moment. "Hm. Why don't you tell me a story?" she replied. "I know you've been writing a lot recently."

The young Madite's face lit up with excitement. "That's a great idea...but I can't really think of anything original right now. You've read all of the stories I've written so far. Could I recite a poem from a book of Dreamic folklore I just finished?"

Vanilla nodded.

Raech took a deep breath. "OK, here it goes;

"Eyes as cold as the winter's snow, heart turned black as a midnight crow,
Frail and thin with pale white skin, such is the man named Hollow.

From ashen ruins his soul did rise, in search of the cause of his demise.
Evil claimed his vengeful mind, while rage and hatred made him blind.

Sickened by sorrow he then took flight. 'Revenge,' he said, 'is now right.
Once a soldier of Spirit's lore, I now want death and nothing more.
But even death has left me now, so here I stand with solemn vows.
I will crush all mankind, and sanity—a trash I'll leave behind.

Curse me heavens if you will, but all I know is how to kill.'

*And so the land was strewn with blood, his wrath now seemed a
raging flood.*
Then one cold winter's eve, a sly young fellow sought to deceive...

*'You may have strength of many men, but soon you'll meet a bitter
end.'*
Then the boy with eyes ablaze, silenced the fiend's blood-thirsty craze.

*Peace then came to this distant land, but still some failed to
understand.*
*Too much strength in mortal's hands condemns a nation where it
stands."*

"That's a very interesting story," Vanilla responded. She gave her
daughter a hug and forced a smile.

"Was it too dark?" Raech asked.

The Crescent Horned Punisher shook her head. In the dim light
of the basement, something shimmering gold caught her eye. From a
distance, it appeared to be a coin of some sort. Curious, she got up and
made her way across the messy concrete floor.

As she moved a few dusty sheets and cardboard boxes aside
and held the small object up to the light, her heart sank. It was Zallin's
badge from the 55th Council. The name "Zallin Eddrick Madite" was
inscribed on it along with a crescent-shaped symbol. She flipped it over.
"Lieutenant of the 55th Council" was printed in plain lettering on the
back. "Please come back safely," Vanilla whispered.

"What did you find, Mom?" Raech asked. The Crescent Horned

Punisher held the badge out. "Oh. I see," was her daughter's response. "I'm sure Dad will come back soon. I think we can go back upstairs now. The storm must have passed while I was telling that story."

Without another word, the two girls trudged up the bare wooden steps. Vanilla stopped at the door. "Raech," she said, still facing the door, "what if... Well, never mind. I love you." The door opened and they stepped onto the cold, white tile of the kitchen. They hugged again, this time for a long while, and then said goodnight.

CHAPTER 10
-Prelude-

About a week later, Vanilla awoke to the pale light of a cloudy day. From where she lay, she could hear Raech in the kitchen pouring cereal into a bowl. With a long yawn, she rolled over to look at the small clock on her nightstand. It was 8:14am. Then she remembered that Zero was going to call her. With a sudden burst of energy, she jumped out of bed and got dressed.

"Good morning, Mother," Raech said as Vanilla entered the kitchen.

"Good morning, Sweetie," she replied sleepily. After pouring a cup of coffee for herself, she sat down in the living room to try and wake up. There was a strange and nostalgic feeling about the day. *It's been so long since I've been on stage. I wonder how Lisa and Wake have been doing. It's been so long since I've seen them. Zero seems to have calmed down a bit since the last time I saw him. Other than that, it doesn't seem like he's changed much,* she mused. *I guess I'm kind of glad for that in a way.*

In the quietness of the morning, Vanilla could hear the concert in her mind. She imagined being up on a massive stage with bright light shining on the band. They all wore their signature black gothic clothes. She had a black tank top over a gray striped long-sleeved shirt. Her hair cascaded down to her feet and swept the floor as she walked to the front of the stage. The crowds chanted, "Amp it up! Amp it up!" She took a deep breath and lifted her microphone to her mouth.

"Mom, your cell phone is ringing," Raech's quiet voice broke in. Snapping out of her daydream, Vanilla blinked and retrieved the phone from her daughter's hands.

"Hello, this is Vanilla."

"Hey, it's Zero. We're at a fancy restaurant called the 'Crimson Heir.' It's in Central 5ᵗʰ City Realm and it's really busy so I think we'll be here for a while. Why don't you join us and we can head to our old studio and use their equipment to practice?"

"Sure. I just woke up though, so I still have to shower and stuff."

"You *just* woke up? It's already past Noon."

"Not here. I think it's about half past eight."

"Oh, that's right. Where is 'Crunk,' or whatever you called it?"

"Glunke? I think my husband said that it's like one of the farthest realms to the west of Duevin."

"Huh. Cool. Why don't you just call me when you're about to leave then?"

"Alright. See you soon."

"Later."

"Was that Zero?" Raech asked, handing the jug of milk to her mother. Vanilla uncapped it and poured a generous amount on her cereal.

"Yep. I'm going to meet up with the band in a bit."

"Oh. That's nice."

"Yeah."

Vanilla wolfed down her breakfast and stood back up. "Well, I'm going to get in the shower. I'm not sure when I'll get home tonight. On that note, why don't you come to the concert tomorrow, Sweetie? It would give you something to do."

"OK. What time is it at?"

"You know, I'm not entirely sure. I'll be sure and let you know today when I find out. I can come and pick you up if you don't want go alone."

"Sounds good. I love you, Mom. I hope you have fun with your friends."

"Thanks, Raech. You're always so sweet. I love you, too."

After preparing for her day, the singer said goodbye to Raech and was heading out the door when she had a thought. *It would be kind of fun to pay a visit to Meltdown Music. It's been years since I've set foot in there.* Altering the destination on her transportation watch, she left the gloomy wastelands of Glunke with high hopes.

In an instant she arrived on a smooth platform next to a train station. In front of her was a series of large platforms that created a terrace. It was an unfamiliar sight at first, but soon she knew where she was. *Over there is where the old warp plateau was. They must have just put this new one in a few days ago. Things sure change fast here,* she mused. Soon the rush of the city withdrew her from her pondering, however.

City Realm 5 was as busy as ever. Large crowds of wealthy people hustled along the wide sidewalks, in and out of shops, and across the streets. The air smelled of factory smog and gourmet food. Bullet trains zoomed by on elevated rails overhead. Vehicles such as cars had long since been outdated by transportation devices and were now considered an unnecessary luxury.

As she descended the long stairway from the last part of the terrace, Vanilla noticed a group of teenagers standing in a circle. As she stepped onto the sidewalk, it became clear to her that someone was rapping to a beat on their cell phone. The Crescent Horned Punisher scoffed at them and rolled her eyes. "That's not even music," she muttered disdainfully.

Quickly making her way through narrow alleys and shady corridors, she came upon a dented metal door with a broken neon sign on it. Two men were leaning against the wall next to the door. One of them looked over at her. "Hey Vanilla, is that you?" he said, sounding quite surprised. He was a Mandian of about 40, in obvious denial about his age. His orange hair was spiked with red highlights and plenty of conditioner. He had a gold chain around his neck and a shirt that had "*Death by Love*" written on it in jagged red letters.

"Um, yeah. How do you know me?"

"It's me, Monty! Don't tell me you've forgotten who *I* am."

"Scythe! Oh my gosh, it's been so long I didn't recognize you! How have you been? It's been ages!"

"Oh, I've been alright. The real question is how have *you* been, little miss runaway? You've been gone from the Musician's Guild for over ten years! Sometimes I'd hear people say that they saw you here and there, picking up groceries and stuff, but I just figured you were gone for good. I was worried sick. I don't know what I'd do if something ever happened to you. It was hard enough when Zero went his separate way… He still refuses to talk to me."

"Well, it's a very long story."

"In that case, why don't you and I go have a drink and you can tell me all about it?"

"Actually, I'm not really into bars anymore. We'll have to make it coffee, or lunch, maybe."

"Ah I see. You've gone straight edge? That's cool."

"Sort of. I still drink a bit, but not like I used to. I've got a family now."

"Finally settled down, eh? What brings you here then?"

"I'm meeting up with my old band for a one-shot gig. I just wanted to stop here for the sake of nostalgia."

"You mean *To the Power of 10*? That's great! Simply marvelous! Grand! Other big words that mean the same thing! Is that the concert tomorrow at Felix Park?"

"Yes! Will you be able to make it?"

"Sadly, no. I'd love to, but I'll have my hands tied with some legal matters at that time. Nothing too big, just some kids in a garage band who thought they could claim rights to a song on my new album, that's all. Parker will be around, won't you, Mate?"

Scythe motioned to the other man, who had been standing stock-still since Vanilla had arrived. He was a lean redhead of 6'3". His hair was spiked and he wore a hooded sweatshirt with baggy jeans and a thick chain dangling from one of his pockets. He grinned, revealing two perfect rows of bleached teeth with braces. Scythe patted him on the back as he came closer.

"Vanilla, this is Parker. He's our new bassist. Jerry quit a few months ago because his wife had a baby. Damn babies. Heh."

She smiled and shook hands with the young man.

"I've heard a lot about you, Vanilla. I'd be glad to attend your concert," he said.

"Oh thanks. It's been so long since I've been on stage...I'm afraid I might not live up to your expectations," she replied.

Scythe cleared his throat loudly. "I just had a thought," he said, "Vanilla, I have your bass guitar from when you were with *To the Power of 10*. Would you like it back?"

"Oh of course I would! Thank you so much! Where did you find it? The last time I saw it was at my old apartment...which I kind of abandoned. I mean it wasn't there when I went back to get my things after I moved."

"Well, call it crazy but I was looking at online auctions for a new guitar. Someone had it listed as Xypher's guitar. They must have been incredibly stupid because guitars don't have five thick strings and their necks are shorter—unless it's a baritone guitar, I suppose. Also, I don't think Zero would buy a purple instrument—well, maybe. Anyway, the bid was already up to 17,500 Gold Crests and there was only a few minutes left, so I bid 20,000 and won. I asked Steve Pulltuck to keep it under lock and key until I found a use for it and now I have! Why don't you come inside with me? I think Steve is still here."

Vanilla agreed and followed her former guardian through the beat-up back door. The atmosphere changed instantly. The store's interior was decorated with small glowing blue lava lamps. Integrated lights dimly illuminated the navy floor. Both the walls and ceiling were painted deep sapphire and gave the building a dreamlike feel. A steady stream of smooth indie rock played over the PA system. Fans and musicians of all kinds were gathered in groups talking or browsing through the merchandise.

Unlike the many of the shops in the City Realms, the layout was intentionally crowded, but cozy, creating the illusion that the store was much smaller than it really was. Guitars and basses were hung in endless rows on the walls and amps of all sizes and brands were stacked around the perimeter. A couple of old wooden stools were situated in front of some of these, implying that they had been tested recently by customers. The isles in the center of the room were very close together, chock-full of cables, chord books, albums, and band merchandise. At the end of each row there were massive lava lamps that acted as pillars reaching to the ceiling and emanated a soft glow.

The back of the store, where Vanilla and Scythe had entered, had a pair of old leather couches adjacent to one another—both backed up against the walls. There was a small end table between them to fill the gap. Underneath it was a filing cabinet with vintage issues of various music magazines, each featuring a now deceased musician.

Scythe led her down isle after isle of products that ranged from retro music chips to signature guitars until they reached the front of the store. A heavyset man in his late 50s was sitting behind the counter, tuning an acoustic guitar by ear.

"Hey, Steve, look who I ran into!" Scythe said, raising his voice a little. The man didn't seem to notice them at first, but after Scythe tried again a bit louder, he looked up.

"What's that?" he said, twisting a strand of his thick gray mustache. Then he saw Vanilla. "Well look who finally decided to come out of hiding! Why, it's been more than ten years since I last saw you. How's life been? You look great, by the way. More, um, stable I might add."

"It *has* been a long time. I've been through a lot of major life changes, but all for the better. I'm married now and have a fourteen-year-old daughter. I haven't really been in hiding…just super busy with life."

"Married? And here I thought the day would never come. You were a wild one in your younger years. You seem to be a lot different now though—I can see it in your eyes. I'm glad you've grown up. There are enough celebrities ruining their reputation with scandals and whatnot. So tell me about this family of yours. What does your husband do for a living?"

"Well, I actually shouldn't stay too long. I'm meeting up with Zero and the other in a bit to—"

"Oh, a reunion? Well, why didn't you say so? I've got the perfect microphone for you. It's the X3 Crystal, Light Fracture's newest must-have for singers. It will cost you, but nothing good in life is free. I'm willing to give you a discount since this is a special occasion, though. It'll be all yours for only—"

Scythe interrupted with a drawn-out smoker's cough. "Steve, I'd like to pick up that bass I got from the auction. Could you bring it up for me?" The rotund musician stopped and sternly looked Scythe in the eyes for a moment before bursting out in a jolly laugh.

"I'm just messing with you, kid! Of course I will. In fact, I just finished adjusting the action on it yesterday. Hang on one second." Withdrawing a keychain with far too many keys from his pocket, the humorous storeowner waddled over to a door on the far side of the room marked, "STAFF ONLY" and disappeared inside.

Several minutes passed before he came into view again. He was carefully carrying an odd-shaped purple bass guitar. It had been buffed and cleaned recently, making it gleam mystically in the cool blue lighting. "DX 10 Custom" was written in angular blood-red lettering on the body. The storeowner skillfully plucked each string and listened to see if it was in tune. "Sounds like everything's in order—that's a Light Fracture product for you. Take good care of it, Vanilla. It was great to see you again and I hope you'll come visit us again soon." With a wink and smile, he handed the instrument to the singer.

It was very heavy, but there was something wonderful about it to her. She slung the wide black strap over her shoulder and ran her fingers over the strings. "It's just like I remember it," she thought, taking a moment to admire the jagged curves of the body and headstock.

"So," Scythe said, "how does it feel? It's just like old times, isn't it?"

"Yeah. It brings back memories. Thank you so much for rescuing this, Scythe."

"Of course! I couldn't let your old bass go to some nobody."

"I'll pay you back somehow. It doesn't feel right just taking something that cost you so much."

"Ha! You really *have* changed. I never thought I'd hear the day you'd say something like that."

"I mean it."

"Well, there's no need to pay me back, OK? Just keep it."

"But—"

"Vanilla, you're like a daughter to me. You know that. I'm just glad that you're alright."

"Thanks," the singer said, wiping a tear from her eyes. "I guess I'd better go and meet up with Zero and the others. They're probably wondering where I am." Reluctantly, she began heading for the exit.

"Oh, hold up! What's your phone number? I'd still like to take you out for lunch sometime," Scythe called out, running up to her.

"Oh! Sorry. How could I forget? It's G7-Q89-32A-767-20A. I should be free next week."

After saying their goodbyes once again, the two old friends parted.

As she walked out onto the sidewalk, the overpowering noise of the city filled her ears again. Gossips chattered in huddles, angry pedestrians shouted at one another, children cried or squealed playfully while running from their mothers. The Crescent Horned Punisher found it hard to focus as she typed a message to Zero with her phone. "I should have asked for the coordinates before leaving," she muttered. Before long she had the address of the Crimson Heir and was on her way.

The classy restaurant was situated in the heart of Central City 5, the most expensive sector in the realm. There were no old, dilapidated buildings in sight; only sleek, futuristic ones. There was no garbage on the streets, no dark and suspicious alleys, not even a single homeless person begging for cash. Everything was much quieter, too.

To Vanilla, it felt eerie and unnatural. As she neared her destination, she noticed that quite a number of cars were parked along the sidewalk outside the entrance. Each one looked exotic and unnecessarily fast. "Jeez, why do these people buy things like that? Nobody needs a car anymore. Only showoffs spend money on those things," she grumbled, starting to feel a bit jealous.

Suddenly, there was a *bang* nearby. Although it wasn't loud, it appeared so in the surreal stillness. Vanilla jumped and nearly lost her balance. Seconds later she realized what the sound was. Someone had slammed their car door and was pulling away. The singer blushed and quickened her pace, casting nervous glances to her left and right to see if anyone had witnessed her reaction.

Soon she was standing before the Crimson Heir. Gorgeous red and black flowers were displayed the behind the safety of the windows. The address was written above the entrance in flowing cursive. From where she stood, she could smell the delicious food. Her mouth began to water as she opened the door and went inside.

The restaurant was much larger than it appeared from the sidewalk. The first thing that caught her attention was the length of the main room. What the building lacked in width it made up for in depth. Decorative mirrors were hung on the walls at intervals, making it seem even bigger. Soft, red tablecloths were draped over each table and garnished with silverware and a vase of black roses. The customers were dressed in fancy and ornate clothing, some of which Vanilla recognized as celebrities. Then she noticed Lisa and Zero, who were sitting at a table to her right.

The blue-haired Grenzel Blind Demon looked up and smiled as he saw the instrument in her hands as she walked over to them. "Hey, I haven't seen that in years! I thought you must have thrown it away."

Vanilla laughed and shook her head, no longer feeling out of place. "Well, I stopped by Meltdown Music on my way here just for the sake of nostalgia. I saw one of my old friends there. It turns out that he found it on an online auction and bought it for 20,000 Crests."

"What the hell? 20,000 Gold Diamonds!? Damn, I wonder how

much *my* guitar is worth then…"

"I know, right? So anyway, he just handed it to me—or Steve did, actually. He said that he couldn't hang on to it now that he knows I'm still doing music. It was my first bass, after all."

"Shit. That's crazy. Small world, isn't it?"

Lisa nudged her. The athletic Mandian was dressed in a red T-shirt and black running shorts. She was wearing her long curly brown hair down, just as she always had. Its spirals were evenly spaced—a natural perfection of sorts. Fourteen years may have passed, but time had been remarkably kind to her—perhaps the result of her passion for martial arts and healthy food. The shine in her vivid green eyes was as bright as it had been when she first joined the band as a teenager.

Vanilla looked over at her and smiled. "Hey Lisa! My gosh, it's been so long since I've seen you."

"I know! I was so excited when Zero told me he had run into you last week. We've got a lot of catching up to do. How have things been?" the keyboardist signed with her hands.

Vanilla nodded. "We certainly do. Gee…where do I even begin? A lot's happened since I last saw you. Let's see… for starters, I'm married now and have a fourteen-year-old daughter."

Lisa set down her fork to reply. *"Whew. I'm glad you haven't forgotten sign language. What's your daughter's name?"*

"Raech."

"Is that short for Rachel?"

"Nope. Just Raech."

"I see. What's your husband's name?"

"Zallin. He's a Madite."

"What does he do for work?"

"Um…well, right now we're just living off savings. He's looking

231

for work though. He's kind of a member of the 55th Council."

"Really? Wow. How did you two meet?"

"Oh jeez. It's a crazy story. I might have to save it for another time." She gave a hesitant glance around.

Lisa nodded. *"Have you been playing your bass much lately?"*

"Yeah. I mean, I've been practicing like crazy this past week so I'll be ready. That reminds me. Hey Zero, what's the plan for today?" she asked, nabbing a piece of chicken from her ex-boyfriend's plate and taking a bite. Before the blue-haired guitarist could answer, Wake burst into the restaurant.

He was obviously flustered. His face was red and sweat was beading on his brow. "I ain't short, you bastards!" he shouted behind him. Two spoiled-looking teenagers in expensive clothes were standing outside snickering at him.

When the vertically challenged drummer turned back around, his face was red with embarrassment. The customers stood frozen in a horrified silence staring at him. A plate fell from one of the waiter's hands. Wake cleared his throat. "Well, th-they started it," he stammered.

After a prolonged pause, the manager of the restaurant appeared. He was a stout man of forty or so. His jet-black, curly hair had an unnatural shine about it that was almost disturbing. It was as if he had just showered and used wax for shampoo. His face was crimson with anger, perhaps a nod to the restaurant's namesake, although the band found it hard to take him seriously after noticing his cartoon-like handlebar mustache. Zero snorted and cupped his hand over his mouth to hide his laughter. "Is there a problem, sir?" he asked innocently.

The answer came like the roar of a hungry lion. "Yes, sir, there *is* a problem! Your foul-mouthed companion's profane ranting has disrupted my restaurant! And why do you people have musical instruments here?

This isn't a concert hall. This is a five-star diner in 5th City Realm! Take your…your rock and roll *garbage* and get out!"

Vanilla nervously retreated behind Lisa. Zero smirked and was about to speak when Wake butted in. "Take that back, you bloated pig! I don't have a dirty mouth! The only dirty thing here is your face, you tub of lard! Go back to the bakery, fat ass!"

The expression on the manager's face was a mixture of burning rage and complete shock. He stuttered like a machine gun as he struggled desperately to find a suitable comeback. The band could see his pulse in his temples, his veins bulging like worms beneath his skin. The side of the manager's mouth twitched so rapidly that it looked as though he was having a seizure.

Now genuinely frightened, Vanilla tugged on Lisa's sleeve. "Shouldn't we go now?" she whispered timidly.

Lisa reached back and held her hand to reassure her, signing, *"Don't worry."*

Sensing the singer's anxiety, Zero took a deep breath and said, "Right…let's be on our way then." He stood up and motioned for his comrades to follow. With everyone still staring at them, the band went back out on the streets.

Once they had assembled themselves on the sidewalk, Zero punched wake in the arm. "Wake, you dumbass! You made a scene in front of the whole restaurant and you scared Vanilla!"

"Wait," Vanilla cut in, "why did you have to hit him?"

Zero stopped and furrowed his brow as if he had never been asked the question before. "I was just standing up for you," he replied rather sulkily.

Seizing the opportunity, Wake clocked the tall guitarist in the face. "How do you like *that?*" he jeered. Zero wiped a bit of blood from

233

his bottom lip and charged at the drummer. Lisa quickly stepped between the two ruffians and gently shoved them apart. The threatening look in her eyes made them stop instantly. The keyboardist's stare was so intense that even Vanilla was petrified momentarily.

"You guys really don't *have* to fight all the time. I think the band would be better as a whole if we all got along," she added hesitantly. Wake and Lisa both glanced at each other, and then at the singer.

"Whoa, Zero was right. You've changed *a lot*!" the drummer said, looking slightly bewildered.

"Well I've been through a lot over the past few years and it's made me realize that fighting doesn't get you anywhere. Even if you win an argument, you don't always gain anything."

"Jeez. Listen to you. I'm fallin' asleep already. When I saw you in that electronics store years ago I thought you were just…I dunno, acting or somethin'. You sound like a freakin' church lady now."

Zero stepped up to Wake and drew himself up to his full height, which was just over six feet. "Hey, don't you talk smack to my ex, you redheaded baby," he growled. The Crescent Horned Punisher could clearly see that her wisdom had fallen on deaf ears.

"Oh, never mind! Look, are we going to the studio to practice or not?" At the mention of the studio, the tension between the two men seemed to have vanished.

"Yeah! Let's go," Zero said with a hint of excitement in his voice. "I'll be glad to get away from this stuck-up asshole's restaurant." After yelling a few cusswords toward the storefront and making rude gestures, the guitarist and his comrades transported.

When they arrived, they were in a different part of 5th City Realm, standing atop one of the numerous warp plateaus. Towering skyscrapers of silver loomed overhead, their mirror-like windows shining like beacons high above the clouds. Below them, the streets were alive with pedestrians, vendors, and businessmen bustling about. The air was tainted with the familiar remnants of smog, a testament to the centuries of political warfare between big corporations and environmental activists.

The group of musicians descended the warp plateau's long concrete steps together, eventually setting foot on the rough gray sidewalk and making their way toward their destination deep in the heart of one of the city's numerous industrial districts.

Meltdown Music Studio was just as Vanilla remembered. The same old, fading brick building was nestled between a clean office building and a large warehouse. The surrounding area was open and desolate, as it was the second largest and most vacant business park in 5th City Realm. Only a few trees and park benches dotted the vast expanse of grassy fields and empty parking lots. She stood for a moment, basking in the nostalgia.

"Come on, Vanilla," Zero called, motioning to her from the entrance. After taking one last second to sit in the black and white feelings of her memories, she caught up to her old friend and followed him indoors.

Unlike the outside, the studio's interior was much different than she remembered it. The old, faded posters of unsung bands had been replaced with that of more recent musicians and well-known names. The only two of which she recognized at first were *To the Power of 10* and *Death by Love*. Directly in front of the exit, where a pair of sagging sofas had once been, was a counter with a small sign on it that read, "Rules." A young man was reclining in an office chair behind it with a newspaper over his face.

"Hey Joey, wake up or I'll wake you up with my fist," Zero jeered, playfully bopping the boy on the head. Startled, the young man jumped up, letting the newspaper glide to the floor.

"I'm sorry!" he blurted out instinctively. His skin and hair was white, like Vanilla's, and fell almost to his shoulders. Two slim gray horns protruded from either side of his head and curved upward, also similar to hers. His eyes lit up when he saw the singer.

"Excuse me ma'am, but I see that you're a Crescent Horned Punisher too," he said shyly.

Zero stepped in front of Vanilla and said, "Don't you be trying anything funny with my ex, kid, or I'll take that name badge of yours and shove it up your—" he began, but Vanilla shoved him aside.

"Let him talk, Zero. Jeez. And stop being so protective of me."

Embarrassed, Zero shrugged and sulked over to the others.

"I'm sorry. Joey, was it?"

"That's quite alright. I'm used to it. And yes, my name is Joey."

"Does he always treat you like this?"

"I guess, but it's nothing, really."

"I'll have to have a talk with him then."

"It's fine. Don't worry about me."

"Oh stop it. You deserve to be treated like a real person. But I'm curious, how did you end up here? I mean, it's very rare to see a Crescent Horned Punisher above ground. Were you born here?"

"I was rescued when I was a baby and raised with a foster family. It's not something that I like talking much about though."

"Oh I'm sorry. I was a runaway myself, but anyways… Uh, I'd better start practice with my band. It was nice to meet you, Joey. Maybe I'll see you again sometime."

"Wait, I didn't catch your name, ma'am."

"It's Vanilla. Vanilla Lamberschvak."

Joey furrowed his brow for a split second at the sound of the singer's last name. "I see," he said slowly. Reclining his feet again, the young man stared at his shoes as if lost in thought. Vanilla had already pushed through the heavy double doors to the next room and had taken no notice of this unusual behavior.

The room the band had chosen to practice in was situated at the back of the building. It was spacious, like a small dining hall, and had cushioned panels on the walls to absorb noise. At one end, close to the door, was a booth with state-of-the-art audio equipment. Directly across from it was a stage lit by blinding overhead lights.

Vanilla walked up to the stage and clumsily climbed onto it. Her fellow musicians had already finished preparations and were waiting patiently for her. "Zero, where's the cord for this?" she asked, holding up her bass.

"Here, catch," the lean guitarist tossed a long black cable toward her. The singer reached out to grab it, but it fell to the ground with a dull thump more than a foot from her hands.

"You know I can't catch," she grumbled, plugging it into her instrument.

"Alright, we're starting off with 'Deadened Life.' That's the third track from our fifth album, Vanilla. Do you remember the lyrics? It's that one that we kept putting off recording."

"I think so. Just start playing and that'll jog my memory."

"OK. I can sing, too, if that helps you. We can just use the stage's microphones here. I think they're already on."

"Sure. I don't know the bass line, though. I only played bass for our first four albums, remember?"

"That's fine. That's why this is practice, after all. Just play around with it and see what you can do. If all else fails we can have Lisa play bass at the concert for this one and just cut out the keyboard part."

"Couldn't we just use a prerecorded piano track?"

"Like a freaking rapper? Hell no! I'd sooner eat my own shi—"

"Alright, I don't want to know!"

"I was gonna say sh—"

"Just no. Wake, start the song."

Wake tapped his drumsticks together four times and the band began to play. Zero stooped over and began headbanging to the rhythm. His blue hair flew wildly as he played. Then he looked up and stepped toward the microphone.

"I don't know what's made me ill.
I think I've just lost all my will.

My head throbs from the knife wound,
My heart has gone and my eyes are dark,

From all the bodies that lay strewn,
I know my mind will be dead soon."

At this point Vanilla had begun to remember the lyrics and was singing along in a clear, powerful voice.

"Deadened life!
They crippled me with their words!
Deadened life!
They can't see the way it burns!
Deadened life!
You might think that it's absurd,
Deadened Life!

But death to me if I go unheard!
You can't see my despair, not that you'd even care.
Hell no! Hell no!
Carry me on wings above and fly me home, devoid of love.
I don't know what's made me ill,
All I know is how to kill."

The song came to a close, leaving the singer trembling with energy and excitement. She grabbed hold of her bass's neck to steady it and leaped in the air. The band stared at their animated partner in astonishment.

"I don't know what you're smoking, but hook me up after practice 'cause I've never seen a thirty-some-year-old woman jump like that," Zero laughed. "Are you ready for the next song then?"

Vanilla nodded, bending forward to catch her breath. "Yup. Just… just hang on one second. I didn't know I could jump like that, either."

"Well hell, I didn't think you *would* jump like that with that shirt you're wearing."

The Crescent Horned Punisher shot him a glare. "You better not have been staring at my boobs."

"Heh. I wasn't."

"That doesn't sound very honest."

"Well it was kinda hard not to when you bounce around like that."

"Zero!"

"Alright, sorry. I'll turn around and play with my back to you if it makes you happy. See?"

"Whatever."

The band continued practicing and discussing their plans

throughout the day. When evening had come at last and the musicians could play no longer, they each left for home; Wake and Lisa to their apartments in 1st City Realm, Zero to his trailer in 3rd City Realm, and Vanilla to Glunke.

The house was dark as the white-haired singer opened the front door. She soon discovered that Raech had gone to bed, though night had not yet come to the gloomy purple planetoid. "Tomorrow night I'll be on stage! I can't wait!" the singer said to herself.

A soft knock on the door made her jump. Her heart raced as she stood petrified. *Who would be at the door at this hour? It can't be Zallin. He'd just come in.*

The knock sounded again, this time a bit louder. Trying to move as silently as possible, she hid behind the couch. Then a disturbing thought came to mind. *What if that person thinks nobody's home and breaks in? And if Raech wakes up…I'd better do something soon!* Hesitating for what seemed like an hour, she eventually scrambled to her feet and crept over to the front of the room. Her knees shook as she bit her lip and slowly turned the knob.

To her surprise, Joey was standing a few feet away from the house, glancing around nervously. He was still wearing his work uniform, but something about him was different than before. He stood hunched over, tense with anticipation. "Hello Mrs. Lamberschvak," he said quickly. "I'd like to have a talk with you, if you don't mind."

"Joey? How did you find out where I live?"

"It's a long story. Does anybody else live here?"

"My husband and daughter do. Why?"

"But your husband is away, correct?"

"Wait a minute. You're not suggesting—"

"No, not that! I wouldn't dream of *that*! I find it offensive that you would even assume that about me. Hm. This certainly makes things harder. I wasn't expecting to have to talk out in the open, but I suppose you'd be even more suspicious of me if I asked if we could go inside and talk."

"Joey, look. I don't know what this is all about, but I don't feel comfortable with you stalking me like this. This isn't appropriate. In fact, I'm almost obligated to call the Royal Guard. I have my concert tomorrow and—"

"I work with the Royal Guard, Vanilla. That's how I know where you live."

"Can you provide proof?"

"Certainly."

The young man retrieved a round, silver badge from within his shirt pocket and held it out for Vanilla to see. "Private Investigator and Spiritan Civil Protection Agent Connor Boldermore" was written across it along with a set of ID numbers.

"So 'Joey' is just an alias?"

"More or less."

"Still, I can't say it's easy to trust you, Mr. Boldermore."

"I understand that. But please…" The undercover detective's eyes were honest and serious. He retracted his badge and systematically stowed it in his pants pocket. The rock star took a cautious step backwards, debating whether or not to slam the door and lock it. The young man simply held his ground, taking no notice of her movement.

"OK, we can go inside. But know that my daughter has powers, so you better stay true to your word." As the words came out of her mouth, she realized that what she said had sounded more cinematic in her head. *Dang it. I can't make these things sound cool like Zallin does,* she thought, stepping aside to let the detective in.

Once inside with the door closed, he turned to her and spoke in a hushed tone. "Vanilla," he began, "there may be someone after you."

Vanilla's heart skipped a beat. "Who? What have I done?" she interjected, forgetting to keep her voice down.

"I don't know all the details yet, but let me just explain what I know so far. There's been a criminal group that's been kidnapping well-known musicians all over Spiritia. You may have heard about the most recent incident on the news yesterday. A pop star named Kendal Thymen was reported to have been abducted from her home in 5th City Realm just hours before a concert. On top of that, seven other reports of similar kidnappings came in over these past two weeks. We think that the kidnapping is being done by a group that opposes the Musician's Guild, as the victims are always musicians who are members, and the Musician's Guild's database was hacked shortly before all this started happening."

"What do you suggest I should do?"

"If you see any suspicious activity around the concert you're attending, call me right away. I'll give you my number. It's T7-89Y-37H-413-888."

"Hang on. My phone takes a second…so your name is Connor Boldermore, correct?"

"That's correct."

"He's lying, Mom!" a voice said from the hallway.

The young man's face turned bright red. "I-I…" he stuttered.

Raech appeared from behind the open doorway. She was in her pajamas, loosely hugging her long white pillow. "His name is Oliver Daresh. I can see it clearly in his mind."

Vanilla quickly got up and ran to the other side of the room. She fumbled with her cell phone and then started to dial a number.

Oliver stood up and pleaded with her. "Mrs. Lamberschvak,

please don't! I can explain!"

"And explain you will: to the authorities! You're full of lies!"

"What if your daughter verified what I'm going to say? Would you be willing to hear me out then? It's obvious that she can tell if I'm lying."

Vanilla stopped to think. As she did, someone picked up on the other end. "Hello, this is the Spiritan Royal Guard. Your call will be recorded for quality and legal purposes. What can we help you with this evening?" She glanced at the young man, who was still standing in place, looking worried.

"Oh, sorry…wrong number," she said into the receiver and hung up.

The phony detective sighed with relief. "Thank you."

"Yeah, sure. Now explain yourself, *Oliver Daresh*."

"OK. As you now know, my name is Oliver Daresh. I am twenty-one years old and was born in the Darfey Underworld in Mouldor." He stopped and looked at Raech, who nodded and politely motioned for him to continue.

"I was rescued from there shortly after I turned two. My parents still live in the Underworld, though. I was placed in an orphanage in 3rd City Realm and later adopted by a former government employee. I lived with him until I was eighteen, at which point I had acquired dangerous knowledge about the Old Government and many other secrets. One year later, my guardian passed away from a heart attack—or at least that's what most people think. I believe that the government killed him remotely with biodegradable nanochips that were implanted in his body. I faked my death to bide time before government agents would come looking for me. From then on I created false credentials and took on multiple jobs to hide myself. I continue my quest for truth through some of these occupations. My reason for finding you is still the same as I stated before, however. There aren't many Crescent Horned Punishers on the Overworld, so whenever I meet one I usually see if there's any way I can help them."

Vanilla glanced doubtfully at her daughter, who nodded again to show her approval. "That's a hundred percent true, Mom."

Oliver took a deep breath and relaxed.

"So, you have my number and my full name now. There's no reason you can't trust me. Even if I were to do something bad, you could easily track me down and prosecute me. That being said though, please keep this a secret; my life *literally* depends on it."

"Alright, Oliver."

"Oh, and one more thing: if you see me in public, act like you don't know me. And if I'm using an alias, please refer to me as that."

"Yeah, I get it."

"I think we're done here, then. Like I said before, call me right away if anything comes up."

"OK."

"Goodbye, Vanilla."

The singer hurriedly closed the door behind the mysterious man and locked the handle and deadbolt. "My *gosh…*" she said with a frustrated sigh. "What kind of man invites himself into a married woman's home and convinces her that he's somebody he's not? Raech, steer clear of boys like that. Deception is like their native language."

"Yes, Mother. But I'm a bit worried about whom or what is following you. He was telling the truth about that, you know."

"Probably him."

"No, I don't think so. I'm not even sure if he knew, exactly."

"Some help he was, then. I'm going to bed. If anybody knocks on the door, just ignore it."

"OK. Goodnight Mom."

"Goodnight Sweetie."

Vanilla went into her room, undressed, and flopped down on her bed. Loneliness started to creep in as she watched the blades on the ceiling fan go around. Its occasional soft clank and the faint pattering of Glunke's slimy rain were the only sounds that could be heard in the stillness of her room. The stress of the numerous events throughout the day was beginning to take its toll and soon the musical maiden fell fast asleep.

CHAPTER 11
- The Concert-

The next morning was quiet and peaceful, a stark contrast from the previous evening. To Vanilla's delight, Raech made breakfast for her and the two of them ate together in the living room. Though no animals inhabited their lonely planetoid, they both felt as if birds were singing happily somewhere.

"So Raech, my concert is at seven tonight, City Realm time. I have to get there an hour early or so for the sound test and to help set things up. Will you be OK with staying out a little late? Concerts always seem to run later than expected."

"Oh, yes! I'm excited to hear you sing, Mom. I wouldn't miss this for the world!"

"Well, I certainly hope I don't disappoint you. I've been practicing quite a bit lately, but only around the band. Being in front of an audience is a completely different story."

"I believe in you. If you could do it once and your band members still do, you can do it again!"

"Aw, thanks Sweetie. That really helps me a lot."

"You're welcome."

"After I shower, I'm going into town for a bit. I just want to look at some amplifiers for my bass. You're welcome to come along if you'd like."

"That's OK. I was planning on reading the last few chapters in my biology textbook."

"Alright. I'm so proud of you, Raech. You're so grown up."

"Thanks Mom. I wouldn't be here without you and Dad, so thank *you!*"

Vanilla smiled and patted her daughter on the shoulder. *Time sure has flown,* she thought, looking into the young girl's expressive, yellow eyes.

"Well, I'm off to take a shower then. Have fun reading!"

"Thanks, I will!"

With much effort, Vanilla rose from the saggy couch and headed for her bedroom. As she entered, she glanced outside and found that the clouds had parted for the first time in years. *It must be a good sign. There's no way this could be a coincidence.*

After gathering her clothes, she closed her bedroom door and went into the bathroom to undress. As she stepped out of her pajama pants, she glanced at her reflection in the mirror over the sink. Her gaze fell upon the tattoo on her upper thigh. It was an arrow-struck heart with the name of her ex-boyfriend written across it. Sighing heavily, she tossed her pajamas aside and turned the water on. The white noise from the showerhead did little to drown out the noise within, however. Again, she looked down at the tattoo.

No. It's over between us. That's a closed door now. I can't go back to the way things were. The best I can do is focus on the present and cherish the memories I have.

The warm water was soothing. The Crescent Horned Punisher quickly found herself singing songs from her old band as she reminisced. Soon she was completely lost in her past.

It was her sixteenth birthday and she was sitting at a table in a restaurant surrounded by her friends. Zero was there, along with Lisa and Wake. There were others, as well; many of them she had long since forgotten. Many were fellow musicians, though their names and faces were unclear.

"So, what'd you guys get me?" Vanilla asked with a mischievous smile, leaning forward to press her large breasts into the table seductively.

"Heh. I'll give you your present tonight," Zero responded, tossing a salty fry at her ample cleavage and missing.

"You gave me that last night," she said, flicking the warm food item off the table. "How about something like an expensive necklace? There's that silver one with the purple stone in it down at The Platinum Prestige."

"You'd rather have that?"

"No. I want both."

"Well, I can't afford the necklace. You know that."

"So? Steal it."

"Yeah, *sure*. You remember what happened last time I tried stealing something for you, don't you? I got my ass handed to me. I was lucky that Royal Guardsmen was a fan of our band."

In response, she toyed with the dangerously-thin straps of her tank top, sliding them off her shoulder and tugging on them. "Maybe your reward for getting me that necklace will make up for the trouble," she said slyly.

"Shit. You're making this hard," the Grenzel Blind Demon laughed, tossing another fry.

This time it landed between her breasts. "Hey!" she exclaimed, instinctively plunging her hand deep into her shirt to retrieve it. "You asshole! It slid into my bra! Now it'll have grease stains…"

"Want me to help you get it out?" Zero snickered.

"Hmph. You just want to touch my boobs. Well, fine! Go on, you jerk."

The flashback ended abruptly as the Crescent Horned Punisher shook her head to clear her mind. Blushing, she held her hand to her chest and took a deep breath. *Jeez, we were so bad. I guess we were one in the same that way, though. Still…at least Zero seems a bit calmer now than he was back then. What will Zallin think when he finds out I met up with him?*

She felt the urge to cry as her thoughts turned to her husband. Leaning up against the wall and casting her eyes to her feet, she watched the water stream down her body and into the drain. Her tears were indistinguishable from the swirling river at her feet.

When she was all set for the rest of her day, the white-haired singer said goodbye to her daughter and set out for 5th City Realm with high spirits. With her mind running through every musical concept she had ever been taught, she navigated through the bustling streets of the wealthy metropolis. The noise from leashed animals, spoiled children, public transport, and people huddled in circles gossiping was drowned out by the ecstasy that she felt inside. Soon she had reached the dreary passage to the back door of Meltdown Music.

The alleyway that the entrance was located in was surprisingly quiet and empty. A pale young woman dressed in a gothic style outfit sat against a dumpster with her head hung. A thin stream of light gray smoke drifted up from a bent cigarette that was pinched between her index and middle finger. As Vanilla walked by, the woman looked up, smirked, and then exhaled a large cloud of smoke. The Crescent Horned Punisher coughed and quickened her pace until she was clear from the overpowering stench. "*That* was rude, but I can't let this ruin my day," she told herself. She looked behind her. The young woman was still sitting by the trash, curling her black hair around her index finger. It was then that she noticed the woman's tattoos. There was a monster tattooed across both her breasts, skulls on both her arms, flying devil-like creatures on her legs, and black stripes on her neck, among other things.

"You got a problem, Whitey?" she called out, sticking up her middle finger.

"No."

"Then stop staring."

"OK, sorry!"

Vanilla's heart was racing from the frightful confrontation. Fortunately she had already reached the door. Eager to escape the shady alley, she burst into the cool music store, coming face-to-face with Steve Pulltuck.

Steve blinked and gave a hearty laugh. "Well look who we have here! You didn't break that bass already, did you?"

"No, not at all! I was going to check out some amplifiers for future reference."

"For future reference or future purchase?"

"Future purchase."

"Of course! Hahaha! Well, take your time. Since you don't have your bass with you, feel free to use one of ours. Oh, and feel free to purchase one too! Ha!"

"Thanks Mr. Pulltuck."

"You know to just call me Steve. Everyone does. Now if you'll excuse me Vanilla, I've got places to be and people to see."

Vanilla stepped aside to let the large man through. He sang joyfully and drummed on his rotund stomach as he waddled down the dark alleyway, stopping every now and then to catch his breath. The door slid shut, leaving her to wonder how anybody could be so exuberant in such a state of poor health.

Time passed rapidly as she tested the store's wide selection of equipment. By the time she had comprised her wish list, it had long since passed lunchtime. The light outside was fading and the singer's stomach grumbled from hunger. Finally pulling herself away from shopping, she decided to head back home to prepare for the evening.

As she entered the house, a delicious smell wafted through the air. Her mouth began to water as she took off her shoes and tossed them aside. "I'm home!" she called out, rushing for the kitchen. On the counter near the oven sat a large mixing bowl and a cooling rack stacked with sugar cookies. Raech was putting a heavy brown cookbook back into its place on a shelf when she entered.

"Hi, Mom."

"Hi Sweetie! I see you made cookies!"

"Yes, sugar cookies. I was going to make chocolate chip, but we didn't have chocolate chips, so I decided on these."

"May I have one?"

"Why of course! This is your kitchen. I'm just blessed with the privilege of using it."

"Well it's a blessing to have you as my daughter."

Vanilla picked up a warm cookie and took a bite. "Wow, these are great, Raech! You really have become a good cook."

Raech blushed and smiled. "Thank you," she replied with an elegant curtsy.

Once she had eaten a more substantial supper, the white-haired singer set about preparing for the concert. She dug her bass and microphone back out of her closet along with some of her old band clothes, carefully choosing the most modest outfit she could come up with. When it was time for her to meet up with the others, she collected her things, went to Raech, and the two of them transported to Felix Park.

It was already dark out in 3rd City Realm. The streetlights shone their orange glow onto the sidewalks, attracting swarms of moths and mosquitoes. An old flatbed hover truck was parked near a collapsible stage that had been set up in the center of the park. A number of fans had already gathered and were mingling with the band. Vanilla and Raech walked up to them and were met by enthusiastic cheers and whistles.

"It's Vanilla!" one fan exclaimed, jogging up to meet her. Soon the small crowd of early arrivers had encircled her and were asking questions, giving praise, and holding out their albums in hopes of getting an autograph.

"Thanks, everyone. Just so I make myself clear: I'm not getting back together with *To the Power of 10*." The fans made disappointed groans and begged her to reconsider. "Nope. I'm married and have a daughter. I just don't have time for preforming full-time anymore," she replied firmly.

Once the excitement had been pacified and the metalheads had given her enough space, Vanilla climbed onstage and set up her equipment. Zero sat beside her on his amplifier, tuning one of his guitars.

"So I see you brought your bass. Do you feel confident enough to play?"

"I think so. I got some practice in today, actually. I was at Meltdown Music trying out some amps."

"Oh cool. Did you find any that you liked?"

"Yeah, a few. I just wrote the names down for future reference. I didn't want to purchase one just yet. I hope you don't mind if I use the one that's here."

"That's what I brought it for. I figured that you didn't have one, so I asked Lisa to bring hers."

"Oh, thanks. That was thoughtful of you—and her."

"Yup."

The guitarist stood up and strummed his red V-shaped guitar. Its heavily distorted sound seemed to hang in the air for minutes, resonating throughout the vast expanse of fields and walkways. He looked up and shook his head. His lengthy blue hair swung to the side but still covered his eyes. "What time is it?" he asked, not fully directing his question at anyone. Vanilla fished her cell phone out of her purse and glanced at it.

"It's six-thirty."

"Ah, thanks. My transportation watch stopped displaying the time a while ago and I can't find anyone that will fix it since it's an old one. It's bullshit—I mean crap."

"Hm. Well I don't know what to tell you then. Hey, shouldn't we run through the songs once more before more people start showing up?"

"We already did. I guess we could go through them one more time if you want."

"We don't have to if you don't want to. I just thought it might be a good idea."

"Eh, I dunno. I'll only do it if you want to. Hey, didn't you bring your daughter with you?"

"I did. Why do you ask?"

"I thought she would be hanging around you."

"She—"

Her heart skipped a beat. "Oh shoot! Raech! Raech, where are you?" she called toward the mass of fans. After a couple seconds with no reply, she jumped off the stage and ran up to them.

"Have any of you seen my daughter?" she asked desperately, raising her voice over the noisy chatter. A sickening wave of anxiety overcame her as she imagined her daughter taking a cigarette from a group of rebellious teenagers or being picked on by a bunch of mean older girls. Then, to her relief, she saw the Madite mingling with a few of the less extreme individuals at the edge of the crowd.

"Hi Vanilla," one of them said when he noticed her walking up to them. "Your daughter is amazing! She can read minds and use magic!"

Raech blushed shyly at the compliment and smiled. Vanilla put her arm around her and sighed with relief.

"I didn't know where you had gone. I almost had a heart attack."

"Oh, I'm so sorry, Mom. I didn't mean to make you worry. When you headed for the stage I assumed that you knew I was back here."

"It's OK, Sweetie. I'm not upset or anything. I just love you, that's all. Who are your new friends, by the way?"

The Crescent Horned Punisher motioned toward the two teenagers that Raech had been talking to. The shorter of the two stepped forward and introduced himself. "My name's Tom and this is my friend Darren. We both love your music!"

Tom had short, spiked hair that had been dyed black. He wore a long sleeve button-down shirt with dress pants and a silver nametag on his shoulder. Besides his height and formal attire, Vanilla noticed a piercing on his tongue when he spoke.

Strange, she thought to herself, *he doesn't seem like the type of kid that would get a piercing there. Well, maybe.*

Next, Darren stepped forward. He was a chubby blonde with thick, round glasses—obviously a freshman in high school.

"I-I know Tom already did the honors me, but I must insist on doing so myself. I am known as Darren James Godsberg, the eldest of my three siblings. It is truly a pleasure to make your acquaintance, O Great Maiden of Metal." Vanilla forced a smile and reluctantly shook his fat, sweaty outstretched hand, trying her best to hide her distaste.

"Well it's nice to meet you two. I've got to get back onstage now. Raech, why don't you stand in the front row? That's always the best place at concerts. Trust me."

"Oh, alright. Which side of the stage will you be on?"

"Center. I guess that's not really a side, but…"

Raech winked, signaling that she had understood her mother's thoughts about the two boys.

"Allow me to escort you to the front and centermost region of this magnificent audience, O Young Princess, daughter of Vanilla the Great and Musical," Darren cut in.

Raech shook her head and replied, "Thank you for your offer, but I'll be fine on my own."

Vanilla smiled, turned around, and then hastily made her way back to the band.

"Good luck, Mom!" Raech called after her.

After climbing back up and taking her place next to Zero, she picked up her bass and slung the strap over her shoulder. "Are we ready?" she asked. The Grenzel Blind Demon shook his head. Then, reaching behind his amp he withdrew a slim performance headset.

"Here, put it on."

"But I have a microphone already."

"Yeah, but how the hell are you gonna play bass while you're holding a microphone?"

"I was going to put it on a stand."

"We'll be moving around a lot though. It'd look weird if you were just standing there."

"No it wouldn't. Lots of musicians stand in front of a microphone while they play an instrument."

"Just put the damn thing on. There's only a few minutes left and we have to lower the curtain now."

"Curtain?"

Just as she had finished speaking, a red velvet curtain dropped in front of her. It was wet and smelled strongly of gasoline. Startled, the singer jumped back. "You're not going to light this on fire, are you?" she asked, hastily fitting the new microphone around her head.

"Yup. We're gonna burn it as we start the first song."

"Are out of your mind?! That's dangerous and there are people out there that could get singed!"

"Don't worry. I've done this like a million times already. Nobody's ever gotten hurt."

"Zero, my daughter is in the front row! This is absolutely ridiculous!"

"Relax. She'll be fine."

"Zero!"

Before the dumbfounded Crescent Horned Punisher could do anything, he gave the signal to Wake to start the drumroll. Struggling to swallow her concern, she shot a glare at the carefree guitarist and readied herself for what was about to happen.

The platform lit up and the curtain began to rise. The crowd screamed and cheered as Zero broke in with a guitar solo, headbanging wildly. A tiny spark flashed from his lighter, which was being used by Lisa, and then the red velvet curtain burst into flames. When it was reduced to ashes, Vanilla stepped into view. Her long white hair cascaded all the way down to her waist and shone brilliantly in the overhead lighting. The dark high heels that she wore clacked as she walked to the edge of the stage.

"Thank you all for coming! We are *To the Power of 10*! Are you guys ready to rock?" she called out, looking confidently into the audience. The reply was a roar of enthusiasm louder than before. Fans new and old jumped up and down, pumped their fists, and screamed at the top of their lungs.

Vanilla closed her eyes and took a brief moment to soak in the glory. Time seemed to stand still as adrenaline welled up inside her. "One, two, three, four!!" Wake shouted from behind his drum set. She opened her eyes, slid her fingers down the thick strings on her bass, and started to play. Even with the little practice she had had, the rhythm flowed as if she had been born knowing it.

"Do you feel the darkness in the rain?
Can you feel my sorrow and my pain?

I'm back from hell again.
I'm back from the darkness within.
I'm back from hell again.
I'm here for revenge.

Can you see me through this pain?
Have your eyes cried my tears?
Or have you cowered in fear?

Will the world turn cold again?
You've just lost your only friend.

A hardened heart bleeds blood of sorrow,
Eyes half open and waiting for tomorrow.

The day is gone. You have no one.
The day is gone. Your death has come.
The night consumes. Your shadow's won.
Darkness looms. Where is your hope?

Do you feel the darkness in the rain?

Can you feel my sorrow and my pain?

I'm back from hell again.
I'm back from the darkness within.
I'm back from hell again.
I'm here for revenge."

Upon the closing of the first song, a deafening applause erupted from the audience, accompanied by fervent whistles and shouts. After a short pause for the band to bask again in their enthusiasm, Wake signaled the beginning of another song and then they continued.

As the drums built up tension, Vanilla closed her eyes and turned her face to the sky. A sudden gust of wind blew her long white hair to the side majestically. It wound around her left arm like vines for a moment until it was cascading back behind her like a waterfall. Skillfully, she slid her fingers down the thick strings of her bass and began to play. Her timing was perfect. The instrument in her hands felt so natural her mind toyed with the idea that it was part of her. The melodies flowed from her soul, blending with those of her comrades and filling the night air with an undying energy. When the time had come, she opened her mouth and sang, crying out from the very core of her being.

"A bridge that was burnt,
A punishment well earned,
This is what I deserve;
To never speak another word.

You carried me on these broken wings.
Out from the ashes my heart sings.

But this is the end where all grows still,
I've lost my hope, my iron will.

Die in my arms, my beautiful, my immortal.
Bleed to black and fade to dust.
Feed this insatiable bloodlust!"

The night steadily drifted onward. Darkness had already covered the sky in a veil of deep purple and blue. A few street lights dimly flickered on and off, as if pleading for the performers to cease their noise.

Finally, the concert came to a close. Zero unplugged his guitar. His amplifier responded with a thundering boom. Startled, he jumped back and cursed loudly. Vanilla smiled and covered her mouth to keep from laughing. *Well, some things never change,* she thought to herself.

CHAPTER 12

-Return-

It was half past 11 o'clock when the last of the lingering fans were finally on their way home. The cheers and fist-pumping of hard rockers and metalheads had long since subsided. Felix Park had faded back into its serene and restful state. The four members of *To the Power of 10* sat on the edge of the collapsible stage, recounting their past shows and memorable moments together.

Zero combed through his long blue hair with his fingers and reclined against his amplifier with a big smile on his face. "Thanks guys," he said, his voice dry from singing.

Vanilla sat down next to him, uncapped a water bottle, and chugged it down. Her skin was wet with sweat, and her hands were shaking slightly with tiredness, but the flame of passion and excitement still burnt bright in her large, round eyes.

"I wasn't sure if I could pull that off. It's been so long…"

"You did great though, Vanilla. For someone who hasn't performed at concert level in fourteen years, you really nailed it."

"Thanks Babe—no wait, not that! I meant to say 'Zero.'"

"Don't worry. I know what you meant."

"Good. I'm married, so I shouldn't have said that."

"Yeah I know. You've told me that three times already. I'm not stupid and I know you didn't mean to say, 'Babe.' It's just funny."

"Alright, alright. Enough."

At that moment, a red sneaker hit Zero on the side of his head and bounced onto the ground. He flinched and angrily jumped to his feet, nearly tripping over the cable that was plugged into his amplifier. "What the hell, Wake?!" he shouted, throwing his arms in the air.

The red-headed drummer was standing in his socks on the other side of the stage, his right arm poised and ready to strike with his other shoe. "See? I can kick you anytime I want, you freakin' tree!"

Quickly grabbing a broken drumstick from the floor of the stage, the tall guitarist hurled it at his short comrade and missed. Wake snickered and taunted, "You still can't hit me, even from this distance! I know little kids that can throw better than you!" Flustered, Zero stuck up his middle finger and spat in his direction.

Before the two roughnecks could make a move for each other, Lisa stepped in. Her ornate dress seemed to flow heroically like a superhero's cape in the cool night breeze. She forced two fingers into Wake's chest without hesitation. The rowdy drummer grunted and fell to the floor, swearing.

"Lisa! You didn't have to *hurt* him! What if you broke his ribs or something?" Vanilla exclaimed.

"Pressure points," she signed.

Just then, Raech approached onstage. It was apparent that she had not seen what had just happened.

"Mom, that was spectacular! You really have an amazing voice."

"Oh, thank you, Sweetie. I'm glad you liked it. I wasn't sure what you'd think of dirge metal."

"Well, I can't say it's my favorite genre, but I believe one of the most beautiful things about music is the diversity."

"That's a very wise statement. We can head home soon. Let me just spend a little more time catching up here."

"Yes Mother."

Raech retreated to a nearby park bench. Zero glanced over at the quiet teenager, who was now gazing contently at the clouds in the night sky.

"So Vanilla, what kinda guy is your husband?"

"You mean species or personality? Why do you ask?"

"Personality. I'm just curious. Your daughter is a lot calmer than most kids her age. I was just wondering if that had something to do with her dad."

"Raech? She's been that way since she was very young. As for Zallin, he's an introvert, as well. The two are quite alike. Zallin's a bit more forward when things get out of hand, though. I mean, he's nice—just not afraid to speak up when there's something wrong."

"Ah, I see. That makes sense. Seems like all Madites are like that."

"Not all of them. You know, I should probably get going. It's late."

"OK. The kid has school tomorrow, right?"

"No. She's actually exempt from school. At the beginning of every year, she goes to take a huge exam at Longstein's Institute in 5th City Realm. It determines if she needs to go to school that year. So far she's passed it every time."

"What? That's crap. You've gotta be joking."

"I'm not. You can ask her yourself."

"Jeez, you're lucky."

"I guess you could say that. But really, I should be on my way now. It was good to be able to perform again. Thanks for giving me the opportunity. We'll all have to hang out soon. I'm really glad I could meet up with you and the band again, Zero."

"Yeah! I'm glad you were able to sing with us again. If you ever wanna do it again, let me know."

"Thanks! I probably will. Bye guys!"

Lisa, Wake, and Zero waved farewell to their old friend and watched her as she gradually disappeared from view.

As two women neared the edge of the park, Raech tugged on her mother's sleeve. Vanilla could sense something was worrying her even before she spoke. The young girl's hand was trembling. "Mom, I'm going to transport us from here."

"Why? We're still in the park's warp barrier, aren't we? I didn't think we could transport until we reached the street."

"We just passed out of it, actually. I'll explain later. Please hold my hand."

"Alright, Sweetie, whatever you say."

Hastily, Raech took her mother's hand and teleported with a blinding burst of blue light.

A few yards away, sitting motionless on a bench in the shadows was a woman dressed in gothic clothing and a baseball cap with a skull on it. The flash had illuminated her face for only a split second. Her eyes were purple and her lips were colored metallic black, a stark contrast to her unhealthy pale skin. Long, black strands of curly hair were draped over her right eye. There were tattoos on her arms, legs, neck, and chest. The tops of her ears were pierced with numerous silver rings and her lobes were gauged with thick ebony disks.

After a few seconds, the woman rose to her feet like a reanimated corpse. She reached into the front of her corset and took out a box of cigarettes that had been stuffed between her breasts. "Hm... *That* was smart. It doesn't matter where you run. I'll find you, Vanilla Lamberschvak," she grumbled and lit them with a spark from her fingernails.

Back at the house, it was pitch dark as Vanilla and Raech came through the front door. Zallin had been out on active duty for five months. To the two girls, the house seemed lifeless. Even for his reclusive personality, life felt hollow without the honest spellcaster. Vanilla did her best to keep positive and dwell on what she was thankful for. Each day presented an increasing struggle with loneliness. She had never had to deal with her husband's prolonged absence before.

Raech flicked the light switch and the house was illuminated. It was even lonelier now that the lack of activity was visible. A thin coating of dust could be seen on the furniture as the lights gradually brightened. Zallin's blue armchair looked almost sad. A bit of stuffing was bulging out of a tear on the right armrest and the seat cushion was drooping, as if sulking about its owner's vacancy.

Vanilla sighed quietly and stood gazing at the chair. After a short pause, she set her purse by the front door and trudged across the living room to sit down. The chair was softer than ever. Performing with her band late into the night was starting to take its toll on her. The hour hand on the wall clock was positioned at nine, while the minute hand lazily slipped to eight. She closed her eyes and instantly fell into a deep sleep.

In what seemed like only a few seconds, she was awakened by a gentle hand on her shoulder. Startled, she jolted into an upright position and found Zallin half-asleep on the couch adjacent to her. His arm was outstretched toward her and his head was back. The royal blue mage's cloak he wore was torn and mud was smudged on his face. There was a tattered bandage wrapped tightly around his forearm, which looked as though it had been singed. He was home; he was alive.

Tears of joy streamed down Vanilla's face. Using what little energy she had, she leaned over and kissed him. The yellow eyes on his hat opened slightly, and then closed again from exhaustion. There they wept together, tired, but at peace.

Golden rays of morning light beamed down on the Crescent Horned Punisher. Strange, shadowy patterns danced on the floorboards as the curtains rippled in the breeze from the ceiling fan. The house was still and silent. Dawn had arrived.

She propped herself up in the navy blue armchair. The aroma of fresh coffee filled the air. "Raech doesn't drink coffee," she mumbled sleepily. Then she remembered: Zallin had come home last night. She was elated. The months of loneliness were finally over. Vanilla got up and hurried to the kitchen as fast as her tired body would allow.

To her surprise, Raech *was* the one making coffee. Zallin was slumped over, face-down at the table. His arms hung weakly at his sides like a doll. Vanilla's sudden outburst of naïve joy vanished as the reality hit her. She had expected her hero to sweep her off her feet or serve her a steamy cup of coffee. Guilt set in as she realized that no soldier would have that much energy right after coming home from a battle. *What was I thinking?* she thought. *That was selfish of me... I'm just glad he's home.*

"Good morning, Mother," Raech said quietly. "Dad asked me if I'd make coffee for you." She handed her a cup of coffee. Vanilla took it and forced herself to continue smiling.

"Thanks Sweetie," Vanilla said distantly. A long silence fell between the three of them.

Zallin broke the stillness with a loud, labored cough. "Vanilla, I'm sorry I'm not the knight in shining armor that you thought I would be. I know you wanted me to sweep you off your feet, but that's not how it is for Council members. When I recover, I'll take you out to eat."

The spell caster's voice was dry and raspy. It sounded like a whisper. With much effort, he lifted his head so he could look his wife in the eyes. "I love you, Vanilla," he said.

Tears started to trickle down the white-haired maiden's cheeks. What her husband said added to her burden of guilt. She rubbed her eyes with her arm. "I love you too, Zallin. As long as you're alright, that's all that matters. You'll always be my hero."

Zallin let his head fall limply back onto the table. He coughed hard and then started weeping. Vanilla walked over to him and embraced him. His skin was clammy and pale. Even the blue color from his hat seemed to have faded into a grayish tint. "You need to rest, Hon," she said sympathetically.

The old grandfather clock in the dining room struck ten. Its regal pendulum shook as the bell sounded. For a few seconds, all other noises seemed to fade into the loud chime.

"Here, I'll help you up." Mustering her strength, Vanilla slid one arm under her husband's shoulders and stood up. To her surprise, his body was fairly light. A flashback went through her mind.

Delicate snowflakes drifted gracefully to the ground. Trees had long since lost their leaves, revealing their skeletal network of branches to the cold air. A beautiful sheet of fresh snow covered 1st City Realm. Pedestrians hustled across the busy streets and sidewalks, frantically searching for last-minute gifts. Ice skaters slid across a frozen pond. The careless few who decided to run joined in on the slipping, although not by their own will.

Zallin sat on a park bench with his hands clamped around a warm beverage. He was bundled up in a thick, gray coat and scarf. Raech was playing in the snow next to him. Unlike her father, the cold didn't seem to faze her at all.

Out on the ice, Vanilla was skating elegantly. She carved perfect figure eights in the frozen pond with her skates. "Zallin, why don't you come out on the ice?" she called out.

"I don't know how to ice skate."

"Oh come on. You're not scared are you? And here I thought it would be more frightening to be in the Councils than to try ice skating."

"I fail to see the humor in that."

At that moment, Vanilla slipped and fell backwards. Her head hit the ice hard. She gasped and began crying.

Reacting quickly, Zallin jumped to his feet and rushed over to her. He knelt down and gently lifted her up. "You'll be OK. Try to take a deep breath and hold still. I'll call Raech over and we can head home," he said reassuringly. With a mere wave of his hand, he numbed the pain for her. "I'll always be here to help you up when you fall, Vanilla."

The flashback faded. There she was, holding Zallin up with her skinny arms. It was ironic, Vanilla thought, that now she found herself saying almost the same thing to her husband that he himself had recited many times. They were still a team despite their vast differences.

"Do you need help?" Raech asked.

Vanilla shook her head. "That's alright, Sweetie. Thanks, though."

When she reached their bedroom, she clumsily kicked the door open and laid Zallin down on their bed. He was breathing slowly, like he was asleep. The eyes on his hat were still open, but evidently he was out cold.

With one last glance back, Vanilla left the room and carefully closed the door. Her heart sank as the sound of her husband's painful coughs rang out. She could feel his suffering.

Hastily, she opened it again to find Zallin sitting up in bed, his right arm held up to cover his mouth. "Vanilla, could you please bring me some tissues," he asked in a husky whisper.

Vanilla nodded and sprinted to the kitchen. *Zallin is an experienced healer. I wonder why he doesn't heal himself? I'm sure there's a reason. I know he has his limits, especially in this condition. Poor Zallin...*

As she pondered over this, she had an idea. "Raech, could you come here for a second? I have a question." The box of soft, white tissues tumbled off the shelf and bonked her in the head just as Raech entered the room.

"Yes Mother?"

"Do you know if a healer can heal another healer?"

"I don't see why not. Is this about Dad?"

"Yeah. I know that you have some healing powers of your own. Do you think you could try?"

"I'd need to know what's causing his illness…I've never actually healed a person before though. I mean, I've read about how it's done and practiced the basic spells, but I'm not sure I want to risk trying without more prior experience. If I were to mess up, I could potentially make things a lot worse. I'm sorry, Mom."

"Oh there's no need to be sorry. I was just curious. Thanks anyway." Vanilla patted her daughter on the shoulder and made her way back to the bedroom.

"Hon, here's a box of tissues for you. Do you need anything else?"

"Thanks Vanilla. If I need anything else, I'll let you know. I'm going to try and rest for a bit. I'm not sure what I've contracted, but I think I just need sleep."

"Alright. I love you."

Vanilla lingered at the doorway for a moment.

"Um, Zallin?"

"Yes?"

"Is it OK if I…rest beside you?"

"I-I'm sorry. I'm really not ready for that now. I'm not sure if what I have is contagious, so wouldn't want to get you sick, either."

"No, no! I didn't mean *that*. It's just…I really want to spend time with you, even if that means lying next to you while you sleep. You've been gone for so long and it's been so lonely. I just—" Vanilla felt the tears welling up inside her.

Zallin saw this and looked down. "I'm sorry. I hope that didn't sound cold. Of course you can. This is your room, too."

Vanilla shook her head and wiped her eyes with the back of her hand. "No, it's fine. I guess I said that kind of weird."

The Madite moved the box of tissues off the bed and onto his nightstand, clearing a space beside him. The Crescent Horned Punisher gently closed the door and behind her and climbed into bed.

In the darkness, Vanilla sat deep in thought, holding her husband's hand. Gradually, his grip began to weaken as he drifted off to sleep. Vanilla listened as his breathing became slow and more peaceful. She smiled and closed her eyes, too.

The hours slipped by. Part of her felt like falling asleep as well, but her worry kept her awake. Eventually, she quietly got out of bed and tiptoed to the door. The sound of Zallin's cough made her jump before she could leave the room, though. She turned around to ask if he was alright, but quickly realized that he was still asleep.

Yikes. Zallin's usually a light sleeper. He must really be exhausted. I sure hope he's able to recover from this quickly.

Out in the hallway, Vanilla closed her bedroom door and turned around. "Oh!" she said, almost bumping into Raech. "Sorry, Sweetie, I didn't see you there."

"That's OK. How's Dad doing?"

"He's still feeling pretty sick. I guess whatever he has will take some time to recover from."

"Poor Dad…"

"Yeah… Say, healers *can* heal themselves, can't they? From illnesses, I mean. I know that they can heal their wounds and stuff, and they can heal other healers, like you told me a bit ago."

"They usually can. Sickness is usually a bit trickier to heal than wounds though—using the technique that Dad specializes in, that is. If the illness is caused by a virus or bacteria, then it requires the healer to either track down every virus or bad bacteria—or most of them—using psychic vision and kill it with very precise magic…or create a magical antibiotic. It's a very difficult thing to do even for experienced healers and it has a lot of risks. Whenever you're using magic to destroy microscopic organisms within someone's body, there's always a possibility of harming good cells. That's why you don't see many mages healing themselves of sicknesses. It's also why services that use magic to heal people are so expensive. The amount of focus it takes is… Oh, I'm sorry. I was starting to ramble. I hope I didn't bother you."

"No, you're fine. That was really interesting, actually. I guess it makes sense."

"Would you like me to continue?"

"Um, maybe some other time. Hey, what time is it?"

"It's twelve thirty-five."

"Oh, no wonder I'm so hungry. Have you had lunch yet?"

"Yeah."

"What did you have?"

"Pasta."

"Hm. That sounds good. Is the water still on the stove?"

"No. I already dumped it out and cleaned the pot. I'm sorry."

"No worries. You were doing what you were supposed to. I can't argue with that."

"Do you want me to bring the water to a boil? I can use magic to make it boil a lot quicker."

"Well, I guess that's alright. I don't really like the idea of using fire magic in the house, but I don't want to wait. Go ahead. Just make sure you don't use too big of a flame."

"I won't."

In the kitchen, Raech retrieved the pot from the cupboard beneath the stove and filled it with water while Vanilla got out a bag of egg noodles. Gracefully, the teen set the pot on the stove and turned on the heat. Her mother stood watching with curiosity—and slight concern as the Madite held her hand near the side of the pot and closed her eyes. There was a little flash from her palm and instantly the water began bubbling. Impressed, Vanilla raised her eyebrows and gently clapped her hand against the bag of noodles. "Wow, I wish I could do that."

"It's not hard."

"Maybe for you it isn't. I can't use magic, remember?"

"That's OK. We all have our own strengths."

"True. Thanks, Sweetie."

"You're welcome."

Vanilla poured a bit of pasta into the water and set the timer on the stove. *Sometimes I wonder what our world would be like without magic,* she thought, glancing back at Raech, who was just leaving the kitchen. *I suppose the military would be a lot different. We probably wouldn't have the Five Pillars...that would be really weird.*

When her food was ready, Vanilla sat down at the table and began eating. *I should ask Zallin if he wants some. Hm...he hasn't eaten lunch yet, either.* Carefully picking the plate up with one hand, she headed toward the bedroom.

Zallin was still asleep when Vanilla entered the room. *Maybe I shouldn't bug him right now. I'll offer him something when he wakes up,* she thought. As she was turning to leave, he began coughing loudly. She winced at the sound and almost dropped the plate. She waited, half-expecting him to say something, but he hadn't awoken.

I really wish there was something I could do to help him. I also wish his captain would just leave him alone now that's he's technically not part of

271

the 55th Council. *I don't like the idea of him getting hurt or sick from these missions,* she thought, giving one last look at her husband before quietly exiting the room.

Out in the living room, Vanilla sat by her stereo paging through her immense song library. The console's holographic screen projected album covers in front of her, which she mindlessly scrolled through by flicking her finger sideways in the air. Eventually she came across her first *To the Power of 10* album. It was black with a picture of her as a teenager, half-naked and posing with her hands on her chest as if she was basking in the shower. Embarrassed, she blushed and quickly slid it aside. *That was awkward,* she thought with a nervous glance behind her. *It's a good thing Raech didn't see that. Jeez, what was I thinking back then?*

A small cough from behind her made her jump. Zallin had appeared in the doorway. He was gingerly clutching his stomach and squinting.

"Oh, are you alright?" Vanilla asked quickly. *That was dumb. Of course he's not alright,* she thought the moment the words left her mouth.

Zallin forced a smile. "I'll be fine. Don't worry about me."

"Can I get you something to eat?"

"No, that's alright. I had some yogurt just a few minutes ago. Thanks though."

"Oh. I didn't hear you. I thought you were still in bed."

Zallin shrugged weakly and forced a smile.

"Are you going back to bed?"

"Not yet. I wanted to find a certain book. I think it's in that cabinet below your stereo."

"Here? Which one is it?"

"It's called *Advanced Healing: Psychic-Driven Solutions.*"

"OK. Let's see... This?"

272

"Yes, that's it."

"Here."

"Thanks."

"Will you be able to heal yourself?"

"Maybe. I think I figured out what's causing this."

"What?"

"I may have accidentally breathed air that was intoxicated by a Meglorab during my mission. If so, it's a miracle that it didn't kill me."

"Wait, what? Are you going to be OK? What's a Meglorab?"

"The fact that I'm still alive means that I'm not in any danger—if that's what's causing this illness. A Meglorab is a blob-like Melbruitz. Luckily there aren't any in Spiritia."

"So does that mean you were in Medrunt-Baritz? I thought you said you were going to be in Spiritia."

"We were, but Crescent changed his mind at the last minute."

"That man...I don't know how you can put up with him."

"I have to. It's my job."

"I wish it weren't. Anyway, isn't it against the peace treaty to go into Medrunt-Baritz?"

"For Spiritans who are residents of Spiritia or affiliated with the government, it is."

"Aren't the Councils affiliated with the government?"

"Not officially. We're still considered an independent military organization. That's why not all of the Councils help Spiritia, even though they're supposed to. Still, since I'm a resident of Spiritia, it *was* illegal, but...I have to obey Crescent."

"I see. I can't believe a man like him can be the leader of a Council..."

"Well, there's nothing we can do about that. Hm. This looks like the one… Yeah. It is."

"You found the right spell?"

"I believe so. Stand back for a moment."

"OK."

A mystical green light filled the room as Zallin set the book down and closed his eyes. Energy flowed from his body and created ripples in the air around him. She could feel a calming aura pulsing past her and watched in wonder.

Suddenly, the magic ceased. The sick Madite stooped over and coughed loudly. Vanilla was at his side instantly, supporting him with her arms. "Are you OK? What happened?" she asked worriedly.

He shook his head. "I guess I was wrong. It must be something else."

"So that wasn't the right spell?"

"It would have been, had this been caused by what I thought it was. I'll have to do more research later. I'm too tired now, though. I think I'll rest some more."

"Well, you do seem to be a bit better than you were a while ago. Maybe you'll be able to recover naturally."

"I hope so."

"Hang in there. If you need anything, let me know."

"Thanks."

Zallin slowly retreated to the bedroom, limping slightly like a wounded animal. Vanilla winced in empathy as she watched him. It tore at her heart to see him in agony. She was about to offer him assistance, but he suddenly fell face-first onto the hardwood floor. She rushed over to him and knelt down, putting her right arm around his back to help him up.

"Zallin, are you OK? Are you hurt?"

"No...I'm fine. I just lost my balance."

"Seriously? Babe, this is *not* OK! I'm worried about you. I'm going to call a doctor. You're *not* fine."

"Vanilla, if I can't heal myself, what could a doctor do?"

The motherly Crescent Horned Punisher was about to object, but stopped and thought. *I guess he's right. He's a healer for the 55ᵗʰ Council. If he can't fix this, there aren't too many people that can.* She shook her head. "But I can't just sit and watch as you suffer. Please, let me do *something,*" she replied.

"What can you do though?"

"I...I...don't know. Maybe someone I know is a healer or something. Let me think."

"I'll be fine Vanilla."

"Would you just stop it? Zallin, it's OK to rely on other people once in a while! You're always helping me, so it's only right that I help you. Besides, you're my husband."

Zallin said nothing and gazed quietly at his feet. Vanilla was near tears, but she forced herself to smile and look confident. "I'm here for you, Zallin. You don't have to do this alone."

"Vanilla..."

"I'm *going* to help you."

The Madite stared at his wife in wonder. A small tear trickled down his cheek, which she gently wiped away with her hand. "I..." he began, but coughed hard. "Thank you, Vanilla."

"Dad? Are you alright? What happened?" Raech's voice came from behind them. She was standing in the doorway, her right hand gently resting on the doorframe.

"I'm fi—" Zallin tried, but was quickly interrupted by Vanilla.

"He's still not feeling well. Raech, do you know anyone who

might be able to help?"

"I don't think so. I don't really know that many people…I'm very sorry."

"That's alright, Sweetie. No need to apologize. I just thought it was worth asking."

"Actually, I think I may have thought of someone."

"Really? Who?"

"Well, I don't really know her personally, but she's one of Grace's friends."

"Grace Hyten?"

"Yes."

"Do you have her number?"

"No. I'd need to get it from her. Let me go get my phone."

"OK."

Minutes later, Raech returned with her cell phone. "I just texted her. She said she'd be over shortly."

"Thank you so much, Sweetie! I hope she can figure out what's wrong and fix it."

"Me, too."

At that moment, they were interrupted by a light knock on the front door. Raech sprinted to the front room to answer it. From the voice of their guest, Vanilla concluded that she was an adult. *Good,* she thought, *there's some credibility to start with.*

When the woman entered the hallway, Vanilla realized that she was a Madite as well. Her hat was reddish pink with yellow eyes. She wore a modest but casual outfit. It was obviously not her work uniform. There were three decorative rings on her right index finger and gold bracelets on either of her wrists. In her hands was a brown folder stuffed with papers. *Even better,* Vanilla thought. *Since she's a Madite, she definitely uses magic.*

"Hello. You must be Raech's mother."

"Yes. My name's Vanilla."

"It's a pleasure to meet you. My name's Atlyn. I'm a doctor at—"

"Atlyn?" Zallin cut in. "Wait…you weren't part of the 55th Council, were you? No… You couldn't have been. She was… No. I'm sorry. Never mind."

"Hm? Do I look like someone you know?"

"N-no. Never mind. I'm Zallin, by the way."

"Zallin? I can't say I recognize you. Anyway, it's nice to meet you, Zallin. Tell me what's going on."

Zallin coughed. "I just got back from a mission with my Council and I've been very sick. I haven't been able to pinpoint what's causing it."

"What symptoms have you been experiencing? Aside from coughing, that is."

"Fatigue, fever, coughing, and loss of balance."

"Hm…those are very generic. Are you able to tell me what you and your Council were doing?"

"I'm not sure if I'm allowed to go into detail of our previous mission."

"I see. The only reason I ask is because it may help me figure out what might have caused this affliction. I usually try and gather as much information as I can from my patients before I do a body scan for abnormalities."

"That's an interesting way of doing things. I was always taught to do a body scan first. That way you can start treatment while you're locked on to the problem with psychic vision."

"Ah, so you must be a healer, too, then."

"Yes. It's my role in the 55th Council. Or it was, I guess. I still assist them from time to time, though I'm no longer an official member."

"Oh, *that* Council. I didn't realize you were talking about *those* Councils. I thought maybe it was something else. Well, I suppose I can start with a body scan, though I'm not sure if I'll be any better than you, considering that you're a Council member—er, ex-member."

"I think it's still worth a try. This illness may have impaired my previous attempts. Even a simple body scan requires immense focus, which I'm struggling to achieve at the moment."

"Alright. I'll need you to sign a waiver, though. I have one in this folder. Hang on." Atlyn opened her folder and hastily paged through it. "Let's see… Ah, here it is! I'll have you read this over real quick. Here's a pen, too. If that one doesn't work, I probably have another one somewhere that you can try."

Zallin took the sheet of paper and glanced at it. Vanilla peeked over his shoulder curiously, but he was finished and signed it before she had even read the first line.

"I probably should have asked for your insurance card or proof of citizenship before having you sign anything. Sorry about that. I'm a bit disorganized right now since this isn't a typical work setting for me."

"That's alright. Let me go get it."

"Actually, you know what? I won't charge you for this. Think of it as a little thank you for all that the Councils do for keeping our dimension safe."

"No, I couldn't let you do that. You have to make a living somehow."

"And I do. Really, it's fine—just this once."

"Thank you very much. I don't really know what to say."

"No need to say anything. Now, shall I begin the body scan?"

"Sure. I suppose I should lie on the couch. It'd be more comfortable than the floor."

"Whatever works."

With the help of both Vanilla and Atlyn, Zallin stood up and walked to the living room. When he was situated on his back, Atlyn told Vanilla and Raech to stand back and Zallin to lay still and relax. The Madite doctor then sat on the floor by the couch and closed her eyes.

Vanilla waited, expecting some visible pulse of light or perhaps even a sound. At first, it seemed as though Atlyn was simply meditating, but the Crescent Horned Punisher quickly noticed the woman's eyes moving back and forth rapidly beneath their lids. *Is she even using magic? I thought I'd be able to see something—or maybe even feel something,* she thought.

To her surprise, Atlyn opened her eyes after only a few minutes. She looked shaken, like she had seen a ghost. Her face had lost its peach color, fading into a tint that was almost as white as Vanilla's. Taking a controlled breaths to calm herself, she slowly rose to her feet and glanced cautiously at the family.

"What's wrong?" Vanilla asked, starting to panic a little. At the sound of her voice, Zallin opened his eyes.

"I...I'm not sure how to tell you this," she said hesitantly, "but it appears as though you've contracted a strain of Moxica."

Zallin instantly went pale as well—more so than he already was. Raech, who was behind Vanilla, gasped and covered her mouth with both hands. "Oh no! Dad..."

"Wait a minute. What's 'Moxica?'" the Crescent Horned Punisher asked, her mind beginning to race.

"Vanilla, do you know why 2nd City Realm was abandoned a few hundred years ago?" Atlyn asked with a grave look in her eyes.

"Wasn't it overrun with crime?"

"N-not always," Zallin replied. "Long ago, during the Old

Government's rule, there was an outbreak of a deadly super virus called 'Moxica.' It's considered to be one of the most devastating viruses to plague Spiritia's history because it can infect every living thing—including plants. It's also highly contagious and there's no known cure for it... Not even magic, as it completely neutralizes most kinds. Moxica causes an illness known as the Doomsday Plague, which usually kills its victims within a week, but not before they experience the worst suffering of any known disease... There have been many cases on record in which the victims committed suicide just to escape the pain."

"The Moxica pandemic in 2nd City Realm spiraled out of control and the Old Government decided to quarantine the entire realm—as it remains today," Atlyn added. "But before we go any further, let me just say that I get the idea that the viruses in your body, Zallin, are severely crippled."

"Really? What led you to believe that?"

"First of all, when I discovered them as I was looking over your cells, I noticed that they weren't behaving normally. Moxica uses the body's cells to replicate its own—and also to hide them from your immune system. These were just out in the open in your bloodstream and none of the adjacent cells seemed to be afflicted. I think they may be crippled—the Moxica, that is. Also, the fact that you're still alive says something. From what I gather, your symptoms have been going on for a few days and you haven't exhibited any of the severe signs of the Doomsday Plague. Said symptoms occur in full twenty-four hours after infection. In other words, I have a feeling that you're going to live through this. Still, we should all be cautious. Vanilla, Raech—you'll probably start feeling sick soon and so will I. I want all of you to stay here in the house until you've recovered. In fact, it might be a better idea to go to a disease control center—just make sure you let them know you've been infected with Moxica before you go there. They may want to escort you to a quarantined area. Do you have any plants?"

"We have some in pots upstairs. There's a vase with flowers in it over on that end table, too," Zallin replied, pointing to a bouquet of beautiful purple and white flowers.

"I see. I hate to say this, but I advise you to incinerate them as soon as possible. There's a chance that they may be infected, too. You might want to throw out any fruit and vegetables you have, as well. I would say all of your food, but you have to eat something, of course. Perhaps you should get rid of everything edible once you've recovered enough to go out grocery shopping."

"Yes, I was starting to wonder about that. I will see to it shortly. What will you do? You may have been infected by now, too."

"That's a good question. I may need to be transported to a quarantined room at a facility that specializes in this sort of thing. First though, I think I'm going to notify the Research and Development Branch, and then my office. If this were a normal sickness, I'd never think of getting the government involved, but as you already know, Moxica is not to be taken lightly. They might try to contact you."

"That's not a problem. I know many people who work for the Research and Development Branch. The 55th Council usually works alongside the Spiritan government, so it's nothing new for me to be contacted by a member of it."

"I assumed as much. Anyway, I regret to say that there's really nothing that I can do for you but give advice. Actually…I have an idea. Zallin, would you permit me to take some blood samples? Maybe I'll be able to make a vaccine! Then again, I suppose if it hasn't been done by now, it may be nothing more than a pipe dream."

"It may be possible. You don't have the proper equipment with you, do you?"

"I can access it via pocket space."

"I see. I've never met a normal person who has taken the time to learn to use pocket space. That's quite interesting. Aren't you worried about contaminating its contents?"

"Yes, I am. That's why I'm a bit hesitant to do so. Also, this area isn't exactly a clinic…I don't mean this to offend you, but there's no telling what kinds of germs could be around here. You certainly *do* keep your house clean. There's no denying that. It's just—"

"I understand."

"Good. Hm… I would almost consider using magic to extract blood, but that's kind of a frowned upon method. Besides, I don't have anything on hand that could be used to keep it in. Not without accessing pocket space, at least."

"We may have to settle for something a bit more makeshift then."

"I know, but it's against my practice. I could get fired for using unclean equipment of any kind. I probably seem like a pansy to you since I'm sure you've had to do plenty of medical procedures in the field under worse conditions."

"It's a very different work environment in the Councils, that's for sure. I don't consider you weak at all. It takes many years to become an accomplished healer. It's very much a lifelong journey. Obviously when we're out on the battlefield, we don't really have the option of preforming treatments in a sanitary environment."

"Excuse me, Doctor," Vanilla said, "but are you sure we'll be safe? I mean, if Zallin is really infected with Moxica, even if it's crippled, isn't it still dangerous? Will we be OK?"

"I… There's no way to know for sure, but the odds seem to be very much in your favor. If Zallin's case was deadly, he would be suffering severely right now. Zallin, I can rescan you just in case. I'd like to scan both you and your daughter as well, Vanilla. This is something that's never been seen before—crippled Moxica, that is. Zallin's body is obviously fighting it. His fever tells me that much. I did notice his white blood cells working quite hard around the viruses when I did that body scan. It's another sign that his body is aware that it's been infected and is working to solve the issue."

"I-I see. I have another question. You mentioned that 2nd City Realm is still quarantined. My ex-boyfriend was born there. Is it possible that he could be infected?"

"I don't think so. How old is he? If you don't mind me asking, that is."

"He's thirty-five now. He's lived in 3rd City Realm since he was a kid, though."

"Well I guess the fact that he's lived in a different realm that long is proof enough that he's never had it. If I remember correctly, all life in 2nd City Realm was lost within a few months of the initial quarantine. It's been a black mark on our dimension's history, mainly from an administration standpoint. In fact, I thought it was still illegal to live there."

"It is. He told me that he...he used someone's modified watch to escape. It's a long story. I don't know if he'd like it if I told someone."

"Don't worry. I'm not judging. We all have different pasts. That's one of the many things that makes us all unique. A while ago I was treating a patient who was apparently the child of a famous rock star. He told me that he was adopted away when he was a baby and now he's dead-set on becoming a Sheneephiism Revivalist pastor, or something. Obviously I can't say his name for legal reasons, but we'll call him Bob. Bob was quite an interesting young man. His foster parents are farmers, so naturally that's what he does for a living. I learned more about plants talking to him than I did in my natural healing classes. I regret to say I don't really have an interesting life story like that. I was just a regular kid who went to school in 1st City Realm and went straight to college after I graduated high school. Like I said though, diversity colors the world."

"I agree. Diversity colors the world… I'm curious. What species was that guy?"

"I'm not allowed to say. Sorry. Why do you ask?"

"No reason. I was just curious."

"I see. I think I'm going to try and get in touch with the Research and Development Branch now. Excuse me for a moment." Atlyn walked into the hallway, leaving the family to exchange uneasy glances. Vanilla strained her ears to try and hear the doctor's conversation, but was interrupted by a coughing fit from Zallin. When he had finished, she began to feel a tingle in her throat. *Oh, no,* she thought. *I must be getting sick now too!*

Before long, Atlyn returned. The expression on her face told the family that she had bad news. "It looks like they want to take us to 4th City Realm for some tests," she said, shaking her head. "I don't know how long we'll be held there, but they said we don't have a choice."

"Why not? That's kind of suspicious," Vanilla replied, remembering the many rumors she had heard about people disappearing after being escorted somewhere by the government.

"Think about what this means to the government. They didn't see what I saw and it'd be foolish of them to take their chances with this."

"But what if this is just a ploy to capture us and use us for experiments?"

"Um, I don't think we have to worry about that."

"Vanilla, I'm guessing you're thinking about Garntell, right?"

Zallin asked. "If so, you needn't worry. That was during the Old Government's rule. Our current government is a lot more ethical and transparent. I've actually been to 4th City Realm numerous times to meet with people from the Research and Development Branch. They're not bad people."

"I know, but…"

"We're all in this together," Atlyn added with a small smile. "They might even be able to produce a vaccine like I was talking about, although it would have been nice if I was the one to get the credit…oh, well. You can't win 'em all. Besides, my patients' recovery is much more important to me than fame."

Before Vanilla could reply—much less think—four men in white armor suits appeared in the house with a bang and a flash of blue light. Each of them had a long device in their hands and an oxygen pack on their back. Their helmets, which were connected to the pack by two tubes that ran along either side of their suit, were shiny and had a black visor. Zallin was about to attack, but quickly realized that they were government workers and relaxed.

"Zallin? I wasn't expecting this," one of them said from behind their mask.

"Ein, is that you?" Zallin asked, squinting to see through the dark visor on the man's helmet.

"Yes. Well, there's not much time for small talk. I have orders to escort you all to 4th City Realm. Do not be alarmed. We're here to help. Unit 3 and 4, you stay here and make sure this area is Moxica-free. Sweep it from top to bottom. If you find any, destroy it immediately. If it's on food or plants, dispose of it with your incinerator. If it's on something else, try to cleanse it the best you can. If you can't get it one-hundred percent, use the warp bag to send it to quarantine."

"Roger," one of the men said.

"Do they have to search the whole house?" Vanilla asked, a hint of panic in her voice.

"Yes," Zallin replied.

"Don't worry, ma'am," Ein said. "Unless my men find something illegal, they're bound by law to confidentiality. We're not here to judge you or your lifestyle."

"Th-that's not what I meant! I just…it feels weird to have strangers searching my house, that's all."

"I understand. I'd feel the same way. Rest assured that we're only looking for Moxica. The moment the area is cleared, my men will leave."

"OK, but…"

"Everything will be alright. Your husband and I go way back. I wouldn't let any harm befall him or his family—or their belongings. We're going to teleport everyone now. There will be a loud noise similar to the one just a second ago as we break through your house's warp barrier. Don't worry; it won't cause any damage to you or the house."

Once again, before Vanilla could prepare, there was a loud bang. Her surroundings changed instantly. She was now in a long metal corridor. Above her, green lights pulsed through translucent black canals, creating the illusion of motion in the dimly lit hall. Every time it passed, she caught a brief glimpse of her comrades. Zallin was calm and quiet. The eyes on his hat stared straight ahead, unwavering like the trained soldier he was. Raech, on the other hand, was apprehensive and struggling to hide it.

Vanilla reached out and put her hand on her daughter's arm. She flinched, but then smiled. "Mom, I love you."

"I love you too, Sweetie."

Raech nodded, but didn't seem any less distressed. The two men in suits walked the group down the passage in an unnerving silence. Ein was at the front, followed by Zallin, Raech, Vanilla, and Atlyn. The other man, whose uniform bore the words "SBHC Unit-2," was at the rear.

Eventually the party came to a metallic, sealed door. It was no bigger than the ones in Vanilla's house, but it was much more high-tech. From the outside, it looked as though it would have to slide upward to open. To its left, there was a blank pad, mounted securely to the adjacent wall. Ein waved his hand over it and the door began to open like the iris lens of an old camera.

Somewhere behind them, there was a dull thump. Startled, Vanilla turned around, only to find that another door had appeared, preventing them from going back. Ein walked through the opening and waited patiently for the rest of them.

The room was small and hexagonal. Like the corridor, it had no windows and was lined with dense metal. A large rectangular table sat in the center. It was shiny and very clean. Vanilla could see the reflection of the ceiling perfectly in it, right down to the smallest details. Aside from it and an unmarked cabinet, there were no other furnishings.

Another suited man was standing in the room when the group entered. He was about the same height as Ein and the others, but his helmet was conical and twice as tall. The black visor was located on the upper half as well, hinting that he might be a Madite. Zallin seemed wary of his presence, but said nothing. Vanilla could sense her husband's distrust and began to worry even more.

The man, obviously aware of this, bowed and spoke with an electronically-generated voice. "Welcome. Please be at ease. You are in good hands."

Zallin nodded, but still remained tense. "I don't believe we've met before. My name is Zallin."

The man gave a small bow again. "It's a pleasure to meet you, Zallin. I would like to tell you my name, but for security reasons I think it would be best if I remain anonymous."

"I apologize if that was intrusive."

"That's quite alright. Now then, I hear you've contracted Moxica."

"That is correct."

"Hm. I shall heal you then. Please brace yourselves."

The mysterious man held out his hands and concentrated. There was a burst of energy and for a brief moment, the family and Atlyn felt an unbearable surge of heat rushing through their veins. It was as if someone had replaced their blood with magma. When it was over, Vanilla's head was spinning. The last thing she heard was her husband's voice calling her name. The world around her faded into white, and then all was still.

In the darkness, she saw a distant light, as though she was submerged in a sea of ink, looking up at the sky. With each passing second, she drew nearer to the surface. As she did so, blurred shapes and splotches of color appeared. At first they looked amorphous, but soon they took on the form of people. She was still too far away to see them clearly.

One seemed to be a Madite with a dark, red hat. He was standing with his back to her atop a mountain and casting a spell that radiated a dark aura from his hands. Just as he began to turn around, everything was swallowed by eerie shadows once again.

When she awoke, she was lying in her bed with her feat elevated by a pillow. Zallin and the others were nowhere in sight. *What happened?* she thought, gingerly propping herself up on her elbows. Then she remembered Ein, being transported to 4th City Realm, and the strange man in the suit. "Oh, no! Zallin! Zallin!" she called, quickly climbing out of bed. As she did, her foot caught on the folds of the covers and she fell to the floor with a thump.

"Vanilla? What's wrong? Are you alright?" Zallin asked, appearing in the doorway seconds later. He extended his hand to help her up.

"Ow...Zallin, I thought they had taken you!"

"Who?"

"The government!"

"No. They teleported us back after you fainted."

"Oh, I thought it was only me."

"No. Raech is here, too."

"What about the doctor?"

"She went back to her lab."

"Are you sure?"

"I'd assume so. Our government isn't evil, if that's what you're worried about."

"What about that Madite in the suit? The one who attacked us."

"He didn't attack us. He used a healing spell...a slightly overpowered one. In fact, I've been wondering what exactly it was. It's not something I have ever witnessed before."

"But... You seemed suspicious of him. I could feel it."

"I was."

"Why?"

"It's a bit of a long story. I don't want to make you distrust our authorities, so I think it's best if I keep it to myself."

"I'm not a child, Zallin. I can think for myself."

"I know, but—"

"But you think I'm easily influenced and led astray? Is that it?"

"Vanilla, you're putting words in my mouth. That's not what I meant."

"Then tell me."

He breathed out through his nostrils. "Fine. There was once a Madite named Osshkven Kepht who worked for the Old Government. From the little information that I found in my time with the Councils, he was a genius with magic. The records say that he died, but it wouldn't surprise me if he's still alive somewhere. Ever since I read about him, I've had this feeling that he's still around. When I saw that Madite back there, I couldn't help but think of Osshkven. Looking back, I may have been a bit too quick with my assumptions, but I can't shake the feeling that something was a bit…off about him."

"Like what?"

"Well, when I asked is name, I was testing him to see if he would lie. I wasn't able to read his mind, which is a given, considering that he's a trained member of the government. Even so, I would have still been able to tell if he was lying when he spoke. The problem is, he very cleverly avoided answering my question directly without lying."

"How?"

"He said that he couldn't tell me for security reasons, which is only partially true. Technically government workers in 4th City Realm aren't allowed to tell their names to civilians, but I'm not a civilian and he knew that. In fact, it seemed as though he actually recognized me, which is a bit unsettling."

"How do you know?"

"From subtle hints in both his body language and the little that I could sense of his soul. I suppose it's entirely possible that he just didn't *want* to tell me. But that brings me to the electronic voice from his helmet… There's no reason someone in his position would need to have that. Seeing *how* he healed us, I know his psychic powers are very strong, so even something like telepathy would have been an easier yet equally effective option if he wanted to disguise his voice."

"I was wondering about that, too. I mean, if he was mute or something, couldn't he just heal himself since he's such a good a healer?"

"Probably. There are also a number of medical procedures that can give a person their voice. Come to think of it, isn't one of your friends mute?"

"You mean Lisa? Yeah. She could have something done about it, but she thinks of it as a reminder of where she's come from."

"I guess that could be the case with that man. Hm. I can't believe I was so quick to judge."

"Maybe you were on to something, though. You could ask your friend."

"Ein?"

"Yeah."

"That might be taking an unnecessary risk."

"Why?"

"If he works with that man... Well, it would just be unwise. Besides, this really isn't any of my business. I shouldn't have gotten started about all this."

"Huh. Anyway, you seem to be feeling a lot better."

"Yes, I do. How are you feeling?"

"Fine."

"Good. That was quite an event."

"Did those government guys take any blood samples?"

"No. Like I said before, they escorted us out right after you fainted."

"Oh. Hey, what time is it? I'm hungry."

"It's almost suppertime. What would you like to eat?"

"Anything's fine."

"OK. I think I'll make some rice and beans. I could also cook that chicken that's in the fridge."

"Didn't those people get rid of our food?"

"They did. I was at the grocery store a little while ago. In fact I got back about ten minutes before you woke up."

"Really? How long was I unconscious?"

"A couple of hours. Raech stayed home with you while I was out."

"Gee…"

"I'll go start supper."

"OK."

CHAPTER 13

-Sister-

It was evening on Glunke. The sky was dark and engulfed in gray clouds. A slight breeze blew gently against the old house. Vanilla sat on her amplifier in the living room with her bass, fingering the strings skillfully. The low rumble from the amplifier shook the windows when she hit certain notes and rattled the pictures hanging on the wall. The musician's long white hair cascaded down the side of the instrument and gracefully rolled off the sides of her legs. Each movement of her head sent a wave down her silky, flowing locks.

Raech was sitting quietly on the couch with her hands in her lap, listening intently to her mother play. The eyes on her hat followed the Crescent Horned Punisher's left hand as it slid up and down the bass's neck.

After a while, Vanilla stopped and looked up.

Raech smiled and clapped. "That was very beautiful, Mother."

"Thanks, Sweetie. It feels good to just play after something stressful happens."

"You mean when Dad was sick?"

"Yeah... That was really scary. I've also never been to 4th City Realm before."

Raech stared lovingly at her mother. "They usually don't allow civilians in because a lot of important government facilities are there."

"I know. I'm just glad we're all OK." She glanced down at her bass. "But anyway, music is kind of my go-to for stress relief. I can just lose myself in it."

"Maybe I'll start playing an instrument sometime. I like how music is so structured and organized. It's a bit like math, in a way."

"Some of it is. Have you ever heard of the Glitch genre?"

"I may have. What's it like?"

"It's very random. Zero hates it, but I'm OK with it. I've only heard a few songs of that genre, but they're kind of neat. I guess it's an acquired taste, so to speak. If I had some of the songs on my stereo, I'd play them for you."

"I see. I'll have to research it. It sounds interesting."

"It is. Say, where's your father?"

"He's getting supper ready."

"Ask him if he needs any help. I suppose I'd better do something constructive before the day is over."

"I can help Dad with supper. You can keep playing."

"Oh, alright. Thank you, Sweetie."

"You're welcome."

After a quick hug, Raech headed for the kitchen. *She sure is a good kid,* Vanilla thought as she listened to the sound of food being prepared. *I always thought being a parent would be really stressful, but it's not. Maybe it's because Raech is a Madite. I guess I got lucky.*

Within minutes, dinner was ready. The family sat down together at the table. Zallin had cooked a delicious-looking casserole and Raech had prepared a small salad. Vanilla eagerly helped herself to both the moment she had a plate in her hands.

"So, how was your day?" Zallin asked, smiling at her.

Mouth full with food, Vanilla simply gave a thumbs up and nodded.

"Oh, sorry. How was your day, Raech?"

"It was good. I finished reading my physics textbook today."

"Good. Do you understand everything OK?"

"Yeah. It wasn't that hard, actually."

"What will you be working on next?"

"I think I'll try biology."

"Haven't you already done that?" Vanilla asked, wiping her mouth with a napkin.

"I did the first and second semester of it. It's really interesting, so I want to keep learning more about it."

"What was your favorite part?"

"Um, maybe evolution. It's fascinating how almost all Mandianoid Spiritans can be traced back to Origin Spiritans—even Madites. They still haven't found out why we became the way we are today, though. The earliest Madite skeleton on record was found in Dreamic, so some scientists believe that there was a genetic mutation caused by one of the now extinct plants there. Being that some plants in areas such as the Zangrot Swamp give off a sort of radiation, it's very possible that was the case."

"Hm. That reminds me. Zallin, we should go for a walk in Dreamic again. I'd like to take a different trail this time though—one that we haven't done before. Maybe one higher up in the mountains."

"Yes, perhaps this weekend we can go. The mountain trails can be pretty strenuous though. Are you sure you'd be up for it?"

"I'll be fine."

"Alright."

"This tastes great, by the way."

"Thank you."

"Say, why don't you try getting a job as a chef? It'd be a lot better than what you do now—safer, too."

"Because some dreams aren't meant to come true."

"Oh, stop it. Maybe some dreams don't come true because you won't give it a chance."

"I suppose. Unfortunately, I don't think I can just walk away from my current occupation."

Vanilla shook her head. "I don't know why you do it, Zallin. I'm afraid that one of these days you won't come home alive…"

"It's for the better of the dimension. Thankfully I'm not getting called in for duty that often."

"But technically you're not Crescent's lieutenant anymore, right? Didn't he say he replaced you when we got married?"

"Yes, technically; but he still calls me Lieutenant and has me go assist the 55th Council with missions here and there."

"I know that, but…it just doesn't seem right. If you're not a member, why do you have to go?"

Zallin hesitated. "I… I don't really know how to explain it," he said after a long pause.

Vanilla sighed. "Promise me one thing."

"I can't make any promises."

"Zallin!"

"Vanilla, please. I don't want this to turn into an argument."

"…Alright. I'm sorry. I just…"

"I will search for another job when I can."

"Good."

When she was finished, she picked up her plate and rose to her feet. "Here, I'll take it," Zallin said, holding out his hand. She thanked him and handed it over.

"Mom," Raech said, "are you going to play your bass any more tonight?"

"Maybe. I wasn't really planning on it. Why? Are you going to study some more?"

"No, I think I'm done for the evening. I was just hoping I could listen to you play again."

Vanilla smiled. "It's kind of late for me to be playing heavy metal riffs. I guess I can try something a bit calmer though. Just let me sit and digest for a moment."

"OK. No rush. I'll just be in my room. Please let me know when you're ready."

Vanilla nodded. As she reclined back in her chair, a thought came to her. *I wonder if I should get back with my band. I feel like I have plenty of free time since I don't have a job. My social life already takes me to the City Realms, so it wouldn't be much of a change. Raech is practically independent now, too. The only reason she's not on her own is because she's still fourteen. It's not like I need to be here babysitting her while Zallin's at work or anything.*

Eventually Vanilla got up and made her way to her daughter's bedroom. The door was ajar, but she knocked softly on it anyway. The young Madite looked up from a heavy textbook and smiled. "Oh, are you ready?" she asked politely.

"I was about to ask you that."

"I'm ready."

"Alright, then."

Raech followed her mother out into the living room and sat down on the couch. Vanilla pulled her amplifier out from beneath the end table and retrieved her bass guitar from its case. "Hang on," she said, plucking one of the strings repeatedly. "I think it's a bit out of tune." Raech waited patiently as her mother skillfully tuned the instrument by ear and plugged it into the amp.

Vanilla sat down on the amp, being careful not to let the long neck of the bass hit anything, and began to play with the gain turned almost all the way down. Instinctively, she tapped her foot to keep tempo. Raech listened intently, unconsciously starting to tap her foot to the beat as well.

After an hour or so, she stopped and leaned her bass up against the couch. "I think I'll get ready for bed," she claimed, turning off the amp and unplugging it from the wall socket.

"Me too. I enjoyed listening to you," Raech said.

"Thanks. I'm glad I didn't make your bored or anything."

"Oh, not at all! It's very inspiring to listen to real musicians."

"That's good."

"Will you be practicing again tomorrow?"

"Probably. You know, if you ever want me to teach you how to play, I'd be more than happy to. Just let me know when."

"OK! I'd like that. Maybe sometime next week?"

"Sure."

Vanilla stood up and made her way toward the master bedroom. As was going down the hall, she noticed that the light was on in Zallin's study, so she peeked around the corner. As expected, the blue-hatted Madite was sitting at his desk, buried in books and loose sheets of notepaper. The small lamp on his desk shone just bright enough for him to read.

"Hon," she said, "do you need more light?"

Startled, he looked up and said, "No, that's alright. Thanks anyway."

"I don't know how you can read like that."

"I prefer lower light levels for reading at night. It's relaxing."

"Alright. I'm going to bed."

"OK. I'll be there in a bit. I just need to finish this."

Vanilla just smiled and nodded. *Sometimes I wish I had motivation to read like that. I get bored of textbooks pretty quick,* she mused.

Back in her bedroom she closed the door partway, slipped out of her clothes and into a silky purple nightgown. It felt good against her bare skin. Climbing onto their king size bed, she threw the covers over herself and reached for the lamp to turn it off. There was a familiar click, and the room was engulfed in an inky black.

In the darkness, her imagination veered to the history of 2nd City Realm and she pictured the devastating aftereffects of the Moxica virus. The jungle of concrete, metal, and glass was silent and empty. The trees were blackened and withered and ponds in all of the parks had lifeless fish floating on the surface, their cold dead eyes gazing vacantly at the sky.

She shuddered and pulled the covers over her head, reminding herself that it was all in her mind—a memory she had never had, nor ever would. Sleep eventually came, but not without a struggle.

The next day, Vanilla awoke to her cell phone ringing. Zero was calling. It was almost Noon according to the time on its display, but it still felt like morning. Reaching for her nightstand to retrieve the small device, she squinted at it for a moment before picking up.

"Hello?" she said sleepily.

"Hey Vanilla. You sound tired," the guitarist replied.

Vanilla propped herself up with a pillow and yawned. "You know I'm not a morning person, Zero."

"But it's past lunchtime!"

"Not on Glunke. There's a time difference, you know."

"Oh shit—I mean crud. Sorry about that. What time is it there?"

"Eleven fifty-three A-M."

"Hey, that's not morning! Wake up, fool!"

"I'm trying. What do you want?"

"Well, Steve Pulltuck is playing with his old group at Meltdown

Music in North 5th City Realm right now. I was just wondering if you wanna go see them."

"Hm. Let me think…"

"This could take a while."

"Oh hush. If I'm free I'll be there in one hour or something."

"I can barely do sixth grade mathematics and I can tell you that 'or something' doesn't work with numbers."

"Bye."

"Hahaha. OK, bye."

With a heavy sigh, Vanilla rolled over and let the phone slip from her hands. She closed her eyes to try and go back to sleep. Much to her dismay, however, it rang again. With an exasperated groan she picked it up.

"Hello?"

"V-Vanilla? Is that you?"

The voice that came from the other end seemed vaguely familiar. It was high pitched and timid, but still somehow like that of an adult woman.

The world became still as Vanilla was hit with a rush of memories. "It can't be…" she whispered distantly. Though her comment was more to herself than anyone, the lady on the other end heard it and responded.

"Oh I'm sorry! Please don't be mad at me. I must have the wrong number!"

"No, wait! *Nyla?* Is that really you?"

There was a long silence. It appeared as if the line had been disconnected. Just as Vanilla was ready to hang up, the quiet voice spoke again.

"Y-yes, this is Nyla. Um… Sis, do you still hate me?"

"No not at all! Nyla, I've changed since we last saw each other."

"But you told me you never wanted to see me again a-and-and that I was just a tool and-and-and I was stupid a-and—"

"Nyla, I don't hate you. You're my one and only sister. I'm glad that you called. I didn't think I'd ever get to hear your voice again... But first things first: I'm sorry for how I treated you when we were kids. I take back everything that I said, every name that I called you, and every mean trick that I played on you. I was wrong and my selfishness really hurt you. It was my fault for everything. Will you forgive me?"

"Aw Vanilla, that's so nice...! I-I thought you'd be mad at me forever. Katie told me that I should call you someday and—"

"Katie? Who's that?"

"She's the girl that I'm staying with. She makes breakfast for me every morning and tells me how special I am. She has a bunch of friends that I get to talk to."

"Ah I see. Well I'm relieved that you're OK. It's been what, twenty-two years since I've seen you? I started to think that something horrible happened. Why don't I come visit you today? Where do you and Katie live?"

"Oh would you really do that? That'd be great! I'd have to ask first. Katie has a boyfriend who comes over sometimes. He's scary 'cause all guys are mean. He acts like a nice person, but I think he's evil like every man."

"Nyla, men aren't evil. There *are* some guys that are jerks, but there are many that are really nice. You can't say every one of them is bad."

"Yes they are, 'Nilla! They're all rotten! I don't like them at all."

"Wow...I guess I don't really know what to say to that. Oh wait a minute. How would you like to come over to my house instead? That way you could meet a nice man. My husband, Zallin, is very kindhearted

301

and—"

"You got married? Why?"

"Nyla just come over. I can give you the address for your transportation watch, if you have one."

"Only if the man isn't there."

"I can't just tell my husband to leave. That would be awfully rude."

Ironically, Zallin walked into the bedroom. Noticing that his wife was on the phone, he lingered at the door and waited politely for a moment to speak.

"Hang on Nyla," Vanilla said and pressed the phone against her chest. "Zallin, guess what? My sister is on the line!"

The Madite blinked. "Really? I'm glad to hear that. How did you find her number?"

"Actually she found mine somehow. I'm glad she's alright."

"Me too. That's a relief. Why don't you invite her over?"

"I did, but she's scared of coming over."

"Why?"

"I think she's afraid of men."

"That's unfortunate, but I suppose it's not out of the question though, given her childhood experiences. Raech and I were going to go to Meltdown Music in 5th City Realm to listen to a band. We'll probably go to the library after that. Perhaps you and your sister could spend time together while we're away."

Vanilla nodded. "Yeah, I'll ask." She put the phone back up to her right horn. "Hey are you still there?"

"Yeah."

"Good! I've got an idea. My husband and daughter are going to be out for a while. You could come over once they leave and we'll have some time to catch up. How does that sound?"

"You're not tricking me, are you?"

"Not at all. Do you have a transportation watch?"

"I think. Is that like a teleportation watch?"

"Yup. They're the same thing."

"Oh. I have one that somebody gave me a long time ago, but I'm too scared to use it. Katie says that she's willing to teach me how when I'm ready."

"Well, it's actually pretty easy. I'll tell you how."

"But Katie said—"

"Alright, so if it's not lit up on the top panel, press the little button on the side that says 'Power' on it."

"OK. I did, I think. I don't know if I should be—"

"Next, touch the top of the watch with your finger."

"I just did. Should I ask if—"

"Then a keyboard should pop up."

"Ooh! That's pretty! How does it do that? It's like, floating and green. Can I poke it?"

"Nyla, I want you to type something now."

"I don't know how."

"Press the buttons on the hologram. Just put in 'G-L-U-N-K-E,' and then hit 'Enter' twice. Since my house is the only one in the realm, it should automatically send you here whether or not you get the house number right."

"G... L... U... N... What does that mean?"

"It's the name of a realm. Now when a number pad comes up, hit the number one and press Enter again."

"OK. Which one is G?"

"Wait, you don't know how to read?"

"Letters are boring!"

"Ugh. How did you find my number in the first place?"

"Katie helped me."

"Is Katie there?"

"I think."

"Ask her to type it in for you."

"OK."

There was a long silence. Vanilla waited patiently, curling her hair around one finger. After what felt like ages, Nyla returned to her phone.

"'Nilla? Are you still there?"

"Yeah."

"Oh good! I thought maybe you'd hung up."

"Nope. I'm still here. Are you ready?"

"For what?"

"To come over!"

"Oh yeah. I forgot."

"Wait, did you get Katie to help you?"

"With what?"

"Typing Glunke into your teleportation watch."

"Oops. I forgot."

"…That's alright."

"Should I go get her?"

"Yeah, if you really do need help finding the right letters."

"OK. I'll be back."

Vanilla waited again, this time drumming her fingers on her thick thighs. Luckily, Nyla was back in less time than before.

"I'm ready!"

"Good. Now just press 'Send.'"

"Which one is that?"

"If your watch is like most, it should be the button in the center right below the screen."

"What does it look like?"

"What? The button or the word?"

"The word."

"It's four letters long and starts with an 'S'—er, a squiggly line. It's like a snake."

"I don't like snakes…"

"Neither do I. Just find the button and press it."

"This one? It's not doing anything."

"Are you outside? You probably won't be able to teleport from inside."

"No. It's scary outside. There are men there."

"Just go into the backyard or something."

"OK. I'll try…I'm there."

"Good. Now hit Send again."

At that moment, the phone cut out. Vanilla closed her eyes and took a deep breath. "I feel like I'm teaching an animal. She certainly isn't the brightest."

The doorbell rang. Startled, she jumped out of bed. She grabbed her bathrobe from the chair by Zallin's desk. Draping it over herself, she headed to the front door. Her heart was beating so rapidly it felt as though it was going to jump out of her chest.

She flung the door open and grinned. Outside was another white-haired Crescent Horned Punisher. She was clothed very much like Vanilla would have been long ago. A loosely-fitting pink tank top with dangerously thin straps displayed her ample cleavage. The words "Show & Tell" were written across it in big gold letters. At first it appeared as if the woman had only her undergarments to clothe her lower half. On second glance, however, Vanilla realized that her curvy sister had a pair of very skimpy, bright yellow shorts. The girl's face seemed to have gone pale from her older sister's dramatic welcome, although her skin *was* already white as snow.

"Hi," she said shyly. With a squeal of joy, Vanilla rushed forward and hugged her long-lost sister. Instinctively, the well-endowed beauty flinched and let out a small scream.

Vanilla drew herself back. "Nyla, what's wrong? I'm not going to hurt you or anything." They stared at each other, Nyla in fright and Vanilla in confusion. Neither of them moved for a matter of seconds. Both were unsure of what to do. Finally, it was Vanilla who broke the tense silence. "I'm sorry if I startled you. Please don't be afraid of me. I've changed."

"Oh 'Nilla, I can't help it. I just get so scared sometimes. I'm not used to being touched so suddenly. I don't think you've ever hugged me, either…"

"Well maybe you just need to be hugged more. Now come on inside. We've got a lot of catching up to do." Nyla nodded and cautiously followed her older sister into the house with a bewildered expression.

Upon setting foot in the living room she dropped her gaudy pink and gold purse and let out a little sigh of ecstasy. A self-portrait of Raech had caught her eye. In the painting, the young Madite was sitting in a patch of vividly green grass, wearing a modest, dark purple and black dress. Rotund birds were perched on a tree branch above her, adding contrast with their brilliant red and orange feathers.

Noticing that her sister had been so easily distracted by the artwork, Vanilla put her hands on her hips and grinned proudly. "That's a painting that my daughter did last spring on a trip to the Blaine Islands in Missk," she said, using the most casual voice she could muster.

"She's so beautiful…" Nyla murmured dreamily. "She's not married, is she?"

Vanilla stopped and blinked. "Um, Nyla, I have a question. Please don't take this to offense, but are you by chance a…lesbian? I'm just curious."

"Yeah, don't judge me!"

"I'm not judging you. I just wasn't expecting that, I guess. I'm sorry if that sounded judgmental. I don't have any problem with that, really. But, um, do you realize that Raech is your niece?"

"I'm an uncle?"

"*Aunt.*"

"Oh. I am?"

"Yeah, you are. Do you mind if I show you the rest of the house now?"

"OK! Do you have any more pictures of that girl?"

"I do, but let's save that for another time, OK?"

"Oh fine."

The sisters meandered down the hallway, through the kitchen, into the master bedroom, and eventually wound up in Zallin's library. Vanilla had purposefully skipped over Raech's room for fear that Nyla might become invasive.

They stood together quietly gazing at the bookshelves looming high overhead. Zallin's collection was made up of massive encyclopedias and deteriorating textbooks about magic and complicated sciences. Ancient symbols and strange titles were present such as, *Molecular Breakdown through the Malachi Function*, and *Bridging the Gap of Soulmor with Velshted Endire*, or *Liberation of the Central Power Core*. Some even looked as though they had been entirely handwritten. For how intriguing they all looked, not one of them was without a coat of dust.

A heavy antique desk sat in the far corner of the room piled high with crooked stacks of the mysterious tomes. Most of them simply acted as paperweights for loose documents, many of which appeared to be Zallin's own research.

Nyla had taken an interest in these and was trying to read them—or at least pretending to do so. The look on her face was complete bewilderment. She scratched her head and squinted hard at the writing. "'Nilla, I can't read this. Will you read it to me?"

Vanilla shook her head. "I'm not sure if I can. That's all about advanced science and magic. Honestly, I wouldn't have a clue. Besides, I thought you said reading was boring."

Her younger sibling put the papers down forcefully and crossed her arms. "Well I didn't know," she pouted.

"That's fine. What's with the whiny voice all of the sudden?"

"I'm *not* whining!"

"Alright, alright. My family may be home soon. I think we should—"

"Can you introduce me to that girl from the painting?"

"You mean my daughter?"

"Is that who that was?"

"Yes. I just said that a few minutes ago."

"Ooh. Have you told her about me?"

"Um… She knows who you are, but that's about it since I haven't seen you for so long. Like I said, she and Zallin will be here soon. That doesn't upset you, does it?"

"Who's Zallin again?"

"Nyla, I've already told you that, too. He's my husband."

"Why does he have to be here? I don't like men."

"Yeah, I know you don't. He lives here because we're married and

I'm not going to make him leave. I thought we had this conversation earlier today."

"Maybe, but I forgot."

"Well if you want to meet Raech you'll either have to deal with my husband being here or we'll have to find a time in the near future where just us girls are home and invite you over."

"Hm. When's the 'near future?' It sounds kinda far away."

"I don't know. I'll have to work things out with Zallin."

"Why does *he* get to decide when the future will be? Men shouldn't have so much control!"

"Ugh. That's not what I was saying. Let's go back in the front room. I'll teach you how to transport back."

Reluctantly, Nyla followed her older sister to the front door. She dragged her feet and sulked, making sure to look as helpless and defeated as possible. Vanilla simply ignored her childish behavior and proceeded to instruct her dimwitted sibling once they had stepped outside.

"Now since you've used your transportation watch already, the 'History' button should work. It displays a list of up to twenty of the most recent places you've gone. If you tap the name of one of those places, a little conformation box should appear. Press 'OK,' and it'll transport you back to that place."

Nyla stared blankly at the watch. "I still don't get it," she said.

With a small sigh of frustration, her older sister repeated her directions again, ending with, "Just try it, Nyla."

The simple-minded beauty gingerly poked at the hologram as her sister had told her. Before she knew what had happened, she had teleported back.

Vanilla took a deep breath and exhaled slowly. "That was fun," she grumbled sarcastically. *Well, I'm glad she's doing alright. It's been years since*

I've seen her. I still feel bad about abandoning her in that park when we were kids...I don't know if I can ever forgive myself for that. I should go visit her later this week. I'm curious to know who this "Katie" is. As she turned to enter the house, her cell phone rang. She quickly dug it out of her pocket and answered it.

"Hello?"

"Hey Hon, it's me."

"Oh hi. How are things going?"

"Good. Raech and I are still at Meltdown Music. We'll be home in a couple minutes though. Did you get to spend some time with your sister?"

"Yeah."

"That's good. How was she doing?"

"She was doing alright...I guess she's really ditzy."

"Hm. Well, it takes all kinds to make this world."

"That's true. I'm a little worried though. Like, I think maybe she has a really low IQ or something."

"Hm. Well, not having met her, I'm certainly in no position to make assumptions. What led you to believe that?"

"Just the way she talks. She's really forgetful."

"I see. I suppose it's entirely possible her traumatic past could have had an effect on her mental development."

"Maybe..."

"You can tell me more about it when we get home, alright?"

"Alright. I'm surprised Raech wanted to stay there so long. She's never been too into musical instruments."

"Well, she says it's more of the culture that she's into. Also, she made a new friend here, so she's been talking with him."

"*Oh* I see. What's this young man's name?"

"I believe it's Soul Ampth. I wouldn't make any assumptions about him, though. He just seems like a regular kid from 5th City Realm, albeit more kindhearted and understanding."

"Really? That's interesting. Do you know what species he is?"

"He's an Origin Spiritan."

"Origin Spiritan? I think I've heard that somewhere a long time ago."

"I'm sure you've seen them before. It's the politically correct way to refer to his species. They were supposedly the first Spiritans to exist. Some people mistakenly call them Destruction Dynasty Members, but that's—"

"Zallin, get Raech out of there quickly! Remember that guy named Dan? He was a Destruction Dynasty member, so that kid might be, too!"

"Vanilla, don't be so quick to judge. Just because someone looks like a member of the Destruction Dynasty doesn't mean they are. In fact, that's actually a racist assumption. I was just about to tell you that, in fact. Besides, the people of that cult always carry their swords with them and they wear very plain clothes while in public. This kid isn't armed and he has designer shoes and a jacket made from very expensive material."

"He could have stolen them."

"I don't think so. Just trust me. Oh, here comes Raech. We'll be home in a second. Bye."

"...Alright, if you say so. Bye."

Moments later, the two Madites appeared a few yards from the front door. Vanilla was still standing outside, so she went over to meet them. Questions about her daughter's new friend were rapidly building up in her mind.

"So Raech, I heard you met someone at Meltdown Music."

311

"Yes! His name is Soul. He lives with his parents in one of the mansions in North City of 5th City Realm. He said that he could teach me how to play guitar for free!"

"Neat. Was he nice?"

"Yes."

"Was he handsome?"

"Um…I don't really know how to answer that. May I ask what your intentions are with that question?"

"I'm just curious, that's all."

Zallin interrupted with a gentle tap on his wife's shoulder. Vanilla cleared her throat and stood up straight. "So, uh, what else did you guys do?"

"Not much. We exchanged phone numbers though."

"Oh, I was talking about you and your dad, not Soul."

"Oops! Um, we looked at some books in the library. I couldn't find anything interesting enough to check out, though. The librarian asked me if I was lost when she saw me paging through a college textbook."

"Really? What did you say to her?"

"I told her I was trying to find something to new learn. She just smiled and wished me luck."

"I see."

By now the family had reached the front door. Zallin stepped ahead to hold it open for the other two. They thanked him and went inside.

CHAPTER 14
-Good Guys, Bad Guys-

It was evening on Glunke and the Lamberschvaks had just finished supper. While Zallin cleaned up the dining room, Vanilla reclined on his blue armchair in the living room. There was a thick magazine in her hands which she casually paged through. The soft light of the tall lamp beside her cast a spotlight around the area.

Suddenly, Raech came to her with an unexpected question. "Mother," she said hesitantly, "Soul was wondering if we would like to come to his house for dinner tomorrow at six."

The Crescent Horned Punisher set down the latest issue of *The Musician's Expression Magazine* and smiled. "Why of course Sweetie! I was starting to wonder what ever happened to your friend. You've kept so quiet about him lately."

Raech's face lit up with excitement. She took a deep breath to calm herself, but it did little to quell her overflowing joy. Even though she tried her hardest to maintain her formal mannerism, the young Madite's enthusiasm was hard not to notice. "So it'd be OK then? Oh thank you Mom!"

"You're welcome. I'd like to meet this nice young man myself," Vanilla said, picking her magazine back up.

Raech turned around to leave the room and almost ran into Zallin.

"Oh, sorry Dad!"

"That's alright. What's going on?"

"Soul invited us to dinner at his house tomorrow."

"Is that so? What time?"

"Six o'clock."

"I see. Hm. Perhaps we should have a little talk."

"Oh, is something the matter?"

"Not at all. I just think it would be good if we discussed some things before you go see him."

"Oh, OK."

Vanilla smiled. *I knew this was coming,* she thought. *I'm just surprised he didn't have "the talk" with her earlier.* She looked at her husband and mouthed the words, "Should I do it?"

Zallin shook his head. Raech looked behind her curiously, wondering what her father was replying to. The Crescent Horned Punisher simply nodded and said, "I think I'll go practice scales in our room for a while. Call me if you need me."

Back in the bedroom, Vanilla pulled up the wooden chair by her husband's desk and sat down with her bass. Strumming over the strings, she noticed it was slightly out of tune. "It must be all this humidity from the rain," she said to herself, flicking off the overhead fan so she could hear better.

Skillfully, she sang a low E and simultaneously picked the corresponding note on her bass. She listened to the two sounds for a second and then gently muted the string with her hand. *That doesn't sound too bad. It must have been the A string then… Yup. It's out of tune. I'll just tune it to itself I guess.*

When everything was in order, she began to play, keeping time with her foot. Even with her bass unplugged, she could feel each note resonate in her chest. The instrument's heavy wooden body vibrated as she went up and down the neck, practicing major and minor scales with little more than muscle memory. She closed her eyes and pondered over the upcoming dinner and the similarities between her daughter meeting Soul and where she had met Zero. Before she knew it, she was composing a song.

"I met you at a music store,
In that city of neon light.

It doesn't matter anymore,
But I'll never forget that night.

You gave me hope for a better life,
I believed you then, though now's it's passed.

A fleeting dream is not what it seems,
Along the way, there was mostly strife.

Come back and take me home,
Come back so I'm not alone.

Soon my suffering burns to ash,
And nothing good will ever last."

She paused for a moment to remember that fateful day she first encountered Zero in front of a local music store in 3rd City Realm. He was a scrawny 13-year-old with worn jeans and a dirt-smudged shirt that was a size or two too big. She could picture his shy smile as she playfully leaned against him. His response came to her so vividly that it was as though she was really in the past.

"You're weird."

"No I'm not!" she replied in the best Alking she could muster.

"You talk strange. Where are you from?"

"Where are *you* from?"

"Some shitty place."

"What does that mean?"

"What does what mean?"

"'Shitty.'"

"It means really bad. Like shit."

The 10-year-old Crescent Horned Punisher stopped smiling and thought for a moment. "I'm from some shitty place too," she replied quietly.

The Grenzel Blind Demon looked around and whispered, "Do you...not want to go home?"

Vanilla shook her head.

"Neither do I. My dad's scary..."

The Crescent Horned Punisher nodded, wiping a tear from her eyes.

Not knowing what else to do, he cautiously patted her on the back. "Hey, maybe you can stay with me. I live with these guys who play music. One of them is kind of weird, but he's nice."

The flashback faded, leaving Vanilla feeling choked up and ready to cry. She gave a heavy, quivering sigh and set her bass on its stand. *It had to be fate,* she thought. *I learned so much growing up with him. And Scythe taught us to read and write and to play music. He was more of a father to us than anyone ever was. I still remember my eleventh birthday at the house...it was the first time I had ever gotten a present. When I think about it, Zero and the guys from* Death by Love *are like a true family to me. Even when I made mistakes and did bad things, they were still there for me.*

A voice from beside her brought her out of deep thought. "Vanilla, are you alright?" It was Zallin.

Startled, she jumped and almost knocked over the tall stack of books on the desk behind her. "Oh! Zallin, you scared me."

"Sorry. You looked like you were about to cry. Is everything alright?"

"Yeah, I was just thinking about the past…"

"I see."

"Did you finish your talk with Raech already?"

"Yes."

"Good."

"I think I'll get ready for bed."

"Oh, I didn't realize it was that late. Is Raech in bed already?"

Zallin nodded. "Are you going to stay up?"

"No, I think I'll get ready for bed too."

"Alright."

The next morning—or Noon—Vanilla awoke to the smell of pancakes. She struggled for a few minutes with the decision of sleeping in or getting food before finally crawling out of bed. *I wonder why Zallin's making pancakes this late,* she thought, slipping on a pair of pink sweatpants and heading for the kitchen.

Instead of her husband, she found Raech at the stove, flipping a batch of the mouthwatering breakfast item. She was wearing her father's blue apron, which was a little too large for her.

"Good morning, Mother. Would you like some pancakes?" she asked.

"Oh, sure. I thought it was your father making breakfast—or lunch now, I guess," Vanilla replied, adjusting the left strap of her purple nightgown.

"I thought it would be a good learning experience to try making these. Dad suggested it because it was quick and easy."

"That's nice. Did you use a mix?"

"No. I made the batter from scratch."

"Oh. It's good to know how to make things from scratch for when you're married. Home cooked meals are always the best."

"Um…y-yes, I agree."

"Or if you're lucky enough to find a husband that cooks, that would be nice."

"I don't mean any offense, but I'm, uh…a bit young to be considering marriage, aren't I?"

"Oh I don't know about that. The earlier you start thinking about it, the less you'll have to worry when the time comes."

"I… Um…"

"I'm just teasing you."

The embarrassed Madite nodded. "H-how many would you like?"

"I'll have three to start."

"OK. Here you go."

Raech plopped three warm pancakes on an empty plate and handed them to her mother, who thanked her and sat down at the table.

"Mmm. These are delicious. I think you've inherited your father's talent for cooking," she said after taking a bite.

"Do you really think so?"

"Sure."

"Thank you! I'm glad you like them. Let me know if you want any more."

"Will do."

When she was done, she set her plate in the sink and quickly rinsed her hands off. "You can just put the rest of the batter in the fridge. We can use the rest of it tomorrow morning."

Raech nodded. "OK."

"After I shower, I think I'll go into City Realm 1 today and visit with Lisa for a few hours. She recently moved into a new apartment. I won't be gone too long."

"OK. I hope you have fun."

"Thanks. Where's your father?"

"I think Dad's in his library."

"Oh, alright."

Vanilla yawned and walked toward her room. As she was exiting the kitchen however, the edge of her right horn caught on the doorframe. "Ow!" she cried, recoiling and holding it with both hands.

"Mom, are you OK? What happened?" Raech asked, rushing over to her.

"I'm fine. It just startled me. I was stretching my arms like this and I didn't realize how close I was to the doorframe."

"Oh. Didn't it hurt?"

"Sort of. I'll be fine. It woke me up at least."

"I'm sorry."

"Well, that's what I get for not paying attention."

The clumsy Crescent Horned Punisher tried again, this time taking care not to bump into anything. When she reached the master bedroom, she closed the door and began to gather clothes.

Operating on autopilot, she went through each level of her dresser, picking out an article of clothing from each. Like her room, every drawer was a mess—a stark contrast to Zallin's. Where her husband's clothes were so well-organized that they could have put any library to shame, hers were carelessly together, vaguely grouped by what part of the body they belonged with. Her short sleeve shirts were clumped together with her long sleeves and tank tops, and a few bras that she was too lazy to put with the rest. Her colorful, skimpy panties were in the next drawer down and all her pants—whether shorts or jeans—were stuffed in the bottommost compartment.

Pulling out the bottom drawer, she found that there were no jeans, much to her dismay. *Damn it, I forgot to wash clothes again. I guess I'll have to wear these sweatpants. I should probably change before we go to dinner though since these are a bit see-through, especially with that black V-string underneath.*

After her shower, Vanilla gathered up her transportation watch and cell phone—which had just finished charging, and headed for 1st City Realm.

Lisa's new apartment was located in the heart of South City. It was warm and bright when she arrived. The golden shimmer of the summer afternoon shone down upon the realm from the cloudless sky and reflected off the many tall buildings like stadium lights. Vanilla squinted and raised her hand to shield her eyes. "Well, it's certainly that time of year," she mumbled to herself, moving steadily through the endless sea of people in the busy streets.

In less than 10 minutes, she had reached the tall building where her friend lived. Inside the fancy lobby, she pressed the intercom for Suite 342. "Lisa, it's Vanilla. I'm down in the lobby." As expected, there was no response from the mute keyboardist.

After a short wait, she sighed and took out her phone. "I guess it would have been a good idea to text her first. Oh well. Maybe she's out with the band or something."

There was a metallic ding from the far eastern corner of the lobby and one of the elevators opened. The Crescent Horned Punisher looked up, hoping to see her friend. To her dismay however, it was only a young couple who could barely keep off each other. *Let's see how long that lasts.*

Marriage isn't going to be like that for very long, she scoffed, feeling a small twinge of envy.

Just as the obsessive couple exited out the revolving front doors of the building, someone slipped past them heading the opposite way. She was an athletic Mandian with curly brown hair and green eyes. It was Lisa. She was wearing a sweaty gym uniform and carrying a duffle bag that bore the unmistakable logo for Supreme Sport Co. There was a patch on one end that said, "I can kick your boyfriend's ass!" She smiled when she saw Vanilla and came over to her.

"Did you just get back from the gym?" the Crescent Horned Punisher asked.

Lisa nodded.

"Oh. I was just coming over to see if you wanted to hang out for a while since it's been a long time. I can always come back another day if you're busy."

The Mandian slung her bag over her left shoulder and signed, *"That's OK. We can hang out. Let me just eat something and take a shower."*

"Oh, are you sure?"

"Yeah, it's fine. I'll give you a tour of my new place."

"OK, cool. Lead the way."

Lisa led her friend into the nearest elevator and pressed the button for the third floor. When the doors had securely slid shut, they began to rise.

"So, are you still going to the same gym?"

"No, Spirit Fit closed down a few months ago. I'm at South Heights Fitness over by the old noodle place we used to go to."

"You mean Poodles 'n' Noodles?"

Lisa nodded.

"Are they still in business?"

321

The Mandian shook her head.

"Ah, that's what I thought. That place was good. I remember when we'd get done with practice and just pig out there with Zero."

"Those were good days."

"They sure were. I wish we had more time. That's what sucks about being an adult…"

"True."

"I'm actually going to dinner this evening at my daughter's friend's house. He invited us all over."

"Is that Raech's boyfriend?"

"I think he will be. I don't know any guys who just casually invite a girl and her family to meet their family. I'm really curious to know what kind of person he is. I don't want her to get involved with some jerk who will manipulate her or something."

"I agree."

Finally, they had reached the third floor. They stepped out into a long hallway with numbered doors on each side. Vanilla followed Lisa until they came upon one marked "Suite 342." The Mandian set down her bag and took a small golden key from her pocket. Inserting it into the lock, she turned the knob and pushed the door open to reveal a nice, spacious room. It was fully furnished with a couch, a hologram TV, cabinets, a table, and a small kitchenette off to one side.

Lisa stood aside to let her friend through. The Crescent Horned Punisher thanked her and entered the cozy living space.

"I'm going to make a protein shake for myself before I rinse off. Help yourself to anything you can find."

"Oh, that's alright. I already ate. Thanks though."

Suddenly, a fat orange tabby cat came prancing up to meet them. He looked at Vanilla with his wide, green eyes and meowed. She knelt down and extended her hand to pet him, but he backed up and turned his bushy tail toward her, as if the whole exchange was simply a set-up to snub her.

"I see Boxer's still as friendly as ever," Vanilla said sarcastically.

Lisa smiled. *"He's always like that."*

"I think all cats are like that. Say, didn't you rescue one recently?"

"You mean Benny? He's around here. He's probably just hiding."

"Hm. I guess that kind of figures."

Lisa set her bag down on the floor by the couch and walked over to the kitchen. Vanilla took her shoes off and sat down in front of the TV. She patted the cushion next to her, hoping to get Boxer to sit by her. The fickle feline looked the other way as she did so and ignored her.

"Come on, Boxer! Come sit up here. Boxer! Hey, look!"

Boxer bent over and licked his paws, glancing up at her to see her reaction. Finally, Vanilla gave up and reclined in the comfy seat. Moments later, Lisa started the blender, which made the cat jump and run for cover in one of the other rooms.

"This is a pretty nice place. I like how the red couch and decorations contrast the darker cabinets. And that lamp you have in the corner is cool," the Crescent Horned Punisher commented once her friend had finished making her shake.

Lisa came over and leaned against the wall opposite her. *"Thanks. I had a friend help me decorate. I can't put anything on the walls, so that kind of sucks,"* she signed with her right hand while holding up her beverage to her mouth with her left.

"Oh, was it anyone I'd know?"

"Probably not. I met her at the gym a couple weeks ago. She's a realtor in 5th City Realm."

"Huh. Why was she at a gym in 1st City Realm then?"

"She lives in East City here because it's cheaper and she can save more money doing that."

"I guess that makes sense."

"Alright, I'm going to take a quick shower. You can turn on the TV and surf around if you want. I'll try to be out in ten minutes."

"You're done with your shake that fast? Wow, and here I always thought Zero ate fast."

Lisa smiled and handed her the remote. The Crescent Horned Punisher took it and said, "Have a nice shower."

When her friend had gone into the other room, Vanilla flicked the TV on and put her feet up on the coffee table. As if in response, Boxer jumped up on her lap and started purring. He swished his fluffy tail from side to side, sending long strands of orange fur into the air. "Jeez, *now* you come up here. Sit down, Boxer, you big ball of fluff."

There was a movie on with two Madite researchers in white lab coats. One of them was holding a clipboard with one hand and entering data into a hologram computer with the other. His partner was beside him staring at a projected screen with a few complex programs displayed. They appeared to be in an underground laboratory of some sort.

"I just don't get it," the second one said, scratching the side of his hat. "The data just doesn't add up. There's no way that could have happened given the circumstances."

"I don't know what to tell you. It happened and that's why we're running these tests," the first Madite said.

"The only thing I can think of is that K35-97 was somehow subject to some kind of dark energy radiation from one of the colony's decommissioned generators...but that still wouldn't explain the encrypted message it left. I mean, the chances of it having that effect are just too slim."

"Stranger things have happened."

"I can't help but wonder if this is all part of some big scheme…"

The first Madite stopped for a moment before continuing to type.

"Do you think—" the other started.

"Conspiracy theories are a slippery slope, Coil. You know that."

"Don't tell me the thought never crossed your mind. Those guys at Central are in the perfect position to pull something like this. Think about it."

"I don't want to get involved in this, Coil. Just keep your theories to yourself. It's better that way for both of us."

"Michael, you told me once that you would have gone to school to become a detective if this agency hadn't hired you right out of high school."

"Stop."

"This is the perfect opportunity to—"

"Coil, just drop it! I have to trust Central whether I like it or not. If you knew what was good for you, you'd keep your nose clean and pretend like nothing ever happened after we've presented our findings to the agency."

"But we haven't done that yet. Don't you see? There's still time to—"

The scientists were interrupted by a low, sinister voice from behind them. "Bickering are we, gentlemen?"

A man stepped out from the shadows. He was a Madite as well, but wore a black suit with a white undershirt and tie. His hat was gray with green eyes—one of which was disfigured.

"Elcom? What are you doing here?" Coil asked, obviously surprised.

"Oh, just some janitorial work. Central told me there were a couple of rats running around the underground. They sent me out to dispose of them before they could multiply," the man said, a wicked smile creeping across his face.

Both scientists inched away nervously. Coil tripped over the power cord to one of the computers and fell backwards. The well-dressed villain was upon him instantly and struck him down with a flash of magic energy. Michael turned around and ran for the exit as fast as he could, but Elcom, who was much more fit, quickly caught up to him.

They fought wildly, but it was evident that the frightened scientist was no match for the trained assassin. In desperation, Michael drew a vial of purple liquid from within his coat and threw it on the ground, right before his attacker's feet. There was a fizzing sound as sparkly blue gas billowed from the puddle the chemical had made. Both Madites covered their mouths and squinted.

A red emergency light flashed overhead and a loud siren sounded. The sprinkler system activated, spraying water down upon them. Elcom jumped back and shielded his face with his arms just as the chemical mess exploded, sending Michael flying into the elevator shaft on the opposite side of the room. With his last bit of strength, he pressed the button for the ground floor and passed out just as the door closed.

Completely engrossed in the movie, Vanilla was on the edge of her seat and failed to notice that her friend had already finished taking a shower. Lisa stood behind her quietly watching the TV. It was not until Boxer leaped from the Crescent Horned Punisher's lap to the back of the couch that she noticed her.

"Oh! Lisa, you're done already? You scared me. This movie is intense. I didn't even hear the water turn off."

"You seemed to be enjoying yourself. I didn't want to interrupt you."

"That's alright. I'm here to see you, after all. Besides, I have a TV at my house. But I'm curious, what's this movie called?"

"I think it's Project K35-97. It came out last summer."

"Hm. I guess that makes sense. I heard one of the characters say part of that name. Anyway, Boxer was sitting on my lap the whole time. He let me pet him."

"He's a big attention hog, isn't he?"

"Yeah. I like cats who are like that though."

"Me, too."

"Oh, I've been meaning to ask you something. Do you know of any place that teaches self-defense? Like for women without powers. I was thinking it would be nice to learn a few things. I know that it's very situational, since I couldn't really do much if someone with magic came after me, but at least I'd have some peace of mind if I'm ever walking through an alleyway in the City Realms or something."

"It's funny you should bring that up. I actually started working at a dojo every Monday and Wednesday as an instructor for hearing-impaired students. That's how I'm able to afford this apartment."

"Really? Wow, talk about ironic! What's the name of the place?"

"Lightning Dragon Martial Arts. They're located here in South City right off of Main Street and 3456ᵗʰ Avenue. They're affiliated with the dojo I trained at when I was a kid, Twin Dragon Dojo. I know the CEO, actually. I met him at a competition years ago."

"Cool! Is it expensive?"

"For personal lessons it's 250GD a month, which is really cheap."

"Awesome! I'll have to check it out sometime."

"You should. It's a great place. The building's pretty new, too, so it's clean and well-maintained."

"I'll bet. So, what have you and the band been doing? Have you guys written any new songs lately?"

"Not really. Zero's having a hard time composing. I think the situation with the band has really gotten him down. We still can't find a good permanent bassist. I mean, I fill in sometimes, but you know how it is with only three people. He's also had a number of failed relationships recently."

"Yeah...I really wish I could join you guys again."

"Why don't you?"

"It's just...I don't know. It would feel weird. Besides, I have a family now. I don't know if I could do it."

"I bet you could. Raech isn't a little girl anymore."

"That's true. She certainly isn't going to set the house on fire or anything when she's home alone. Still, my family comes first. I like spending time with them whenever I can. I want to give my daughter a better childhood than I had."

Lisa nodded solemnly.

"...And I don't want her to be alone all the time. Loneliness is like a disease. It eats away at you..."

"I understand."

Vanilla smiled weakly. "We both know it, don't we?"

Her friend nodded again.

The Crescent Horned Punisher stretched her arms and yawned. "Anyways...I still need a tour of this place."

"Oh, right. I forgot about that. Sorry. Follow me."

The Mandian led her friend into the next room, which was a small bedroom. There was a keyboard in the corner near the window with a laptop and headphones sitting on it and a stereo beneath it. There was a stool behind it with a sweater thrown over it for extra cushion. On the other side of the room was a mattress with cat-themed sheets on it—and orange fur, which Vanilla presumed was from Boxer. A travel case for a bass guitar was leaning against the bed. It had stickers on it of playful cartoon cats.

"*This is my bedroom. Sorry it's a bit of a mess,*" Lisa signed.

"That's OK. My room's a mess, too. Boxer must like your bed."

"*Yeah. He sleeps on it all the time with Benny.*"

"Aw, that's cute."

"*Yup. This is basically the only bedroom. The room next to it is a bathroom, which is where I keep the cats' litter box and food. There's an extra room over there, but I'm just using it for storage right now, so there's not much to look at in there.*"

"Huh. That's cool. Are you planning on doing anything with it in the future?"

"*Probably. I just need to reorganize things a bit and go through my boxes. But I haven't had the time to do that yet. I'll probably have my realtor friend help me with that sometime next month.*"

"That'll be nice. Hey, can I try out your bass?"

"*Sure. It's the same one I've always had, so don't expect anything special.*"

"That's alright. It's a good bass. The Big Mamma basses from 3027 to 3036 play really nice. I've tried a few of the new models at Meltdown Music and I didn't really like them all that much. I mean, they were OK, but they just felt a little too generic. I know they changed the tone circuitry for the optional input back in 3045 and they've sounded different ever since."

"*Interesting. I didn't know that.*"

"Yeah, it kind of sucks. You can get a reproduction board to replace the one in the new models, but it just doesn't sound as good as the old one. That and it'll void your warranty. Light Fracture products cost too much to *not* have warranty."

"*Yeah.*"

Vanilla climbed over the piles of stuff and grabbed the travel case. She slid it onto the bed and opened it up. Inside was a large gold-colored bass guitar with a thick, round body and wide tuning knobs. It had "Big Mamma" written in tribal tattoo-like cursive on the lower half of the body, just under the bridge.

The Crescent Horned Punisher strummed the strings and listened. "Yup, it's in tune," she said, more to herself than anyone. She sat on the edge of the bed and played with her eyes closed.

Like a ninja, Lisa snuck over to her keyboard and turned it on quietly. She waited until her friend had reached the end of a measure before adding in her own riff. Vanilla smiled and continued her bass line, not opening her eyes. Together they jammed, just like old times. The hours passed like minutes and soon it was time for her to leave.

"Well, I'd better get going. I have to get ready for that dinner. It was good seeing you."

"You too. I'm glad we got to hang out. You're welcome to come over any time."

"Thanks. I'll definitely look into that martial arts place when I get the chance."

Lisa nodded and smiled. With one last goodbye, the Crescent Horned Punisher made her way out of the apartment and back onto the bustling streets of 1st City Realm. It was still light out, as it was only 5:10 in the evening.

Glancing at her phone, she saw that Zallin had called her twice. "He's probably worried I forgot," she thought, pulling out her teleportation watch and pressing the Home button.

The house was warm and welcoming when she arrived. The outside lights had been turned on, presumably by Zallin. Stepping through the front door, she was met by Raech, who was pacing while looking at her phone. The teen looked up when she heard the door open.

"Oh, hi Mom. How was your visit with Lisa?"

"It was good. Are you texting someone?"

"Yes. Soul just texted me his address."

"I see. What is it?"

"5687 West Prestige Street in 5th North City."

"Whoa, 5th City Realm? And North City at that. He must come from a really rich family."

"Oh, I thought I already told you he was from 5th City Realm."

"Hm. You might have. I don't know why I was thinking it was 1st or 3rd. Actually, I remember your father saying something about that before. Never mind. Where is he, by the way?"

"Dad?"

"Yeah."

"I think he's finding a tie."

"Alright. I need to go change into something more formal. That dress looks nice on you."

"Thank you!"

Vanilla headed straight for the bedroom, where her meticulous husband was combing through his black hair. "Are you ready to go?" she asked, digging through the closet for a somewhat modest dress.

"In just a few minutes. How about you? I tried calling you a while ago."

"I saw that when I was leaving Lisa's."

"Hm. I would have preferred if you had at least told me where you were going."

"I told Raech. I figured she'd tell you."

"Still, I think it would have been better if you would have told me directly or at least sent me a text."

"It's not like I'd be running off with another man or barhopping, you know."

"That's not what I was saying. I just think it's good to communicate things like this."

"I just did."

Zallin was quiet.

"Oh come on, don't be like that, Zallin."

"I don't know what you mean."

"Yes you do."

"Vanilla, I don't want to argue with you."

"Well, whatever. Hey, can you help me with this dress when you're done grooming yourself there?"

"I wasn't 'grooming.' I was combing my hair."

"It looked a bit more like grooming to me."

"I don't see the humor in that."

"Alright, sorry. Jeez."

"What do you need help with?"

"Just lacing up the back."

"OK."

"Thanks."

"You're welcome."

"Well, I think I'm ready to go."

"Me too."

Together, they walked out into the living room to find Raech and transport.

The weather in North 5th City Realm was perfect when they arrived. Vanilla walked with her arm around her husband's, doing her best to keep up with his long stride in her high heels. Raech was practically skipping with joy and anxiety—an unusual behavior for the reserved teen.

Looking at her immediate surroundings, Vanilla was astonished at the size of the houses around her. Behemoth mansions loomed over well-kept yards with stately but secure fences around them. Vibrant flowers and exotic trees dotted each estate, creating the appearance of numerous private paradises. *They're like little self-contained worlds,* she thought.

As they walked along the smooth sidewalk near a tranquil park, a hovercar drove up noiselessly. Raech stared in awe at the vehicle. It was sleek and jet black, sporting a silver badge that read "Mergrand Dahlto" in fancy, thin letters. Even in the dim evening light, the metallic beauty glistened like polished onyx. The car just idled, levitating a foot from the smooth pavement.

Then, with a mechanical swoosh, the tinted passenger side window rolled down. A man in a gray business suit looked at the family from behind triangular shades. "Are you the new neighbors?" he asked in a somewhat annoyed tone. The family shook their heads. "Good, I didn't think so. You guys look like something that crawled out of the sewer and shit doesn't belong on the sidewalk!" He cackled and rolled his window back up before anyone could reply. With a gust of warm turbulence and a loud thruster noise, the rude man took off down the road.

Raech's eyes began to water, so Zallin put his arm around her and said, "Don't listen to him. People like that can't see past their pride. Your identity should never come from what others say about you—especially people like that." Raech dabbed her eyes with her sleeve and sniffed.

"Zallin!" Vanilla said. "You should have done something! How dare that man say something like that? People like him don't deserve to have anything."

"He didn't leave me time to say anything. Besides, what good would replying have done? I'd rather not feed the issue. The best thing to do is ignore people like him."

"Well you could have... Oh, I don't know! You should have hit his car with magic or something."

"Vanilla, I'm not a criminal and I don't intend to become one. That wouldn't have solved anything anyways. There's a time and place for everything and a right and wrong method."

"You can't be OK with what he said to us, though."

"I'm not. Let's just forget it and move on."

"Easy for you to say..."

After walking one more block, they reached the wrought iron fence that surrounded the Ampths' massive property. Neatly trimmed hedges created a wall behind the metal bars for privacy. Coming up to the gate, they noticed that it was intertwined with pretty, flowering vines.

"So *this* is where he lives, then?" Vanilla asked skeptically. Raech nodded and looked around for a way to notify the Ampths that they had arrived. To the immediate left of the gate was a small silver button with a speaker and microphone above it. "Call" was printed on the device's metallic faceplate in shiny black letters. She pressed it and waited. There was a short pause followed by a scuffling sound over the speaker.

"Who is it?" asked a gruff voice.

"That must be Soul's dad," Raech whispered to her parents. "Good evening, sir. My name is Raech Lamberschvak and I'm here with my parents for dinner. We were invited over yesterday by Soul." For a moment it seemed as if the man hadn't heard her. Then, still without verbal acknowledgement, the gate started to open. Vanilla was half-expecting it to creak, but it did no such thing.

A long stretch of sidewalk led up to the house. Wooden arches were placed at intervals, creating a partial tunnel. The hedges on either side of the walkway grew too tall to see over. Raech began to wonder if it was part of a garden maze.

Finally, the family reached the house. It was grand, like something that might have belonged to a royal family or foreign ambassadors of a powerful nation. The outside walls were painted white and looked very sturdy. Towering arched windows were situated evenly along the front of the building. The roof was made of heavy clay tiles that were colored a gray-blue. A fancy banner of black, silver, and gold hung above the doorway. The door itself was in a small inlet at the top of marble steps. Above it was a balcony supported by fancy stone pillars.

Hesitantly, Raech rang the doorbell. It was a deep, dissonant, bellowing sound that would easily wake even the heaviest of sleepers. The decorative handle on the door rattled with a resonation that sustained for what seemed like years, even after the bell had faded into silence. The family took a step back and waited.

They heard the sound of someone yelling angrily while passing by the door. "Soul, get down here right now! Your guests are here!" Footsteps thundered from the second floor. A moment later the door swung open and the family was met by the rich teen.

His white hair was slicked back and shiny from being wet. Unlike his father, who stood behind him, the long lines under Soul's eyes were dark gray and not pure black. He smiled and greeted them. "Pardon me, I was in a hurry to answer," he said buttoning up the end of his blue dress shirt. Blushing, he shook hands with his guests, starting with Raech. "Hi Raech! It's good to see you. You look great!" Raech blushed at the teenager's compliment, but thanked him.

"Hello again, Mr. Lamberschvak. I'm so glad you could make it."

"Why thank you, Soul. I appreciate you inviting us." Soul nodded and moved on to Vanilla.

"Hello there! You must be Raech's sister."

Vanilla waved her hand at the comment, "Pfft. Oh, I don't think

I look *that* young, but thank you. You sure know how to flatter a woman. My name is Vanilla. There's no need to address me with 'Mrs.' though."

"Oh, I think I may have heard of you before. Were you in a band called, *To the Power of 10?*"

"Yes! I'm surprised Raech hasn't told you that already."

"I didn't want to brag," Raech chimed in.

"That's alright. Wow, it's really an honor to meet you in person! I have all of your albums and like twenty T-shirts from your concerts. I met Zero once at Meltdown Music. He's really a good guitarist! You're an amazing singer, by the way."

"Awesome. Thanks for supporting my band. I was actually in concert with them recently. Zero's my ex-boyfriend. I ran into him in 1st City Realm a while ago and he asked me if I'd preform with them one last time."

"That was the concert in Felix Park, right?"

"Yup. Did you go?"

"Yeah! I wouldn't have missed it for anything!"

"Did you hear me mess up the bass line on the last song?"

"No, not at all. It sounded perfect to me."

"Oh, well, it really wasn't."

"Ah, that's OK. You guys are a lot better than me when it comes to music. Then again, I suppose most people are. I'm more of a listener than a performer. So anyway, you're not planning on getting back into the band?"

"No, unfortunately. Life's different now. A band is a full-time job and I just don't think I have the time or energy anymore."

"Aw, that's too bad. Oh, where are my manners? Everyone, come in."

Soul stood aside for the family to enter. They thanked him and stepped inside. The house's interior was gorgeous. The front room was small, but merged with a much larger living room. It was furnished with rosewood cabinets, leather sofas, and expensive-looking lamps. In the north corner there was a massive hologram TV. There was a reality show on a wealthy-looking man talking to two beautiful women, but it was muted.

Raech noticed a strange bronze sculpture sitting next to a tall bookcase. At first glance it appeared as if the metallic object was formed in the image of a person. On further inspection however, she realized that it was far from a normal being. It had sharp claws in place of fingers, scaly skin, and the head of a horned boar. She shuddered at the sight of it and looked away. "I see you're getting acquainted with my father's decorative styles," Soul joked, noticing her reaction. "I can give you guys a tour of the house later if you remind me," he continued, looking at Zallin and Vanilla.

Zallin nodded and said, "So Soul, you haven't introduced us to your family yet. Who all lives here with you?" Vanilla looked at him nervously. Her mind had wandered to her memory of Dan.

"Just my father, stepsister, and stepmom. We'll be eating very shortly. I can introduce you before we all sit down," the teenager replied.

Moments later they entered the dining hall. It was massive; like a school cafeteria, only much fancier. Gold and crystal chandeliers hung from the ceiling by polished silver chains. The walls were lined with large antique paintings, some of which looked strikingly similar to priceless works that Raech had once read about in a book. The walls themselves were a rich royal blue, giving the room an even more regal appearance. Toward the southern wall underneath three tall windows was the dinner table. It was long and narrow and made from a very dark wood. A blue and gold tablecloth stretched the entire length, providing a platform for a cluster of flickering candles.

"Here we are," said Soul, turning around to face his guests.

"Wow, this is breathtaking!" Vanilla said, taking in the dignified atmosphere.

"Why thank you ma'am. This estate is the earning of a very successful man; yours truly," said a deep, apathetic voice from the other side of the room. Everyone looked in the direction it had come from.

Standing at a window with a stern, but prideful look on his face was a well-dressed middle-aged man. His back was as straight as a board, but his hands rested on a black and gold cane. The sleekness of his white hair seemed almost unnatural as it glistened in the overhead light. He gazed indifferently at the family with his black and yellow cat eyes. Vanilla felt a chill run down her spine.

"Allow me to introduce myself," he said somewhat begrudgingly as he began walking toward them. "My name is Richard Devon Ampth. I am Soul's father and an ex-member of the Destruction Dynasty. I am a distant relation of the highly esteemed Leonox Royal, the mightiest emperor ever to rule my people."

"It's nice to meet you, Richard. I'm Raech's father, Zallin Lamberschvak."

"The pleasure is mine. You are a Madite, are you not?"

"That is correct."

Richard's mouth twitched. "I see. And this Crescent Horned Punisher is your wife, I presume?"

"Yes. Her name is Vanilla and this is my daughter, Raech."

The young Madite curtsied and smiled. "I'm honored to meet you, Mr. Ampth. Thank you for—"

Richard interrupted with a small cough. "Yes, of course. Welcome. Now if you'll excuse me, I must retrieve my daughter. Make yourselves at home. Dinner will be ready in five minutes sharp."

As their rude host retreated to the next room, the family couldn't help but feel put off by his aloof attitude. They did their best to hide it, however.

Soul seemed not to notice. "Why don't we all get seated? Feel free to choose whatever spot you want. Just reserve the seat at the head of the table for my dad," he said.

The family obeyed and sat on the side opposite the windows so they could look outside. The chair cushions were soft and surprisingly comfortable. Soul casually plopped himself down next to Raech. "So, how was everyone's week?" he asked.

Feeling a bit more comfortable now that Richard had left the room, Vanilla was first to reply. "It was OK. I can't say any of us had anything special going on. I went out for lunch with a friend of mine last Tuesday. Have you heard of a place called, 'The Carefree Cake Walker?' They have all kinds of amazing desserts there."

"No, I've never heard of it. Where is it located?"

"It's in the West section of 1ˢᵗ City Realm. If you know where Truman's Library is, it's just about a block away from there."

"I actually don't do much shopping in any of the other City Realms. Most of the stuff I buy I can get in the Blackstone Mall."

"Oh," Vanilla said, sinking back in her chair. She had stopped herself from asking, "Isn't that really expensive?" seeing that Soul was very wealthy.

"So, I hope you don't mind me asking this, but where do you guys live?"

"We live on a small planetoid realm called Glunke. We're currently its only inhabitants—strangely enough," Zallin replied, leaning forward in his chair.

"Really? That's pretty cool. Why doesn't anyone else live there?"

"I'm not too sure. It may be because of the weather. It's almost always cloudy and it tends to rain four or five times a week. Also, the temperature rarely gets up to eighty."

"That wouldn't be so bad. I know a few people that love places like that. Rain is—"

"Do they like slimy purple rain?" Vanilla interjected, raising one eyebrow.

"Um... What?"

"It rains purple slime on Glunke instead of water."

"That's weird. No offense or anything."

Just then one of the double doors on the far side of the room opened. A red-headed woman came toward the table with a cart of food. She glanced nervously at the visitors as the cart came to a halt. Soul stood up and helped her set large plates of delicious-looking food on the table. There was lobster, turkey, salads, fruits, nuts, wine, custard, and numerous other delicacies.

Vanilla couldn't help but gape at the meal. She had never seen so much expensive food all in one place aside from on TV shows or in magazines. Zallin, on the other hand, had been to a number of royal banquets with the 55th Council, most of which were much larger. Raech sat with her hands in her lap and smiled politely.

Once everything was in order, Soul cleared his throat and said, "Everyone, this is my stepmother, Ann. Ann, this is Zallin, Vanilla, and Raech Lamberschvak." The family smiled and greeted the red-headed woman, who in turn gave a shy wave and kept her eyes fixated on the floor. Her knees were shaking and she seemed to have trouble making eye contact.

Suddenly, a flustered teenager burst through the same double doors and marched up to the table. She wrenched an empty chair back and sat down. Unlike Richard and Soul, her skin was a shade of peach. Her brilliant red hair was short and curly, and her eyes were hazel. She folded her arms and reclined, glaring sharply at Raech.

Soul took a deep breath and sat back down. "This is my stepsister, Maria. Maria, these are my—"

"I don't care who or what they are!" Maria interrupted angrily.

Richard rushed up behind the rebellious teen and put his hands heavily on her shoulders. "Please excuse my daughter. She's had a dreadful day today," he said, struggling to keep his cool. His grip tightened threateningly on Maria's shoulder.

Vanilla's attention was on the food, however. It was as if she hadn't heard the rude comment. Her mouth was watering and it was all she could do to keep from reaching for the plate of crisp apple dumplings in front of her. "It looks so delicious…" she said dreamily.

Zallin put his hand on hers and whispered, "Vanilla." She jumped and blinked like she had been brought out of a trance.

"Oops, sorry," she whispered back.

"Ahem. Now we may eat," Richard said after he had seated himself at the head of the table. With a sharp glance at his daughter, he took a napkin from beside his plate and tucked it in his fancy shirt.

The food was heavenly. Every ounce of mashed potatoes, turkey, and prime rib were cooked to perfection. The salads were so fresh that anyone could have assumed the vegetables were picked that very day. Even some exotic delicacies were laid out toward the end. Vanilla ate to her heart's content and then some. It took every last bit of her self-control—and a worried glance from Zallin—to stop eating.

The instant everyone had finished, Maria stood up and whirled around, knocking the chair over with her hand. Richard exhaled loudly through his nostrils, sounding like a bull ready to charge. "Soul, why don't you show our guests the garden?" he said through clenched teeth. The irascible host's face was bright red with suppressed rage. The veins on his forehead bulged and pulsed like the ticking of a time bomb. He and Maria stared fiercely at each other.

"Right this way, everyone," Soul said, turning to the family and motioning to a nearby door. The Lamberschvaks quickly withdrew from the dining hall with Soul. As the door closed heavily behind them, yelling could clearly be heard from the table.

"I wanted *my* friends to come over tonight! It's not fair! Soul *always* gets his way. And that *rat* he brought into our house looks like she's only fourteen."

"Silence! The day your mother brought you into this family was more than enough hell for me, you ungrateful swine! At least Soul has a job and does what he's told without bickering!"

At Maria's reference to Raech as a "rat," Zallin frowned and instinctively reached his hand into his coat. He hesitated, remembering the incident with the man in the hovercar and took a deep breath through his nostrils. The powerful spell caster's muscles relaxed slowly and he drew his hand out. Vanilla bit her lip, wanting more than anything to launch insults of her own back at the spoiled girl. Just when she was opening her mouth, Soul spoke up.

"I'm so sorry you had to hear that, Raech… Don't listen to her. You're beautiful."

Raech wiped a tear from her eyes. "Th-thanks…"

The group walked in silence through corridor after corridor until they came upon a regular-sized door. Up until this point, all the doors they had seen were wide and grand, as to be expected in a mansion of such luxury. This one, however, was plain and simple. The only striking feature was a slightly discolored handle, which appeared to be half brown and half silver.

Soul placed his right hand on the doorknob and stopped. He took a deep breath and looked at his guests. "Raech, Mr. and Mrs. Lamberschvak, I really want to apologize on behalf of my family. Both my dad and my stepsister have been incredibly rude to you guys. I feel terrible, especially since this is your first time meeting them," he said, motioning to Vanilla and Zallin.

The Crescent Horned Punisher sighed and carefully inspected Soul's face to see if he was being sincere. "You know Soul," she said after a moment, "I really don't feel comfortable letting my daughter be around your father and your stepsister. From what I've witnessed so far, there are a lot of problems here."

Soul swallowed hard and nodded. "I understand. It's OK if you don't—" he began, but Vanilla interrupted.

"Now just hang on. I wasn't finished yet. As I was saying, there are definitely some things in this family that I don't approve of, but I can see that you're different from them. Call it a woman's intuition, but I know that you've been through a lot in life and that you've chosen to pursue the right path. I'm totally OK with you dating my daughter as long as you guys don't hang out here. No offense to you, Soul. I have nothing against *you*."

Soul blushed, but looked relieved. "How did you know I wanted to date Raech?" he asked, nervously glancing in the young teenager's direction.

"Oh you didn't think you could hide these sorts of things from a mother, did you? It's not every day that a young man invites a girl and her parents over for dinner to meet his parents."

Raech couldn't help but beam with excitement at their

conversation. "I'll go out with you, Soul!" she blurted out. Soul smiled and gave her a hug.

"I'd still like to see this garden before we get out of here, if that's alright," Vanilla added after letting the new lovers have a moment.

"Oh, right," Soul replied as he flung the door ajar and stood aside.

The sight that lay before them was majestic. The Ampths' backyard stretched on for what seemed like eternity. In front of the family was a wide walkway made from smooth, light-gray stones. Much like the front yard, tall flower-filled arches loomed over the path, making a sort of tunnel. Walls of dense green hedges ran on either side of the tunnel. From steps where Vanilla stood, she could see beyond them.

To her right was a large glassy pond with an ornate fountain in the center. A variety of colorful fruit trees encircled the small oasis, which would provide plenty of shade on a hot summer day. Though most of the Photose had already sunk from the sky, leaving it dark out, Vanilla still felt inclined to meander over to the pond and sit on the grass beneath one of the trees. It was a welcoming sight and a stark contrast from the dark and regal theme of the mansion.

Turning to her left, she saw an exact mirror of the oasis. Even the fruit trees seemed to be the same height and shape as the ones on the opposite side. *This whole place must be symmetrical,* she mused.

Soul's voice brought her out of deep thought. "We should probably stick together. This garden is easy to get lost in. Also, your transportation watches or powers won't work here. My dad had a warp barrier installed so nobody would cause mischief."

As they walked along the big steppingstones beneath the roof of vines and flowers, Vanilla couldn't help but wonder what happened to Maria after everyone had left the house. Though the rebellious youth had been very rude, Vanilla began to feel sorry for her. Finally, she mustered the courage to ask. "Soul," she said, choosing her words carefully, "It seems that your stepsister doesn't get along very well with you or your father."

The young man glanced back at her. "Yeah. To tell you the truth, none of us do. Over time I've come to the realization that it's best for me to just try and be respectful. There are many things that my father and I disagree about, but feeding conflict with anger and insults will never resolve it. I'm sure you're probably wondering about Maria's punishment, but really, it's OK. She'll be fine."

"Soul," Vanilla said sternly, putting her hand on his shoulder. He stopped and looked her in the eyes for a brief moment, and then blushed and stared at his feet. "Soul," she repeated, "is your father hurting you?" Zallin and Raech had stopped, too, and were standing on either side of the young man. He bit his lip and gazed more intensely at his spotless designer shoes.

"Yeah," he said quietly. His voice cracked as he spoke.

Vanilla hugged him and patted him on the back. "It's alright. We can help. I've gone through something similar."

Zallin stepped forward and also rested his hand reassuringly on the teen's shoulder.

"You don't have to do anything. I'll be fine. Really," Soul replied, struggling to keep from crying. He tried to move away, but Vanilla held him in her embrace.

"We're going to help you whether you like it or not. That's what friends are for."

"But I…I don't need help. Don't worry about me. I can manage this."

"No, Soul. You can't. I couldn't manage what happened to me and it caused me to have an adolescence that was full of bad choices and regret. Stop trying to act tough. There are battles you can't win on your own."

"How can you help me, though?"

"If I remember correctly, you're seventeen, right?"

"Yeah, why?"

"You're going to stay with us for a while. It'd be different if you were a year older and could rent an apartment, but for now you can take refuge in our home."

Upon hearing this, Zallin opened his mouth as if to object, but then thought better of it, hoping to avoid an assault from his wife's verbal armada. "Will your father be upset?" he asked after thinking for a second.

Soul shrugged. "Probably, but he won't chase after me. I've run away once before. He didn't come looking for me, but he did get violent after I came home…"

"Well, is there anything you need from the house?" Raech asked. She had been quiet the whole time, so it surprised everyone when she spoke.

Soul thought for a moment, and then shook his head. "I can buy what I need. I have my wallet and cell phone with me."

"Soul! Come inside and clean up your dishes!" an angry voice called from somewhere close by. Everyone froze. Vanilla reached for her transportation watch, but Soul shook his head. Then Vanilla remembered what he had said before and nodded.

"So, if we can't transport, how will we escape?"

"Easy. Just follow me."

Taking out a silver ring from within his jacket, the young man closed his eyes and slipped it on his index finger. There was a flash of grayish-blue light, and then a sword appeared in his hands. It was like nothing Vanilla had ever seen before. The handle was short and encrusted with tiny rubies and wrapped with black leather. Its guard was minimal; merely a thin disc of steel that bore ancient letters on it. What caught her eye most was the blade. It was thicker and more cylindrical than most swords, which made it appear to be very heavy. Four deep grooves marked where it was segmented into individual parts. Each piece had two wicked hooks sticking out on either side.

Zallin eyed the sword suspiciously and furrowed his brow.

As if he had read the soft-spoken Madite's mind, Soul quickly explained as he skillfully swung it at the air. "This sword belonged to one of my ancestors. It was left to me in my grandfather's will because of my mother's close connection with him. I don't like to use it because I'm not proud of my heritage, but it'll do. I'm going to cut a path to the street."

"Are you sure? It'd be a shame to ruin this nice garden. I can probably break through the warp barrier and at least get us to the street," Zallin said, but Soul had already begun hacking away at the shrubs.

As they reached the fence line that bordered the sidewalk, they heard Richard shout gibberish in rage from somewhere deep within in the garden. "It looks like he found the path I've made," Soul said dismally, "so there's no turning back now. We should be clear of the barrier now. I'm ready to transport when you guys are." Vanilla grabbed his hand and pressed the Send button on her watch. Instantly they were teleported to the front door of the house on Glunke.

"Wow that was sudden!"

"I'm sorry. Are you OK?" Vanilla said.

"Yeah I'm fine. It's no big deal. I'm just...well, never mind. So is this where you guys live then?"

"Yup. It may be kind of...well, modest compared to what you're used to. I hope you don't mind."

"It's fine. I like it. Where are Raech and Mr. Lamberschvak?"

"They should be here any second. Sometimes it takes—"

Vanilla was interrupted by a flash of bright blue light beside her. The two Madites had appeared and smiled. "Sorry it took us a while. Dad wanted to apologize to Mr. Ampth. We thought it was the right thing to do. He didn't take it too well, though." Vanilla tried to smile, but found it hard. Seeing that it would be unwise to argue, she simply nodded and unlocked the door.

Zallin stopped as he entered the living room. His eyes were fixated on a dim, flickering light that shone eerily from the kitchen. He signaled for everybody to stay still and they obeyed. Like a cat stalking its prey in the inky night, the spell caster crept stealthily toward the doorway that led into the kitchen, readying his staff. The air was thick with anticipation as he silently pressed himself against the wall and slowly raised his staff.

Suddenly the lights flicked on. "You didn't think you could sneak up on me, did you Zallin?" a jolly, booming voice said. "I was wondering how things were going so I decided to pay you another visit. When I got here it didn't look like anybody was home so I let myself in. You have a terrible security system, by the way. A blindfolded baby could have broken in. But hey, here I am."

Zallin stood up straight and saluted as a towering, 7'2" tall man walked into the living room, stooping low to avoid the doorframe. His long hair was colored pale shades of red, blue, green, yellow, and purple, except for the very top, which was silver. His chin was as square as a box and his eyebrows were thick and bushy. In his hands he held a massive, wicked scythe with a small broken skull at the end of the handle. A metal lantern hung loosely by a chain wrapped around the top of the weapon.

Flustered, Zallin put his staff away and took a deep breath. "Sir," he began, but the tall brute interrupted.

"Well, look who we have here! It's that young man whose mother

348

tried to fight me years ago! Saul, was it?"

Soul's eyes narrowed. Biting his lip with his pointed teeth, he took a shaky step forward. A tear slowly worked its way down the pale teen's cheek and fell onto his fancy shirt. "What kind of coward kills a woman?! What kind of sick mind even contemplates robbing a little kid of his mom?!" he roared.

The crude captain of 55th Council raised one eyebrow and let out a long sigh. "Kids these days are just idiots. Your mother—Nenphii was it? Hell I don't remember. I don't keep track of names. All I see is weaklings—like her! Anyway, she was a Darklord and it's my job to kill Darklords before they cause trouble. Killing an evil fiend like her was the right thing to do. Maybe you'll understand when you're a bit older."

Burning with rage, Soul charged forward, brandishing his sword. Crescent readied his scythe. There was a loud bang and flash of blue light, followed by a thump. Raech had teleported between the two men and had taken both blows. Vanilla screamed in horror and fell to her knees weeping. Zallin quickly grabbed his staff and was pointing it at Crescent. Soul let go of his sword and stared in shock at Raech who was still standing but had closed her eyes and was stone-still. Her mouth was open slightly and a bit of blood was trickling from it.

Seemingly unmoved the scene, Crescent turned his head and looked Zallin straight in the eyes. "Lieutenant Zallin, put down your weapon," he said coldly.

Trembling with fear and anger, Zallin stood his ground. "Not on my life," he replied in a quivering voice.

"I'll say it again, Zallin. Put down your weapon, or I will break your arm off and kill you with it." The spell caster refused to budge, so the irascible captain grabbed his hand.

Instantly, however, he let go and stepped back, clutching his stomach. A bright red splotch had appeared by the lower half of his ribcage. "What the hell!?" he yelled, drooling from pain.

"Three of your ribs are broken," Raech said, opening her eyes and removing the gigantic scythe's blade from her shoulder. Everyone stared in awe at the young Madite.

"That's impossible! How did you survive that?" the dumbfounded Crescent exclaimed, and then coughed up a glob of blood onto the carpeting.

"Less than a nanosecond after your scythe pierced my skin, someone passed on their power as a Chosen to me. I am now one of the Seven Chosen like you."

She took a breath and continued. "Had you hit me any later, you would have lost all your power in accordance with the Scrolls. Any sooner and I certainly would have died. The only reason I was able to harm you was because I weakened your ribs by misusing a little-known healing spell that reallocates calcium to other parts of the body. Being that it was entirely passive magic, it was able to bypass your Central Power Core. After that, the strain put on your ribs from your muscles contracting was all it took for them to break."

Crescent winced and drew himself up to his full height. The sickening sound of his bones cracking more could be heard as he did so. "You're lying! That was just a fluke! I'm gonna freakin' kill you now!" he shouted angrily, wiping the bodily fluids from his mouth with the back of his sleeve.

"Do you really want to take that risk? I'm sure you know what will happen if you attack me now."

The brute's face scrunched up in a hateful scowl. "No! That's not fair! I always win! I have to!" he screamed, throwing his hands in the air and wildly stomping large holes in the floor. The pain from his broken

350

ribs seemed to have been numbed by his rage.

"That's enough!" Raech said, raising her voice. "Leave this place at once and never return. Should you cause any harm to my family in the future, I can easily find a way to make you lose your power."

Seething with animosity, the 55th Council's captain transported, but not before uttering the most abominable remarks he could think of at the family.

The room was filled with silence, aside from heavy breathing from Soul. "I-I don't...I don't know. Raech, are you...? No," he panted. "He was the one... He killed my mom! That bastard! I'll get him, even if I die trying!"

Raech put her hand reassuringly on his shoulder. "I'm sorry about your mom, Soul... We were incredibly lucky this didn't get any worse. Are you alright? Let me get you a glass of water." Feeling strong nausea setting in from the frightful encounter, the child prodigy Madite slowly stumbled toward the kitchen. Still shaken, Soul ran to her side and supported her with his strong arms.

Zallin had rushed to Vanilla's side the moment Crescent left and was tending to her. She had fainted shortly after the young girl had been hit and was lying on her back behind the couch. "W-we survived," he said to himself in bewilderment.

CHAPTER 15
-As The Ashes Settle-

A slight chill hung in the air, lingering from the night before. It was morning on Glunke. Vanilla lay awake under the soft covers thinking about the events of the previous day and fidgeting with the ends of her sheer purple nightgown. Her mind was filled with a menagerie of emotions as she pictured Raech throwing herself in front of Crescent's attack to save Soul. Even though the girl had survived, the vivid image still stung her heart, all too reminiscent of Zallin's sacrifice less than a year before. She squinted at the ceiling, her eyes automatically following the wooden blades of the fan as it cycled around endlessly.

Slowly, she pulled herself out of bed and stood for a moment, staring out the window at the eternally cloudy sky. Then she returned her attention to the room.

It was messy—a familiar sight. Her clothes lay strewn around her dresser; socks partly hidden by the bed skirt, threatening to disappear until the next time Zallin did a thorough cleaning of the house. A pair of her sweatpants were draped over the Madite's chair and several of her tops were piled on the floor.

There was an empty bag of sea salt potato chips, her latest comfort food, at the end of her dresser that had missed the trashcan. The silvery inside of its light blue foil wrapper glinted as the light of dawn shone down upon it.

Suddenly, she heard a light knock on the door, which had been left partially ajar when Zallin exited the room that morning.

"Um, Mrs. Lamberschvak," Soul's voice came from the other side.

She blushed and grabbed the sheet, holding it in front of her. "Hang on, I'm not dressed!"

"Oh s-sorry!"

She took a deep breath and sat on the edge of the bed, still clutching the sheets. "It's OK. How did you sleep last night?"

"Um, not…not too well."

"I'm sorry. We'll go shopping later today and get you a regular bed. I guess we really haven't ever had a reason to use our guestroom before."

"No, no, it's not that. I just…"

She gave a weak smile and looked down. "I'm guessing it's about what happened yesterday."

"Y-yeah… That. Thanks. I don't want to be a burden for you guys."

She shook her head, though he couldn't see since he was still on the other side of the door. "It's alright. You don't have to worry about that. I'm glad we can help you."

"If there's anything I can do, just let me know."

"I'm sure there are some things that you can help with. Talk to Zallin about it, though. He'll have a better idea of what we can have you do while you're living with us."

"OK."

"Did you already have breakfast?"

"No, not yet. I was going to ask you about that. Is it OK if I just find something myself? I don't really know how you guys do things here."

"Yeah, that's fine. It's all fair game."

"Thanks."

She hesitated. "Hey Soul?"

"Y-yeah?"

"I'm so sorry to hear about your mother. I can't believe Crescent did that… You must have gone through a lot."

There was a long pause. Eventually, the teenager replied with a barely audible "It's OK," and started to walk down the hallway, but Vanilla stopped him again.

"I'm glad you're OK."

He sniffed, obviously holding back tears. There was a twinge of anxiety in her stomach, but she couldn't think of what else to say, so she remained silent and waited to see if he would reply.

When she heard him finally move away from the door, she got up again, still holding the sheets over herself just in case, and closed it all the way. *I guess we'll have to get in the habit of keeping this closed in the morning,* she thought, looking down at her body.

Retreating to her dresser, she squatted down and pulled out the drawers to retrieve a change of clothes; a pair of her favorite black jeans, a spaghetti-strap tank top with a band logo, and a matching pair of pink undergarments.

She cast a glance at the bathroom. Her stomach rumbled, the familiar clawing of hunger taking center stage. Setting the pile of clean clothes down on the edge of her dresser, she grabbed her silky robe off of the chair in front of her vanity and put it on over her nightgown. Then she opened the door and headed out into the hallway.

The house had a different feel than before. She could sense a shift in the energy of the air, though it was hard to put her finger on how exactly things had changed. She thought back to her first time in the cabin—when it was *only* a cabin. The walls, which were once barren and unpainted wooden boards, were now adorned with family photos and paintings that Raech had done. The carpet was no longer the off-white dust trap that it had been when she first set foot upon it after being rescued by the Raech of the future. It was now clean and soft against her bare feet—a comforting feeling that she had come to look forward to at the end of a long day or the start of a new one. It was home.

As she was passing the guestroom where they had hastily set up a sleeping bag and lamp for Soul the night before, she heard weeping. Part of her expected it to be the Origin Spiritan, but it was too high pitched to be a man. It was familiar as well. She would have recognized it anywhere.

Panicking, Vanilla ran to Raech's room and opened the door. The 14-year-old Madite was sitting on her floor looking at her hands through tear-glazed eyes.

The protective Crescent Horned Punisher's eyes darted around the room. Nothing seemed out of place, however, and the girl didn't appear to be hurt. She knelt down by her side and put her right hand on her daughter's cheek. "Sweetie, what's wrong?"

"I-I broke the door!" she sobbed, pointing behind her.

Vanilla's gaze followed the direction she had motioned to. Sure enough, on the inside of the room, the brass knob was completely destroyed. Strangely, it looked as though it had been crushed by an industrial trash compactor. The shiny object was now only a mere fraction of its original size, looking more like a mangled hairpin than anything.

She returned her attention to the crying teen. "W-why did you do that?" she asked, her voice trembling with uncertainty.

"I didn't m-mean to! I'm so sorry, Mother! I didn't mean to…"

"But…how did it happen?"

"I can't control my strength!"

Vanilla thought for a moment, revisiting the events of the day before in her mind. Then it dawned on her. "Is it because you're one of the Seven Chosen now?"

She sniffed. "I-I think so." Raising her hand to wipe her nose, she stopped herself and continued crying. "I'm scared! What if I hurt myself or someone else?"

Vanilla dug around in the pockets of her robe for a few seconds before retrieving a handkerchief. Gently, she wiped the girl's eyes and then her nose.

"You don't have to apologize, Sweetie. I know you didn't mean to do it." There was a sinking feeling in her chest as the uncertainty began to rise. *Is this something she'll get used to?* she thought, casting an apprehensive glance at the girl's slender, beautiful fingers and wondering how anything so fragile-looking could hold so much destructive strength.

"I'm afraid to touch anything now."

Vanilla bit her lip. "Where's your father? Maybe he has an idea of how to help you get used to your new powers."

"I don't know. I haven't been out of my room today."

"I'll go find him and see what he has to say, OK?"

"OK."

She got up and turned around, stopping for a moment to look at the damaged door handle for the second time. A chill ran down her spine as she thought of the immense power that her daughter was now tasked with learning to control. Leaving the door open, she headed back into the hallway and made her way to Zallin's study.

When she arrived, the door to the room was shut. She paused for a moment to press her right horn against it and listen. It was silent. Withdrawing, she knocked softly three times.

"Come in," the Madite said.

Vanilla opened the door and stepped inside.

The room was small, only made to appear smaller by the large bookshelves and mountains of research papers. The one window on the west corner of the room was partially obscured by the arching back of an old white couch and the leaves of a potted plant next to it. Desperate for natural light, the fragile flora had grown at an angle to maximize the time it spent basking in it each day. It was an unusual organism—something one of her old friends had given her for her birthday several years ago.

Zallin was sitting in an armchair at his desk at the northern end of the room reading an old book titled, *History of The Seven Kingdoms: The Fall of an Empire*. He had his feet up on a cushion that he had taken from the couch. His hat's yellow eyes, which were half-lidded, were still scanning the book as she approached.

Vanilla cleared her throat. "Hon?"

There was a short pause before he replied. "...Yes?"

"Um, I think Raech is having trouble controlling her power. She...she accidentally crushed the knob on her door."

He looked up from the dense pages and frowned. "I see..."

"Is there something you could do to help her?"

He gave a barely audible sigh through his nostrils. "It's something that she'll have to get used to."

"But...can't you at least do something to reassure her? She's crying and she says she's really scared that she might accidentally hurt herself or someone."

He put a plastic bookmark in the tome and set it down on the desk with a dull thump. "Alright," he said quietly. Placing his hands on either of the chair's armrests, he slowly rose to his feet.

As he was doing so, Vanilla's stomach growled again. She had the urge to ask him about breakfast, but quickly reconsidered.

As if he had read her mind, he stopped at the door and said, "I'm sorry, but could you please make something for breakfast this morning?"

She blinked. "Er, y-yeah, of course!"

"Thank you."

He disappeared into the hallway, leaving her standing amidst his personal library. *I wonder if that means he hasn't eaten yet,* she thought, furrowing her brow. As she neared the door, she came face-to-face with Soul. He peeked around the corner right as she took a step into the hallway.

"I'm sorry!" he said, backing up.

"It's OK. You startled me. Did you find something to eat?"

"Yeah."

"What did you have?"

"A bowl of cereal. I was going to ask, do you want me to wash my dish or put it in the dishwasher?"

"Either is fine. It doesn't matter."

"OK. What's this room? Is it a library or something?"

"This is my husband's study."

"Mr. Lamberschvak sure has a lot of books. Has he read them all?"

"I think most of them. He likes to read in his spare time."

"Oh. That's cool. Does he play any instruments like you?"

She shook her head. "No. He's not really the artistic type." She stood aside and motioned for him to come in the room. "You can take a look around if you want. We didn't really have time to give you a tour of the house yesterday with all that happened…"

Soul entered and looked around at the towering wooden shelves, chock-full with a plethora of encyclopedias and other archaic learning material. His eyes lit up with curiosity as his gaze landed upon a book with foreign letters. "Does he speak different languages?"

"Quite a few, yes."

"Do you?"

She hesitated. "Just Alking," she lied, praying she could avoid questions about her childhood in the Gar Underworld.

"How did you two meet?"

"It's kind of a long story. I'll have to tell you another time."

"OK. You don't have to tell me if you don't want to. Sorry if that was intrusive."

"No, it's OK. We get asked that a lot, actually. I think I'm going to go get some breakfast. Make yourself at home."

"OK."

Back in the hallway, she made her way to the kitchen. The clawing of hunger was getting stronger. With shaking hands, she opened the refrigerator and looked over its contents briefly. Nothing stood out, so she closed it.

Then she stood in front of the cupboards for a few minutes staring in indecision, a hand on either handle. There were colorful boxes and bags of food, but none of them looked appetizing enough for her fickle preferences. Her eyes scanned over the labels, not reading a single one.

The sound of something shattering pierced the stillness like cannon fire on a quiet night. Startled, Vanilla whirled around.

Raech was standing on her tiptoes, looking down at the floor where the fragments of a broken glass had slid in all directions from the point of impact at her feet. She looked equally as shaken as her mother.

"I'm so sorry!" The girl had begun to sob again.

Vanilla closed the cupboard door and carefully leaned over to reach the pantry, being careful not to step on the sharp shards of glass. "It's OK, Sweetie. What did your father say about your powers?"

"He said I'll have to adapt."

She frowned. "Did he have anything you could try to help you get used to it?"

She shook her head.

"I see. Well, don't worry about breaking things, OK? We can just get your father to repair them. He seems to be pretty good at that. Just do your best to be careful and I'm sure you'll get the hang of it."

When Vanilla had safely reached into the pantry, she groped around for a bit before coming across the handle of a broom and dustpan. Grabbing it, she pulled it out and began sweeping up the fragments of broken glass.

When she had finished, she emptied them into the garbage can and put the broom away. Then she turned back to her daughter and said, "I can make you something for breakfast. What would you like?"

"Maybe something that I don't have to use a fork or a spoon for."

She thought for a moment. "How about a grilled cheese sandwich? That's something I can probably make without any trouble."

She nodded. "Thank you, Mother."

"Just have a seat at the table. I'll work on that right now."

"OK."

Cautiously, the young teen sat down, keeping her hands together in her lap. Her shoulders were tense and she squeezed her arms together to make herself as thin as possible.

Vanilla went to the refrigerator and got a block of cheddar cheese, pausing for a moment to look for any existing slices before closing the door and setting it on the counter. Then she retrieved some slices of bread from the pantry and a pan from the drawer beneath the stove. After carefully and unskillfully slicing a few uneven pieces of cheese and placing them on the bread, she plopped it onto the hot pan and waited, drumming her fingers on the edge of the counter and humming to herself.

"Um, Mother?" Raech said.

"Yes Sweetie?"

"Has Soul eaten anything yet?"

"Yeah. I just spoke to him a minute ago and he said he found something. Do you know where he is right now?"

She thought. "He's in his room. I can sense it."

"Oh. Have you always been able to do that?"

"To sense where people are?"

"Yeah."

She shrugged. "Kind of. I tried just now and it was a lot clearer than it's ever been." She paused. "I felt like I could see everything in the entire realm all at once. I've never been able to do that before. It must be from becoming Chosen…"

"Hm. Oh, looks like your grilled cheese is done." Vanilla got out a plate and slid the hot food item onto it. Then she carried it over to the table and set it down in front of her daughter. "Do you want anything to drink?"

She hesitated. "No, thank you."

"Are you sure?"

"I…I'm afraid I'll break something again."

"Well you don't want to get dehydrated. What if I put a straw in a cup? Then you can just sip it."

"It's not just my hands that are strong. It's everything…"

"Even your lips?"

She shrugged. "I think so."

"Well if you accidentally crush a straw, that's no big deal. It's worth a try."

"OK."

Vanilla quickly got a glass of ice water and put a straw in it. Then she set it down on the table next to the plate of food.

Raech was already attempting to lift the grilled cheese sandwich to her mouth. She had wrapped her hands around it with movements slower than a sloth and more careful than a brain surgeon. As she raised it up, her finger twitched and her apocalyptic strength kicked in, squashing the bread instantly. Her lips trembled.

Vanilla reached over and rubbed her back. "Hang in there. It might take some time, but I'm sure you'll get the hang of it."

She took a shaky breath and bit into the cheesy mess. Her mother watched her empathetically until she was done. "I can get your dishes," she said, collecting them off the table and bringing them over to the sink. *I should probably make something for Zallin now,* she thought.

Returning to the fridge, she got a few eggs and cracked them over the pan, which was still hot. "I'll make some scrambled eggs for both of us," she thought out loud.

When they were done, she divided the eggs into two portions, putting each on separate plates. Then she went off to find her husband.

Zallin was back in his study again reading the same book from before. The bookmark had traveled almost to the end, some 500 pages or so. The eyes on the Madite's blue hat flickered from side to side, scanning the text at amazing speed, despite the weary look on his face.

Vanilla set the plate of scrambled eggs down on the side of his desk.

"Thank you," he said quietly.

"You're welcome, Hon. You know, you'll have to look for a job now."

"Yes, I know. Please let me put my feet up for a while though. I need to rest for a bit."

She nodded. "OK. I wasn't trying to pressure you."

"I appreciate that."

She hesitated. "Hon? I'm sorry to interrupt you again."

He looked up. "That's alright. What do you need?"

"I was just thinking about everything that's happened this year..."

"I see."

"The cursed book, Raech getting kidnapped, you going to Medrunt-Baritz with the 55th Council..." Her lips trembled. "I just want a normal life..."

He nodded. "I do, too. We've been through a lot."

She sighed. "Sometimes I don't even know what to think."

"Hm."

"You're always so collected. I don't understand how you do it."

"It's something I had to learn during my years with the 55th Council." His voice was quieter than before and he broke eye contact as he spoke.

"I'm sorry. The way I said that came out wrong. I didn't mean to sound accusing."

He shook his head. "I didn't think you sounded accusing."

She turned around and took a step toward the door, but stopped. "Hon..."

"Yes?"

"What happened there?"

"'There?'"

"...When you were in Medrunt-Baritz with the 55th Council."

He finally set the book down and was silent for a few seconds. Then he spoke slowly, his eyes downcast and his fingers steepled. "...We were sent there to exterminate a Darklord that the Spiritan government had been tracking. It was just like any other mission of its kind. We did our job and filed a formal report to the government." He paused. "... That's all."

She waited. "I see," she said, searching his eyes. "I'm sorry for interrupting you."

"That's alright. I love you."

"I love you too." Turning around slowly, she walked out of the room and closed the door carefully behind her.

Out in the hallway, she made her way to the guest room. Soul was sitting on the floor, paging through the messages on his Call Ring. The holographic display flickered at random intervals, denoting a need for servicing.

Vanilla knocked on the open door softly.

Startled, he looked up. "Oh, Mrs. Lamberschvak."

"Hey. What are you working on?"

He sighed and glanced back at the ring-shaped multi device's display. "Just trying to figure out how to block my dad's number."

"Did he try calling you?"

He nodded.

"I see. You said he wouldn't come looking for you though, right?"

He shrugged. "I don't *think* he will. I'm just kind of worried…"

"Hm. Well, in fifteen years of living here, the paparazzi have never found me, so I don't think he'll find you anytime soon."

"Thanks."

"I know what it's like to run away from home. Regardless of what your dad might think, you're doing the right thing. You deserve better."

"It's hard to stop worrying though."

"I know. Just give it some time. Our home is your home now." She leaned down and gave him a hug.

He blushed and turned his head to the side to avoid staring at her deep cleavage. "Is Raech awake?" he asked quickly.

She straightened back up. "Yeah. She's been awake for a while. She's still trying to get used to her new powers."

"Oh."

"I'm trying to process everything myself."

"Me, too…"

"Well, I should get in the shower. You're welcome to use the guest bathroom down the hall. We can go shopping today for clothes and toiletries or whatever you need. We also need to get some furniture in here for you."

"I can help pay for it."

"You have money?"

"Yeah. I'd feel bad if I didn't pitch in."

She smiled. "That's very mature of you. Alright, I'll come get you when we're ready to go out, OK?"

"OK. Thanks again for everything, Mrs. Lamberschvak. I really appreciate this."

"Of course."

She left the room, closing the door partway behind her. Back in the hallway, she went straight to her bedroom. As she walked the length of the soft white carpet, she thought about her first year living in the house and smiled. At one time, each room felt new, despite its obvious age.

Zallin was in their bedroom when she arrived. He appeared to be reorganizing his formal shirts in the closet. He sifted through shades of blue and gray, swapping their positions with the precision of a machine. Every movement was calculated and articulate. He looked up as he heard her come in. "Vanilla, I'd like to talk to you about something."

"What?"

"Could you close the door, please?"

She frowned for a fraction of a second. "Uh, sure." Gently, she slid the plain wooden door shut and returned her attention to him. "What do you want to talk to me about?"

He hesitated. "I'm a bit concerned about this arrangement. Please hear me out."

"You mean with Soul staying with us?"

He nodded.

"But—"

"Vanilla, please listen to what I have to say."

She pursed her lips together and shifted in place.

He continued. "I'm afraid that having Raech's boyfriend stay with us will create temptation for them."

"You mean...?"

He nodded. "It's very difficult to live with the person you love without occasionally desiring intimacy."

She swallowed, her thoughts turning to Zero. "That's true...Raech is only fourteen. If she was eighteen, it wouldn't be so much of an issue. I mean, if it was four years in the future."

"Actually, I don't want Raech sleeping with a man she's not married to. Even if she was eighteen, that would still be a problem."

Vanilla frowned and folded her arms across her chest. "Why? *We* did."

He sighed and spoke carefully. "The circumstances were... different for us."

"Zallin, if you're seriously dating someone and you're an adult, it's good to know if you can satisfy each other sexually."

"I don't think that that's an excuse to have sex before you marry someone."

She shook her head and ran a trembling hand though her hair. "Well, I think having a healthy sex life is important to a successful relationship. It's obviously not *everything*, but it's like...I don't know. Like, if you were in a relationship with someone who never wanted to have sex, but you did, it would never last. Remember what we talked about on our wedding night?"

"I was willing to compromise for you."

"Right. So—"

"It doesn't mean that Raech should sleep with Soul before they're married."

She took a deep breath and closed her eyes for a few seconds. "I really don't agree with you, Zallin. Once she's eighteen, I'm fine with her and Soul sleeping together, as long as he takes responsibility."

"But we need to be on the same page in terms of parenting, even if we disagree individually."

"So you just want me to do things your way again? My opinion is just as valid as yours, you know."

"Yes, but think about her future. Let's say that five years from now she had a child with Soul and then they broke up. Being a single mother is a very difficult thing, especially for someone at that age. She would have to provide for her child financially and emotionally all by herself. Not only that, but it could be emotionally hard on the child."

"But people get divorces, too. Being married doesn't *prevent* people from going their separate ways."

"I know, but there's an element of commitment in marriage that isn't as present in a dating relationship."

"Not necessarily. We both know couples who have been through a divorce. I understand what you're trying to say, but it's not true."

"Please. I don't want this to turn into a fight. All I'm asking is that you try to see things from my perspective."

"No, all you're asking is that I agree with you, which I don't."

He sighed heavily. "Vanilla—"

She threw her hands in the air and rolled her eyes. "Alright, fine. Whatever."

"I'm not trying to discredit your opinion or—"

"It's fine, Zallin. Just drop it, alright?"

He nodded. "...Alright. Thank you."

She trudged over to her dresser and picked up the pile of clean clothes she had set there that morning. "I'm going to take a shower," she said flatly.

"OK," he replied.

In the bathroom, she set her change of clothes by the sink and took off her robe, tossing it over an empty towel hanger. Then she slipped out of her sheer purple sleepwear and climbed into the shower.

Though temporary, the white noise of the water running drowned out the worries of the real world. It was calming, like the ambience of a light rain at night.

Vanilla ran her fingers through her long white hair and took a deep breath of steam. *Soul seems like such a kindhearted young man. It's terrible that his father was hurting him...* As the hot water streamed down her back, she closed her eyes and thought back to her years as a teenager, living with *Death by Love* and Zero. *I guess we both had saviors now.*

About the Author

Hailing from the mystical land of southern Wisconsin, Mitch "The Ninja" is an artist of multiple trades who has an undying passion for world-building, swords, and fantasy. He has been working on creating fictional universes for over 20 years and plans to continue doing so until the day he keels over like a dried up sardine and takes his last breath. He spends his free time working on his books and dreaming up new ideas to incorporate and expand upon.

For inspiration, he listens to music, takes long walks in nature, and pretends to be a ninja, much to his neighbors' chagrin. He delights in the cheesiest puns and will not hesitate to tell you that, "The kiss of death comes from the 'apocaLIPS.'"

CPSIA information can be obtained
at www.ICGtesting.com
Printed in the USA
FFHW011053240819
54430200-60119FF